Mrs Hudson an
Ca...

Martin Davies grew up in north-west England. All his writing is done in cafes, on buses or on trains, and all his first drafts are written in longhand. He has travelled widely, including in the Middle East, India and Sicily. In addition to the Holmes & Hudson Mysteries, he is the author of four other novels, including *The Conjurer's Bird*, which sold over 150,000 copies and was selected for the Richard & Judy Book Club and *Havana Sleeping*, which has been shortlisted for the 2015 CWA Historical Dagger award. He works as a consultant in the broadcasting industry.

Also by Martin Davies

A Holmes & Hudson Mystery

A Holmes & Hudson Mystery

MRS HUDSON

AND THE

CHRISTMAS CANARY

MARTIN DAVIES

CANELO

First published in the United Kingdom in 2022 by

Canelo
Unit 9, 5th Floor
Cargo Works, 1-2 Hatfields
London SE1 9PG
United Kingdom

Copyright © Martin Davies 2022

The moral right of Martin Davies to be identified as the creator of this work has been asserted in accordance with the Copyright, Designs and Patents Act, 1988.

All rights reserved. No part of this publication may be reproduced or transmitted in any form or by any means, electronic or mechanical, including photocopy, recording, or any information storage and retrieval system, without permission in writing from the publisher.

A CIP catalogue record for this book is available from the British Library.

Print ISBN 978 1 80436 100 9
Ebook ISBN 978 1 80436 099 6

This book is a work of fiction. Names, characters, businesses, organizations, places and events are either the product of the author's imagination or are used fictitiously. Any resemblance to actual persons, living or dead, events or locales is entirely coincidental.

Cover design by Dan Mogford

Look for more great books at www.canelo.co

Printed and bound in Great Britain by Clays Ltd, Elcograf S.p.A.

1

Today I visited an old student of mine. He lives not very far away, just across the park, and he was eager to share with me a scientific paper he'd just reviewed. At my age, it's always nice to be remembered.

So I walked there, across the park and along the Serpentine, enjoying the crisp sharpness of a bright December afternoon. Five days till Christmas, and a band was playing carols, and there was something in the smiles of passers-by, in the excited voices of the children rushing past me, which put me in mind of the Christmases of my youth, back when the streets were still cobbled and the lamps lit by gas.

I enjoyed my visit. My host was excellent company and the paper a good one. As I was leaving, I noticed a picture hanging in his hallway, a framed print of a painting that had once been rather famous. The young man saw that it had caught my eye and looked slightly embarrassed.

'My grandmother's,' he explained. 'Rather out of fashion nowadays. My wife thinks it a bit indecent.'

I watched his eye wander over the young ladies lolling in the foreground, then he shook his head and helped me on with my coat.

He obviously didn't notice anything. But of course, why should he? After all, I'm very much older now, and wearing many more clothes. *And I never thought it a very good likeness in the first place.*

In the park, the band was still playing. I walked home smiling to myself.

Chapter 1

It was an evening when London seemed to smell of Christmas. Clouds of aromatic smoke rose from every street corner, proof that the chestnut sellers were doing excellent business; and all the way along Regent Street, boys were dispensing beakers of spiced wine or Bishop's Nose from steaming pans, filling the night with cinnamon and nutmeg, and a familiar hazy sweetness which lingered in the air long after their barrows had passed on.

It was hard not to feel a little excited. Not quite a fortnight into December, yet already the streets were growing festive. Despite the bitter cold, the pavements were crowded and, from Piccadilly to Oxford Circus, hansom cabs jostled for space. Fires burned brightly in every tavern, and lamps shone in the windows of the big shops, touching the pavements with splashes of reds and greens and golds, drawing tangled knots of late shoppers to marvel at the lavish displays.

But it was a night to go carefully. It was so cold that despite the trotting horses and the eddying pedestrians, the cobbles were already beginning to freeze, and my skirts, splashed with a good helping of mud, felt icy through my petticoats. Too cold for snow, Dr Watson had said that morning, examining the sky from the comfortable warmth of his bedroom, and it seemed he was right. When I peered up, past the glowing gas lamps and the smoking chimneys, I could glimpse the stars, fierce and clear, and not a snow cloud anywhere to be seen.

I would have been happy to stay out longer, peering into shop windows and listening to the music drifting from the public houses, watching the street performers and the shop buskers and the old women selling sprigs of mistletoe; but I still had chores to do and dishes to wash and the beds to turn down. Christmas or no Christmas, it was time to be getting home.

However, my homeward journey did not prove entirely uneventful. More than once I had to step off the pavement to make my way through the crowds, and when I reached my destination, I found the little gate in the railings, the one that led down to the kitchen door, was blocked by a young man with ruddy cheeks and a gamekeeper's bowler hat. He was dressed in the sort of smart Sunday suit often chosen by a visitor up from the country, and he was clearly very intoxicated.

I had already steered my way past various groups of similar young men that evening, all in very high spirits and some of them distinctly unsteady on their feet; but this one appeared to have become detached from his friends and was now relying on the Baker Street railings to keep him upright. Even so, I realised, he might easily have slithered to the floor had the folds of his heavy coat not become snagged in the spike of one of the palings, effectively tethering him to the spot.

'Can't move!' he told me plaintively as I approached him, in a slight West Country accent. 'Want to move, young lady. Want to go home. Just can't seem to. London pavements. Very tricky.'

He attempted a smile which, although rather lopsided, did not seem threatening, and I deemed it safe to approach him.

'I think your coat is caught,' I told him. 'If you just allow me...'

He lurched a little as I tugged the fabric free, but managed to steady himself, and then frowned and reached inside his coat, as though feeling for his waistcoat pockets.

'Had a ring. Two rings...' His frown deepened for a moment, then cleared completely. 'Not rings anymore. Gave them to Humphrey. Up in town to see a friend, you see. A very good friend. Generous friend. Name of Humphrey. A very good egg, Humphrey.'

And he seemed to find this last statement so hilarious that he let out a peal of laughter, and had to grab the rails to keep his balance.

Tipsy young men were not an uncommon sight in town in the weeks before Christmas, but they tended to be found in the livelier thoroughfares or around the railway stations, and it was unusual for one to wander into Baker Street. I was beginning to worry what I was to do with him, when he took a deep breath and straightened.

'Got a train to catch,' he announced. 'Better be off. Young lady, would you be good enough to tell me where I am, and which way for Victoria?'

He raised a finger and waved it, as if to clarify.

'Station, I mean. Not Queen. Looking for railway, not royalty.'

'This is Baker Street,' I told him, 'and it's that way for Victoria, but it's not a short walk. Perhaps I could find you a cab?'

'No, no!' he replied sternly. 'No cab. Can find my way. Never get lost.' He paused to blink rapidly for a moment or two. 'Baker Street, you say? 'S right. I remember now. Came here to find Mr Sherlock Holmes. Wanted to ask him something. Something very important. Very important.'

He took a deep breath and peered down at me as though perhaps I were a little blurry.

'Wanted to ask him, who painted all the Christmas trees?'

And with that strange question hanging in the air, he touched his hat to me, and turned, and made his way rather gingerly along the pavement, then across the road, till I lost sight of him in the gloom between two lamp-posts.

Dr Watson always used to say that there was no more welcoming place in the whole of London than Mrs Hudson's kitchen on a cold winter's evening, and on that particular evening its warmth wrapped me up from the first moment I stepped inside. The fire was blazing, a pan was burbling on the stove and a smell of ginger and cloves crept from the oven. The housekeeper herself was scrubbing down the kitchen table with her sleeves rolled up, her round, muscled arms creating almost perfect circles of soap-suds as she worked. She greeted me with a nod and gestured towards the range.

'Dinner's in the pan, Flotsam, my girl, and there'll be ginger shortbread later if you fancy it. Now, gloves off and hands by the fire, and tell me how you found things at Trevelyan's.'

I did as I was told without demure. Now I was home, in the warmth, I realised again just how cold it was outside.

'Oh, Mrs Hudson,' I told her happily, 'Trevelyan's is looking ever so wonderful. It's hard to believe that Scraggs has been able to turn that empty old shop into something so gorgeous!'

I said it with pride, because I had known the young man in question since the night I first met Mrs Hudson, when he had found me tiny and lost and hopeless, wandering the streets in rags. Back then he had been a simple grocer's boy, but one with a quick wit and a keen nose for business. In the years that followed, his advancement had been rapid, until, only a few months previously, he had taken on the lease of an old tea merchants' store on Bridle Lane with a view to opening a shop of his own.

And not a small shop, either. With the help of an investment from old Mr Trevelyan, who himself had started out selling Shrewsbury biscuits from a barrel on the corner of Cork Street, the premises Scraggs had settled upon could – if properly opened up – rival in size those of such fine establishments as Ostermann's and Throok's. And although his shop had neither the eminent location of the former nor the grand architect of the latter, it was, with its marble counters and old mahogany fittings, undoubtedly rather splendid.

Mrs Hudson listened to my description of the latest developments with some satisfaction, although I couldn't help but notice a very tiny furrow in her brow.

'It is a bold undertaking, Flottie, and young Scraggs is undoubtedly risking a great deal, in the face of some redoubtable rivals. But, of course…' And here her face brightened and the furrow faded slightly. 'Of course, you and I both know, Flotsam, that if anyone can make a success of such a venture it is Scraggs. Now, no more chatter. There's stew in the pan, but barely time for you to taste it, because Mr Holmes is impatient for the evening editions and has asked for you to take them up as soon as you got back.'

I moved straightaway to gather up the pile of newspapers I'd brought home with me, but Mrs Hudson stopped me with a stern glance.

'Food first, Flotsam. I daresay the gentlemen will be able to last another ten minutes or so without the headlines. Meanwhile, if we don't want cinders with our tea tomorrow, I'd better be seeing to that gingerbread...'

I found Mr Holmes and Dr Watson comfortably ensconced in their study, the shutters closed, the coals glowing in the grate and a mellow air of contentment pervading the room. I had barely seen either of the gentlemen that day, for they had been up all night, and for many nights previously, keeping watch on the potting shed in Sheen where the Hammersmith Counterfeiter had been storing her ill-gotten gains. Now, with that business brought to a satisfactory conclusion, and with neither gentleman stirring till just before noon, both appeared well-rested and unusually tranquil. Sherlock Holmes, in one armchair, was looking over an article about railway crime; Dr Watson, in the other, sipped at a glass of brandy-and-shrub and thumbed through the Society pages of a popular magazine.

'Ah, Flotsam!' Mr Holmes greeted me as I entered. 'Your arrival is timely. We are in need of news, and are both hoping that the late editions will deliver us a baffling mystery to rouse us from our torpor. There was nothing of any interest in the morning papers other than an item about more stolen jewellery being melted down, but there's little to intrigue us in that. Meanwhile, I'm sorry to say there hasn't been a knock at the door all afternoon, and I believe this morning was similarly quiet.'

'Yes, sir,' I confirmed, placing the pile of newspapers on the low table between the armchairs. 'Only a lady wanting to know if you helped people with their crossword puzzles, and another urging you to sign a pledge about giving up tobacco.' I hesitated. 'There *was* a person outside a few minutes ago, a rather inebriated young man, with a question about Christmas trees. But he hurried off to catch a train.'

'Christmas trees, eh?' Dr Watson sighed and shook his head. 'Have you noticed, Holmes, that people seem to be putting them up earlier and earlier every year? I can't say I approve of it. I like nothing better than dressing a tree on Christmas Eve, but nowadays people are doing it a good three or four days in advance of that. We'll be having Christmas carols in mid-December next! And look at this piece here, Flotsam,' he added, passing me his magazine. 'Instead of standing firm, it seems our stately homes are going the same way.'

'Third Time Lucky!' I read aloud, peering at the passage he'd indicated. 'News reaches us of a series of singular misfortunes at the Sussex home of Lord —, where preparations for the festive season are already underway. It appears that a certain fir tree, chosen from his lordship's woods to be the centre piece of the festive adornments, and having been felled one evening in preparation, was found the following morning with its upper branches cruelly hacked away by an unknown hand. A second tree of similar appearance, having been selected to replace the first, was brought from the woods the following day, only to suffer a similar fate during the hours of darkness. Happily, we can report that a third tree, by all accounts a much larger and possibly even finer specimen than its predecessors, suffered no such ill-treatment, and has already taken its place in the grand hallway of his lordship's country residence.'

It seemed a peculiar little incident, and I said as much, passing the magazine to Mr Holmes as I did so.

'Peculiar, Flotsam?' Dr Watson accepted my verdict with a vigorous nod of his head. 'I should say so! Putting up a Christmas tree halfway through Advent! Lord So-And-So, whoever he is, should know better. Wouldn't you agree, Holmes?'

But the great detective was gazing intently at the article in the magazine, and barely seemed to hear his friend's question.

'As Flotsam says, Watson, this is a peculiar story. Lord who, I wonder?' He gave a little twitch of his lips as if in exasperation. 'Really! It is too bad that these wretched magazines persist in hiding everything that is helpful or informative behind a line of dashes. What purpose can such coyness possibly serve?'

'I suppose they don't want to embarrass the fellow, Holmes.' Dr Watson took another sip of his brandy-and-shrub. 'After all, it can't be nice for him to know there's a lunatic loose on his estate, cutting the heads off Christmas trees.'

'A lunatic, you say, Watson?' Mr Holmes looked at his friend, then across at me, one eyebrow very markedly raised. 'It would seem unlikely.'

Still holding the magazine, he settled a little deeper into his armchair.

'It is maddening that the article tells us so little, but I would be inclined to believe that the actions described are not those of a madman, but of someone with a very clear purpose. What that purpose is, of course, I can't be entirely certain. But I *would* conjecture that the stately home, should you wish to identify it, is one that boasts a galleried entrance hall. And should the unnamed lord wish to acquaint himself with the decapitator of his trees, I would urge him to look for a member of his own domestic staff less than three hundred and fifty-two days into their employment, in vigorous health, most probably male, whose post does not require him, on any regular basis, to climb ladders.'

And with a contented smile, the great detective turned to his pipe, and resolutely refused to say another word on the subject.

I didn't think a great deal of it at the time. After all, Mr Holmes was always seeing significance in details that no one else particularly noticed.

Of course, if I'd known then that those damaged trees had their roots in the dark soil of an impossible puzzle, a tale of lost love and lost treasures, a mystery that for nearly a quarter of a century had baffled Scotland Yard – well, I suppose I'd have paid a bit more attention.

The following morning, I was up well before the lark, or even the pigeons, cleaning out the grates and laying the fires, while the city outside still shivered in the dark. By the time the sun rose, I had washed and dressed, and was eating breakfast in my smartest clothes, while Mrs Hudson pinned my hair into a fashionable arrangement most unusual for a housemaid. It was my day to visit Bloomsbury for a science lesson, a weekly ritual reaching back for almost as long as I could remember; because Mrs Hudson was a great believer in education for young women, and ever since the night I was first dragged from the muddy streets and thrust into her presence, she had insisted I spent nearly as much time learning as I did cleaning, and nearly as much time reading as polishing.

Rather surprisingly, one of those pressed into service to further my education was none other than the Honourable Rupert Spencer, nephew of the Earl of Brabham, a young man of impeccable social graces, who had known Mrs Hudson ever since his childhood at Brabham Hall. There she had once provided him with refuge after an incident involving ducks in the ballroom – an act of compassion so greatly appreciated by the young man that he seemed to feel my lessons in the natural sciences went only a small way towards repaying the debt.

As a result, one morning every week, I would forget about the stains on the Baker Street carpets and the mystifying scratches on the skirting boards, and would cross London with a spring in my stride, heading for Bloomsbury Square, where Rupert Spencer lived with his uncle and his uncle's ward, Miss Hetty Peters, a very lively young lady who was required to act as chaperone during my lessons. How much of biology or chemistry Miss Peters gleaned in the course of these sessions it was hard to tell, but I certainly learned from her a great deal about bonnets, and fashions in lace, and about what colours never to wear with pearls.

Thankfully, because Mrs Hudson's rigorous regime had taught me good manners and good vowels, and equally good posture, these visits had never struck me as intimidating. In fact, they'd been part of my life for so long, they seemed to me perfectly normal; and from being a ragged waif unsure of my own name, I had somehow become a young woman of perhaps seventeen (I never could be certain of my own age) who was almost as capable of *taking* tea in polite society as I was of serving it.

That particularly morning – another bright, clear one, and bitterly cold – the door was opened to me by Reynolds, the Earl of Brabham's butler and an old friend of mine. I could tell at once by the slightly pained expression on his face, that the earl was at home that day, because no one could ever be truly at ease in a house containing the Earl of Brabham. Widely known in Society circles as the Irascible Earl, his ill-temper was notorious, although, because almost everything annoyed him equally, it was seldom directed at any one person in particular for any great length of time.

'His lordship is upstairs, Miss,' Reynolds warned me, 'and is in one of his more colourful moods. It would appear there has been some sort of confusion concerning a delivery, and it has not made for a tranquil morning.' He allowed himself a little sigh. 'Meanwhile, you will find Miss Peters in the library, Miss. She is eager to see you – something to do with the Bible, I believe.'

This was undoubtedly rather surprising, as Miss Peters had never struck me as someone with urgent theological needs. I found her in the lovely book-lined room that looked out over the square, pacing up and down by a window bright with low winter sunlight. She greeted me with a warm and very lovely smile, and advanced to place both her hands in mine.

'Flottie! Just the person. I need to ask you: have you ever felt as though you were a butterfly being kissed by a moonbeam?'

I confess this utterance alarmed me, because Miss Peters was not generally given to whimsy, and it was hard to think of any more whimsical utterance. Furthermore, it was not at all what Reynolds' warning had led me to expect.

'It's Clara Fazakerley, you see,' she went on, leading me by the hand towards the window seat which looked out over the square. 'Clara is a very old friend, but now she thinks herself in love and is spouting all sorts of nonsense, and instead of being pleased for her, I just want to throw things. Because it turns out, Flottie, that nothing in the whole world is quite as dull as listening to someone tell you, over and over again, that they're tiptoeing on sunbeams, or that they feel like a flower-filled meadow stirred by a wild West Wind.'

She gave a little sigh, then sank elegantly onto the grey silk cushions.

'Especially when that someone is Clara Fazakerley, who avoids sunbeams like the plague, and has never set foot in a field of flowers in her life, because she's terrified of creepy crawlies and thinks long grass is going to make her sneeze.'

Miss Peters paused, and pulled me down next to her on the window seat.

'So you see, Flottie, yesterday evening, at the Wilkinsons' *soirée*, I'm afraid I rather lost my temper with her, and told her that whenever *I* felt stirred up by a wild West Wind, it generally turned out to be indigestion. Which just shows how very annoying she was being, doesn't it, Flottie, because I'm such a *patient* person. But last night

I was particularly out of sorts, mostly thanks to Rupert, who instead of dancing, spent hours talking to old Lady Prendergast about her collection of Burmese figurines.'

She sighed tragically at the thought, then rallied her spirits.

'Anyway, I thought it would serve Rupert right if I danced with the Billington boys instead, because even though they barely have a thought in their heads between them, they can both manage a very passable waltz. But last night they didn't manage any waltzes at all, they just flopped about in the rose garden like limp old socks. You see, it turns out they've had their heads completely turned by Hortensia Portman's beautiful younger sister, who is barely seventeen and who, according to Rupert, has eyes like silent forest pools, and was wearing a creation of emerald green silk that was so divine it made me want to cry. And all the time I wasn't dancing, Potty Peasmarsh was showing me magic tricks, and really there are only so many times you can watch someone's fob-watch disappear and pretend to be surprised. So, Flottie, what with the dress and the forest pools and old Lady Prendergast, you can imagine that I wasn't at all in the mood to hear Clara Fazakerley compare herself to a skylark.'

She paused for breath, and I seized my opportunity.

'So, Hetty, who exactly is Clara Fazakerley in love with?'

'Well, that's just what makes it all so ghastly, Flottie!' Miss Peters declared, shaking her head as she did so. 'Because the person she says she's in love with is none other than Dumpty Boynton, who can dance much better than either of the Billington boys, but really is about as different from a wild West Wind as it is possible for anyone to be. And the thing is, Flottie, I'm not at all sure he's suitable.'

She gave a little wave of her hand.

'Oh, I know the Boyntons are perfectly respectable. The older brother is in the Guards, and the mother raises vast amounts of money for fallen women and things. But there's something about Dumpty Boynton that strikes me as just a little *seedy*, if you know what I mean, like a bad egg which only smells when you open it. You know, Flottie, the sort of young man who was a little too pleased with himself as a schoolboy, and who has never quite grown out of it. I wouldn't be at all surprised if he was interested in fallen women too, but in a very different way from his mother.'

'Goodness, Hetty.' I couldn't help but admire Miss Peters' ability to paint a picture, even if she used a great many brush strokes with which to do it. 'But Reynolds mentioned you were asking about the Bible. Is that something to do with Clara Fazakerley too?'

'The Bible? The Bible?' At first Miss Peters seemed completely at a loss, but then she smiled brightly. 'Oh, no! That was something completely different, Flottie. I was asking Reynolds if he knew anything about the Philistines, because I overheard Rupert talking about them last night, and Reynolds strikes me as the sort of person who probably paid attention in Sunday School. But he just wittered on about Samson and Goliath, and I can't see why Rupert would have been talking about either of those two, because, for all his faults, Flottie, Rupert isn't really the sort of person who talks about the Old Testament at parties. Are you, Rupert?'

At some point during this explanation, Mr Spencer must have entered the library. Looking up from the window seat, I saw that he was now leaning, grinning, against one of the bookshelves.

'Hetty is quite right, Miss Flotsam,' he assured me. 'Although, to be honest, at the sort of gatherings Hetty drags me to, the topic seldom arises.'

He crossed the room to shake my hand, smiling again as he did so. He was undoubtedly a good-looking gentleman, with brown eyes and a firm handshake, and a sense of humour lively enough to withstand a great many domestic tribulations of the sort caused by Miss Peters and the Irascible Earl, indeed sometimes by the two of them simultaneously.

'However,' he went on, 'I think the conversation Hetty overheard was on a rather different subject. Tell me, Miss Flotsam, has there been much talk in Baker Street about the recent reports of stolen gems turning up out of their settings?'

I nodded, although it was not only in Baker Street that the subject was being discussed. For some months, the newspapers had been full of such stories.

'A little, sir, although Mr Holmes has not shown any great interest in them. Do I take it, then, that the Philistine you were discussing last night was the Buckminster Smelter?'

Mr Spencer nodded, and was about to reply, but was interrupted by a little cry of protest from Miss Peters.

'The Buckminster *what*?' She gave an elegant toss of her head. 'Really, you two, sometimes I think you talk in riddles deliberately to annoy me. *Philistines, smelters...* What exactly *is* a smelter? Is it some sort of fish? No, Rupert, don't say a word! Flotsam will explain, won't you, Flottie?'

And I would have done, only before I could even begin, I was startled by the library door bursting open, revealing the intimidating figure of the Earl of Brabham. His face was very red, and he was scowling.

'Rupert! Where on earth is my old horsewhip?' he demanded in a booming voice, without any preamble whatsoever. 'I shall be needing it at once. Honour is at stake!'

I confess I always felt more than a trifle nervous in the presence of Mr Spencer's uncle, and that day his countenance struck me as particularly ferocious. It was almost as though he carried his own storm cloud with him as he marched into the centre of the library, where, on noticing my presence, he halted abruptly.

'What's this?' he began, angrily. 'Visitors? At this hour? Hmph!' He let out a snort, the sort that might have been made by an angry dragon. 'I remember the days when anyone stupid enough to pay calls before noon at this house would have the dogs set on them! We used to borrow a pair from next door, then return them in the afternoon, when my father was finally out of bed. That soon put an end to charity callers, I can assure you! Anyway, Rupert, you'd better stop yapping and send this one her on her way while I get to the bottom of this poultry business.'

'This is Miss Flotsam, Uncle,' Mr Spencer told him calmly. 'You have met her before.'

All three of us had risen at the earl's entrance, and now he peered at me from beneath fearsome, shaggy eyebrows.

'Flotsam? Flotsam? Ah, yes! I remember. The intelligent one. Not so intelligent that she doesn't call at stupid times though! Now, Rupert, about this morning's delivery. Reynolds says we can't return it so I've a good mind to call the police, and have them track the joker down. Then we can get to work with the horsewhip!'

Mr Spencer turned to me with a smile, apparently completely unperturbed by the earl's fiery expression.

'My uncle took delivery of a rather strange gift this morning, Miss Flotsam,' he explained, 'and is eager to discover its sender.'

'Gift? Gift? GIFT??' The Earl of Brabham sounded as though he might explode. 'That was no *gift*, my boy. It was a deliberate and devilish insult! By someone intent on mocking us publicly! Someone seeking to besmirch the family name! Reynolds says it is impossible to work out where it came from, but we'll see about that. I've a good mind to call out Scotland Yard this very morning. What do you say, Miss Flotsam?'

As so often in the earl's presence, I found myself lost for words, and once again Mr Spencer came to my rescue.

'We had a large parcel delivered this morning, addressed to my uncle,' he told me calmly. 'When unwrapped, it turned out to contain a small crate, which when opened...'

'*When opened?* Don't mince your words, sir! It wasn't you opening it, or Reynolds, or Hetty here. I opened the damned thing myself, because I was expecting five copies of *The Bloodstock Breeders' Almanac*. And what do you think flew out, Miss Flotsam, the moment I had the lid a few inches open? A blasted chicken! Flapping and clucking and whatnot, all around my study. Had to use my own top hat to catch the thing!'

'A chicken, sir?' I asked faintly.

'A chicken! A hen! A fowl! Can't think of any other way to describe it! And no note, no card, no return address, just black and white squares on one side and my name on the other with a little scribble underneath it. The damned coward didn't have the backbone to own up to his own prank, you see! What sort of bounder finds a trick like that amusing? Answer me that, eh, Miss Flotsam? Well, I'll tell you. A blasted imbecile, that's who! My word, I wouldn't want to be in his shoes when I track him to his lair!'

Mr Spencer cleared his throat very politely.

'Reynolds seems certain, Uncle, that there's simply been an error on the part of the delivery boy. He thinks there must have been two parcels to deliver and the labels were somehow switched. The boot boy has been sent to call at every house in the square, to find out if anyone has been expecting a live hen of any description.'

'An error? An ERROR?' The earl's cheeks had turned very purple. 'Reynolds is an ass, and I told him so! He can say what he likes, but I recognise a practical joke when one's played on me! That dashed crate had my name on the label, and the label was tied on with a piece of twine stout enough to hang Reynolds by his ankles from that chandelier, which frankly would have been a much better use for it! I'm telling you, my boy, that wretched fowl was meant for me, and if you believe otherwise, you're a bigger fool than I already take you for!'

'And tell me, sir,' Rupert Spencer replied, his air of calm unruffled, 'where is the bird in question now?'

His uncle snorted again.

'Told Reynolds to get rid of it, of course! You don't think I wanted to keep it, do you? Do I look like the sort of man who keeps hens? And I certainly didn't want to eat it. Goodness knows what it might contain. So I told Reynolds to send it to the Secretary of the Board of Trade. He likes hens. Always being an annoyance at the club, going on about his black Orpingtons. How a man like that can be trusted with affairs of state defeats me entirely! Now, that horsewhip, Rupert. If you remember seeing it around anywhere, tell Reynolds to bring it up straightaway. Need to get in some practice!'

And with that, his lordship was gone. My lesson that day was about astronomy, but I wasn't at all sure how much of it I was going to retain. It was hard to concentrate on the Great Bear or Orion's Belt with the voice of the Irascible Earl still ringing in my ears.

It was only later that I realised just how important that lesson was.

Chapter 2

When I stepped out from Mr Spencer's house later that day, I found Bloomsbury Square cloaked in the gloom of a wintry December afternoon. The clear skies of the morning had been obscured by a blanket of thick, sullen clouds, and a chill wind licked into every corner of the square. It was barely one o'clock but already the light was murky, threatening an early dusk.

By rights I should have hurried directly back to Baker Street because I had the doorknobs to polish and a lot of work to do on the silverware. But I couldn't resist making a small detour to Trevelyan's in Bridle Lane in search of Scraggs. So busy had he been with the opening of his new venture, that it was a little while since I'd seen him, and our recent encounters had all been hurried and rather unsatisfactory. On each occasion I had thought him rather short, as though his mind was elsewhere, and I longed for the opportunity to talk to him properly, to tell him what a very fine store Trevelyan's was becoming, and how very impressed I was by all his efforts. I wouldn't say I was missing him – obviously, I was far too busy for that – but it would have been nice to have a few moments with him, nonetheless.

My little diversion ended in disappointment, however. Trevelyan's looked as welcoming and bright as ever, and was busy with shop assistants, both young men and women, polishing the counters and tidying the shelves. The shopping floor itself, however, was not busy, so it didn't take me very long to realise that Scraggs was not present in the front of the shop; and when I enquired of a pleasant-looking gentleman overseeing the arrangement of umbrellas into a striking display, I was told that Mr Scraggs had left the premises an hour before and was not expected back before closing time.

A little surprised by this, and saddened to have missed him, I could think of no excuse to linger, so stepped out once again into the murky streets, my collar turned up against the wind, and made my way home towards Baker Street. If possible, the clouds seemed even gloomier than before.

However, in Mrs Hudson's kitchen, a cheering welcome awaited me. The fire was bright; there were apples stewing in a pot on the stove, filling the kitchen with the sweet smell of fruit and cinnamon; and Mrs Hudson herself was in excellent humour, having successfully removed a mystifying green stain from the upstairs skirting board with a blend of Everard's paste and baking powder. In answer to her queries about affairs in Bloomsbury Square, I told her all about the Earl of Brabham's unsolicited hen and about Miss Peters' frustrations with Clara Fazakerley.

She seemed to find the first of these things as amusing as I did, for when I told her the earl had been forced to capture the bird in his own top hat, her eyebrow gave a little twitch. At the description of Miss Fazakerley's romantic entanglements, however, she looked more serious and nodded.

'I know very little about the Boyntons, Flotsam,' she told me, 'but old Mrs Fazakerley, the young lady's grandmother, was something of a Society favourite back in the days of bell-shaped skirts, and I'm told she too was given to flights of romantic fancy. It's said that she used to write her own sonnets and send them to minor poets with dubious reputations, although, of course, there was nothing very dissolute about the man she eventually married. Mr Fazakerley made his fortune manufacturing nerve tonics in the North, and was old enough to be her father. So Miss Peters perhaps has some grounds for hoping that the current infatuation will pass.'

That afternoon, however, as I set about the brass doorknobs with vinegar and a soft chamois, I couldn't help wonder about the question Miss Peters had asked me: whether it was possible for one person to meet another, and, in that moment, to find themselves utterly changed. It happened in novels, I knew – I had read a great many of them – and I'd always liked to believe that such tales had at least some foundation in real life. But when I tried to think of examples known to me, although I tried very hard, I struggled to find any.

And then I thought of Scraggs, and hoped that everything was all right.

There really wasn't time for any moping about however, for after the doorknobs there were the stair-rods to see to, then Dr Watson's collection of small brass toby jugs, and then the gentlemen's various pieces of silver, which were in great need of a polish before they could be brought out on Christmas Day.

The silver cupboard at Baker Street was a small, walk-in affair, situated at the top of the stairs immediately opposite Mr Holmes' study. By a twist of providence, if the study door was left only a little open, anyone at work polishing the silver was afforded a surprisingly clear view into Mr

Holmes' favourite room; and even if the study door was only ajar, voices from there carried quite clearly to the little room outside. That evening, as I worked on the silver platters that had been a gift to Mr Holmes from the Crown Prince of Denmark, I was aware of the two gentlemen engaged in quiet conversation.

'Lord Evershott, Lord Markham, Lord Empingham...' Mr Holmes appeared to be listing random peers. 'Lord Cottesbrooke, Lord Saltby. And possibly Lord Kettleford. It really is impossible to say, Watson.'

'Eh? What's that, Holmes?' Dr Watson had evidently not been devoting his full attention to his friend. 'I was just reading something about the Rutherford Tiara. It's a grim business.'

'Indeed, my friend.' But I could tell from his tone that the great detective was not greatly interested in the Rutherford Tiara. 'Now, you will argue, no doubt, that Lord Kettleford should not be on the list, because his family seat is in Northumberland. But you may recall that he does in fact own a property in Sussex through Lady Kettleford, albeit a modest one.'

'Kettleford... Saltby...' The good doctor sounded a little desperate. 'I'm sorry, Holmes, you've lost me. Why were we talking about these chaps?'

'Those Christmas trees, Watson! You remember. The ones which were vandalised before they could be taken in and decorated. I've been through our copy of the Peerage, and it seems to me that the events in question must have taken place at the homes of one those six men, because I can find no other lords with homes in Sussex that I know to contain galleried halls. Of course, Watson, there are plenty of big houses in Sussex with grand, high-ceilinged rooms, I'll give you that. But I rather think there must be a gallery if the disfigured trees are to make any sense at all.'

Precisely how Dr Watson might have replied to this I cannot tell, for at that moment the serenity of the evening was disturbed by a forceful rapping on the front door.

Aware that Mrs Hudson was engaged in the messy task of cleaning the oven, and confident that my own apron was reasonably clean, I laid the Danish platters carefully to one side and hastened downstairs to admit the caller, who turned out to be a distinguished-looking and smartly dressed gentleman of around fifty years of age, with a neatly trimmed grey beard and rather striking blue eyes. He addressed me politely but firmly, stamping his feet to keep out the cold as he did so, telling me that he had an urgent need to consult Sherlock Holmes on a matter of great importance, and asking if that gentleman was at home. The card I carried upstairs to the study was of superior quality and bore the name of a Mr Horace Denham.

'Denham, Watson?' Mr Holmes studied the card with a slight frown. 'Is the name familiar to you, my friend? No, nor to me. But I suppose we'd better see what the fellow wants. If you would be so good as to show him up, Flotsam, and then perhaps return to your duties in the silver cupboard, where you will be most conveniently placed.'

This latter remark was accompanied with a very partic-ular little nod, one that reminded me that Mr Holmes was every bit as aware as I was of the strange acoustic qualities of the silver cupboard. Latterly, you see, I had come to realise that my employer, instead of deploring the thought that his housemaid might overhear the confidences of his clients, had rather warmed to it. For, as he frequently declared, efficiency was everything when pitting his wits against his criminal rivals, and the better Mrs Hudson and I understood his needs, the more his clients would benefit. To Mr Holmes, I had quickly learned, confidentiality was far less important than results.

That's why, after showing Mr Denham up to the study, I didn't feel the least pang of guilt about retiring to the silver cupboard and continuing my work, especially as Mr Holmes made a point of asking me to leave the study door open a little – in case, as he put it, the excellent fire made the room grow stuffy. This allowed me, through the crack in the door of my tiny workroom, a surprisingly clear view of our visitor as he was welcomed in, and urged to settle himself into his host's armchair. I had already closed the shutters against the night, and the room looked warm and inviting in the lamplight.

'So how can we be of assistance, sir?' Mr Holmes began from his familiar position leaning against the mantelpiece, while Dr Watson hastened to provide the visitor with a glass of whisky-and-soda-water to keep out the cold.

'It is good of you to see me at this hour, Mr Holmes,' the newcomer began. 'I wish to consult you about a serious matter, one that affects me greatly, but one that affects a lady of my acquaintance very much more. I may speak in complete confidence?'

My employer nodded gravely, without even the smallest glance towards the study door.

'You have my assurance, sir, that anything you say within these walls will be treated with the utmost discretion.'

'Then I shall begin.' Mr Denham settled himself a little deeper into the armchair. 'You have heard, I take it, of Maximillian Cortado, the violinist? For these last twenty years he has been one of this country's most eminent musicians – perhaps *the* most eminent – constantly in demand both at home and abroad. You must surely know of him?'

'Cortado?' Dr Watson was still at the drinks tray, pouring himself a substantial helping of brandy-and-shrub. 'I've certainly seen his name on posters and things. And didn't I hear talk of him being knighted in the next honours list?'

'Indeed, sir. And many would argue that such an honour is long overdue.' Mr Denham shifted a little in his seat, and I could hear the unease in his voice. 'My fear is that, unless something is done quickly, then any such honour might never be bestowed. You see, Mr Holmes…' And here Mr Denham shifted again. 'You see, Maximillian Cortado has disappeared.'

A little silence followed this statement, but if the speaker was expecting Mr Holmes and Dr Watson to express great astonishment, I knew he would wait in vain. I had lost count of the many cases brought to Mr Holmes' door that involved individuals thought missing, and very few of them ever proved of much interest to the great detective. Far too many of them had simply decided to go somewhere else for a little while.

Perhaps Mr Denham sensed this. It was hard to tell in the firelight, but even from where I was standing, he appeared to blush.

'Of course, gentlemen, my consternation as I say those words can only be properly understood by those who know Mr Cortado as well as I do. You see, Max is a musician – disciplined, dedicated, a creature of rigid routines. For something like this to occur is utterly out of character, and the grave concern felt by those close to him cannot be overstated.'

Mr Holmes gave the very slightest of nods.

'Perhaps, sir, if you were to acquaint us with the facts…?'

'It happened three days ago,' Mr Denham explained after taking a further moment to gather himself. 'Ever since the death of his wife, Maximillian has lived alone in Bromley Place. But his servants are all devoted to him, and they have been able to give a very clear account of what occurred. On the day in question, he spent the afternoon practising in his rooms for a private recital he was giving that night. At about half past four in the afternoon, he called for his coat and gloves, saying that he wished to get a little air before dressing. It was not unknown for him to take a constitutional around the square, even after dark and in bad weather, so the servants were not surprised in the slightest. They fully expected him back within the half hour. But Mr Cortado did not return that afternoon, gentlemen, and has not returned since. He failed to appear at that evening's *soirée*, and sent no word of explanation. As far as I can ascertain, gentlemen, not one of his acquaint-ances has heard anything from him.'

Mr Holmes, who had taken up his pipe without showing the slightest intention of lighting it, appeared to give this some thought.

'And you can offer no explanation for such an abrupt disappearance?'

'Absolutely not, sir.' Mr Denham spoke with great conviction. 'Max has a reputation for hard work and stead-iness. His wife, Margaret, used to say that no musician in the country has ever worked harder at his craft.'

'You can appreciate that, can't you, Holmes?' Dr Watson remarked, returning to his armchair, drink in hand. 'Mr Holmes is something of a violinist himself, you see,' he explained to Mr Denham.

'A mere amateur, sir,' the detective assured his guest with the faintest of smiles. 'But I have played enough to appreciate the many hours of dedication and discipline that a violinist of Mr Cortado's calibre must have devoted to his art. Now, sir, perhaps you could be good enough to tell us a little more about the gentleman. He is a widower, you say?'

'He is, Mr Holmes. His wife passed away two years ago, after twenty-four years of marriage. Maximillian, of course, is still a comparatively young man — forty-eight years old at his last birthday, I believe, for he married young — and he retains all the vigour and energy of youth. But as I say, he has always channelled his energies into his music, and has allowed himself few other interests. Certainly nothing that could explain such aberrant behaviour.'

'And you are a particular friend of his, Mr Denham?' Mr Holmes asked the question lightly, but looked up from his pipe as he asked it, as if to study his visitor for a moment.

'I…' Mr Denham appeared to hesitate. 'Well, I am an old acquaintance of his, Mr Holmes, but in coming to see you tonight I am, first and foremost, representing the interests of another. I think I mentioned a lady? Well, the lady in question is Miss Lavinia Burrows. You may have heard of her. She is a renowned patroness of the arts, especially of music. She and I have known each other since we were children. And this inexplicable business has left her devastated, Mr Holmes.'

Mr Denham paused to clear his throat, evidently a little embarrassed.

'Miss Burrows has been close to the Cortado family for many years, first as a very close friend of Margaret Cortado, and then, since that lady's death, as a supporter of her husband. Although she is a handsome woman of independent fortune, she has never married, although I had perhaps at one time thought...'

Our visitor seemed to be on the brink of imparting a personal confidence, but hastily drew back.

'What I mean to say, Mr Holmes, is that since his wife's death, Maximillian and Miss Burrows have grown increasingly close. She keeps him up to his practice just as his wife once did, and is his most eloquent advocate in public. It was widely understood – by their whole circle of acquaintances – that Maximillian intended to take the opportunity provided by this week's recital to propose marriage. After all, as I've said, he's still in the prime of life, and Miss Burrows is a fine-looking and gracious woman only three years his junior. They seem admirably matched. So when Mr Cortado failed to appear at the recital, it left Lavinia – Miss Burrows – doubly distraught. And the longer he stays away, sir, the more anxious she becomes.'

As Mr Denham continued, his voice seemed to grow more urgent.

'In addition, Mr Holmes, although I have not spoken of it to the lady in question, I cannot pretend that ugly rumours are not beginning to circulate. I've heard it said – by a blackguard who should know better – that Maximillian has simply taken himself off on a drunken spree in order to delay his engagement for as long as possible. "Cold feet" is the phrase he used. Which is why he must be found, Mr Holmes, and the full truth revealed, without a moment's delay!'

'The full truth?' The great detective raised an eyebrow. 'Can you be completely certain, sir, that the rumour-mongers are incorrect? A widower who was happily married for so long may surely have certain qualms about replacing his beloved first wife with a second?'

'I can assure you, sir, that Mr Cortado had no doubts whatsoever about his course of action.' Mr Denham made the declaration with such certainty that I felt sure he was speaking the truth. 'Only last week he and I spent an evening together. At no point did he express even the slightest hesitation about entering into a second marriage. On the contrary, we spoke frequently of what a fine woman Miss Burrows is, and what benefits the connection would bring him, not only personally, but also to his career.'

Dr Watson heard this with a frown.

'If not cold feet, sir, do I take it you suspect foul play?'

'What other conclusion can I reach, Doctor?' There was a note of desperation in his voice. 'After all, I know his finances to be sound, his health excellent, and his reputation impeccable. He has achieved great fame in his chosen career and he was about to enter into an engagement which would have assured him a comfortable home life and sustained professional success. Knowing this, Lavinia – Miss Burrows – and I are both convinced that something terrible must have befallen him that afternoon, as he walked the streets in the dark.'

'Let us return to that afternoon, Mr Denham.' In contrast to his visitor's, Mr Holmes' voice was crisp and devoid of emotion. 'You say he left the house to go for a short walk. Were his servants able to provide a description of what he was wearing?'

'A very complete one, sir. A brown lounge suit of the sort he always wore for practice, a grey silk cravat, a dark overcoat and – rather unseasonably – a straw boater. That's not as unusual as it sounds, Mr Holmes,' Mr Denham added hastily. 'Max is well known for wearing his boater all year round. It's a little eccentricity of his. Lavinia – Miss Burrows – likes to say that from October onwards it makes Max stand out from a crowd, while from May he simply disappears into one.'

'Mr Cortado is not a striking-looking individual, then?' Mr Holmes asked. 'Boater apart, not someone who would attract attention on a busy London street?'

'Well, he's a good-looking fellow, Mr Holmes, but I don't think you would call him a striking one. Dark hair just beginning to turn grey, clean shaven, average height, slim-build. So no, there's no particular reason why a passer-by would notice him. Other than his hat, of course. They'd be bound to notice that.'

'A hat can be removed, Mr Denham,' the great detective observed calmly. 'Now, can I assume he took nothing else with him on his walk that afternoon? No bag of any sort?'

'Nothing, Mr Holmes. Just his cane.'

'And you have relayed your fears to the police, no doubt?' Mr Holmes was studying his pipe with great care.

'I have, sir.' Mr Denham paused to swallow. 'Mr Cortado's servants became concerned when he was not back within the hour, and sent out a party to search for him in the surrounding streets. When they found no sign of their master, the butler thought to send for me, and I advised them to call the police at once. But the police investigations, rather than clarify matters, have simply muddied the waters.'

Mr Denham tailed off, and Mr Holmes cast an eager glance in his direction.

'Go on, sir. Precisely what theory have the police formed to explain Mr Cortado's disappearance?'

'I don't believe they have formed any theory, Mr Holmes. At first they told me that he had probably called in on a friend. But when he failed to appear for his recital that evening, they did at least agree to make enquiries at the railway stations. And unfortunately, a railway clerk at Victoria reported selling a second-class ticket to Bognor Regis to a man in a boater about half an hour after Max left his house.'

'Bognor Regis?' Dr Watson sounded slightly alarmed. 'That's on the south coast, isn't it? Now why on earth would your friend decide to head off down there on a chilly winter afternoon? Does he know anyone in Bognor?'

Mr Denham shook his head.

'Not as far as I'm aware, Doctor. Which is one reason why I refuse to believe that the man at Victoria was Max.'

Mr Denham turned from Dr Watson back to Mr Holmes.

'That is why I called here tonight, sir. The police think Mr Cortado has taken himself off on a jaunt. They have sent his details to the force in Bognor, and are refusing to investigate further until they hear back. Meanwhile, as you can imagine, Miss Burrows is desperate for answers. She is certain that something terrible has happened, and cannot understand why the police are ignoring the evidence that's staring them in the face.'

'Eh?' Dr Watson looked slightly alarmed, as though afraid he'd missed some crucial point. 'What evidence is that?'

Mr Denham looked at him in surprise.

'Why, the violin, Doctor. The Monteverdi violin. One of the finest instruments in the world, and the only one that Mr Cortado will ever play. I've never known him make any sort of journey without it. Even on an overnight visit to a friend, he will take it with him so that he can practise. But it's still there, Doctor. Still in its case. So I don't care how many men in boaters went to Bognor that afternoon, sir. If Maximillian Cortado has left it behind of his own volition, well then, gentlemen, he's no longer the man I know.'

In the silence that followed these words I could hear the grandfather clock ticking, and somewhere outside a slightly drunken voice was calling for a cab.

'Very well, then!'

Mr Holmes straightened suddenly and stepped away from the mantelpiece.

'A world-famous violin virtuoso of regular habits, with no known problems and pleasing future prospects, steps outside one winter's afternoon and disappears completely, leaving his precious violin behind. Our friends in the police are convinced he has travelled, without luggage, to Bognor Regis, a conclusion that rests entirely upon the assumption that no other gentleman in Victoria Station that afternoon could possibly have been wearing a boater out of season. Such asinine thinking almost demands to be punished, and it is, I suppose, a fairly interesting little puzzle.' He looked down at Mr Denham a little sadly. 'Although I fear that a great many possible solutions present themselves, and the large majority of them are extremely mundane. Nevertheless, you may reassure Miss Burrows that we shall look into it. It may be necessary for us to talk to her in person, you understand?'

Mr Denham, rising from his chair with an expression of great relief on his face, assured Mr Holmes that Lavinia Burrows would be more than happy to receive the two gentlemen, and would be overjoyed to know that the great Sherlock Holmes was acting for her.

And yet it seemed to me that his own joy at this outcome was not completely unalloyed, for as I showed him out, I noticed the firm set of his jaw and, as he pulled on his gloves, it seemed to me that he gave an almost imperceptible sigh. He had a kind face, I thought. But it was hard not to conclude that Mr Horace Denham, for all his honourable motives, and however hard he tried to disregard the fact, might be struggling with an unwelcome truth: that for him personally, his friend's sudden disappearance was not without its compensations.

It turned out that my duties for the evening were not quite complete, for no sooner had Mr Denham taken his departure than a pull on the bell summoned me back upstairs, to Mr Holmes' study. I found the two gentlemen seated in their armchairs, Mr Holmes' pipe, still unlit, cradled in his hand.

'And so, Flotsam,' he greeted me, without preamble, 'Dr Watson and I are intrigued to know what you made of our guest.'

There would have been a time, and not long since, when such a statement would both have astonished and alarmed me. But latterly Mr Holmes seemed to take a certain satisfaction in such questions, perhaps because they made me arrange my thoughts in a clear and logical order; because it was true, I think, as Mrs Hudson often remarked, that Sherlock Holmes would rather hear common sense from a guttersnipe than nonsense from a duke. And in the excitement of a new case, he sometimes seemed to forget the roles that Mrs Hudson and I performed in his household. For Mr Holmes, I think, distinctions of class were irritating distractions if they clouded the clarity of his thoughts, and the washing up of dirty dishes was an unforgivable frivolity compared to the conviction of a dangerous felon.

So, that evening, I was not unprepared for the question put to me, and I had my answer ready.

'Well, sir, Mr Denham is clearly an extremely wealthy gentleman, but I don't think he mixes very much in high society. And he owns a small dog.'

'Good lord, Flotsam! A dog?' Dr Watson was clearly impressed. 'I never guessed that. What did I miss? Don't tell me the fellow came here with hairs on his trousers!'

'His cane, Watson.' Mr Holmes sounded slightly pained. 'Surely you must have noticed? There were a great many bite marks on it of the sort made by a playful canine, but none were above the height of his knee, strongly suggesting that the animal in question is low to the ground. What of the rest, Flotsam?'

'Well, it was his hat, sir. That told me a lot. When I took it from him, I noticed it was from Lock's, and only the very wealthy buy their hats there. But it was far from the latest fashion. And it was the same with his clothes, sir. I could tell they were all of the very best quality, but none of them were at all the sort of things a gentleman would wear who wanted to show off his wealth.'

'Hmmm...' Dr Watson pondered this. 'The sort of chap happier in the background than in the limelight? Yes, I can see that.'

'And perhaps,' his friend added, 'his natural reticence is why he has remained a bachelor for so many years.'

'A bachelor, Holmes? Did he mention that?'

The great detective eyed his friend affectionately.

'Did you notice his waistcoat buttons, Flotsam?'

I screwed up my eyes and tried to recall them.

'I think they had little acorns on them, sir.'

Mr Holmes looked pleased.

'They did indeed, Flotsam. Which is a sure sign that Mr Denham is a member of the Beaufort Club. But the buttons were not new, were they, Flotsam? You will have noticed that, although polished, they were not shining. They had a patina of age, suggesting that Mr Denham has been a member of the Beaufort for a good number of years.'

'Ah! I see, Holmes!' Dr Watson leaned forward in his chair. 'And only bachelors may be members of the Beaufort. Members are required to resign the moment they become engaged.' He considered this for a moment. 'Makes me feel a little sorry for the fellow. Couldn't help noticing that he spoke very fondly of Miss Burrows.'

Mr Holmes placed his pipe on the arm of his chair and rose to his feet.

'As I told Mr Denham, the disappearance of this violinist may prove to have the most trivial and common-place explanation, but we must do what we can. What would you say, Watson, to calling at his house in Bromley Place tomorrow and seeing what can be gleaned from his servants?'

'Absolutely, Holmes!' Dr Watson also rose, as if to show that he was ready for action. 'We should go first thing.'

'You forget, my friend, that tomorrow we are expected in Scotland Yard to lay before Inspector Merivale the full facts of the counterfeiting case. But we should be finished there by four o'clock at the latest, so I suggest you visit Bromley Place then. While you do that, I have a mind to visit Victoria Station. The boater hat is an interesting detail, Watson, but I feel it may mislead more than it assists.'

I saw that Dr Watson's face had fallen.

'You wish me to go to Bromley Place without you, Holmes?'

I had known Dr Watson for long enough by then to understand that his reluctance to undertake such investigations on his own was not, as some have suggested, because of any lack of confidence on his part. Although a master of self-deprecation, I knew him to be perfectly capable of any such task, and suspected that his rather unassuming and affable manner sometimes elicited information which would have eluded a more intimidating questioner. But the good doctor was a sociable man by nature, and, if given the option, would generally have preferred a tedious task in company over a congenial one that required solitude.

And I think Mr Holmes understood this quite as well as I did, for he was already shaking his head.

'Go alone? Far from it, Watson,' he replied. 'You will no doubt garner a great deal of valuable intelligence, and someone to assist would be invaluable. I am sure Flotsam here will be delighted to accompany you.'

At first Dr Watson looked very pleased at this suggestion, and I couldn't help but blush slightly at such a very flattering proposal. However, I was also aware that I had a number of errands to run the following afternoon, and was just about to explain that Mrs Hudson had already made plans for my time, when I saw Dr Watson's face fall.

'Delighted to have you with me, Flotsam,' he explained. 'No one shrewder, always thought so, you know that. But surely, Holmes, won't it be considered a little *unconventional* for Flotsam to assist me in such a matter?'

But Mr Holmes, having retrieved his tobacco pouch from the mantelpiece, simply set about filling his pipe.

'And what is that to us, Watson? As I recall it, we weren't able to unmask the Watford Tea Gang by acting in accordance with convention. And there was nothing conventional last month about your method of stopping that fellow Saundersfoot from throwing the rabbit off the roof of St Paul's. Convention, Watson, is an umbrella for the cautious, and if people dislike our methods, they are welcome to take their business elsewhere. And now, Flotsam,' he went on, after pausing to reach for a match, 'if Dr Watson is to have your assistance, I daresay a word with Mrs Hudson will be in order. Perhaps you would be good enough to send her up?'

It seemed Mrs Hudson had no objection to Mr Holmes' proposal, although her permission was withheld until the two of us had worked out how, by rising earlier than usual, we might squeeze the tasks and errands of the day into the hours before four o'clock.

And then, that evening, when the last chores were finished and the last floor mopped, as we sat by the kitchen fire enjoying a moment of peace, she surprised me by returning to the subject of Mr Denham's visit.

'You say, Flottie, that you felt today's visitor was an honest gentleman?' she asked me, brushing some invisible crumbs from her skirts as she did so.

'Yes, ma'am. He had a nice face. And, as I think I said, I could tell he had a dog, because...'

But she held up her hand before I could continue.

'Yes, indeed. It was a shrewd piece of observation, Flottie. But for now, I'm more interested in your instincts than in your deductions. And you seem to feel that Mr Denham came here today because he was genuinely perplexed by recent events, and was seeking an explanation.'

'Yes, ma'am. He seemed baffled by the whole business.'

'And yet... Well, never mind.' She broke off, and rose from her chair. 'It is another cold night, child, and Christmas is less than two weeks away. The cake is made, the pudding is maturing nicely, and I've been topping up the mincemeat with rum for the last six weeks. I think we deserve a glass of the Morley Madeira.'

I was certainly not going to argue with that. It was only comparatively recently that Mrs Hudson had begun to allow me occasional sips of the many bottles that emerged from our cellar, but for me the Morley Madeira already stood out. I was, of course, aware of its reputation, and knew that the only bottles in England were all in the hands of Lord Grimsby, who guarded them with understandable jealousy. But his lordship had a long memory, and for reasons that were not completely clear to me – something to do with his favourite niece, an Austrian dancing master and a missing pastry cook – he made a point of having a single bottle delivered to Mrs Hudson every fourteenth of October. It tasted of sweetness, and orange blossom, and of warm nights in foreign lands.

The careful pouring of such a liquid was not something to be rushed, so by the time Mrs Hudson was once again seated next to me, I had almost forgotten that we'd been discussing that day's visitor. But the subject was clearly still very much on Mrs Hudson's mind.

'Before you visit the Cortado house tomorrow, Flottie, I think I should tell you that, although I know next to nothing of the missing violinist, his late wife, Margaret Cortado, was not entirely unknown to me.'

I noticed a tiny furrow between her brows as she spoke.

'She was, I'm afraid to say, the sort of woman who is unkind to her servants. Very strict and demanding, and always very quick to scold. I remember one particular young woman, a perfectly respectable lady's maid when she worked with me at Brabham Hall, who after six months in the service of Margaret Cortado had lost her nerve completely, and ended up as parlour maid to an admiral in Gibraltar.'

I raised my tiny little glass towards my lips but didn't drink, wanting to savour the anticipation.

'I suppose, ma'am, that's the side of someone's character that their friends don't always see.'

Mrs Hudson nodded thoughtfully.

'Quite right, Flottie. I've heard it said of Margaret Cortado that her husband would never have achieved the prominence he currently enjoys had it not been for her. Mr Raffles once told me that Maximillian Cortado had been a very fine cricketer in his university days, and a rather dashing fencer, but had given all other pursuits up on his marriage, in order to concentrate on his music.'

My first sip of the Morley Madeira filled me with a warmth which seemed to begin at my toes and work its way up. It was the sort of warmth that made you want to think well of people, and I hoped that perhaps Margaret Cortado had shown enough kindness and devotion in her marriage to make up, at least in part, for her lack of consideration elsewhere.

My second sip put Mrs Cortado out of my head altogether. After all, Mr Cortado had been a widower for two years. His wife's terseness to her servants could have nothing at all to do with his sudden disappearance.

That night, when I finally made my way to bed, I left Mrs Hudson still sitting by the fire. She had taken up the magazine which Dr Watson had been reading the day before, and which Mr Holmes, apparently, had drawn to her particular attention. When I said goodnight and closed the door, she was studying the item about the damaged Christmas trees, and a puzzled frown had formed between her eyebrows.

Chapter 3

The next morning I was up long before dawn, cleaning the fireplaces, lighting fires and refilling all the lamps. Outside, the night had been a clear one and the cobbled streets were treacherous with ice. When the collier's cart drew to a halt outside, the great dray-horses steamed in the gloom.

With so much to be done, Mrs Hudson and I allowed ourselves only a hurried breakfast, taken just as the sun was beginning to rise. By then, the blazing coals had done their work; the kitchen was warm and bright, the study had already lost its chill and, when I came to put on my coat before embarking on the morning's errands, I found that Mrs Hudson had spread it out in front of the kitchen fire so that it was as cosy to slip into as any fine fur.

'Now, Flottie,' Mrs Hudson warned me, handing me a heavy basket, 'there's a lot to get done. There's a jar of pickled eggs in here for Mrs Dawson, and a bottle of my rosehip syrup for old Tom Mallows in The Strand. And I'm afraid I've put in three large jars of my Christmas chutney for Mrs Richards, because the Penhursts are always nagging her for it, and last year they'd eaten the lot before the end of Advent. Then there's the shopping list, and you'll need to get to Lamingtons before noon or the best cuts of Wiltshire ham will all be gone...'

I assured her that all would be done, and set about my tasks at a great pace. Walking quickly was a good way of keeping warm, and I was eager to finish as early as possible. If I were to keep my appointment with Dr Watson at four o'clock, I would need to be back in time to wash and tidy myself, and to change into my best clothes.

Happily, things progressed smoothly, and by eleven o'clock all but two items were ticked off my list. As I stepped out of Lamingtons, having secured some excellent cuts of ham, and having arranged for the delivery of two brace of cold partridges, I became aware of my name being called, and the Earl of Brabham's very grand carriage drawing to a halt beside me. Its window was down, and Miss Peters, her head and shoulders protruding, was waving from it.

'Ahoy! Flotsam! I was *sure* it was you! Do come aboard! I've been wanting to talk to you all morning!'

I tried to explain to her that my time was accounted for, and that I still had errands to run, but she was having none of it.

'Oh, don't worry at all about them, Flotsam, darling! Carrington will take you wherever you want to go, won't you, Carrington? And it will be ever so much warmer in here, and *much* less muddy, and we've nearly finished anyway, haven't we, Carrington? We're supposed to be picking up Rupert outside his club at a quarter past, but if we're late he won't mind waiting. Well, he may mind a bit, but he *will* wait, because he's surprisingly patient like that.'

The coachman, Carrington, listened to all this with a nod of greeting and a little grunt, but it was not an unwelcoming grunt, and by this point a good many pedestrians had paused to observe us, so it seemed to me altogether easier and less awkward to do as I was told.

'I was heading for Trevelyan's,' I explained as Carrington descended from his box to hand me in. 'But that's the other side of Regent Street, and the traffic is terrible...'

'Oh, don't worry about the traffic, Flotsam!' Hetty reassured me brightly. 'Carrington doesn't mind traffic at all, do you, Carrington? It gives him something to curse about, and I suspect that Carrington can be rather inventive with his language when the occasion requires. But perhaps we should collect Rupert first, just to be on the safe side, because I don't want him in a bad mood tonight at the Ellingworths' *soirée*. What do you say, Carrington?'

The Earl of Brabham's coachman was an old acquaintance, and thoroughly good-natured beneath a stern exterior, and he confirmed that it would indeed be more sensible to call at Mr Spencer's club before making our way to Bridle Lane.

'Trevelyan's?' Miss Peters asked me, as I settled myself beside her, wriggling slightly so that I sank as deeply as possible into the gorgeous seats of the earl's coach. 'Isn't that the new place?'

I told her that it was, and that it was ever such a beautiful shop, and full of the most amazing and wonderful things, and that she really must visit it. But a look of doubt remained on Miss Peters' face.

'Isn't it just a little bit out of the way?' she asked. 'And why would anyone go there when they can go to Ostermann's or Throok's? No, please don't look at me like that, Flottie!' she added hastily. 'I'm all for trying something new myself, but remember when that Russian opened his

47

store at the wrong end of Regent Street, and Lucinda Cullompton was seen buying gloves there, and then it turned out the gloves were all made of something that wasn't really silk, and there was a terrible fuss, and Lucinda Cullompton never lived it down? Well, of course, I'm sure the things at Trevelyan's are every bit as good as you say, but nobody wants to be the next Lucinda Cullompton, do they, Flottie? Which is why everyone carries on going to Ostermann's, and probably always will.'

My spirits sank a little at this, for although I was certain Scraggs had created a shop that was every bit as impressive as its rivals, I did recognise the truth in Miss Peters' words, and I wondered how the people with most money to spend were ever going to be persuaded to go there. Because if they did not, then it didn't really matter how many other customers Scraggs managed to attract; Trevelyan's would quickly become that dreaded thing, *the unfashionable shop*. And if that were to happen, I was terribly afraid it would break Scraggs' heart.

Miss Peters, although unaware of my particular attachment to the new store, apparently sensed my anxiety, for she gave my hand an extra-firm squeeze and began to prattle on merrily as if in an effort to restore my spirits. To my surprise, she returned to a subject that she had touched upon the previous day.

'You see, Flottie, you never did get a chance to explain it properly, and Rupert seems to be worried about it – something to do with a friend of his and a family heirloom. And I know he'd tell me all about it if I asked him to, but he'd be bound to take such a terribly long time about it, and would probably become a tiny bit pompous, so I thought it would be much better if I asked you to do it instead.'

'You mean, to explain about the Buckminster Necklace?'

Miss Peters looked a little exasperated.

'Yes, of course, Flottie! Haven't I just been saying that? I need someone to explain why everyone is so cross about this Buckminster Smelter person.'

And so, while the carriage trundled slowly towards Mayfair, I settled back into the hugely comfortable seats and told Miss Peters everything I knew about the individual who had become known in the newspapers as the Buckminster Smelter; starting with the discovery by customs officers in Liverpool of an unusually fine diamond in the possession of a rich American lady about to embark on one of the fast steamers for New York.

It was a fairly simple tale. The lady in question, a Mrs Toft-Hauer, had purchased the diamond the day before, in the lounge bar of the Adelphi Hotel, from one of those smartly dressed salesmen who hawk their wares around the plush lounges of upmarket establishments, the sort of salesmen whose business cards boast impressive addresses that seldom prove to be genuine.

Mrs Toft-Hauer, it turned out, had a good eye for a diamond. She had bought the stone in good faith, and had paid a substantial sum for it, albeit a sum that turned out to be only a fraction of its true worth. She had been perfectly willing to declare her purchase to the customs officer at the Albert Dock, who, with remarkable shrewdness, recognised the stone at once as part of the Buckminster Necklace – an historic and priceless piece that had gone missing from the stately home of Lord Buckminster some ten years earlier.

This discovery had caused an uproar – not because of the gem's value, but because it was no longer in its setting.

'You see, Hetty,' I explained, 'the Buckminster Neck-lace wasn't just any old string of diamonds; it was much more than that. It was a medieval masterpiece. Lord Buck-minster had turned down any number of requests to have it displayed in the British Museum.'

Which was why news of the necklace's destruction had caused such outrage. It's said Lord Buckminster turned grey overnight, and that the Queen's jeweller wept for a week. Twenty-seven of Europe's finest goldsmiths signed a letter to *The Times*, condemning the vandalism and demanding the immediate arrest of the person or persons responsible. And a consortium of Hatton Garden jewellers offered a substantial reward to anyone who could bring the culprit to justice, on the condition that the blackguard was given a very sound thrashing in the process.

No such rough justice was ever administered, however, for the perpetrator of the outrage remained at large. Worse still, in the months that followed, the discovery of various other notable gemstones – a ruby here, an emerald there – began to suggest that Lord Buckminster's necklace was not the only rare piece to have met such a fate.

'But really, Flottie,' Miss Peters asked, 'why would anyone do such a thing? The thief must have known that the stones were worth much more *in* the necklace than out of it.'

'Yes, Hetty. But according to Inspector Faraday of Scotland Yard, it can be almost impossible for a criminal to dispose of very famous pieces of jewellery. They're bound to be recognised, you see. If they do try, the inspector says they nearly always get caught.'

As I was speaking, the carriage had pulled over towards the kerb, and before Miss Peters could reply, the door was pulled open from the outside, revealing the smiling face of Mr Spencer.

'Exactly on time for once, Hetty!' he began cheerfully, then noticed that Miss Peters wasn't alone. 'Hello, Flotsam!' he went on. 'Has Hetty kidnapped you? If she's trying to persuade you to go shopping for hats with her, you must stand firm. It can take days, or even weeks.'

'Rupert, you beast!' Miss Peters protested loudly. 'We are taking Flotsam to Bridle Lane, and we are not talking about hats or about anything like that. We are talking about crime. Flotsam is telling me all about the Buckminster Necklace, and I imagine she knows a good deal more about it than you do.'

Mr Spencer, who had clambered in beside me, nodded briskly at this.

'She probably does, and a very sad story it is, too. The thing that perplexes me about it though, Flotsam,' he continued, as the carriage lurched into motion, 'is why the necklace should be broken up now, after such a long time. Because it's not just the Buckminster Necklace. The newspapers seem certain that the Rutherford Tiara has gone the same way, and that has been missing for nearly thirty years. And it's two decades since anyone last saw Mary Queen of Scots' emerald earrings, but the stones turned up in Amsterdam only last month.'

'Well, sir,' I told him politely, 'I heard Inspector Faraday of Scotland Yard tell Dr Watson that someone new is at work, someone who is willing to purchase such well-known stolen items at an acceptable price, and to take upon himself the risk of breaking them up and disposing of all the different bits.'

Miss Peters, who had a lively appreciation of fine jewellery, was looking appalled.

'Why, this smelter fellow is a monster! But I suppose, Flottie, that your inspector must be looking for someone quite rich, who does it for the thrill.'

I think both Rupert Spencer and I must have looked similarly bemused.

'And just why would they be doing that, Hetty?' he asked her.

Miss Peters looked at him with genuine astonishment.

'Why, Rupert, because smelting things must be quite a hot and messy job, so I don't suppose he does it for fun. And obviously he doesn't do it for the money, does he?'

It was unusual to see Mr Spencer quite so taken aback, but he made no attempt to hide his confusion.

'But how can you be so sure?'

Miss Peters gave a little sigh and turned to face us again.

'Well, I may not know much about smelters, Rupert, but I do know a bit about hats. And if you think about it, Lord Buckminster's necklace is a bit like an out-of-fashion bonnet – very beautiful, but impossible to sell. Now, being a man, and terrible at shopping, you probably imagine that you could buy a bonnet like that for next to nothing, because the milliner will be desperate to get rid of it. But the milliner knows what all the feathers and silks in the bonnet are worth, and she will never sell it for less than that. Why should she? After all, if she had the time, she could take it apart and re-use them herself. You see?'

It was clear from his expression that Mr Spencer didn't see, so Miss Peters rolled her eyes and carried on.

'I don't really know how I can make it any plainer for you, Rupert. You see, if someone *does* eventually buy the bonnet, then they will have to pay enough to cover the cost of all the feathers and ribbons and things, or very close to it. So how could they possibly make any money by pulling it apart and selling those bits? Sometimes, Rupert, I think you don't understand money at all.'

I saw the light dawning in Mr Spencer's face.

'My word, Hetty. I see what you mean.'

Miss Peters gave a little yawn.

'There really is no mystery to it, Rupert,' she told him airily.

Mr Spencer grinned at her, apparently unchastened by this reproof.

'Well, speaking of mysteries, Hetty, I have news of something infinitely more mysterious than the fate of the Rutherford Tiara. It really is the most peculiar thing. If you'd care to hear it, that is…'

He paused to straighten his cravat, and Miss Peters, who had stopped yawning, gave a little 'tut' of annoyance.

'Oh, really, Rupert! Don't be such a tease! Tell us at once, or I shall kick you in the shins.'

The young gentleman smiled.

'Very well…'

Then he leaned forwards and rubbed his hands together.

'You see, I was talking to some fellows at the club today, and I found myself telling them about the extraordinary delivery my uncle received yesterday. As I expected, it produced a bit of merriment, especially the bit about him chasing the hen around his study, and I would have thought no more about it if I hadn't noticed that the only person not smiling was young Tommy Merriman, who was looking at me as though I'd just made his hat disappear into thin air. "Tell me all that again," he insisted, so I did, only this time no one was laughing, we were all watching Tommy. And when I'd finished, he looked a little puzzled and shook his head, and announced that exactly the same thing had happened to his father, two days before.'

Mr Spencer looked across at me, then over at Miss Peters, before he went on.

'Well, obviously, the first thing we did was compare details, and the circumstances of the two deliveries seem remarkably similar. Neither hen was expected, neither was accompanied with any details about the sender, both were addressed directly to their recipients on labels attached with strong twine. From my uncle's description, it sounds as though both labels were similar too, with a black-and-white pattern on one side and just the name and a little scribble on the other. I confess I couldn't remember a great deal about Uncle's hen because I barely caught a glimpse of it, but it seems both creatures were mainly black.

'Well, there was a lot of talk about pranksters then, and speculation about what sort of person would find any humour in that sort of thing. But there was one aspect of the whole thing that puzzled everyone...'

And here Mr Spencer paused, as if rehearsing it all in his mind.

'You see, nobody could suggest anything at all to connect my uncle with Merriman's father. The two don't appear to know each other very well socially, they have widely different interests, they belong to different clubs and, as far as any of us could make out, they have completely different circles of friends. So, there's your mystery, Hetty. Why were two such different people selected as victims of the same joke?'

And I might have found that question even more inter-esting, had my brain not already been full of Christmas trees and violinists, and had we not, at that very moment, pulled up outside Trevelyan's. I could see at once through the large windows in its main doors that very few customers were in the store, but more importantly, I could see Scraggs in the process of leaving, his shoulders hunched miserably under his overcoat.

'Excuse me,' I mumbled to my companions, my hand already on the carriage door. 'I really have to go.'

And I was gone before either of them had time to reply.

—

I caught up with Scraggs some twenty yards further down Bridle Lane. He turned when he heard my footsteps trotting in pursuit.

'Hello, Flot!' He managed his familiar smile and my heart gave a little leap. It seemed too long since I'd seen it. 'Are you looking for me?'

'I've been looking for you for ages, Scraggs,' I told him, taking the arm he held out for me. 'Tell me, how are things going?'

He gave a little shrug and pursed his lips.

'It's hard work, Flot, but we're getting there. The old store's come up a treat, don't you think? Makes me proud to look at it.'

'It looks... amazing,' I told him. 'Much finer than Throok's. It makes me happy just to step inside. But what about trade? Are things still a little... a little quiet?'

He gave my hand a squeeze.

'Don't worry about that, Flot. Things are still very slow, but I've always expected that. When I worked out the figures, I gave us six months to catch up with Throok's. And Christmas will help too, if we can get a few more people in.'

Still walking arm in arm, we turned into Brewer Street where the pavements were busier. Very timidly, I told him what Miss Peters had said about her friends staying loyal to Ostermann's.

'These things take time, Flot,' he reassured me. 'We'll win them over in the end, I know we will. I know we will. No, my most pressing problem at the moment is Mr Trevelyan – persuading him that everything's all right. That's where I'm going now. He's a nice old man, but when he sees the shop floor mostly empty, he gets jumpy. We'll be needing a whole load more stock in the New Year, and he'll need to stump up for it, and if he doesn't, well, the whole thing collapses. So my main job at the moment is keeping his spirits up.'

'You'll manage that, Scraggs, I know you will.' And I hugged his arm a little tighter, then stopped dead in my tracks. 'But what am I thinking! I'm supposed to be at your tea counter right now, with a big order for Baker Street!'

So with a hurried goodbye, and with my fingers crossed for his meeting with Mr Trevelyan, I retraced my steps as rapidly as I could, with a bounce in my stride that hadn't been there a few minutes earlier.

Chapter 4

My high spirits carried me all the way back to Baker Street, my tasks completed in good order, all my deliveries made, and the kitchen clock showing only a few minutes after noon. I still felt anxious about Scraggs, and about the future of Trevelyan's, and I knew that Scraggs was anxious too. But somehow talking to him had revived my spirits wonderfully. And if anyone could make a success of things, I was sure he could.

I said as much to Mrs Hudson as I tumbled into the kitchen, brandishing my ticked-off list, then depositing the parcels I'd brought with me into an untidy pile on the kitchen table. And there was something hugely comforting about the steady manner in which she began to tidy things away, all the time asking me detailed questions about my expedition. Had Tom Mallows recovered from his shortness of breath? Were the Penhursts back from Paris? Was there Northumberland grouse to be had at Lamingtons? When I told her Mr Spencer's story about the second chicken, she raised an eyebrow but made no comment. For a happy ten minutes, everything seemed very *ordinary*. It was good to be home.

But no sooner had my purchases been put away and the kettle boiled for tea, than our tranquil interlude was brought to an end by a knock at the front door and the arrival of a small boy with a telegram for Mr Holmes.

'Saw it when it came in,' he confided in a whisper as he passed me the envelope. 'Sez it's urgent. Can't read the long words, but I do know "urgent". It's one of my favourites.'

Back in the kitchen, I relayed this information to Mrs Hudson and the two of us looked at each other for a moment, then looked down at the envelope on its little silver tray.

'Mr Holmes thought he might be at Scotland Yard till four o'clock, ma'am,' I remarked, 'and he was probably going straight to Victoria Station after that. So if it really *is* urgent… But, of course, it might be about a personal matter.'

'For Mr Holmes, child?' Mrs Hudson looked at me pointedly.

'We should probably open it then, shouldn't we, ma'am?' I decided. 'Because if it really is very urgent, I could always take it to him at Scotland Yard, even though he doesn't like to be disturbed.'

'Most sensible, Flotsam,' Mrs Hudson replied, slicing open the envelope with one deft flick of her finger. 'I agree entirely. Now, what have we here?'

> URGENT DEVELOPMENT RE CORTADO STOP VITAL YOU ATTEND RUMBELOW SOLICITOR ONE PM TODAY STOP SEND ASSOCIATE IF UNAVAILABLE STOP DENHAM

The two of us regarded this breathless communication in silence for a moment, then Mrs Hudson looked across at the kitchen clock.

'Am I to run down to Scotland Yard with it, ma'am?' I asked, trying to work out in my head how long it would take me.

'Certainly not, child.' Her voice was calm but very firm. 'By the time you've made it all that way, and then persuaded someone to find Mr Holmes for you, the appointment will already be missed. So either Mr Denham will have to be disappointed, or else...'

She rubbed her hands together briskly.

'Now, Flottie, your best clothes are already laid out. If you give your face the quickest of washes, I'll sort out your hair, and if you hurry you should be able to make it.'

I looked at her in astonishment.

'You want *me* to go, ma'am?'

'Why ever not, Flottie? You'll still be able to meet Dr Watson in Bromley Place at four o'clock, and you'll be able to tell him all about it then. And Mr Denham does make a point of insisting that, should Mr Holmes not be available, he must send someone in his place.'

'But, Mrs Hudson, ma'am, I'm sure he didn't mean someone like me. I think he meant...'

'Mr Denham is in no position to choose,' Mrs Hudson told me firmly, placing her hand in the small of my back and beginning to guide me towards the door. 'Perhaps I would think differently were it a different solicitor, Flotsam, but Mr Rumbelow has known you since you were a tiny scrap of a thing, and is fully aware of the high regard in which you are held here. As for Mr Denham, well, he will find Mr Holmes' assistant to be a composed and intelligent young lady. Although, unless you get that smudge of soot off your chin, he will not think you a very elegant one.'

'But would you not like to go yourself, ma'am?' I asked, pausing on the threshold.

'Good lord, Flottie, I've no time for that. Those part-ridges will be arriving, I've got mince pies to make, and I want to talk to the sweep about the flue. What's more,' she added, waving vaguely at the kitchen table where Dr Watson's society magazine still lay, 'Mr Holmes has asked me to go through a list of country houses in Sussex, jotting down my recollections of their entrance halls. Now be off with you, or I'll ask the sweep to send you up the flue in person.'

It was a bit of a rush – partly because Mrs Hudson insisted on arranging my hair in a very fashionable style, and partly because the busy-ness of the streets rather hampered me in my progress – but I made it to the solicitor's offices with five minutes to spare.

Mr Rumbelow was a portly gentleman of some sixty years of age, who had known both Mrs Hudson and Mr Holmes for a great many years, and whose occasional visits to Baker Street – sometimes above stairs, sometimes below – had been a part of my life for as long as I could remember. On this occasion he seemed delighted to see me, rising from his enormous mahogany desk to shake my hand, and to enquire how he could be of assistance. When I explained what had happened, and that Mrs Hudson had sent me in response to Mr Denham's telegram, he simply nodded sagely without showing any obvious sign of surprise.

'Indeed, indeed,' he replied, offering me a seat in one of the deep leather chairs reserved for visitors. 'A most sensible precaution, and one of which I'm most certain Mr Holmes would approve. Mrs Hudson has always been the most sensible of women. Of course, my client...' He paused, as though choosing his words with caution. 'My client might find such a substitution rather unorthodox, but he is perfectly free to proceed without you if he wishes. Now, I believe that must be the sound of his arrival. If you wait here, Flotsam, I shall greet him in the outer office and prepare the ground...'

And so I waited nervously in my chair, partly afraid that Mr Denham would refuse to countenance my presence there, partly afraid of the immense responsibility upon my shoulders should I be allowed to remain. From the room beyond, I could hear the two gentlemen exchanging greetings, then Mr Rumbelow's voice sounding brisk and business-like.

'Indeed, sir, indeed. Mr Holmes has, as you suggested, sent someone in his place. She is awaiting us in my office.'

'*She?*' Mr Denham's bewilderment was clear from his tone. 'Can that be right? Or has there been some confusion? When I sent that telegram, I rather intended to suggest Dr Watson...'

'It seems, sir, that Dr Watson is also unavailable. Of course, if you do not wish Miss Flotsam to attend...' He cleared his throat politely, then lowered his voice slightly. 'Sir James Croxton was singing her praises to me only the other day. You recall that failed assassination attempt in Brunton Street in the autumn...? The details are never to be made public, but you may recall that one or two of the newspaper accounts mentioned a young lady present at the scene...?'

'My word!' Mr Denham sounded genuinely impressed. 'I *do* recall some such thing...'

I couldn't quite catch the exchange that followed, but it was clear from Mr Denham's rather admiring expression when he was shown into the room that Mr Rumbelow had not been backward in recommending me.

It was also clear that Mr Denham didn't recognise me, not even in the slightest. The housemaid who had taken his hat and coat in Baker Street the previous evening and the smartly dressed young woman in Mr Rumbelow's office were clearly two quite different people.

'Miss Flotsam,' he began, greeting me with an outstretched hand, 'I had been warned to expect the unexpected when dealing with Sherlock Holmes, and perhaps you will allow me to say that this is a most agreeable surprise?'

It was said very pleasantly – neither condescending nor flirtatious – and I forgave him for not recalling our previous encounter. I did look very different. And he still struck me as a likeable gentleman.

'Now, Mr Rumbelow,' he went on, 'perhaps you could explain why you have summoned me here. You have information about Mr Cortado, I think you said? That sounds like excellent news! Is he safe? How can I assist him?'

But the solicitor was already shaking his head.

'Please, I beg you both, be seated.' He took a handkerchief from his breast pocket and began to dab at his forehead. 'I do have a letter for you from Mr Cortado, but I regret to say, sir, that the communication is not a new one. That is to say, it pre-dates his recent disappearance. Perhaps I should explain.'

He dabbed at his forehead again, then reached into a drawer in his desk and took out two thick, creamy envelopes.

'As you may be aware, I have had the honour of assisting Mr Cortado with his legal affairs for a number of years. Generally, it has not been an onerous task. Mr Cortado is one of my steadier clients, and other than occasionally requiring me to read through a lease, he has very rarely had need of my services.'

Mr Rumbelow gave his forehead a final rub, as if for good measure, then returned his handkerchief to his pocket.

'Imagine, then, my surprise when he called at these offices one morning a few days ago and entrusted me with the two envelopes that I have here. His instructions were most explicit. I was to keep both envelopes in my possession until he returned to collect them. But if he had not returned by one o'clock this afternoon, I was to ensure that both envelopes were opened and that you and I were to share the contents. As you will see, Mr Denham, this one is addressed to you. The other is addressed to myself.'

'I don't like the sound of this at all.' Mr Denham was looking extremely worried. 'It's as though he was preparing for something that he feared was coming... When exactly did this take place?'

The solicitor pursed his lips.

'Of course, I was unaware of this at the time, but I now understand that it was on the very morning of his disappearance.'

'I see.' Mr Denham digested this for a moment, still looking very sombre. 'Then I suggest that we read these letters without delay.'

By way of reply, Mr Rumbelow rose in his seat and passed him one of the envelopes. Mr Denham cradled it in his hand for a moment, then broke the seal and extracted a single, densely written sheet of paper.

Dear Horace, he read.

I find myself in the most hideous tangle, and can see no way out of it. I must decide today. If I am a coward, I will do nothing. I will retrieve this note and you will never read it. The world will still admire me, the crowds will still come to hear me play, but I will go to the grave despising myself, full of a self-contempt that will surely destroy me. Or, if I can summon up the courage, I will step from my house today and face my destiny, knowing full well the cost. If I choose that course, it is my belief that you will probably never see me again in this life. There can be no way back. This situation is entirely of my own making, and I have no one but myself to blame. If you ever hear anyone else reproached for the desperate action I am taking, I beg you to correct them, and to assert with utter conviction that the fault is all mine.

Mr Denham paused to clear his throat. He looked shocked, and very pale.

I have only one regret: I know the world will soon forget me, but I fear that you and perhaps one other will attempt to remember. You will have no grave to visit, but you may try to lay flowers at the altar of my memory. I beg you to resist all such temptation. And I must ask you to shoulder for me a sacred responsibility. You are aware of the very profound respect I feel for Miss Burrows, and I, in turn, know you to be her truest and most devoted friend. May I therefore ask you to convey to her my warmest compliments, and to assure her of the very real and profound regret I feel at such

> *an abrupt severance of our friendship. And please*
> *deliver to her, from my house in Bromley Place, my*
> *Monteverdi violin, as a lasting proof of my esteem.*

Mr Denham broke off to reach for his handkerchief, and dabbed at the corner of his eye, then swallowed hard and continued to read.

> *Denham, I would not for the world have Miss*
> *Burrows lose any chance of future happiness*
> *because of me. Therefore, I beg you to endeavour,*
> *by any means at your disposal, to help her to forget*
> *me. A chapter is over. Now the world must forget*
> *and move on.*

> *Your foolish and impulsive friend,*
> *Maximillian Cortado*

These last words were read in a trembling voice, and were followed by a little sob as Horace Denham once again reached for his handkerchief.

'Forgive me, Rumbelow, Miss Flotsam...' he began. 'Such a message... Such news... What can it mean? It is hard to take in. Can it be that he is telling us he intends to take his own life? I can scarcely believe that! Or was he going out to meet some character who he felt certain would do him harm? Both alternatives are appalling! I never knew Cortado engage with anything shady or dangerous. I never really knew him do anything but play the violin...'

With sudden passion, he flung the letter down.

'What a fool! What a damned fool! If only he had talked to us about all this! Whatever his plight, Miss Burrows and I could surely have helped him. But now...

This is great villainy, Mr Rumbelow. And it seems we must fear the worst. The very worst. God knows how I will break the news to Lavinia!'

I watched Mr Rumbelow reach for his own handker-chief, as if to offer it to Mr Denham. However, on realising that the object in his hand was very far from pristine, he returned it hastily to his waistcoat.

'We should certainly communicate this information to the police without delay, Mr Denham,' he urged. 'As for what we should tell Miss Burrows, they will know exactly what is to be done. But first, if you will forgive me, sir, it was Mr Cortado's wish that I should read his other letter. With your permission...'

Mr Denham was busy blowing his nose, but managed to nod as he did so.

The second letter proved to be much shorter than the first, and Mr Rumbelow scanned it swiftly.

'It is very much a simple statement of his affairs,' he concluded, 'reminding me that I am his executor and holder of his will. Let's see...

> My dear Rumbelow, etc... As my executor, etc...
> Fees owing from performances... Prompt settle-
> ment, etc... If any period of time ensues before
> my death is proved, exercise customary diligence...
> outstanding debts and bills to be paid in full...
> salaries of all servants to be paid in full until
> probate granted... Earnings overseas... Rates and
> taxes, etc...

Mr Rumbelow was nodding as he read. 'All very sens-ible and admirably clear. Ah, and here's one last bit that concerns you, sir,' he added.

As per my letter to Horace Denham, it is my stated
wish that my Monteverdi violin should be given to
Mrs Lavinia Burrows promptly, and without any
delay whatsoever, to be her property in perpetuity.
Yours faithfully, Maximillian Cortado, Esquire

The solicitor removed his spectacles and looked up at us.

'A very well-ordered and organised document,' he concluded. 'It suggests that Mr Cortado was very much prepared for the worst, and had given considerable thought to such a contingency. These instructions will ensure that no one suffers any financial hardship from his disappearance. As to his will, well, if it comes to that, I know that on his wife's death he had me draw up a document leaving his entire estate to various charities. But, of course, we need not think of such things now. Instead, sir, I suggest we lay these documents before the appropriate authorities without delay.'

But Mr Denham was still shaking his head, as though struggling to comprehend the import of the letters.

'Maximillian Cortado, gone? The world's greatest violinist? It cannot be! For a great man to have his life snuffed out... And to go to his fate so calmly... Why, sir, it simply defies belief!'

I repeated this remark to Dr Watson when I met him half an hour later in Bromley Square. I had left Mr Denham and Mr Rumbelow together, the two preparing to go to the police. Aware that Dr Watson might well be early, I hadn't volunteered to join them, and I had found the doctor waiting for me, stamping his feet with cold, by the rails in front of the house. Before we'd even rung the bell, I had poured out the whole story of Mr Cortado's letters, concluding with his friend's despairing final exclamation.

'Defies belief?' Dr Watson pondered this. 'Well, I'd have to agree, Flotsam. It would certainly seem to be a rum business. Decidedly rum. Sounds as though the fellow's in trouble with the debt collectors.'

And with that he offered me his arm.

'Come, Flotsam. We have a job to do. Let's go inside and see what strange secrets await us.'

—

Unfortunately, Mr Cortado's house in Bromley Place didn't seem to harbour any strange secrets.

We were greeted by Shapps, the butler, who had been warned of our arrival by a note from Sherlock Holmes himself, and who seemed extremely excited to see us.

'Do come in, sir, madam, do please come in. Let me take your hats, coats… May I bring you something? A little something to keep out the cold, perhaps, sir? Were Mr Cortado here, he would undoubtedly offer you whisky. Later perhaps? Of course. Please, let me show you into the drawing room. I've lit the fire in anticipation of your visit, and it is such a lovely room at this time of day. Mr Cortado rarely had time to enjoy it because of all his practising, but when he did have a moment, he would often comment on the excellent light. I've heard him say that the view of St Bardolph's spire carries his eyes up to the clouds. He has a great fondness for clouds, does Mr Cortado. I have heard him comment on them more than once.'

Shapps, it seemed, was not the silent sort of butler.

'I am more than pleased to answer any questions you may have, sir,' he went on, addressing himself mostly to Dr Watson. 'Everyone here is so worried about the master.

The mood below stairs is one of great anguish. We are all greatly fond of Mr Cortado, you see, and we're quite desperate with worry. Perhaps you would like me to start by telling you about the day of his disappearance?'

Apparently Mr Shapps was the sort of witness who was perfectly capable of interviewing himself, and I grew curious about what other questions he would decide to answer. Perhaps Dr Watson shared my curiosity on the subject, because he simply nodded and allowed the butler to continue.

'Well, sir, that day began as any other. Mr Cortado breakfasted in the morning-room on two poached eggs and a kipper, then took a turn around the square before returning to smoke a cigar. You will, of course, be surprised at this, for you will doubtless be aware of Mr Cortado's reputation for rehearsal. It is said that no violinist has ever worked harder at his craft than Mr Cortado. He is quite famous for it. Indeed, sir, he once told me that he would have been little better than a fairground fiddler had Mrs Cortado not taken him under her wing and instilled in him an understanding of the need for practice!'

The butler clearly considered this the most outrageous and amusing piece of badinage, for he grinned broadly at the memory.

'Certainly, in Mrs Cortado's day, there would have been no walk around the square, it would have been practice straight after breakfast, and practice before it, too, except on Sundays. And no cigar either, because Mrs Cortado believed that tobacco smoke reduced the efficiency of the lungs, and that a great violinist needed every possible ounce of oxygen if he were to give his best performance.'

Dr Watson held up his hand to pause Mr Shapps in his flow.

'So, in your opinion, Mr Cortado has grown less diligent in his practice of late?' he asked thoughtfully.

'Not at all, sir,' Mr Shapps told him firmly. 'If anything, of late he has been much more like his former self. But things got very bad when Mrs Cortado passed away. We feared he was going into decline. He barely touched his violin for days on end. He would rise late, take himself off for frequent walks, and spend a lot of time in the garden doing nothing but stare at the plants. He put on a brave face, sir. In fact, on the surface, he was every bit as affable as before, but sometimes I used to find him out in the square in the evenings, looking at the stars, and the expression on his face then… Well, it's hard to describe, sir. Perhaps our housekeeper summed it up best, because she's very shrewd that way. "The master's longing for what's lost," she used to say. And I could only agree. It was most upsetting to see.'

He shook his head at the memory, then brightened.

'Fortunately, Miss Burrows quickly grasped the situation – she had always been a great friend of the master's wife, you see, and a tremendous admirer of the master's playing. She is a lady of strong character, sir, and once she brought her influence to bear, things quickly became a lot better. Mr Cortado returned to practice, and there was no more moping in the garden after that. With Miss Burrows so frequently in the house, things quickly felt like the old days. And Mr Cortado seemed less lost, sir. Playing the violin, you see, sir… Well, I always thought it distracted him from his worries. Yes, there's no doubt that things have been a lot more regular and ordered since Miss Burrows took a hand in things.'

'Sounds like the sort of chap who lived for his art,' Dr Watson surmised. 'I've known one or two fellows like that. Neither of them the sort you want to sit next to on a long train journey, though.' He stroked his chin for a moment or two, then returned his attention to the butler. 'So, carry on, Shapps. What did Mr Cortado do after breakfast on the day he disappeared?'

'Well, sir, after the walk and the cigar, Mr Cortado did finally take up his violin. But he only practised for a very short time, sir, before calling for writing things and dashing off a couple of letters. I've no idea to whom, sir, as he insisted on delivering them himself, even though I offered to take them to the post box in person.'

'Yes, we know about those letters.' Dr Watson looked pleased to be a little ahead of the game. 'And we know where he took them. Was he gone long?'

'Rather longer than I expected, sir,' the butler replied, 'but I believe he also visited his bank, and he mentioned that he had looked around some shops. He didn't say so specifically, sir, but I rather hoped he might have been shopping for a gift for Miss Burrows. For some weeks, we have all been expecting an engagement to be announced.'

'Tricky sort of thing, shopping for an engagement gift,' Dr Watson mused. 'Friend of mine who had a passion for antique snuff-boxes ended up in the dog-house for months. Was Mr Cortado more successful?'

The butler looked a little pained at the question.

'I couldn't say, sir. The master would hardly share such a thing with me. When he returned, he got down to some serious practice, and remained upstairs until around three o'clock in the afternoon, when he came down to ask about the afternoon post. And a few minutes after that, he went out, sir. I've had many hours to recall that moment, asking myself if he looked strained or anxious, or in any way out of spirits. But I honest don't think he did. If anything, he seemed very calm, sir. His last words to me were a comment he made on the doorstep just as he was stepping out about how rare it was in London to see the stars so clearly.'

'So let me get this straight...' I could tell by the little frown on Dr Watson's forehead that he and I had been struck by the same detail. 'Mr Cortado had been practising in much the way he always did, until he broke off to enquire about the afternoon post. And then, only a few minutes later, he left this house, never to be seen again. What do you think, Flotsam?'

'It would be interesting to know what post he received that afternoon, sir,' I suggested meekly.

We both turned to look at Shapps, who for once seemed hesitant.

'Well, sir, madam, I really couldn't say. I think there were one or two letters from musical academies and the like. Those are always easy to tell from the crests printed on the envelopes. And probably a couple of bills, sir. As I remember it, there were at least two or three other letters, but that wasn't at all uncommon. Admirers from across the globe write to Mr Shapps, sir. As I recall, he took all the post to his practice room to read, sir, as was his usual custom. There is a small bureau there where he generally deals with correspondence.'

At Dr Watson's insistence, we were conducted at once to Mr Cortado's practice room, which proved a bare, rather cold room near the top of the house, lit by a single small window. It had, Mr Shapps assured us, excellent acoustical properties, but as far as I could see, little else to recommend it. I found my admiration for Mr Cortado's dedication increasing. To spend so long in such a place – practising, practising, practising – must have taken an iron will, and a willingness to forego a great many comforts. Even the chair at the small writing bureau looked rather uncomfortable, and – apart from a stand holding a single violin case – there was no other furniture in the room.

'We should like to take a look through Mr Cortado's papers,' Dr Watson informed the butler firmly. 'But of course the police have probably been here before us.'

'On the contrary, sir.' There was a very clear note of disdain in Shapps' voice. 'The London police have shown no interest whatsoever in any of the master's effects. When they finally accepted he was missing, their first step, apparently, was to check at the railway stations, and once they had formed the opinion that the master had departed for Bognor Regis, they took no further interest in the case.'

'Is it at all possible, please, that he really did go to Bognor?' I asked meekly, still not sure that this large and talkative man would tolerate being interrogated by someone like me. But it was a question he seemed to welcome.

'In my opinion it is not remotely possible, Miss,' he informed me. 'I have never heard the name of that place uttered within these walls. The master has no friends in Bognor, no acquaintances, no business connections of any sort. Mr Cortado was a man familiar with the great cities of Europe. He was not, I am certain, familiar with Bognor.'

'I daresay it was just some other fellow in a boater,' Dr Watson replied soothingly. 'In a city as large as this one, it's only to be expected that someone somewhere is wearing the same hat as you. Now, come on, Flotsam, let's see if we can find that afternoon's post.'

This task, however, did not appear very difficult. On opening the bureau, we found it contained some loose sheets of music paper, a number of old theatrical bills advertising performances by Mr Cortado, and a neat pile of eight assorted envelopes, all of them sealed but for one.

'That's them!' Mr Shapps told us excitedly. 'I recognise them all right. That's the pile I brought in that afternoon.'

But Dr Watson was looking puzzled.

'It's a bit strange, isn't it, Flotsam? Where are all his other papers? Old letters, that sort of thing. It's almost as if he cleared the decks before he went.'

'It seems only one piece of post was opened, sir, but there's no sign of the contents. Look — the envelope's empty.'

So together we searched the bureau drawers, only to find that each was as tidy — and as strangely sterile — as the next. They contained plenty of stationery, some unused notebooks, various pots of ink and a box of Egyptian cigarettes, but no correspondence or writing of any sort.

'Must have taken it with him, damn the fellow!' Dr Watson muttered when our efforts were finally exhausted. 'Seems to me that letter is the key to the whole business.'

'I fear, sir, that I don't recognise the writing.' Shapps had taken up the empty envelope and was studying it. 'It is an unusual, almost child-like hand. The sort, perhaps, that someone might produce who wished to remain *incognito*.'

Dr Watson took the envelope from him and peered at it.

'I'd say you were right, Shapps. It's disguised hand-writing if ever I saw it. What do you think, Flotsam?'

But I wasn't looking at the envelope, or even thinking about the handwriting. I was looking around the room, wondering where, other than in his desk, Mr Cortado might have concealed an important document. The practice room seemed to offer very few possibilities, barring loose floorboards or secret panels. And, after all, it was highly likely that the violinist had indeed taken the letter with him, either to secrete elsewhere in the house, or to carry with him on his mysterious final journey. Even so, I did still have one suggestion to make – but the answer to Dr Watson's next question put it quite out of my head.

'So, Shapps,' the doctor began, 'you've told us that Mr Cortado left the house very shortly after reading a letter which arrived in the afternoon post. A letter that is now missing. But tell me, and this is vitally important, are you certain that nothing else untoward occurred in the days before Mr Cortado's disappearance? No unexpected callers? No telegrams? No unexplained absences? Nothing at all that might explain his peculiar departure?'

'Nothing, sir.' The butler answered with great certainty. 'Mr Cortado is a man of routine, and each of those days was very like any other.'

And perhaps, had he said no more, all the events of the days that followed might have turned out very differently. But just as he began to turn away, a thought struck him.

'I suppose there was *one* thing, sir, one thing that was a little unusual. But it is so trivial it is hardly worth mentioning.'

'And what was that, Shapps?' Dr Watson asked sharply.

'It was two days earlier, sir. But it really was nothing. Just a mix-up of some sort. That morning, you see, sir, quite out of the blue, and for no reason that anyone could explain, Mr Cortado received a delivery addressed to him personally. It proved to be a small crate, sir, containing a lively and rather ill-tempered chicken.'

Chapter 5

'*Another* chicken, Flotsam?'

I wouldn't say that Mrs Hudson looked startled by the news, but I did have the satisfaction of seeing both her eyebrows twitch quite markedly. 'I confess that is a surprise.'

Dr Watson and I had not lingered very long in Bromley Place after Shapps' revelation about the unexpected hen. My companion, of course, was at first somewhat confused by the significance I placed on the incident, and was keen to conduct a full search of the house in the hope of unearthing Mr Cortado's mysterious letter. But my mind was awhirl, and I needed time to think, time to explain things to Dr Watson and to work out what it all meant. I knew I'd be unable to concentrate on any search until I had, and as I pointed out as I dragged him away, we could always return the following day.

On arriving in Baker Street, however, we found Mr Holmes had not yet returned home, and when I mentioned that Mrs Hudson had been making mince pies, it was Dr Watson who suggested that we repaired to the kitchen.

'For it's a beastly cold evening, and it's always warm down there,' he reasoned, 'and nothing beats a mince pie fresh from the oven.'

The suggestion did not greatly surprise me, for I knew Dr Watson always enjoyed his visits below stairs, and it didn't seem to surprise Mrs Hudson either, because she waved us both towards the kitchen table, where a platter was piled with small pies, their pastry so sweet and crumbly that I ate three without pausing, and still went back for a fourth. Dr Watson exercised a little more restraint, consuming the same number of pies rather more slowly, but when Mrs Hudson proposed that these should be accompanied by a glass of the old oloroso sherry, his bliss appeared complete.

And while we revived ourselves, we spilled out the whole story of our afternoon, from my arrival at Mr Rumbelow's to our departure from Mr Cortado's house in Bromley Place. The revelation that Mr Cortado, like the Earl of Brabham, had received a hen quite unexpectedly made her pause in her scrubbing of the draining board.

'So you think these birds must have been sent by the same person, Flotsam?' She considered this for a moment, idly rubbing her forefinger over the bristles of her scrubbing brush. 'We can't be sure of that, of course, but it would certainly seem likely. Now, let's see… Lord Brabham, Mr Fergus Merriman and Mr Maximillian Cortado…'

'They seem an ill-assorted threesome, don't they, Mrs H?' Dr Watson remarked. 'I don't know much about this Merriman fellow, but Flotsam tells me that he and the earl are not well acquainted.'

'I know a little about the Merriman family, sir, but not a great deal. Fergus Merriman is the grandson of Sir Joshua Merriman, and I'm told he's a rather unassuming gentleman, with a very great interest in antiquities. In other words, it would be hard to think of anyone less like the Earl of Brabham.'

'And neither of them at all like Mr Cortado, ma'am,' I pointed out. 'If it is a joke of some sort, it isn't a very funny one. Of course, the earl was very cross about it, and I suppose someone might find that amusing, but most people would simply assume the delivery was an error and wouldn't think of it again.'

'And that seems to have been the case with Mr Cortado,' Dr Watson added. 'According to Shapps, he took a good look at the label, as if trying to work out what it all meant, then said something about it being a very strange thing, and asked Shapps to take the bird away and find a home for it. Apparently Shapps has a nephew in Clapham who keeps hens, so if you ever want to examine the fowl in question, Mrs H, we know where to find it!'

This was clearly intended as a jocular remark, but to my surprise Mrs Hudson nodded with great seriousness.

'Now, about that label,' she went on. 'Is there any suggestion that it resembled the one attached to Lord Brabham's bird?'

I explained that Shapps had been able to tell us very little about the label, only that it had been clearly marked with the name *Mr Maximillian Cortado*, and that there might have been a printed pattern of some sort on the rear of the card. He freely admitted that after seeing his master's name, he had paid little attention to it. He vaguely recalled that perhaps Mr Cortado had pushed the label into a waistcoat pocket after reading it, though equally he might have tossed it into the fire. There had certainly been no trace of it in the violinist's desk.

'A great shame,' Mrs Hudson remarked, but before she could say more, our little gathering was interrupted by a knock on the area door, and the appearance a moment later, warmly wrapped against the cold, of Mr Sherlock Holmes himself.

'Ah! Just as I thought!' he exclaimed happily, acknow-ledging each of us with a nod of the head. 'Forgive my unorthodox entry, Mrs Hudson, but I had a strong conviction that I should find Dr Watson down here at your kitchen table.'

'How's that, Holmes?' Dr Watson asked. 'You're not going to tell me that you could somehow deduce it from the position of the study shutters, or the light in the hallway, or the muddy marks my boots left on the top step?'

Mr Holmes smiled at him fondly as he tugged off his gloves.

'Far from it! But I swear I could smell those mince pies a good ten yards from our front door, and I know from experience that you're not a man who likes to partake of festive fare in solitude.'

His friend acknowledged this with an amiable grunt, and Mrs Hudson put down her scrubbing brush.

'I daresay, sir, on a night such as this, you might find a restorative drink in order. Flottie, would you be so good as to fetch Mr Holmes a bottle of brown ale from the cellar? And a plate for a mince pie too, if you would. And then, sir, perhaps you would let Flotsam tell you all about Mr Cortado's chicken.'

I'm ashamed to say it, but by the time I'd finished repeating the whole story to my employer, there were only three or four pies left on the platter; Mr Holmes had already started a second bottle of beer; and Dr Watson's sherry glass had been refilled for the fourth time. Mrs

Hudson had removed her apron, and had joined us at the table, her own glass cupped delicately in her hand.

When I finished speaking, Mr Holmes thought for a moment, then nodded.

'As you have observed, Flotsam, the unsolicited poultry are hard to ignore, and we would be foolish not to attempt to learn more. In Mr Cortado's case, the arrival of the fowl preceded three actions that were not typical of his usual routine – the writing of letters to Mr Rumbelow and Mr Denham; his insistence on delivering them himself while also spending a period of time elsewhere, ostensibly at shops and at his bank; and, finally, of course, his unexplained disappearance. But we must remember that your average fellow in the street, if asked to consider the sudden vanishing of a distinguished violinist, would consider it much more likely to be brought on by the arrival of a mysterious letter than by the delivery of a hen. Which brings us back to the item of post which arrived immediately before his disappearance. I'm a little surprised, Flotsam, Watson, that neither of you thought to bring the letter with you.'

Dr Watson looked astonished, and a little outraged.

'But we told you, Holmes, there was no sign of it. We searched the writing desk as thoroughly as anyone could. We even checked for secret compartments and false bottoms, didn't we, Flotsam? Of course, I know the letter could have been somewhere else in the house, but it's a big old place, and if we'd started to search the rest of it, we'd have been there all night.'

'Forgive me, my friend.' Mr Holmes, thawed by the fire and warmed by the beer, was clearly in an excellent mood. 'But I had assumed from your description of the place... After all, Watson, a violinist who wants to store something safely would surely turn to the thing he himself keeps most safe?'

'To his violin, sir,' I muttered in a rather small voice. 'The Monteverdi violin. It was there, in the room, sir, in its case. I was just about to ask if we could look there, but then there was the news about the chicken...'

My employer held up his hand.

'It is no matter, Flotsam. No harm is done. Watson and I will pay a visit to Bromley Place tomorrow to take a look at the thing. The letter will no doubt reveal a great deal about Mr Cortado's disappearance, and may even offer clues as to his intended destination that evening.'

'But are we sure Bognor wasn't his destination, Holmes?' Dr Watson asked, his glass of oloroso paused halfway to his mouth. 'I suppose it *might* have been him at Victoria.'

'We can be certain, my friend, that the man the booking clerk remembers was not Mr Cortado.' Mr Holmes placed his bottle of beer on the kitchen table and leaned forward slightly. 'You see, I have been busy myself. After leaving Scotland Yard, I proceeded directly to Victoria Station and made some enquiries about the sighting of the man in the boater.'

'And you've concluded that man could not have been Cortado?'

'I've proved he was not, Watson. What is more, I've actually spoken to the fellow himself. Had the police done their job with even a modicum of thoroughness, they would have done the same. The boater helped, you see. Bognor is a seaside resort, of course, but what sort of man wears a boater to visit a seaside resort in December? Possibly someone like Mr Cortado, who sports the head-wear out of simple eccentricity. But it struck me as much more likely that the boater might have been part of some sort of uniform, something the fellow had donned quite deliberately as appropriate for his destination.'

Mr Holmes retrieved his beer, took another sip, and continued with a contented look on his face.

'Now, Watson, what sort of profession requires its members to wear boaters in Bognor regardless of the season? The obvious answer was that the fellow must be an entertainer of some sort. After all, those sea-front bands which disappear from our resorts in October invariably return for a short Christmas season, still dressed in blazers and boaters as if it were August rather than December. But, of course, a musician would be taking with him the tool of his trade, and as the police were looking for a famous musician, I think even they would have noted the fact that the mystery man in the boater was carrying an instrument.

'So some other sort of entertainer then? To be honest, it made little difference to my next steps. A conversation with the newsboys selling the evening editions, confirmed by the flower girl selling mistletoe by Platform Two, provided me not only with a description but a name.'

The great detective gave a little sigh.

'Our friends in the police, who are happy enough interviewing respectable railway clerks and the like, have yet to learn that the newsboys and street hawkers notice a good deal more. Their livelihood depends on astute obser-vation to identify the most promising customers. From them, I learned the man in the boater that day was not Mr Cortado but a children's puppeteer known as Marlo the Magnificent or, more mundanely, William Hodge of 27 Bird Street in Whitechapel. He confirmed as much to me in person when I tracked him down to his lodgings. At this time of year, he travels to Bognor every Wednesday or Thursday and spends the weekend performing there, and will continue to do so until the end of the pantomime season.'

'So that's that, Holmes,' Dr Watson concluded with some satisfaction. 'Well, it's an end to that particular mystery, at least.'

'Yes, indeed, my friend.' But Mr Holmes spoke hesitantly and was no longer looking at any of the rest of us. He seemed to be studying a point on the far wall, near the French dresser. 'Although, Mr Hodge did have a little mystery of his own. It's a trivial thing, and yet...'

His voice tailed off, then he gave a little shake of his head, and returned to his beer with a smile, apparently considering the conversation at a close.

'Well, out with it, Holmes!' Dr Watson exclaimed. 'You can't stop there.'

'Oh, it's nothing, Watson. Or, at least, it ought to be nothing. It's simply that Hodge remembered that trip in particular, because he boarded the train as normal, placing both his bag and his hat in the luggage rack, then stepped out of the carriage for a moment to buy a newspaper from a boy on the platform. He exchanged a few pleasantries, for as we've discovered, he was a regular traveller and well known to the station hawkers. He then lingered on the platform until the train doors began to shut. But on arriving at Bognor and retrieving his luggage from the rack, he discovered that his boater had disappeared.'

Dr Watson tutted.

'How maddening for the fellow! The same thing happened to me once, on the late-nighter to York. Lost an excellent bowler hat, magicked away somewhere between

Peterborough and Grantham. Still makes me cross to think about it.'

Mr Holmes smiled.

'As you say, Watson, such things do happen...'

Although he smiled, I wasn't sure that he spoke the words with any great conviction.

'Now, to more important matters. Mrs Hudson, how did you get on with that list of Sussex stately homes?'

It seemed to me a little irresponsible of Mr Holmes to be persisting in his interest in the Christmas tree incident when so many questions remained about the well-being of such an eminent gentleman as Maximillian Cortado. Word was bound to reach the newspapers that Sherlock Holmes had been consulted about his disappearance, and when that was the case, the British public had come to expect immediate results. In contrast, no one seemed at all bothered about the two damaged Christmas trees, not even the person who owned them.

But at Mr Holmes' bidding, Mrs Hudson had retrieved a list of names from one of the kitchen drawers and was running through it briskly.

'Evershott House, yes. Frawling Hall, Lord Empingham's seat, yes. Foxton Abbey – that's the home of Lord Cottesbrooke – most definitely. Its galleried entrance hall is famous. But I think, sir, you can cross off Lord Saltby and Lord Kettleford. And as for Strathley Manor, Lord Markham is so reclusive that no one is ever really received there, and given his lordship's reputation for parsimony, it's hard to imagine so much fuss being made about Christmas trees.'

'Very shrewd, Mrs Hudson! I shall take your word for it. So we are left with Evershott House, Frawling Hall and Foxton Abbey.'

'But, please, sir,' I asked, unable to contain myself any longer. 'Does it really *matter* which house it was where those two fir trees were damaged?'

Mr Holmes raised an eyebrow.

'Surely you see that it might, Flotsam? Thanks to Dr Watson bringing that item to our attention, we are now in a position to prevent a carefully planned crime.'

I waited for him to elaborate, but he simply turned back to face his housekeeper.

'Mrs Hudson, I don't pretend to be an expert in the fashionable way to decorate Christmas trees nowadays. In truth, I consider the whole practice unutterably absurd. And Dr Watson here has clearly not dressed a tree since his distant youth, have you, Watson?'

'Eh? Well, probably not, Holmes. But I still understand the principles. Candles, fruits, bits of confectionery, all the brighter the better. Though I can't say I'm in favour of these pricey glass baubles that people are so keen on nowadays. It seems to me that some people don't really care about good taste anymore, they just want to show off how much they've spent.'

The great detective looked delighted.

'My point precisely!' he declared. 'Have I not heard, Mrs Hudson, that in some of our great homes, it has long been the habit to decorate the top of their Christmas tree with an ornament of extravagant value? I am thinking, I suppose, of the Stutely Star.'

Mrs Hudson was nodding at this, her eyes slightly narrowed, as though she were beginning to follow Mr Holmes' line of thought.

'Certainly, sir, the Stutely Star did begin something of a fashion for bejewelled ornaments in some of the wealthier households. That was a great many years ago, of course, and the fashion today tends away from such ill-advised ostentation, with a velvet ribbon often seen as the wiser choice. But certainly, sir, such extravagant items still form the centrepiece of festivities in some of our stately homes.'

'Extravagant enough to be worth stealing, Mrs Hudson?'

The housekeeper nodded slowly.

'The Stutely Star was studded with fine diamonds, sir. And the angel which tops the tree at Kensworth was made by the Tsar's personal jeweller and is said to be dressed with two dozen rubies.'

'Very well.'

Mr Holmes rose to his feet with sudden energy.

'Tomorrow, Mrs Hudson, perhaps you and Flotsam would be good enough to pay a visit to the Earl of Brabham's residence, to find out from his servants what became of the label attached to his lordship's hen. And the same thing at the house of this Merriman fellow, too, if you would be so good. It may well be that someone there thought to retain it. It would be unfortunate if both gentlemen had simply tossed the evidence into the fire.'

He turned to his friend.

'You and I, Watson, shall pay a visit to Mr Cortado's house in Bromley Place, to take a look inside his violin case. But before that, we need to get off telegrams to Lords Evershott, Empingham and Cottesbrooke, warning that, however absurd it sounds, a plot may be afoot to steal the ornament from the top of their Christmas tree.'

Chapter 6

The fourteenth of December seemed reluctant to begin. The dawn was lost behind dark, lowering clouds, and long after I awoke – even after the two gentlemen had breakfasted and left the house – a strange half-light prevailed. Hansom cabbies kept their lamps lit, shop windows glowed bright in the gloom, and the sky remained stubbornly the same colour as the mud-lined streets. Dr Watson, on stepping outside, had pulled up his collar and predicted snow.

The prospect of an expedition with Mrs Hudson should have cast some light into all this gloom, but even that cheerful notion was quickly dissipated – for no sooner had Mr Holmes and Dr Watson been waved off, and their breakfast things cleared away, than a small boy arrived with a note from Scraggs. My heart gave a little leap at the sight of his handwriting, until I realised that his letter was not addressed to me at all, but to Mrs Hudson. She read it with a very grave expression on her face, then sighed and folded it into her apron.

'It would seem, Flottie, that things are not going well with Scraggs.' She rose slowly, without any of her usual energy or sense of purpose. 'It is as he feared. He had an interview with old Mr Trevelyan yesterday, and it would seem that gentleman has begun to regret his investment. Scraggs, of course, has reminded him that the business is still growing at the rate they expected, but he fears that, unless Mr Trevelyan has a change of heart between now and Christmas, then there is a real danger that the shop may not be able to re-open in the New Year.'

I felt a horrid, heavy feeling grip me, as if a very cold and unforgiving stone was suddenly weighing on my stomach. I had known that Scraggs' venture was a risk, but I'd always felt certain he could make it work. My faith in him, however, was of no value at all unless it was shared by Mr Trevelyan.

'Surely there's something you can do, ma'am?' I asked desperately.

'Scraggs has asked me to call upon Mr Trevelyan this morning, Flotsam. If you recall, Mr Trevelyan is an old acquaintance of mine, from the days when he was still in the process of making his fortune. I believe my opinion may still carry some weight with him. But he is very far from the daring young man I knew then – the man who once almost cornered the market in naval provender. I fear he has grown timid in his old age, and now seems anxious to cut his losses.'

'But you can persuade him, can't you, ma'am?' I could feel my fingertips pressed very hard into my palms. 'I mean, you can help him see that Trevelyan's will be all right if he just gives it a little time.'

Mrs Hudson had moved across the kitchen until she stood by my side, and I felt her place a hand on my shoulder.

'Sadly, Flottie, Mr Trevelyan's anxieties are not logical, so there is no point in countering them with logic. I shall try to raise his spirits, child. But the best argument in Scraggs' favour would be a significant increase of custom between now and Christmas. However, as Mr Trevelyan knows all too well, for many people a visit to Ostermann's or Throok's in the days before Christmas is a tradition. So I'm afraid Scraggs has quite a task on his hands.'

I nodded forlornly and pressed a little closer to her.

'Is there nothing else you can do, ma'am? You know so many people…'

'I do indeed, child. But it will surely take a lot more than any one person's recommendation to alter things on the scale that Mr Trevelyan wants them altered. Now, come, Flotsam, fetch your coat. It's still too early for me to call at the Trevelyan household, so let us go to Blooms-bury Square together. After that, I fear, you will have to continue without me.'

On this occasion, we did not call at the Earl of Brabham's front door, but at the service door below street level which led to the servants' hall. There we were welcomed by Reynolds the butler in his shirt sleeves, who ushered us into his pantry, seated us on either side of his cheerful fire, called for tea, and pressed me to take a slice of Madeira cake. I confess, his genial mood went some way to lightening the gloom I'd been carrying with me.

'Don't worry, Miss,' he whispered, when the reason for my low spirits was explained. 'Trevelyan's is shaping up to be a fine store, and I daresay something will crop up to change the old man's mind. Now, Mrs H, what can I do for you?'

So Mrs Hudson explained our interest in the Earl of Brabham's hen, and Reynolds gave us his own account of what had occurred.

'A most peculiar-looking creature, it was,' he explained, as he described the scene he had discovered in the earl's study that day. 'Not like the sort of hens we get from the butcher's.' He hesitated a little awkwardly. 'Well, obviously, Mrs H, it was alive, for one thing. But what I mean to say is that it had a funny, fluffy head. The overall effect was rather comical. And, of course, if you had seen it as I did, peeping out of his lordship's top hat... I've kept a straight face in front of his lordship for nearly thirty years, Mrs Hudson, but I tell you that moment sorely tested me. As for colour, well, it was a mottled sort of creature, but mostly black, as I recall.'

I nodded intelligently at this description, but knowledge of hens was not my strong suit, and I wasn't sure it was Mrs Hudson's either. She passed quickly onto other things, and Reynolds explained to her that the bird had been delivered by a small boy, the sort of willing urchin who in those days was all too happy to run such errands for tuppence. No one had thought to detain this individual when the delivery was made, because why would they? There had been no reason to believe there was anything unusual about that particular parcel, and by the time its contents were discovered the young lad was long gone.

'We did ask around the square,' Reynolds explained, 'because I was sure it must have been a simple error. But no one was expecting a delivery of live poultry.'

'And there was really nothing to indicate who might have sent it?' I asked, because that in itself seemed very odd to me. The breeding of fancy hens was much in vogue at that time, and I knew that the sort of people who indulged in it were the sort who generally wanted to publicise their skills. But Reynolds was adamant that there had been no name of a breeder nor any return address, just a simple wooden crate of the sort used to transport hens to market.

'And what about the label, Reynolds?' Mrs Hudson asked. 'We're worried that his lordship will have thrown it onto the fire in one of his rages.'

The butler nodded solemnly.

'You know him all too well, Mrs H. He did indeed dispatch it to the flames, but not before I'd had the opportunity to study it closely. You can imagine I was extremely curious. But it told me very little. It was, I think, a fairly cheap card, with a black–and–white diamond pattern printed on one side and his lordship's name, written in a neat but unexceptional hand, on the other. There was, in addition, a little pattern sketched below it, but I took that to be a simple embellishment by the writer, the sort of flourish someone might add unconsciously, as it were.'

'And that sketched pattern was...?' Mrs Hudson asked, her voice very calm, but one eyebrow twitching very slightly upwards.

'I'm afraid I didn't pay a great deal of attention to it,' Reynolds confessed, 'but I seem to remember it was a little line of crosses or stars, something like that.'

And how ever strongly we pressed him, he was unable to provide any further details. He was, however, able to furnish us with the address of the Merriman household, and when Mrs Hudson explained that I would be venturing there alone, to question the servants about the Merriman hen, Reynolds cleared his throat very politely.

'If I might be so bold as to make a suggestion, Mrs Hudson? Mr Spencer is upstairs and might perhaps be persuaded to accompany Miss Flotsam. Not only is he well known to the Merrimans, Miss, but he would also be able to tell you all he knows about the three additional hens.'

'*Additional hens?*' I think Mrs Hudson and I spoke in perfect unison.

'You mean there are others, Reynolds?' I continued, and I must have sounded incredulous. 'Other people have received them too?'

Our old friend looked unperturbed.

'Indeed, Miss. I do apologise. I hadn't appreciated that you were unaware. I understand it is something of a talking point at the moment, at both Mr Spencer's club and beyond. And no, Miss, before you ask – the other three gentlemen appear to have nothing at all in common either.'

We found Rupert Spencer in his study, poring over a case of bright green beetles. When Reynolds explained that I was to visit the Merriman household, he proved more than a little eager to accompany me, explaining that Miss Peters was expected back at any moment from a visit to Clara Fazakerley, and that recently she had not returned from such outings in the best of tempers.

'Much better to be out,' he told us. 'Miss Fazakerley is apparently still going on at length about the perfect purity of her love for Dumpty Boynton. It makes Hetty want to throw things. Now, about those hens. You say that Cortado the violinist has received one? Well, he's certainly not alone...'

None of us thought of moving, so the three of us stood with the beetles between us while Mr Spencer explained. It seems that a number of members had been present at his club during his first conversation about hens with young Mr Merriman. Such an intriguing anecdote was bound to be repeated over the next day or so, and it seemed to have been repeated often, by a great many people, with the result that three of Mr Spencer's fellow members had hastened back to the Dampier Club two evenings later with their own excited contributions to the story.

'Freddie Thompson was the first to find me,' Mr Spencer told us. 'It turns out that his great uncle is a member of the Empedocles Club, and he heard two fellows chatting about how Vincent Steel, the liberal politician, had been warned by the Speaker for having a live hen delivered to him at the House of Commons. Of course, Steel protested that he hadn't asked for the hen, and had no idea who'd sent it, but he was given a thorough scolding anyway. He thinks it must have been sent by someone making a point about Free Trade. But, of course, once you know who else has been getting them, the Free Trade thing doesn't really hold water.'

'Sir Vincent Steel…' Mrs Hudson appeared to know the name, although I confess it was unfamiliar to me. 'Very interesting. Not the sort of man to associate with your uncle, sir. And the other two hen recipients?'

'One was Harold Toukens, who used to be a prominent manufacturer in the north of England. Apparently, when his wife died, he retired from business and now lives a quiet life in Haywards Heath, writing a book about the history of Flemish locksmithery. His god-son was staying with him when the creature was delivered, and mentioned the incident to some of his friends at Sharps. And, of course, lots of young men are members of both Sharps and the Dampier Club, so word got back to us at the Dampier in no time.

'As for the last one, I think it's particularly interesting. All the others were delivered to London or the Home Counties, you see. But Teddy Scott lives in Paris. You may remember he was caught up in a bit of a scandal ten or twelve years ago, when his wife ran off with a Canadian millionaire. Well, eventually he managed to divorce her, and he moved to Paris after that. We only heard about *his* hen because he sent a telegram to an old friend of his called Taffy Flinders asking what the devil he meant by it. Thought it was a joke, you see, because Taffy is known for his jokes. But Taffy's been laid up with rheumatism for months, so it couldn't have been him. I happen to be a friend of Taffy's nephew, and he told me all about it.'

Mr Spencer paused, and waved his hands over the green beetles in a gesture that conveyed complete bewilderment.

'So there you have it. As well as your virtuoso violinist, there's a retired industrialist with an interest in old keys, a *bon-viveur* with a house on the Rue de Martignac, the MP for Monmouthshire South, a chap who spends nearly all his time pootling around Norfolk looking for ancient flint mines, and finally my uncle, whose main interest in life is studying the bloodlines of thoroughbreds in the hope of unearthing the winner of next year's Derby. And that's only the ones we know about. It would seem that their secret admirer has eclectic taste!'

'Indeed.' Mrs Hudson nodded slowly, but I noticed that tiny furrow in her brow as she did so. 'But perhaps some additional information will come to light when Flotsam visits the Merriman household. Now, young lady, I must be off to see Mr Trevelyan, so I shall see you back at Baker Street. No need to hurry home, child, as Mr Holmes has enough on his plate today to keep him out for some time, and I'm quite happy to put the carpets off till tomorrow.'

These were kind words, but in the event, I was home and warming myself by the kitchen fire a good hour or more before Mrs Hudson. My visit to the Merriman house near Russell Square proved a very cordial one, but one that provided me with very little information that I didn't already know.

Mr Fergus Merriman, the recipient of the hen, was out of town, but we were received by his son, Mr Timothy Merriman, who was a pleasant young man of about twenty. I felt my cheeks flush a little when Mr Spencer introduced me as 'someone assisting Sherlock Holmes in his investigations', and Mr Merriman certainly looked at me with a good deal of curiosity when he heard the words, but he was quick to make us both comfortable in a warm and welcoming drawing room, and answered all our questions as best he could.

'It's a great shame my father isn't here,' he told us. 'But since my mother died, he seldom stays in town for more than a day or two at a time. He's always out visiting ancient sites and things, and measuring them, and whatnot. Makes him happy though, so I'm all in favour.'

Mr Merriman repeated to me what he had already told Mr Spencer, that as far as he knew, his father had no dealings whatsoever with the Earl of Brabham, and when I mentioned Mr Cortado, and explained that he was a famous violinist, he simply looked bewildered and told us that his father had never been one for mixing in artistic circles.

I'd desperately hoped that one of the other people on my list of hen-recipients would strike a chord with Mr Merriman, but although the names of Harold Toukens, Sir Vincent Steel and Mr Teddy Scott were not totally unfamiliar to him, he wasn't aware of any connection between them and his father.

'You will have gathered, Miss Flotsam, that my father is not a great one for company. And unless anyone on that list has a secret love for prehistoric remains, I very much doubt they would enjoy spending time with him.'

As for the label on the hen-crate, Mr Merriman was not really very helpful. He remembered a printed pattern in black and white on one side, and his father's name on the other. He thought there had been some sort of decoration next to the name, but he couldn't be sure. When he rang the bell to summon both his father's manservant and the cook, neither was able to add anything at all. The delivery boy had gone before he could be questioned. There was no mark of any sender. It was all a complete mystery to them.

The hen itself, though, had clearly made an impression.

'A dashed peculiar-looking sort of fowl,' Mr Merriman told us, 'with an outrageous, fluffy head, like a poodle!'

'We'd never seen the like of it below stairs, sir,' the cook added fervently. 'Edgeworth here said to roast it, but I wasn't going to serve the master anything that looked like it had come dressed in its own hat. So I told the boot boy to see if the coalman would take it, because he likes a fresh egg, and that was the last we saw of it.'

So I returned to Baker Street a little before noon and found no one at home. My spirits were undoubtedly a little low, as the whole business with the chickens seemed to be going nowhere, and was feeling rather silly. Had it not been for Mr Cortado's disappearance, no one would be paying any attention to them, and there wasn't really anything to suggest that Mr Cortado had disappeared *because* he'd received a hen. The letter he'd received a few minutes before going out seemed a much more likely cause. The sooner Mr Holmes found it and returned with it, the better.

If Mrs Hudson had taught me anything, it was that good hard work was a reliable way of distracting someone from their woes, so I dragged the landing carpet downstairs and into the area, and gave it a thorough and energetic beating. It was a heavy carpet, and not at all easy for one person to handle, and rather spitefully I felt it deserved everything it got.

I was in the mood to give the hall carpet exactly the same treatment, but throughout the afternoon my efforts were interrupted by repeated knocks at the front door, all of them small boys delivering telegrams addressed to Mr Holmes. On this occasion I could think of no excuse for taking any liberties with my employer's correspondence, so the telegrams piled up on a silver tray in the hall to await his return. By the time I heard Mrs Hudson's familiar footsteps on the area steps, there were six of them in all.

Mrs Hudson's return proved even better than the carpets at lifting my spirits, for she bustled into the kitchen full of energy and purpose, and immediately set about preparing for the return of the two gentlemen.

'Kettle on, Flotsam, and lay a tray, then if you'd be so good as to cut some sandwiches to go upstairs, and another plateful for us down here, we'll be well on our way. I'll put out a few slices of that ham from Lamingtons, and there's a Dundee cake in the pantry, and that good Cheshire cheese from Lord Memblesbury. Jump to it, child! They'll likely be home any minute.'

We went to work briskly, and while we worked, we talked. I was quick to ask Mrs Hudson about her interview with old Mr Trevelyan. Her answers, though brief, were not disheartening, and certainly her mood contained no trace of pessimism.

'Mr Trevelyan is in two minds, Flotsam,' she told me briskly, as she set to work on the ham. 'And so long as he remains in two minds, then things will continue as they are and Scraggs will have every chance of proving to him that the shop is an excellent investment. Mr Trevelyan is, to borrow a phrase from Scraggs, in a right old dither, and I don't think he will make up his mind either way much before Christmas.'

She sighed, but not despairingly.

'I fear his recent experience with Australian banking shares has shattered his confidence, and Scraggs is suffering as a result. But Scraggs' venture has life left in it for now, which is perhaps the most we can ask.' She brushed her hands together vigorously. 'Meanwhile, Flottie, I have been busy in other ways. It just so happens that my route home from Mr Trevelyan's took me through Westminster, where it occurred to me that I might pay a visit to the Houses of Parliament.'

'To see Mr Vincent Steel, ma'am?'

It appeared that Mrs Hudson, at least, had not yet dismissed the business of the chickens as an absurdity.

'*Sir* Vincent, Flotsam. Exactly so. I confess that I'm not completely unacquainted with the gentleman, having once been able to assist his housekeeper during something of an emergency. A diplomatic mission from the Balkans had descended unexpectedly upon his country house in Kent, and locating, at short notice, an auxiliary butler fluent in Slovenian, was no easy task. Thankfully it is an occasion that Sir Vincent remembers with some gratitude. With the Christmas Recess looming, I thought it highly unlikely that he would have time to see me, but on receiving my note he very graciously agreed to take a turn with me around Parliament Square.'

'And did he have anything to tell you about the chickens, ma'am?' I asked, as she put down her carving knife and moved to where her winter coat was hanging behind the door.

'Better than that, Flotsam. He gave me this.'

And she produced from the coat pocket a little piece of card with a black and white pattern on one side and Sir Vincent's name on the other.

No conjuror producing a white rabbit from his hat could ever have wished for a better response, for I think I may have gasped out loud.

'The original label, ma'am! He still had it!'

'He did indeed, Flottie. And when those sandwiches are ready, I suggest that you sit down and take a good look at it.'

The sandwiches were ready very quickly, for I worked with unusual haste, and when Mrs Hudson was satisfied that the bread was suitably thin and the corners suitably square, I settled down with the card.

Having listened to descriptions of the cards delivered to Mr Merriman, Mr Cortado and to the Earl of Brabham, it was immediately obvious that this card was strikingly similar. It was an inexpensive object, and the chequered pattern on one side was made up of alternating black and white diamonds. On the other side, the name 'Sir Vincent Steel MP' was written in a generous, flowing script, and beneath it the writer had drawn, in the same ink, a little line of stars.

'It isn't very much, is it, Flotsam?' Mrs Hudson was peering at the card over my shoulder. 'But it is certainly something. And as well as giving me this, Sir Vincent very kindly agreed to send telegrams to Mr Toukens and Mr Scott, asking them to provide certain information to Mr Holmes about their own unexpected deliveries.'

She sounded quite pleased, so I tried to hide my disappointment.

'I'm afraid, ma'am, that this label… Well, I don't really see how it helps at all. If all the cards are the same as this one, only with different names, then surely they don't tell us anything?'

She pulled out the chair next to mine and settled down beside me, the little card in front of us.

'Well, let's just see what we have, shall we, Flottie? Let's start with what we know about the people receiving these cards.'

I gave a little dispirited sigh.

'They're all very different, aren't they, ma'am? They don't seem to have anything in common.'

Mrs Hudson rested her hand on my forearm and gave it a little squeeze.

'I don't think that's entirely true, child. Instead of dwelling on the ways they are different, let's think for a moment about how they are similar. For one thing, all of them are men. Then there's their age. None of them are particularly young. They mostly seem to be in their late forties or early fifties, and the oldest would appear to be the Earl of Brabham who has just had his sixtieth birthday.'

I had no choice but to agree. They were all gentlemen of a certain age.

'The other very obvious thing is that they are all men with a certain standing in society. All are at least reasonably affluent, and even if they are not particularly well acquainted with each other, they all move in the same social circles. When I asked Sir Vincent about the others, none of the names were unfamiliar to him. He was certain that he'd been introduced to all of them at one time or another, and some of them – Lord Brabham and Teddy Scott were the examples he gave – have attended a great many of the same events as him. He is on nodding terms with them both, but no more than that.'

There was something about the clear way Mrs Hudson laid things out that made things seem a good deal less complicated. I picked up the little label and looked at it again.

'Do you think someone else may have received a hen, ma'am?' I went on, encouraged by a little upwards twitch of Mrs Hudson's eyebrows. 'Someone we don't yet know about? You see, we have six names on our list, and there are seven stars on the card. Perhaps it's a star for each gentleman, and there's still one more for us to find?'

'It's a possibility, child,' Mrs Hudson agreed solemnly. 'Now, let us think for a moment about *why* these hens were sent...'

She broke off and appeared to listen, and for a moment I felt utterly bewildered, because I was sure I could hear the clucking of a hen somewhere nearby, as though, by talking about hens, I had somehow summoned one up. But apparently Mrs Hudson could hear it too, and we both rose from the table at the same moment, when it became clear that not only was there a hen nearby, but that it was being carried up the steps to our front door.

And to my astonishment, I could hear Mr Holmes' voice, rising above the squawking.

'Not the front door, Watson! Straight downstairs, I think. And go carefully with that crate! You'll have the paint off the railings!'

It was indeed a hen, and as odd a creature as I'd ever seen – mostly black, but speckled with flecks of white, with white feet, a white beak, and a startling crown of black and white feathers around its head, as though it were wearing a very fancy bonnet. It sat in its crate on the kitchen table, clucking softly at the small audience that surrounded it, until on Mr Holmes' prompting, Dr Watson was persuaded to lift it from its crate and display it to us in all its glory.

The great detective gazed at it rather fondly.

'Not our usual sort of visitor, Mrs Hudson,' he remarked, 'but having observed her for the best part of this morning, I'd venture to say she's by no means the least intelligent. She has proved a most equable travelling companion, has she not, Watson?'

'Very well behaved, Holmes. I've grown quite attached to her.'

And it may very well have been a mutual affection, for the bird seemed to nestle very comfortably between Dr Watson's large hands, and began to make a peculiar cooing noise, like a very sleepy pigeon.

'But, sir,' I began, looking for a polite way of phrasing the obvious question, but failing to find one, 'where on earth did she come from?'

'From Clapham,' Mr Holmes replied crisply, as though that answered my question. 'From the nephew of Mr

Cortado's butler, to be more precise. It was he, you may remember, who received the unwanted creature from Bromley Place. She is, he tells us, a very good layer. He also tells us that she is a Houdan hen from France, a breed not particularly common on these shores. Now, Watson, you'd better put her back. Continence is not one of her virtues. A little water would not go amiss, Mrs Hudson, and perhaps any kitchen scraps you have to hand – although she has already feasted royally at Bloomsbury Square.'

Back in its crate, the strange fowl settled comfortably into a corner and continued to coo, while Mr Holmes explained.

'Our morning began with something of a setback, you see. We called at Bromley Place with the intention of examining Maximillian Cortado's famous violin or, to be more precise, with the intention of examining its case, in search of that mysterious letter. Unfortunately, we were informed that Mr Denham had called an hour or so before us, and had taken the violin away to present it to Miss Lavinia Burrows, as per the instructions in Mr Cortado's letter.'

Mr Holmes clearly considered his answer complete, for he took a seat at the kitchen table and began to help himself from the platter of sandwiches that was waiting to go upstairs. It was left to Dr Watson to take up the narrative.

'So we trailed all the way over to Kensington to call on Miss Burrows, didn't we, Holmes? Only to find that she wasn't at home. I thought that might be it for the day, Flotsam, but Holmes here took it into his head that he wanted to see Mr Cortado's chicken. And young Shapps, the hen-fancier, proved to be a very pleasant fellow. When

I said it would be good to know if the others had received the same type of bird, it was his idea that we should borrow this one. So we carted her off to Bloomsbury Square, where Rupert Spencer told us all about the other fellows who've been receiving chickens, and then we followed you to see the Merrimans. Everyone's agreed that she's the same sort of chicken as the ones they received.'

While Dr Watson was giving us this account, his friend, having finished a second sandwich, had taken up the black and white label from the kitchen table and was examining it carefully.

'I see that you too have been busy, Mrs Hudson. I dare not even enquire as to what past service you have rendered Sir Vincent Steel, but the outcome is invaluable. With this in our possession, and with our feathered friend here, we have the complete message.'

'Message, Holmes?' Dr Watson looked up from the hen-crate, where he was pushing a part of his sandwich between the wooden struts.

'Of course, Watson. These things are clearly not intended as gifts, because the person sending them cannot for a moment believe that the recipients want, or are in need of, live fowls. So I think we can safely conclude that these deliveries are intended as a message of some sort. A coded message, if you like, but one that is intended to convey a meaning or instructions. The really interesting feature of this business is that none of the recipients we have identified so far seem to understand that meaning. The arrival of the hens seems to be met with utter bewilderment.'

'So why send them, Holmes?' Dr Watson reached for another sandwich. 'I mean, what's the point of sending people coded messages they don't understand?'

'That is the question at the heart of this matter, my friend. The sender has information to convey. It is clearly confidential information, for they have resorted to this absurd method of cloaking their meaning. Now, one possibility is that they have accidentally made the message so obscure that the intended recipients don't understand it. Alternatively...'

'Alternatively, sir,' I burst in, taking advantage of the great detective's pause, 'the message is intended for someone who *will* understand it, but is deliberately being sent to other people too. That way, no one knows for sure who the real recipient is!'

'Precisely, Flotsam. Of course, we cannot ignore the possibility that there are other recipients we don't yet know about, and that might change everything. And then there is Mr Cortado...'

'My word, Holmes!' Dr Watson turned his attention away from the hen-crate. 'Although he told his butler the thing baffled him, it's perfectly possible that he knew exactly what it was all about! In which case, you'd have to conclude that it wasn't the *letter* which led to his disappearance, it was the hen. Perhaps it was some kind of warning?'

Mr Holmes nodded and looked again at the label.

'The obvious course of action is for us to decode the message, my friend.'

'You mean that line of stars, Holmes? I can't see what sort of meaning could be hidden there.'

But his companion shook his head.

'I should think a great deal of meaning could be imparted using a pictogram of that sort. And remember, there are three parts to the message, Watson. The stars are only one of them.' His gaze turned to me. 'What do you think, Flotsam?'

'Three parts, sir...?' After the briefest moment of panic, my thoughts arranged themselves into some sort of order. 'Yes, sir. There are two things on the label – apart from the names, I mean. There's the drawing of stars, and then there's the printed pattern on the back. The pattern's the same on every card.'

I looked across at Mrs Hudson, who rewarded me with a very slight nod of the head.

'And the third thing, Flotsam?' she asked softly.

'Well, the hen is the third thing, isn't it, ma'am? The hens must have some sort of meaning for someone, mustn't they? And they're not just any old hens, they're very fancy ones.'

Mr Holmes gave an approving snort.

'Nicely put, Flotsam. So, we have an exotic French hen, a line of stars and a harlequin pattern of black and white diamonds.'

'But what could those things possibly mean, Holmes?' Dr Watson asked plaintively.

'I've no idea, Watson,' his friend replied. 'But the more we can discover, the clearer things will become. For instance, if any further deliveries of poultry are reported, we may learn more. Mr Cortado's missing letter may tell us a great deal. And remember, Watson, we're awaiting news from Bognor. Speaking of which, are there any telegrams, Mrs Hudson?'

It took me less than half a minute to retrieve the little silver tray from the hall, and to place it in front of Mr Holmes, who contemplated it with a raised eyebrow.

'Six? Rather more than I expected...'

Mrs Hudson cleared her throat politely.

'I believe, sir, that Sir Vincent Steel, on learning a little more about the mystery of the hens, and having a passing acquaintance with both Mr Toukens and Mr Scott, took it upon himself to ask certain questions of both gentlemen on your behalf.'

'Did he indeed?' The great detective looked across at Mrs Hudson and smiled. 'How very good of him. It is excellent to see one of our elected members show such an instinctive grasp of what is required. Now, let me see...'

He selected one of the six telegrams, apparently at random, and slit open the envelope with a small penknife drawn from his waistcoat pocket.

'From Harold Toukens, Watson, and I don't think we can have any difficulty deciding what questions he was asked. "*Seven stars. Black and white diamonds. Fluffy and ridiculous.*" A pleasingly pithy response, and one that leaves us in no doubt that his delivery resembled the others very closely.

'Next, we have a reply from Mr Scott in Paris, saying exactly the same thing, but with rather less economy of language. "*Seven stars like child's drawing. Black rhomboids on white, repeated. Hen good natured, blackish, looks like feather duster. Valet says has seen similar in farms outside Paris.*" So, my friend, that is all exactly as we might have expected.'

He reached for another envelope.

'Ah, from the station master at Bognor Regis! Let's see... "*Boater was indeed found beneath seat Thursday evening. Shall return to Mr Hodge, Whitechapel, as per your request.*"'

Dr Watson and I exchanged looks of utter mystification.

'Found that magician fellow's hat for him, have you, Holmes?' his friend muttered. 'Daresay he'll be pleased to have it back.'

But the effect of the telegram on Mr Holmes was very marked, and rather dramatic. An expression of intense interest was lighting up his face, and I could sense his concentration as he re-examined the message.

'It was a long shot, Watson,' he said at last. 'An extremely long shot. But when I heard his boater had disappeared on the train…' His face relaxed into a smile, and he tossed the telegram onto the table in front of his companion. 'Chance,' he announced grandly, 'can make fools of us all. And on this occasion, Watson, it appears to have played a rather mean trick on Maximillian Cortado!'

'Cortado? How?'

Dr Watson's confusion was clearly as great as my own, but Mr Holmes was already reaching for the next telegram.

'Ah! As I hoped,' he declared on examining its contents. 'From Lord Cottesbrooke. So let us move on from this business of the missing violinist, which, were it not for the hens and the hat, would be a case almost entirely devoid of interest. This other conundrum is altogether more intriguing, eh, Mrs Hudson? Here's what his lordship writes. "*Housekeeper states always velvet ribbon on top of tree. Value three shillings maximum. Theft unlikely. Cottesbrooke.*"'

My employer's continued interest in the story of the decapitated Christmas trees continued to baffle me, and perhaps even to annoy me a little, so I confess that Lord Cottesbrooke's telegram gave me a secret twinge of satisfaction, appearing, as it did, to contradict Mr Holmes' predictions. It was clear, however, that Mr Holmes' spirits were in no way lowered by it, and he hurried on to the penultimate telegram.

'From Lord Evershott. "*Christmas trees be damned. Pagan nonsense. Won't have one in the house.*"' The great detective placed it on the table with a little smile. 'Very well. So by elimination, the planned theft must be from Frawling Hall. Let us see what Lord Empingham has to say. He will presumably be pleased to have received a timely warning.'

But when Mr Holmes opened the final envelope, the look of triumph that I'd expected to see did not appear. Instead, his eyes narrowed as he read, then his face became very still, as if he were hoping to stare right through the offending telegram, to some hidden meaning beneath it.

'The application of logic,' he said at last, 'is not without its perils. Just take a look at this.'

The telegram that he laid before us was certainly a surprising one.

LORD EMPINGHAM UNWELL STOP
BIDS ME SEND COMPLIMENTS AND
TO INFORM YOU WARNING COMES
TWENTY-THREE YEARS TOO LATE
STOP HAWKINS

'Good lord, Holmes!' Dr Watson chuckled. 'Seems you were right about a theft from Frawling Hall. It's just your timing's a bit off, that's all!'

His friend, however, seemed to find no humour in the situation. He studied the telegram again, his face still full of thought.

'Lord Empingham… Frawling Hall… I knew those names meant more to me than a simple entry in *Burke's Peerage*! Yet had a theft from Frawling Hall been described in the newspapers, even twenty-three years ago, I would surely remember it. What about you, Mrs Hudson? Are you aware of any long-ago scandal at Frawling?'

The housekeeper considered this question for a long time, her face very serious, and when she finally spoke, it was without any degree of certainty.

'That would have been around the time of the sixth Lord Empingham's death, sir. That's the present lord's father. But I know nothing of any untoward or unusual happenings from that time, I'm afraid.'

'Well, Mrs Hudson,' Dr Watson grinned happily, 'it doesn't happen very often, but for once it seems I know more about these things than you do! Not that I know much, of course, but when I was in the army I used to share drinks with a fellow whose family owned the neighbouring estate down at Frawling. Nice chap, he was, and an excellent spin bowler, although I can't recall his name for the moment. But I remember him mentioning Empingham once – it was a particularly hot night, when we were stationed in Bengal, and he told me there'd been some unpleasantness about Empingham's father's will. Don't think he told me more than that, but I remember the incident because it set me thinking about my own will, which rather spoiled the evening.'

Mr Holmes scarcely seemed to be listening, and his brow was still furrowed.

'Do you remember Inspector Dickinson, Watson? He retired years ago, but before he did, didn't he once mention Frawling Hall to us? We were discussing that business of the vanishing opium shipment, if you recall. The one that disappeared from a closely guarded warehouse in broad daylight, and the inspector muttered something about it being just like Frawling. Of course, Dickinson was a terrible one for re-telling old cases at inordinate length, and I remember being quite sharp with him, telling him to stick to the matter in hand.'

Dr Watson shook his head, but before he could reply his companion had risen and was consulting his watch.

'Come, my friend. If there was even a whisper of gossip surrounding Frawling Hall back then, it would surely have found its way into *The Clarion*, and the editor there owes us a favour. I propose that you and I spend the next couple of hours in the archives.'

He tapped the top of the hen-crate, where the odd-looking bird was still nestling comfortably.

'Perhaps you could see this fine lady returned to her home in Clapham, Mrs Hudson? I fear, were she to stay longer, Dr Watson would want to keep her. Now, if you will excuse us… In a few hours' time, hopefully, we will know a great deal more about this Frawling Hall business.'

Which turned out to be true.

—

It had been a busy morning, and Mrs Hudson decided that the hall carpet could wait until the following day. With the two gentlemen gone, the afternoon seemed very quiet, and the gentle, throaty plok-plok-plok of the hen was strangely soothing. When the baker's boy came to take her away, I was sorry to see her go; and in the silence that followed, the quick, sharp rapping at the front door, when it came, was enough to almost make me drop my scrubbing brush into the pail.

Because both Mrs Hudson and I had our sleeves rolled up and our hands dirty, it was decided that I, as the marginally tidier, should pull on a clean apron and attend to the caller. I left Mrs Hudson on her hands and knees, scrubbing doggedly at the awkward patch just in front of the area door.

The clock was striking four as I climbed the stairs, and, outside, the sky was already dark. Even in Mrs Hudson's supremely warm kitchen, you could feel the cold pressing against the windows; it would be a good night to be indoors. At that hour, though, the streets were still busy, the late afternoon traffic of carts and carriages as unrelenting as ever, and the pavements were crowded with pedestrians.

The caller rapped a second time before I reached the front door, and there was something in the knock that made me imagine an imperious and impatient young gentleman of the sort I wouldn't at all like. But the figure I revealed on opening the door was very different from the one I'd imagined – a slim, narrow-faced woman of perhaps forty or forty-five years of age, dressed with extreme elegance, and possessed of a rather charming smile.

'I have called in the hope of seeing Mr Sherlock Holmes,' she told me. 'Is he, by any chance, at home?'

She said it firmly but in a nice way, and when I explained that he was not, she handed me a card and told me that she thought she would perhaps return later. It was hardly my place to read the card, but I couldn't help noticing that the name on it was an unusual one – *Mrs Lawrence Alma Tadema*.

Her business complete, she was just turning to leave when a shriek of laughter erupted from the pavement beyond, so loud above the general hubbub that both of us turned to look, and I saw a little huddle of three well-dressed ladies who had clearly met by chance on the pavement adjacent to our front door and were now chatting with great animation.

'Oh, great heavens!' I heard our visitor exclaim, and before I had the chance to remonstrate, she'd pushed past me into the hallway and had shut the door behind us.

'I do apologise, child,' she told me, peeping out of the little window beside the front door. 'But, you see, my husband wasn't at all sure I should come here today – he's concerned about the smallest sniff of scandal – and I told him that he was being absurd, because no one would ever know. And now, just out there...' She indicated the three chatting ladies with a nod of her head. 'That is a neighbour of ours, Mrs Gilmour, and her two cousins, who are the three most appalling gossips in St John's Wood. Is it very wrong of me to ask for a minute's sanctuary, just until they go away?'

'No, ma'am. Of course, ma'am,' I replied, a little uncertainly. 'But perhaps you should come in and wait in the study?' We were both of us peering at the group outside. 'Those ladies look as though they might be there for some time.'

'Oh, I couldn't possibly impose in such a way. Tell me, child, is there a back door of any sort?'

'Well, ma'am,' I began doubtfully, 'there's the kitchen door into the area, and then up the steps into the street. But if they happened to look your way...'

I saw her eyes move to the gate in the railings at the top of the area steps.

'But that will work!' she decided. 'Look at where the newsboy's standing. You see? He's between them and the top of the steps, so they wouldn't actually see me coming out. And once I've reached the pavement without being observed, it doesn't matter if they *do* see me. So, although it is highly irregular, perhaps you would be so good as to show me to the kitchen?'

And so I showed her downstairs, forgetting for a moment that Mrs Hudson was on her knees by the area door. It was only as I actually entered the kitchen that I remembered, and my first thought was that the housekeeper would be awfully cross with me for showing visitors into the room without any warning.

But when she looked up and saw us, instead of disapproval I saw her eyebrow lift very slightly, as if something had greatly surprised her. Even so, it was our visitor who spoke first.

'Mrs Hudson!' she declared, astonished.

'Why, if it isn't Miss Laura. Miss Laura Epps.' The housekeeper rose to her feet with great dignity, wiping her hands on her apron as she did so. 'It must be all of twenty-five years! But, of course, it isn't "Miss" any longer, is it, ma'am?'

'No, indeed!' As she spoke, the visitor's shoulders seemed to relax and her features seemed to soften, as though, having steeled herself for an interview with the formidable Mr Sherlock Holmes, the unexpected and sudden discovery of a friendly face came as a great relief. 'I'm Mrs Alma Tadema now. My husband is Lawrence Alma Tadema, the artist.'

'And was it Mr Holmes you were hoping to see, ma'am?' Mrs Hudson asked, unpinning her dirty apron.

I think it was the simple kindness in the housekeeper's tone that gave her words such impact, because all at once our visitor's composure began to crumble.

'Oh, Mrs Hudson!' she exclaimed. 'I really don't know what to do! It all sounds so stupid! And it is probably most ridiculous of me to think of bothering Mr Holmes about it… But it's my husband, you see. He's pretending it hasn't affected him, but I know he's terribly anxious about it, and it's affecting his work. And he's about to make sketches of a most eminent subject, so he really mustn't be distracted. But you will think him absurd, I know you will. You see, he just can't understand why he hasn't been sent a hen.'

Chapter 7

Nothing was properly explained to me until all three of us were seated around the kitchen table. Before that, for a good two minutes, I was scurrying around, helping Mrs Laura Alma Tadema out of her coat and into a seat, and allowing her a moment to dab at her eye with her handkerchief. While she composed herself, I was sent to fetch brandy and to lay out the fruitcake and build up the fire, while Mrs Hudson washed herself and replaced her filthy apron with a crisp, clean one.

Only when all three of us were settled at the table, and when our visitor had taken her first sips of brandy and her first nibble of cake, did Mrs Hudson begin to make introductions, telling our visitor my name and explaining that, in the peculiar business of the hens, it just so happened that I knew as much – if not more – than anybody in London.

Mrs Alma Tadema replied to this with a little smile in my direction. I had thought her rather plain when I first saw her, but her eyes, which were deep-set, were full of feeling.

'I was around your age, Flotsam, when Mrs Hudson befriended me. Younger perhaps, for I met my husband at seventeen, and by nineteen I was married. And Mrs Hudson was only with us for a few months, just while the terrifying Mrs Hardacre was recovering from one of her fits of neuralgia. And I'm afraid, Mrs Hudson, I spent most of those months hiding from my family in your kitchen, and crying because I wanted to be a painter and thought it would never be allowed.'

'Not at all.' Mrs Hudson sounded rather gruff. 'You *were* a little upset at the time, but you were always very charming company. And of course, as I told you then, you were always going to be an artist, no matter what anyone told you.' Mrs Hudson turned to me. 'Mrs Alma Tadema is a very accomplished painter, Flotsam,' she explained.

Our visitor's surname hadn't seemed familiar when I saw it on her card, but now there was talk of art and painting, I realised I had heard of it before.

'Why, *Mr* Alma Tadema is terribly famous, isn't he, ma'am? I think I heard Mr Rumbelow saying that he was the favourite artist of the royal family!'

'I believe Mr Alma Tadema has also achieved some success,' Mrs Hudson conceded. 'And I'm sure he has a great talent. But of course a gentleman will always find it much easier to achieve fame than a lady of similar accomplishments.'

Our visitor listened to this with a little smile.

'Mrs Hudson is being as generous as always, Flotsam,' she told me. 'My husband's work is indeed a great deal better known that mine, but rightly so, for he has a very rare talent.' She turned back to Mrs Hudson. 'He and I were introduced only a few months after you left us, Mrs H. He was *so* encouraging, and practically ordered me to paint. And of course he was a widower, and when he moved to London the following year and started giving me lessons, well, one thing led to another, and we were married the year after that, even though he was a full sixteen years older than me.'

She smiled at us both, that same, warm smile.

'And I like to think that neither of us have ever had a moment's regret, for we have painted together and supported each other, and his career has gone from strength to strength, and when it comes to famous patrons, well, he's on very familiar terms with the Prince of Wales and his family, so everything should be perfect. But then there's this peculiar business.'

Mrs Hudson said nothing, but with a nod of the head encouraged our guest to continue.

'It all happened not long after we were married, you see, and we thought it was quite forgotten. It was the Christmas of '73 to be precise. Lawrence had not long moved to this country – my husband is Dutch by birth, you see, Flotsam, but moved to London to escape the Prussian invasion. We were married the following year. And then in '73 we were invited to spend Christmas in the countryside, in the company of a number of genteel and well-connected people, and the invitation made Lawrence incredibly happy. Because, of course, back then he was only just beginning to make a name for himself over here, and for all his jocular manner, I think a little part of him feared that the English might never really accept him as one of their own.

'So that's why it was such a wonderful year for us. Lawrence's paintings were being hugely admired, and my work was shown at the Paris Salon, and then, to top it all, Her Majesty created us denizens of Great Britain, which was a huge honour, and meant so much to Lawrence because he finally began to feel at home on these shores. So we travelled down to Sussex in such high spirits, looking forward to meeting a distinguished company of people, and staying until the New Year's Eve Ball. If we had only known the scandalous events that were to unfold...'

'To Sussex, you say?' Mrs Hudson's eyebrow twitched upwards very slightly. 'May I ask, ma'am, where precisely this gathering took place?'

'Near Amberley,' our visitor replied calmly, unaware of the reaction she was about to provoke. 'A little village near there. We were the guest of Lord Empingham at Frawling Hall.'

—

It was rare for Mrs Hudson to appear startled, rarer still for her to seem lost for words. But on hearing this announcement, I couldn't help but notice that she raised both her eyebrows quite markedly, and waited for a good two or three seconds before replying.

'You must forgive us, ma'am, if we look a little surprised. It is only because Mr Sherlock Holmes is currently very interested in another small matter relating to Frawling Hall. It would be tempting to marvel at the coincidence, were it not for the fact that it is surely no coincidence at all. Let me see... 1873... So this was twenty-three years ago? And the scandal you mentioned, I imagine it involved the theft of a valuable Christmas ornament?'

It was Mrs Alma Tadema's turn to look astonished – and also a little horrified.

'Why, yes, Mrs Hudson! But how could you possibly know? The matter was kept very quiet so as to avoid the scandal becoming widely spoken of. And, as I told you, we had thought it almost forgotten...'

Mrs Hudson gave a little wave of her hand.

'I assure you, ma'am, Mr Holmes knows almost nothing about the stolen item, or the circumstances around its theft. Perhaps, if you have the time, and if you would take a little more brandy...'

So that night, with the winter creeping through the streets outside, we clustered together in the warmth of Mrs Hudson's kitchen and heard all about another Christmas, more than two decades before, when Mrs Alma Tadema was twenty-one and still newly married, and had made the journey down to Frawling Hall full of excitement, knowing that, among the many other treats in store, she and her husband would be allowed a rare glimpse of Lord Empingham's famed and most precious heirloom.

The Empingham Canary, she told us, had been hand-crafted in Damascus, in the workshop of a legendary Ottoman goldsmith, back in the early days of the Queen's reign. It had been commissioned by the fifth Lord Empingham during his travels through Syria, apparently – or so the story goes – to win a wager with a fellow traveller, a keeper of caged birds, as to who owned the finest bird in the Orient. Fashioned out of solid gold and decorated with green and yellow sapphires, the little bird had been famous in the souks and caravanserai of the Middle East even before it had been completed. The cost of the gold and the jewels alone was enormous, but the Empingham Canary had a value far beyond its materials, and Lord Empingham won his bet; for his bird was said to be one of the finest pieces of craftsmanship ever to emerge from a city famous for its goldsmiths, and was hailed by all who ever saw it as an object of rare and mesmerising beauty.

The fifth lord had carried it home with him to Sussex, arriving at Frawling Hall on the night of the winter solstice. The story goes that he immediately decreed a huge fir tree was to be felled and brought into the Hall, to be decorated in the way then fashionable in royal circles, and that the Empingham Canary was to be displayed in all its glory on its highest branch.

The siting of the Christmas tree in Frawling's grand entrance hall – and the placing of the canary upon it – was not perhaps a random whim on the old man's part. Thus placed, not only did it catch the eye of every guest at the moment they entered his home, but also allowed them, by ascending to the gallery that ran around the Great Hall, to study the little bird in detail, at eye-level, at such proximity that they could reach out and run their fingers down its perfectly formed yellow wings.

And so the tradition was established: the Empingham Canary would grace the Christmas tree at Frawling Hall every year, from the week before Christmas Day until Twelfth Night; and at all other times it was locked safely out sight and out of danger in the vaults of Lord Empingham's London bank.

If the little golden bird was an object of joy to the fifth Lord Empingham, then to his grandson Hugo – destined to be the seventh lord – it was an object of magic. Appearing only at Christmas, perched above a towering column of greenery that was bright with flamboyant decorations, touched by candlelight so that sometimes, especially late at night, it almost seemed to move on its branch; close enough to reach if you climbed to the gallery, but somehow, even when you touched it, always unreachable – the little bird won a place deep in his heart. In short, as Mrs Alma Tadema told us, he fell in love with it.

As that small boy grew, his affection for the little bird in no way diminished, and in his fiftieth year, when Frawling Hall finally passed to him, the new lord was determined to maintain the tradition of the Christmas canary. His father, the sixth lord, had been a difficult and cantankerous man, much given to gambling on horse races and prize fights. In his latter years, he had quit Frawling Hall entirely, spending the last twenty years of his life living in a townhouse in Pimlico surrounded by a group of rowdies – louche individuals who enjoyed his largesse every bit as much as they enjoyed his uncanny ability to identify the winners of handicap sprint races. By all accounts, he lavished a fortune on his hangers-on, much of it spent buying up vast quantities of champagne and Parma ham, for which delicacies he had a particular fondness; however, in fairness to the sixth lord, nearly all of these extravagances were paid for by his investments on the turf, leaving his estates at Frawling unencumbered by any debt at the time of his death.

Relations between this prickly individual and his son, it seemed, had not been cordial. Young Hugo's mother had died in childbirth, and he had been abandoned into the care of his grandfather from a very early age. Luckily, a strong bond grew between grandfather and grandson, a bond of great affection, bolstered by a shared love for Frawling Hall and everything in it. Hugo's father, however, considered his son tame and lily-livered, and greatly preferred the company of his nephew, Hugo's cousin, a young man who was generally disliked by everyone else.

This cousin – Adam Snaresdon by name – shared his uncle's interest in both horseflesh and champagne, consuming a great many magnums of the latter while squandering large sums of his uncle's money on the former. But his pleasure was in prize-fighting – it was said that no one enjoyed the sight of broken teeth on the canvas more than he did – and his particular talent was in the management of his uncle who, alone among the Pimlico rowdies, considered him a young man of wit and intelligence.

Hugo, meanwhile, was left with the management of the Frawling estates, and could not have been happier with the arrangement. His feeling for Frawling Hall and for the countryside surrounding it was genuine and heartfelt, and under his stewardship the family fortunes prospered. He bred prize-winning shire horses, took care of his tenants, and maintained all the family traditions. At Christmas-time, he made a point of inviting to Frawling a diverse and interesting group of guests, and the costume ball on New Year's Eve remained the most talked-of social event in the county. His father's reckless existence barely rippled the tranquil waters of Frawling Hall, and when a week before Christmas in the year 1873, news reached Frawling of the sixth lord's death, Hugo – now the seventh Lord Empingham – saw no reason to cancel the seasonal fest-ivities that were already planned.

As she explained this detail to us, Mrs Alma Tadema's dark eyes opened very wide, as if in sympathy with the seventh lord.

'That must sound awfully callous to you both,' she told us, 'and I'm sure nowadays at least a day or two of mourning would be observed. But you must remember that things were a little different back then, and the sour relations between father and son were well known to everyone – they had lived totally separate lives for almost twenty years. And it wasn't only his son who had fallen out with the sixth lord, whose outrageous behaviour over so many years had placed him beyond all decent society, and it almost seemed there was no respectable family in London he had not grievously offended. His insults to the Prince of Wales, for instance, were so brazen and repeated that any show of grief for the man would have been considered in rather poor taste. So the new lord ordered the lowering of the flags and black crepe on the doors in the usual way, then carried on regardless. And there wasn't a soul anywhere who thought any the less of him for it.'

Mrs Hudson greeted this with a solemn nod, and asked our visitor to continue her tale.

'Well, knowing that the family estates were all entailed to him, the new Lord Empingham really seemed to have no cause to regret his father's death. His father, of course, had some personal wealth to his name, and a good deal of Scottish whisky in a bonded warehouse in Perth, but it had been assumed for years that Mr Snaresdon would inherit these. They made no difference to the Frawling estate, and Lord Empingham had no desire to profit from his father's death. So preparations for Christmas proceeded as normal, and we all arrived at Frawling Hall on Christmas Eve that year unaware of the blow that was about to fall upon our host.

'The reading of the will took place in London, Mrs Hudson, on that same day. Lord Empingham's solicitor attended, but I believe his lordship took very little interest in the whole affair – at least until the following day – Christmas Day – when the solicitor, a little fellow called Wadkins, arrived at Frawling Hall, very pale and rather out of breath. Oh, it was awful, Mrs Hudson! We were all aware that something dreadful must have happened from the moment he stumbled out of his carriage. And gradually the word spread through the house party, so when we saw our host so grey and haggard, we all fully understood.'

She paused, her dark eyes still full of feeling.

'You see, Mrs Hudson, while Frawling Hall and all its estates were entailed to the seventh lord, it turned out that the Empingham Canary was not part of the entail. It was the personal property of the sixth lord, inherited from *his* father. So the sixth lord was entitled to leave it to whomsoever he wished. And on Christmas Day, with his guests already assembled at Frawling, and the tree so splendidly decorated, and the beautiful golden bird on top of it, Lord Empingham discovered that the canary had been left to his cousin, Mr Adam Snaresdon, to dispose of as he pleased.'

It had clearly been a very painful discovery, and Mrs Alma Tadema described in detail Lord Empingham's reaction; how his guests saw him staggering from his study after his interview with Mr Wadkins so pale-faced and shocked that he seemed to have aged twenty years. And when he emerged from his room that evening, hollow-eyed and gaunt, it had been widely assumed by his guests that his intention was to curtail the house party and to wish them all farewell.

'But his lordship said exactly the opposite,' Mrs Alma Tadema explained, after another sip of brandy. 'He begged us all to stay. He said that none of his father's cruelties or extravagances had ever yet caused him to cancel the Frawling costume ball, and that he had every intention of going ahead. He told us that our company would help him recover from the bad news he had received. And as for the Empingham Canary, well, he declared that we should all enjoy it while we could, for it would almost certainly be the last time it graced the Frawling Hall Christmas tree.'

Mrs Alma Tadema gave a little sigh and a shake of her head, and helped herself to more fruitcake.

'That night, Lord Empingham took his place at the head of the table for Christmas dinner and made no mention whatsoever of his cousin or the golden bird, talking instead only of the masked ball. The theme was "Harlequin" and those of us staying at Frawling Hall over Christmas had already prepared our costumes – the ladies were all to dress as Columbina, of course, and being very young at the time, I was hugely excited by the beautiful dress I was to wear. It had been made for me in Smith Row out of an expensive Chinese silk, and looking back I always feel terribly ashamed that on such a night, when my host had suffered so great a misfortune, the prospect of attending a ball made me so very animated and joyful.'

At the word 'Harlequin', Mrs Hudson had cast a meaningful look in my direction, and now we both waited attentively to hear what would follow.

'I remember very little about the following day,' Mrs Alma Tadema confessed. 'What we did, how we passed the time… Really, I have no recollection of it at all. I don't suppose any of the other people staying at Frawling Hall will remember much about it either. Because, of course, it was the drama of that evening which really stands out – the thing that none of us will ever forget. I do remember, though, that it started to snow from very early on Boxing Day, so that by the time it got dark, the snow was already quite deep. Lawrence and I tried to walk around the lawns between flurries, but by dusk it was too thick for strolling. A cruel wind had sprung up and was driving it into drifts, some of them as high as my waist, so that when, at about five o'clock, Lawrence tried one of the French windows, he found it impossible to open because of the snow piled against it. He said it looked as though we'd all be snowed in for a day or two, and I suppose that is why we were all so surprised when, just before dinner, we heard a loud banging on the front door.'

The scene our visitor painted for us that afternoon was a dramatic one: Lord Empingham's guests assembled in the library in the company of his lordship and Mrs Graham, Lord Empingham's very infirm great aunt, who acted as hostess on these occasions. Sherry was being served. There was a low murmur of conversation, and a convivial atmosphere despite the blow that had befallen their host, for, as Mrs Alma Tadema explained, it was hard for her and her fellow guests not to feel festive in such a place at such a season, with the fires roaring, the lamps bright, every room festooned with Yuletide decorations and the snow falling outside. A very fine dinner awaited them, with good company and excellent wine. Perhaps, some guests were conjecturing, it had all been a mistake, and the lawyers would soon prove the Empingham Canary to be part of the entailed estate; perhaps Lord Empingham's cousin could be persuaded to sell it back to his lordship at a reasonable price, so that the family tradition could be maintained; perhaps this cousin wasn't so bad after all; one rumour held that he was planning to loan it to Frawling Hall for all future Christmases as a token of his good will.

And then came the loud and angry knocking at the great oak front door.

Mrs Alma Tadema said the room fell silent. So silent, she maintained, that the footsteps of the butler across the marble floor echoed around the entrance hall. They could even hear him clear his throat as he drew back the bolts.

But then, as the door swung open, all was tumult: a male voice, raised in anger, demanding admittance; a second voice, shouting above the roar of the wind; the protestations of the butler; the wild surmise of the assembled company, now gathered in the Great Hall to view the scene; and above it all, Lord Empingham's voice, authoritative and clear.

'It is Mr Snaresdon, Hawkins. You had better let him in.'

The arrival of Lord Empingham's cousin turned everything on its head. Where there had been calm and order and a general sense of well-being, suddenly there was disruption and uncertainty, and according to Mrs Alma Tadema, a little whiff of danger too, as though suddenly no one could feel entirely sure of the ground on which they stood.

'Pleased to see me, Empingham?' the visitor called out across the hall, the sneer in his voice audible to everyone. 'You certainly don't look it. We damned nearly didn't make it, I'll tell you that. Had to abandon the dog-cart the other side of Frawling, and then struggle through on foot. But you can probably guess why I've come. Yes, I'm here for my canary. So don't just stand there gaping, old chap. Hand it over. And quickly, if you please. We need to be on our way, if we're to make it back to the village in this weather. Don't we, my sweet?'

It was this last remark that turned the attention of the assembled company to Mr Snaresdon's travelling companions.

There were two of them, and according to Mrs Alma Tadema, it was impossible to imagine two more different people. One was a very young woman who Mr Snaresdon eventually introduced to the assembled company as his wife, Theodora. The other was a man of around fifty years of age, of broad and solid build, with the gnarled features of a prize fighter – an individual who was never introduced at all, but was always referred to by Mr Snaresdon as Savage, although whether this was his actual surname or simply a reflection of his personal qualities was never made clear.

'He was a great brute of a man,' Mrs Alma Tadema recalled. 'My husband instantly wanted to paint him as a gladiator in the Roman circus, but it would have taken a brave person to approach such a man with such a proposal. As I remember it, he barely said a word, simply stayed close to Mr Snaresdon and did whatever that gentleman asked of him. His wife, on the other hand...'

Our visitor looked across at me.

'She was around my age, Flotsam, not a great deal older than you are now, and my first instinct was to feel sorry for her. She was foreign, you see, from Greece – and she barely said a word to anyone. And the way she looked at her husband, well, it's hard to describe. Not hostile, but certainly not affectionate. As though she could see straight through him. And she was terribly pretty. I don't know if it's true, but word went around that her father trained street-fighters in the slums of Athens and that she had married to escape a world so squalid that even marriage to a man like Mr Snaresdon was preferable. I thought she was probably shy, but that evening I sat next to her at dinner, and I realised she was just watching and listening, and keeping her own counsel.'

'So, ma'am,' Mrs Hudson asked respectfully, cutting her guest another slice of cake, 'how did she come to be sitting down to dinner with you? Given the weather, didn't Mr Snaresdon need to hurry away?'

'Oh, it was all perfectly ghastly, Mrs Hudson! The scene in the hall seemed to last forever, with Lord Empingham attempting to reason with his cousin, inviting him to join the party, to stay for the ball, saying there was no reason why the canary needed to be carried off straightaway. He practically begged for it to be allowed to stay for one last Christmastide. But his cousin was having none of it. He had booked rooms for his party at The Plough in Frawling, and he expected his cousin to provide a carriage to get them there, or men to clear the road if the snow demanded it. He would remain in the house for ten minutes only, and he demanded that his property should be delivered to him within that time.

'Well, eventually Lord Empingham convinced him that it would take a few minutes for the servants to remove the bird from the tree, and that it had its own case, specially built for it, that would need to be brought down from the attic in the West Wing. He promised that it would be handed over within the hour, and Mr Snaresdon rather grudgingly agreed to sit down to dinner with us while he waited.'

Mrs Alma Tadema gave another little sigh.

'As you can imagine, it was a terrible meal. My husband is a jovial man, known for his ready humour and his fondness for practical jokes, but even he sat stony-faced that night. We all attempted to talk amongst ourselves at first, as though everything were ordinary, but it was impossible not to listen to the conversation between our host and his cousin, until eventually we were all sitting in silence while they argued. And it was awful to listen to! One couldn't help but feel for Lord Empingham who was practically begging to be allowed to buy the bird. At one point it seemed he was almost offering to split the

Frawling estate between the two of them, and the more he begged the more his cousin seemed to enjoy the power he had. In the end we all heard him laugh out loud.

'"I already have your father's money, Hugo," he told him, "which is quite enough for me to live on for the rest of my life. At the end of the week, my wife and I shall set sail for Greece. I've bought a villa there, on an island, where I shall get drunk every night for the rest of my life in warmth and comfort. I don't need your money and I don't need your land."

'And at that point, Mrs Hudson, it so happened that the golden canary was brought into the room in its beautiful rosewood box, and Mr Snaresdon rose to his feet and grabbed the box, and opened the lid and displayed the little bird to everyone.

'"Take a good look at it," he told us, "for this is the last time you ever will. You see these sapphires? I've always thought they were wasted on my uncle's ridiculous bird. So I have plans for them. Think how ravishing they will look around the neck of a beautiful woman. Around my wife's neck, to be precise. Because, if you ever see them again, that is where they'll be. I leave here tonight for the village of Frawling, and tomorrow to London, where I intend to have this gaudy piece of nonsense melted down and the stones set in silver. And every time I allow my wife to wear them, I shall think of you, Empingham, and the plucking of your precious canary. And you, my friend, will think of me every Christmas for the rest of your life, every time you put up a Christmas tree, and there won't be a damned thing you can ever do to avenge yourself!"'

'And did he, ma'am?' I asked, breathless at the thought of such wanton cruelty. 'Did he leave that night?'

'Well, no, Flotsam,' Mrs Alma Tadema conceded, apparently aware that this was something of an anti-climax. 'Lord Empingham called for the carriage to be brought round, but the message came back that the snow was too deep even to move it from the coach-house. Mr Snaresdon flew into a terrible rage about it, demanding that men should be found to clear a path to the village, but when he sent Savage out to examine the conditions, the ruffian confirmed that the roads were indeed impassable and that the snow was coming down faster than anyone could clear it. He and Mr Snaresdon might struggle through to the village on foot, he said, but Mrs Snaresdon…'

'An uncomfortable situation for all concerned,' Mrs Hudson observed, rising from the table to put the kettle on the hob.

'Yes, indeed, Mrs Hudson. So yet another horrible scene ensued, with Mr Snaresdon stating quite baldly, in front of all his lordship's guests, that it was a deliberate plot, that the Empingham Canary would be stolen away from him, that the house was full of Empingham's friends and servants, that it was as certain as night follows day that some sort of assault would be attempted upon him while he slept.'

'Not a remark that would have won him many admirers,' Mrs Hudson noted, reaching the teapot from its shelf. 'A good many hosts would have shown him the door on the spot, snow or no snow.'

Mrs Alma Tadema nodded vigorously.

'Precisely, Mrs Hudson. And it seemed that every one of the gentlemen present, my Lawrence included, was about to jump to their feet to remonstrate, but Lord Empingham laughed out loud in a way that silenced everybody. "Very well, Adam," he said, "I think I can guarantee you a safe night's sleep. You can sleep in the Tower Room, and you can lock yourself in. Even you will have to agree that no one can get at you there. And if you're really worried, you can keep the shutters open on the east window. Then if anyone does breach your defences while you sleep, their light will be visible to the whole household. I only hope you don't mind the cold! You can have as many blankets as you like, but I tell you, only a brave man or a stupid one would choose to sleep up there on a night such as this."

'I don't think,' our visitor added, 'that Lord Empingham believed for a moment his cousin would take up the offer. I think he assumed, as we all did, that Mr Snaresdon would see the absurdity of his fears, and would eventually agree to spend the night in a comfortable guest room, perhaps with the canary at his bedside, or perhaps with it locked away, securely and sensibly, in his lordship's safe. But the man was in a strange state that night. We could all see it. Angry and wild, in a sort of frenzy of agitation, and excited almost to the point of mania. At the mention of the tower, his face seemed to light up.

"'I'll accept your offer, Empingham," he declared. "Not for myself, but on behalf of my companion here, who fits your description on both counts, and who won't mind a little chill in the air. Will you, Savage?"

'I remember the contempt in his eyes then, Mrs Hudson, as he looked around at all the gentlemen assembled there. "And it will take a braver man than any of you," he told them, "to wrestle the canary from the arms of a bruiser like him."'

I heard Mrs Hudson give a little sigh, as if in disapproval of such melodramatics.

'I have never had the pleasure of visiting Frawling Hall myself, ma'am,' she interjected gently, 'but I take it that the tower is part of the house?'

'That's right, Mrs Hudson. The oldest part. It stands on the north-west corner of the main house, and a little forward of the more recent additions. I think there used to be an outside entrance, but that had been bricked up years before, so the only way in was through the library. The tower walls are about three feet thick, so even Mr Snaresdon had to agree that his man would be safe there.

'Nevertheless,' our visitor continued, 'I remember there was a lot of wrangling about keys. It emerged that Mr Snaresdon didn't trust his own man a great deal more than he trusted the rest of us, and was planning to keep Savage locked in the Tower Room with the canary, so that no one but himself could open the door. But then it turned out that there were *two* keys to the room at the top of the tower, and at first Mr Snaresdon demanded both should be surrendered to him. Lord Empingham told him that one of the keys had been on his personal key ring for the last thirty years and that the Devil himself wasn't going to remove it, but that he would sleep with his keys beneath his pillow if Mr Snaresdon was really so nervous about the canary's safety. Mr Snaresdon said he *was* so nervous, and that he would sleep with the other key beneath *his* pillow, and that he wasn't worried about Lord Empingham himself making any attempt to remove the canary, because he didn't think his lordship had the nerve for it.

'Well, when he said that, so sneeringly and so openly, I think there were a number of Lord Empingham's guests on the brink of calling the fellow out, but again his lordship just laughed, and said that he had no respect for

Mr Snaresdon and even less for his henchman, Savage, but that he did respect the laws of inheritance, however painful they were to him personally, so he had not the least intention of removing the canary from under that gentleman's nose. But, he added, if the canary were to take wing that night and disappear into the darkness, never to be seen again, it would be exactly what Mr Snaresdon deserved, and he for one would thank the Lord for it.'

Mrs Alma Tadema paused there and looked from Mrs Hudson to me, then back again.

'And that's what this is all about, Mrs Hudson. Because, you see, that's exactly what *did* happen.'

Chapter 8

Mrs Hudson poured the tea.

She did it very calmly and deliberately, in the way she always did, making sure that we all had just the right amount of milk and sugar. Outside, in the darkness, an angry little wind had begun to snap at the heels of passers-by, although the street was much quieter now, the rumble of carriages less frequent. Only when she was settled comfortably in her seat with the linen cosy firmly on the pot did Mrs Hudson return to our visitor's remarkable statement.

'Now, ma'am,' she began. 'You were telling us about the Empingham Canary. Are we to understand then that it vanished from behind those locked doors?'

Mrs Alma Tadema looked a little embarrassed, as though conscious that she might have over-embellished her story.

'Well, Mrs Hudson, it certainly seemed so. You see, I was woken the following morning by the most terrible hubbub. The man Savage had been thumping on the door of the Tower Room, shouting to be let out – he was locked in, if you remember – and yelling that the golden canary had been stolen from under his nose. Unfortunately, it was a little while before anyone heard him, because, as I think I said, the Tower Room is rather remote and has enormously thick walls. But when Mr

Snaresdon unlocked the door, there was no sign of the canary.'

Mrs Hudson was stirring her tea rather thoughtfully.

'So it had been stolen overnight, despite all the precautions?'

'Oh, no, Mrs Hudson. That's what I thought at first, when Lawrence – Mr Alma Tadema – shook me awake and began to explain. But people tell me it must have been stolen in the morning – there were lots of arguments about it, and I never really understood them all. I know that Mr Snaresdon accused Lord Empingham of stealing it, and Lord Empingham said it must have been Savage, and insisted that both he and the room were searched. But my husband always told me it was neither of them – that the bird must simply have flown away. He would say it as a joke, but I know it always worried him. And it still does, although in the end it turned out that Savage was the thief, after all.'

I could see that this piece of information surprised Mrs Hudson, for she took up the teaspoon once again – it was one of the little silver teaspoons that had been a gift from Mr Cremonini, the opera singer – and gave her tea another stir.

'He would seem the most obvious suspect,' she remarked, 'but I had rather thought your tale might be leading somewhere else. So that fellow was actually caught with the bird in his possession?'

But our visitor shook her head.

'Oh, no, Mrs Hudson,' she said again. 'The Empingham Canary was never seen again. But Mr Snaresdon insisted that the police should be informed, and he sent Savage to do it. And after that, Savage was never seen again either. He just set off down the lane for the village and carried on. The police inspector told my husband that he was last seen in Amberley, taking a train for London. Apparently, the police knew all about him, and had been looking for him in relation to a completely different crime. So as far as the Empingham Canary was concerned, we all thought that was that.'

Mrs Alma Tadema took a sip from her teacup and gave a little shrug.

'The theft seemed to dismay Mr Snaresdon and Lord Empingham equally. In one sense, the loss was all Mr Snaresdon's, as he was the legal owner of the bird, and even melted down it would have been worth a very great sum of money. But I think perhaps Lord Empingham felt it more deeply, for he loved that bird, and having it ripped from his possession so suddenly almost broke his heart. The only consolation for him, I believe, is that Snaresdon was denied the pleasure of destroying it in an act of pure, deliberate spite. Now, I'm told, his lordship clings to the hope that Savage sold it to someone who loves it, that somewhere it is still safe. I've heard that Lord Empingham's spirits never really recovered, though. He has been an invalid these last ten years or more.'

There was no doubting the genuine sorrow Mrs Alma Tadema felt as she thought of it. Those warm eyes of hers seemed to fill with pity.

'It was out of respect for Lord Empingham,' she went on, 'that the incident was never really spoken of by those of us who were his guests that Christmas. It was not that we made any pact of silence, of course. But we all understood that an unsavoury incident of that sort would attract a good deal of unpleasant attention. No gentleman wants it known that a house guest has been robbed beneath his roof. And the loss of the canary was such a blow to him... Obviously, the New Year's Ball could not go ahead after that, so the Harlequin costumes were all packed away again, and we tiptoed away from Frawling Hall in respectful silence as soon as the snow allowed it. I heard that Mr Snaresdon and his wife did indeed depart for Greece before the month was out, and I think we all hoped that the incident had been buried beneath the sands of time. Until, that is...'

'Until the hens began to arrive.' Mrs Hudson took a substantial sip from her teacup, then placed it gently back in its saucer. 'I assume that all the gentlemen known to have received one of these birds were also present at Frawling Hall that Christmas?'

'Precisely.' Our guest nodded vigorously. 'There has been so much talk about these chickens in the last day or two, with everyone saying that the people receiving them were unconnected, but Lawrence saw the connection at once. It was a very long time ago, of course, and we haven't seen very much of those others since then, because we have all moved in rather different circles, but when he heard the names – Brabham, Toukens, Merriman – he had no doubt that in some sinister way we were all being reminded of those peculiar events. For the last two days he has been expecting to receive his own hen, but none has arrived. And for Lawrence I think *not* receiving one is making it all worse.'

'But surely, ma'am,' I asked, not understanding, 'if he thinks that perhaps the hens are some sort of warning or threat, then *not* having one sent to him must be a good thing?'

But Mrs Alma Tadema shook her head.

'The last twenty years have been good to my husband. His work is admired, he moves in the best circles of society. But when he remembers our visit to Frawling Hall, he is taken back to a time when he still felt an outsider, when he felt he was being watched and judged by his peers. And he feels very strongly that the disappearance of the canary – the fact that Savage simply vanished and that no one was ever convicted of the theft – leaves a stain on the reputation of those who were present at the time. Of course, men like Lord Brabham and Sir Vincent Steel won't feel it in the same way. Their reputations are impregnable. But for Lawrence it's different. And then, of course, our house was blown up...'

'My goodness!' I blurted out, taken by surprise, because that isn't the sort of thing you expect to hear. But Mrs Hudson didn't seem at all surprised by our visitor's remark.

'I take it, ma'am, that you are referring to the Regent's Canal explosion of 1874? I remember reading in the newspapers that the house of an eminent artist had been damaged in the blast.'

'Indeed, Mrs Hudson. That was our house, and it was all but destroyed. It was a miracle that we escaped with our lives. Of course, I understand now – and my husband understands now – that it was a tragic accident, that the barge exploded because its cargo was, well, highly explosive. But coming so soon after the Frawling Hall affair, Lawrence was convinced at first that it was some sort of reprisal aimed at him personally. You see, even now, when he recalls those days, I think he fears that the finger of suspicion may yet be pointed at the foreigner. And somehow the fact that he has not received a hen makes him feel that he is being singled out, marked as different from the others.'

'These others,' Mrs Hudson asked, 'can you remember everyone who was present at Frawling Hall on that occasion?'

'I don't think I can remember them all. I know William Grey-Wilson was there – he's in St Helena now, you know. He stood out because he'd sprained his wrist and his arm was in a sling, and because he was the only one of the young men who was unmarried. But he was sent to Jamaica the following year, and we haven't seen him since. As for the rest, well, I would have to ask Lawrence. I know he will remember.'

Our cups were empty now, and Mrs Hudson began the process of refilling them.

'There was something else you said about your husband, ma'am… Something that suggested he was not convinced Savage had committed the crime. Is that still the case?'

It seemed to me an innocent enough question, but our visitor's face took on a look that very much resembled despair.

'That's right, Mrs Hudson. And I've never really understood it. But my husband has always maintained Savage was innocent. That's why he makes the joke about the bird flying away. But I think it's also why he still worries so much about the whole affair. He has a sense, I think, that the business is unfinished, and it makes him uneasy. Because after all, if Savage didn't steal the bird, who did?'

It was six o'clock in the evening when Mrs Alma Tadema finally said her farewells. There was still no sign of Dr

Watson or Sherlock Holmes, but she left, I think, greatly reassured that Mr Holmes would not consider her visit a frivolous one. For, as Mrs Hudson explained, the great detective had his own reasons for taking an interest in Frawling Hall, and would almost certainly wish to speak to Mrs Alma Tadema and her husband in person.

'As far as I'm concerned, Mrs Hudson,' Mrs Alma Tadema continued, confidently anticipating the housekeeper's thoughts, 'the sooner my husband begins to unburden himself the better. If Mr Holmes were to meet my husband in his studio, Mrs Hudson, that would be best. Lawrence likes to talk, and if he were busy arranging a scene or positioning a model, well, I think he would hardly notice he was doing it. And I think it would be very good for him to talk to someone other than myself. He has kept his uneasiness about this business locked away for far too long.'

Mrs Hudson assured her again that Mr Holmes would undoubtedly take a keen interest in the matter, and when Mrs Alma Tadema left us – up the area steps, as she had originally planned – I thought I detected a lightness in her step that had not been there when she first descended to the kitchen.

When she was gone, Mrs Hudson stood in thought for a moment, then looked up at the kitchen clock.

'My word, Flotsam. Just look at the time! Our gentlemen cannot be much longer, and we haven't lifted a finger to prepare. We had better make haste.'

I knew enough to do exactly as I was told, but while I was laying a tray for the gentlemen's supper, I ventured to ask what Mrs Hudson made of it all.

'You mean the canary business, Flotsam? Well, it's an interesting tale. The harlequin pattern on those cards cannot be a coincidence, can it? The sender is surely linking the delivery of the hens to the gathering at Frawling Hall.'

I noticed a little frown form between her eyebrows.

'And yet the Harlequin Ball never took place,' she went on, 'so the connection would seem a little tenuous. Perhaps that is why the recipients themselves are not making the connection. Now, if I'm not mistaken, that's Mr Holmes' footstep at the door, so off you go to take his coat, child. And you may mention as you do it that we have a great deal to tell him...'

If I'd been worried that Mr Holmes might feel slightly put out by news of Mrs Alma Tadema's visit, then I did him an injustice. He had spent a long afternoon in the archives seeking information which, in his absence, had been brought to his very doorstep, but the remarkable story of events at Frawling Hall and their connection to the mysterious hens proved ample recompense for the lack of success he and Dr Watson had met with in the archives of *The Clarion*.

'For there can be no doubting the discretion of all concerned, can there, Watson? Not even the slightest rumour of any scandal reached the acute ears of the Press.'

By this point, he and his companion had, between them, demolished the better part of one of Lamingtons' superior hams, a cold guinea fowl, a large bunch of Muscat grapes, some excellent biscuits, a substantial wedge of Clawson Stilton and two slices of Dundee cake. Far from being disgruntled, Mr Holmes looked extremely content.

'I daresay we should go and see this Alma Tadema fellow first thing in the morning, Holmes,' Dr Watson concluded, cradling a large glass of claret in his palm. 'See what he has to tell us about the whole business.'

'It would certainly be sensible to hear what he has to say, my friend,' Mr Holmes agreed. 'But there can be no question of my going tomorrow. You must go without me, Watson.'

'Without you, Holmes? Where will you be?'

'Why, at Frawling Hall, of course, Watson. Surely you must see that all roads lead there? And I would very much like to give Lord Empingham the good news in person.'

'The good news, Holmes? What news is that?'

'Why, that the Empingham Canary will be returned to him before Christmas.'

'*Returned* to him, Holmes?' Dr Watson looked over to where me and Mrs Hudson were still standing by the dinner tray, and gave a mystified little shrug. 'How on earth do you arrive at that conclusion?'

The great detective looked pained.

'Dear me, Watson, the damaged Christmas trees, of course! Those telegrams made the whole situation plain. I don't think it is unreasonable to state that the famous Empingham Canary will be in his lordship's possession before the end of the month.'

His friend cast another glance towards us, and his exasperation was plain.

'Are you telling us, Holmes, that you know who stole the bird?'

'Of course not, Watson.' Mr Holmes looked a little exasperated too. 'The information we have doesn't stretch that far. But clearly somebody intends to return the canary to Frawling, and I think it would be a kindness to inform Lord Empingham at once.'

'But, please, sir,' I asked nervously, for I was every bit as mystified as Dr Watson, 'even if the thief does return the bird, it still doesn't belong to Lord Empingham, does it?'

'Presumably not, Flotsam.' Mr Holmes looked unconcerned by this detail. 'And I confess that I have no idea who, in law, can claim to be the bird's current owner. But at least we can be certain it is no longer Lord Empingham's cousin. For the simple reason,' he continued, anticipating my next question, 'that according to a notice which appeared in *The Clarion* in late November, Mr Adam Snaresdon died of pneumonia somewhere in the Peloponnese in the early autumn. So once again, it would seem, the famous golden bird has avoided falling into his clutches.'

'So let me get this straight, Holmes,' Dr Watson replied rather wearily. 'We don't know who stole the Empingham Canary, but you seem certain – for reasons that I don't begin to understand – that someone is about to return it to Frawling Hall. So where on earth do these wretched hens come into it?'

'An excellent question, Watson, and one that at the moment I am quite unable to answer. But it reminds me that we must write to Mr Denham first thing tomorrow, telling him that we are hot on the heels of his missing friend.'

'Who? The missing violinist? *Are* we hot on his heels, Holmes?'

'Oh, really, Watson! Did the stolen straw boater tell you nothing? Come, I suspect you are teasing me. Perhaps you would be good enough to drop in on Mr Denham in the morning, telling him his friend is alive and well. You could do it after your visit to Mr Alma Tadema.'

I have often remarked on Dr Watson's remarkable good nature, but this was one of the very rare occasions when his expression became a little petulant.

'Must I really see this Alma Tadema fellow, Holmes? Couldn't you go yourself when you're back from Frawling?'

Clearly I was not alone in noticing Dr Watson's peevish tone, for his companion turned to him with concern.

'Why, whatever's the matter, my friend? You need only ask him a few simple questions.'

'Yes, but in his *studio*, Holmes.' Dr Watson put down his wine glass. 'I don't know if you've seen many of the fellow's paintings, but I have. And I'm not saying he doesn't have talent, because clearly he does. But his subject matter… Well, there's a great number of scantily clad young women, Holmes. Some of them, frankly, are not really clad at all.'

I watched the doctor blush.

'Of course, I know it's art, Holmes, and I've no objection to it. I'm as happy looking at that sort of thing as the next man, and there's no denying his paintings are very easy on the eye. But looking at a picture is one thing, gawping at a young lady in person is quite another, and for a gentleman to be hanging around a fellow's studio asking questions about hens, while some young lady might be standing there disrobed… Well, Holmes, you must see that's dashed awkward.'

His companion looked amused.

'Really, Watson? And you a medical man?'

'That's quite different, Holmes,' Dr Watson replied sharply. 'I've never insisted on patients dressing themselves like Grecian slave girls, for one thing.'

'Very well.' Mr Holmes sighed and turned to his house-keeper. 'Mrs Hudson, do you feel that Flotsam here might undertake such a task and emerge uncorrupted?'

Mrs Hudson looked rather stern.

'Flotsam, sir, has this carpet to beat at some point tomorrow. But I daresay the scruples Dr Watson has expressed would not apply in her case in quite the same way. And of course there is no doubting that Mr Alma Tadema is a gentleman. So if Flotsam is willing...'

I was. It was agreed.

'Then Dr Watson and I shall take the first train to Amberley tomorrow morning, and from there to Frawling Hall,' Mr Holmes concluded brightly. 'Perhaps, Flotsam, on your way back from your visit to St John's Wood, you would deliver a message to Mr Denham's house? I shall bring him more news of his friend, Mr Cortado, as soon as I return to London.'

And with that, the conference was over. Mr Holmes took up his violin, Dr Watson muttered something about dropping in at his club, Mrs Hudson began to load the various plates and platters onto the tray; and I, thinking about the two gentlemen catching their train the following day, suddenly understood why Marlo the Magnificent's missing boater pointed the way so clearly to the missing violinist of Bromley Place.

Chapter 9

The next morning brought a note, addressed to me personally, from Mr Rupert Spencer. It was a much brighter day, with clear blue skies and little wind, but the chill in the air was so sharp it felt as though it might cut to the bone. Mr Spencer's note was not a lengthy one, merely two or three lines to the effect that no accounts of any further hen deliveries had reached him. *But who knows?* he concluded. *Outside London, and across Europe, hens may be descending upon every third household for all I know.* When I showed it to Mrs Hudson, she allowed the faintest of smiles to play across her lips.

'I don't think, Flotsam, that we have anything to fear on that score. In fact, I would be surprised if we were to hear of many more of these strange deliveries. Mr Grey-Wilson, for instance, the gentleman Mrs Alma Tadema remembers from that Christmas at Frawling Hall. I very much doubt that he will receive an unexpected hen.'

'No, ma'am,' I agreed heartily. 'He's the governor of St Helena, isn't he? It would surely be impossible to have a chicken delivered all that way.'

But Mrs Hudson didn't look particularly convinced by my reasoning.

'Perhaps so, Flotsam,' she conceded. 'But I confess I was not thinking of the logistical difficulties when I made my prediction. For I believe he is a married man, nowadays.

Now, I've laid out one of the dresses which Miss Peters gave you for your visit to Montrachute House, and if you agree to sit still for ten minutes, I will arrange your hair to match it.'

It is hard to describe how very lovely Miss Peters' old dress was, and somehow just putting it on made me feel more confident and more capable, so that on arriving at Mr Alma Tadema's house in St John's Wood I felt almost no nerves whatsoever. Which is just as well, for it was a house unlike any other I had ever visited – sprawling, and huge, an astonishing confection of great domes and pillars and marble rooms hung with lavish fabrics, so that I felt as though I'd stumbled into a world that was partly ancient Rome, and partly the *Thousand And One Nights*.

And when I was shown – by a silent footman who accepted without question my statement that I was calling on behalf of Mr Sherlock Holmes – to the doorway of Mr Alma Tadema's studio, I could not but feel a sense of awe at the room that lay before me: double height, ornate and richly decorated, with light from above, and a remarkable window of onyx instead of glass, and in the middle of everything, spectacularly out of season yet lush and perfect, a huge bowl of roses set upon a low marble table. I might have been standing in the palace of an ancient Byzantine Emperor. It certainly felt very different from the rest of St John's Wood.

'If you wait in here, Miss,' the footman told me, 'the master will be along shortly.'

Left alone in such a room, I confess for a moment I simply stood in awe, looking up and around, taking in all the details of the decorated ceiling above me, until I realised with a shock that I wasn't alone at all. In one of the room's lavishly draped alcoves – although you could scarcely call it an alcove, for it was deep enough to hold a hansom cab and was capped by a sort of half-dome that shone like silver – in that alcove, leaning against a huge piano, stood a woman of perhaps twenty-seven or twenty-eight years, watching me with amusement.

'It is quite a sight, is it not?' she asked. Her voice was crisp and business-like but not unkind, and she was extremely well-spoken. I saw that she was neatly dressed in clothes that were modest but of very fine quality, so if she were one of Mr Alma Tadema's models, she appeared a very respectable one. 'I believe,' she went on, 'that there is a screen over there, if you need to remove your clothes.'

'My clothes?' It took me a moment to understand. 'Oh, no, ma'am! I'm not an artist's model. In fact, I thought *you* were.'

'Me?' The idea seemed to amuse her enormously. 'I should think my family would have something to say about that! But I'm flattered that you feel an artist would have me, Miss…?'

'Flotsam,' I told her, taking the hand she offered me. She was, I thought, a rather good-looking woman, but perhaps not in the way beloved by artists. Her features were strong rather than sensual, with a rather penetrating gaze and high eyebrows, but a softness in her eyes which belied the seriousness of her expression.

'I am Miss Coburg,' she replied, stating it very decidedly, as if to leave no room for doubt. 'And this is Miss Dalrymple.'

She gestured to the far side of the huge studio, where, I realised, a second figure lurked unobserved. She was an elderly lady encased in a rather old-fashioned and dark-coloured dress, and she was sitting up very straight on a richly upholstered ottoman, peering at me in a disapproving fashion. She had been concealed by a lofty stand of plumed fans when I entered, and had been sitting so still that she hadn't caught my eye. Now she nodded her head very slightly in my direction and sighed audibly, then returned to her silent vigil. As far as I'm aware, she said nothing at all for the duration of my visit, and remained primly upright on the ottoman throughout.

'Miss Dalrymple accompanies me to ensure that nothing improper occurs in these dangerous, Bohemian quarters,' Miss Coburg explained with a smile, 'but of course Mr Alma Tadema is something of an old family friend, and even my grandmother, who is famously quick to disapprove of things, feels it is quite all right for me to come here and sit for him. We have a remarkable collection of family portraits, you see, and my people are always keen to add another. But my visit today is an impromptu one, to discuss the arrangements for my sitting. Now, what about you, Miss Flotsam? What brings you here today, if it is not to be captured for posterity as a nymph or a Roman maiden?'

So I explained to her that I was calling on behalf of Mr Sherlock Holmes as he and Mr Alma Tadema had business together, and then wished that I hadn't said even that much, for Miss Coburg raised her eyebrows in astonishment and drew me further into the alcove.

'How tremendously exciting, Miss Flotsam! May I ask how you come to be performing such a role? I have never thought of Mr Holmes as a man much given to the company of young ladies. But perhaps you are acquainted with him socially? Or perhaps he is a relative?'

'Goodness me, no!' I exclaimed, because the very idea of Mr Holmes having social acquaintances of any sort, let alone young women, seemed both absurd and impossible.

He was much happier in the company of, well, criminals. Or policemen. Or foreign dignitaries with complicated stories to tell about missing heirs and blackmail plots. As for relatives, apart from one brother, I had never heard mention of any.

But in trying to explain to Miss Coburg that my connection with Mr Holmes was that of employee to employer, I somehow found myself telling her rather more than I intended about how very surprising it was – even to me – that I should find myself running such an errand. I've no idea why, on that day, I confided so much. I am usually much more discreet. I think, perhaps, there was something about Miss Coburg that rather invited confidences, a face that suggested both kindness and sagacity. Or perhaps it was simply that she was a stranger, so it didn't much seem to matter.

'What a very remarkable tale!' she declared when I was finished. 'I shall read of Mr Holmes' exploits with quite different eyes in future. But tell me, do you not find it confusing to be a housemaid one moment and something quite different the next?' She smiled a rather sad smile. 'I've learned for myself how onerous it is to perform unwelcome duties, and for you to return to your daily chores after some of the excitements you've described must be terribly hard.'

'Oh, no, ma'am,' I assured her brightly. 'I have a... well, a friend, who teases me sometimes, telling me that I don't know my place. He says it in fun, I know, because he *likes* that I don't. But the truth is I've never really *had* a place. First, I was just a stray, not even sure of my own name. Then Mrs Hudson taught me how to be a housemaid, but she taught me many, many other things too, so being a housemaid was always just one thing, and there are ever so many others. And it doesn't really matter to me anyway, because for now I'm just happy to be where I am.'

This was greeted with a smile of surprising warmth.

'You know, Miss Flotsam,' Miss Coburg began, 'I sometimes hear acquaintances of mine express fears that there are revolutionaries active in our cities, shady characters working to bring about social upheaval – and always the speakers seem to be imagining unshaven, fanatical men plotting violence in basements. But I do believe there's more for those people to fear in that "for now" of yours, than in any number of grubby male plotters!'

I think she was about to explain herself, but just then the door to the studio was thrown open and a portly man sporting a small beard and *pince nez* spectacles bustled into the studio, apparently in great haste. On seeing me, he stopped in his tracks.

'Good lord,' he exclaimed, 'am I meant to be painting?'

His wife had told me that Mr Alma Tadema was Dutch by birth, and although his English was excellent, it was not without a trace of accent. He took a few steps closer to me then held up his hand, one thumb out in an 'L' shape, and appeared to examine me for a moment.

'Excellent, yes. I can definitely use you, my dear. In the Roman baths, I think. Please, let me see your profile.'

I suppose I should have corrected him at once, but such was his enthusiasm, and the urgency of his manner, I found myself turning my head exactly as he directed.

'Very fine, yes, very fine indeed. But, madam,' he went on, as if remembering himself, 'there has been a mistake. I am quite sure I'm not painting today, and I was expecting quite a different visitor. I was told she was here. There has been an error. A most inexplicable error.'

I realised then that, from where the artist stood, Miss Coburg's position by the piano wasn't visible, and I hastened to explain.

'You were expecting Miss Coburg, sir, and here she is.'

'Miss Coburg?' He looked utterly confused for a moment, until the lady herself stepped forward.

'That's right, my friend. Miss Coburg. And here I am. You said in your note, if you remember, that you wished to discuss some preliminary sketches for the portrait?'

'Miss Coburg…?' He looked from that lady to me then back again, as if the presence of us both simultaneously in his studio had rather flummoxed him. Then, finally, understanding seemed to dawn, and he gave a little bow. 'Why, yes, of course! Some preliminary sketches, yes. Most certainly, ma'am. Miss Coburg. The sooner the better…'

'But I fear, sir, my visit is inconvenient, as this young lady has business with you. Miss Flotsam has been sent by Mr Sherlock Holmes.'

'Miss Flotsam…?' He turned to me. 'Ah, yes, of course, I received a note at breakfast. Mr Holmes wants some information about the incident at Frawling Hall, does he not? Well, I'm most happy to provide it, madam. A damnable business, and if Mr Holmes can clear it up after all these years, then I'll be eternally grateful to him. Those events still cast a shadow.'

Miss Coburg signalled across the studio to her companion.

'I shall leave you, sir. You will wish to speak to Miss Flotsam in confidence, and although I confess to an intense curiosity about the incident under discussion, I know much better than to pry.'

This remark seemed to give Mr Alma Tadema something of a start, for he pulled off his spectacles and waved them as if in agitation.

'Leave, ma'am? Why, on no account, I beg you! This low winter light... you must see how perfectly it falls, how it touches the face and plays with the lines of shade. A rough sketch now, while the light is just so, would be invaluable. If you were to give me just five minutes, ma'am...'

Miss Coburg looked across at me and appeared to hesitate, but the famous painter carried on.

'Have no fear about the other matter. With Miss Flotsam's permission, I will answer her questions while I work. It will not interfere with my drawing in the slightest. And of course, ma'am, I have no qualms about discussing the matter in front of you. I know you to be the most discreet person in London.'

And so I stood in that remarkable studio feeling rather out of place while Mr Alma Tadema retrieved the necessary materials from one corner of his studio, then I watched while he directed his sitter into the pose he required, requesting most respectfully that she should remove her hat and loosen her hair. I had heard that great artists could be peremptory, or rude, or careless of the feelings of others, but Mr Alma Tadema seemed almost deferential in his dealings with his sitter, and a good deal more jovial than temperamental. Only when Miss Coburg had achieved the precise position he was seeking, and he had taken up his pencil to draw, did he direct a comment to me.

'And now, Miss Flotsam,' he began, his eyes never leaving his subject, 'what precisely does Mr Sherlock Holmes wish to know about the Frawling Hall affair?'

Although the artist himself wasn't looking at me, Miss Coburg undoubtedly was, and with an expectant gaze, so I found myself feeling rather nervous, anxious that my questioning should make a good impression.

'Well, sir, perhaps if you were to tell me your own recollections of events that Christmas…?'

Mrs Alma Tadema had told us that her husband liked to talk, and I quickly realised she was right, for I barely had to ask him any questions at all. As he drew, he gave his own account of the Canary Affair, from his arrival at Frawling with his wife to the evening when the bird went missing.

'It was an uncomfortable occasion, as you can no doubt imagine, Miss Flotsam. For me especially, as I had seldom before been a guest at one of your great houses, and felt anxious that I would make some terrible error of manners in such very strange circumstances. But for the rest of the company it was most difficult too, I think. Mr Snaresdon, although a gentleman by birth, was clearly not one by conduct. That night, after locking his own servant in the tower, he insisted that we should all join him in the library for drinking. The library, you see, contained the only door into the tower, so that way he could keep an eye on the entrance while he drank.'

'And did he lock that door too?' I asked, struggling a little to understand the peculiar geography of Frawling Hall.

'There was no lock on that door,' the artist replied firmly. 'I remember as much, because Mr Snaresdon complained about it a great deal. But it was no matter – the door led directly to the ancient spiral steps, and at the top of the steps was the door to the Tower Room, where Savage slept with the bird. It was a heavy oak door

– medieval in its thickness one might almost say – and reinforced with iron strips, with an equally sturdy lock. So it seemed to me that securing the door at the foot of the steps – the door into the library – was unimportant. Nobody without a key could pass through the upper door. Even with a battering ram, they couldn't do it, as there wasn't room to swing one.'

'And were there no windows on the spiral staircase, sir?'

'Only those narrow slits for archers, you know the sort. Very ancient and very thin. Not even a small child would be able to slip through them.'

'And did you all remain in the library for very long that night, sir?'

'Not so very long, Miss Flotsam. The atmosphere was not congenial. Some guests barely said a word, and some of us spoke more than was necessary, in order to compensate. Myself, I was one of the latter. I remember talking a great deal about my Harlequin outfit, the one I was to wear for the masked ball at New Year. There had been a mistake, and the costume delivered to me was for a much slimmer young man. I made a great joke of being too fat to squeeze into it, for even then my figure was of generous proportions. But I think my chatter annoyed Lord Empingham, for he told me rather curtly to hang it on my door that evening, and he would have a servant take it away for alterations.'

The memory still clearly pained the artist, for he paused in his sketching and stared for a moment at the high onyx window above his subject. Then he seemed to remember himself and resumed both his work and his narrative without prompting.

'It is funny to speak of that Harlequin suit after all these years, Miss Flotsam, for that night I was woken by a tremendous banging on my door. It was about ten minutes short of midnight, and I quickly realised the person knocking so urgently was Mr Adam Snaresdon. He told me that he had heard someone in the corridor, and wanted me to come with him to investigate. My wife and I had rooms next to his, you see, so it wasn't the case that he was choosing me to assist him over other candidates. Mine was simply the first door he came to.'

'So did you go with him?' I asked, rather breathlessly.

'I did.' He paused to add a series of quick strokes to his sketch. 'Given the unique and difficult circumstances that existed in Frawling Hall that night, I felt it incumbent upon me to keep an eye on things, as it were.'

'And did you see anyone?' It was the question on my lips, but it wasn't me who asked it. Miss Coburg was clearly listening to the artist's account just as breathlessly as I was.

'Alas, no, ma'am. I pulled on a dressing gown and went with Mr Snaresdon, who was similarly attired. Our rooms were in the East Wing, and we walked the length of it, both on the first floor, where our rooms were, and on the ground floor too. But the house was very quiet, exactly as it should have been, in fact. So after ten minutes or so, Mr Snaresdon declared that he was going to the tower, to check that all was well, and would I come with him? Well, it seemed proper that I should – not because I thought he would find anything untoward, but because I didn't really trust the fellow, and thought it would be prudent to keep an eye on him.'

'And *was* there anything untoward going on at the tower?' Again, Miss Coburg asked the question before I could.

'Nothing at all, ma'am.' The artist reached for a clean sheet of paper, secured it tightly, and began a second sketch. 'We entered the tower through the library and climbed the spiral staircase, which wasn't easy because we had only one candle between us, and that was being carried by Mr Snaresdon, who went ahead of me. Those old stone stairs are a bit uneven, and I stumbled more than once. And all the time Mr Snaresdon was shouting at the top of his voice – "Savage! Savage! Is everything in order?" I thought he would wake the entire house. But when we reached the big oak door of the Tower Room, it was clear that Savage was still asleep, because it took a minute or two of thumping on the door to rouse him.'

'You did not go in, sir?' It seemed to me a hugely important question.

'We did not, Miss Flotsam. Mr Snaresdon, you see, hadn't thought to bring his key with him, because when he left his room, he hadn't intended to go to the tower – he had simply been looking for intruders in the corridor outside his room. So Savage remained locked in, and we remained locked out. I could tell by the man's voice when he answered our calls that he had been deeply asleep, and it took a moment or two longer for him to light his lamp, because when he finally did, I saw the light showing beneath the door.'

'And all was in order?'

'According to Savage it was. He assured us that the Empingham Canary was still in its case, right beside his bed. And it was easy to believe him, for how could it be otherwise? So Snaresdon told him to stay awake with the light on for the rest of the night, in case something was afoot, and Savage shouted back that he would. Then Snaresdon rattled the lock to check that it was still secure, and we returned to the library. There Mr Snaresdon tried to interest me in a drink and became quite animated when I refused – so animated, in fact, that he knocked over a decanter which smashed on the floor.

'That calmed him down a little and he agreed to go to bed, but before we retired, he took a chair and wedged it beneath the handle of the door that led to the tower. I pointed out to him that this precaution was of little practical use, as anyone wishing to enter the tower could simply remove the chair and go in. "True," he replied with a smile I considered rather demented, "but I'll know if they do! Watch!" And then the loathsome fellow picked up a small shard from the broken decanter and balanced it on the back of the chair, just where it rested against the door.'

I considered this for a moment.

'I see, sir. So if the piece of glass wasn't there in the morning, it would prove that somebody had moved the chair. But would the thief not have noticed it, sir? Because if they did, all they had to do was to put the piece of glass back when they left the tower.'

Mr Alma Tadema smiled, without looking away from his sketch.

'They would almost certainly have noticed it, Miss Flotsam, if all the lamps had been lit in the library, as they had been that evening when the guests were gathered there. But we were working by the light of a candle, and any thief would presumably have been doing the same. And unless the room was very bright, I don't think anyone would have noticed such a little shard of glass.'

He seemed quite certain of this, so I nodded and reminded him of where his account of those nocturnal adventures had begun.

'You mentioned something about the Harlequin suit, sir?'

The artist nodded.

'Indeed. You see, Miss Flotsam, I had no trouble falling asleep after all that marching around, but before I slept, I remember noticing that my Harlequin suit was no longer hanging behind my door where I'd left it. I remember thinking how strange were the habits of the English country house, that it had been taken away for improvements while I slept. But when I woke next morning, the suit was most definitely hanging behind the door again, unimproved, and the mask with it, just as I had left it. Given the momentous events of that morning, I never asked about it or mentioned it to anyone, so to this day I cannot be entirely sure whether or not I dreamed it.'

At this point, Miss Coburg broke from her pose to rub the muscles of her neck with her fingertips.

'And you were awoken, sir, I take it, with the news that the golden ornament had been stolen?' she asked.

'No, ma'am. I was roused from my slumbers that morning by Mr Snaresdon again, banging on my door a second time. He'd been told by a servant that Savage was causing a disturbance in the tower, and he wanted me to go with him – "in case it's some sort of infernal trap," were the words he used. That was a little before seven in the morning, and we both knew Savage had been locked in all night, so I could see no cause for alarm. But back we went to the library, and Mr Snaresdon started making a huge fuss because someone had moved the chair that he'd left behind the door. But the butler told us he'd moved it,

164

after he'd lit the lamps that morning, and when questioned by Mr Snaresdon, he claimed that he had indeed noticed a little piece of glass resting on the back of the chair. As we climbed the tower stairs for the second time, we could hear Savage rattling the lock, demanding to be let out, and shouting that the golden canary had vanished.'

He shook his head, recalling the moment. I could tell that the recollection still troubled him deeply.

'As you can imagine, ma'am, once the theft had been confirmed, we all found ourselves in an extremely awkward situation. I mean, there could be no doubt that the thief was one of those who had spent the night in Frawling Hall. There's no entrance into the old tower other than through the house, and the house had been secured for the night in the usual way. Furthermore, there was snow on the ground. Even if the weather conditions had allowed a burglar to get as far as the hall, his footprints in the snow would undoubtedly have betrayed him.'

Miss Coburg, to whom he had addressed the remark, nodded sympathetically, in a way that suggested she fully understood why the artist remained so uncomfortable about the whole business. I waited for a moment while Mr Alma Tadema peered very closely at the sketch he was making, then asked him if he could remember the names of all the other guests at Frawling Hall that Christmas.

'I certainly can, Miss Flotsam,' he assured me, his eyes returning to his subject. 'I have thought of them all a good deal over the last twenty years. It was a large party. There were twenty-one of us in all, not including Lord Empingham himself or his great aunt, Mrs Graham, who was something of an invalid. We were ten married couples, all of us under forty and most of us much younger, and then there was Grey-Wilson, who was a bachelor. The married men? Well, there was Touken and Cortado, Steel and Teddy Scott, Fergus Merriman and Lord Brabham, all of them with their wives – they're the ones who've received hens, of course.'

All the while, as he talked, he continued to draw, as though his words and his art came from completely different parts of his brain.

'Then there was Ernest Fuller and his wife Mary, Mr and Mrs Thaddeus Holland, and the Smith-Jacksons. It comes as something of a relief to me that, like myself, none of those have been sent poultry of any sort. How can I be so sure? That's easy, Miss Flotsam. I sent telegrams to all three families asking the question. No doubt they think me an eccentric foreigner, for it is an astonishingly odd question to be asked out of the blue, by a man you haven't spoken to for a dozen years or more. But all three gentlemen replied very politely in the negative.'

'But there must have been many individuals in Frawling Hall that night other than Lord Empingham's guests,' Miss Coburg pointed out.

Mr Alma Tadema gave a little snort.

'Indeed, ma'am. And of course in England it is the first thing everyone thinks of. *What about the servants? What about the servants?* But Lord Empingham's servants had all been in the family for years, and his lordship made it clear he trusted them implicitly. However, the man Savage was a servant of sorts too, of course, which is why everyone was so delighted to blame him for the crime.'

'But he ran away that morning, sir,' I pointed out. 'Straight after the theft was discovered. Surely that suggests he was responsible?'

'I don't believe for a moment that he stole the ornament, Miss Flotsam.'

At this moment, for the first time, Mr Alma Tadema looked away from his work and addressed me directly.

'I don't believe it for the simple reason that I was present when Mr Snaresdon unlocked the door of the Tower Room at seven o'clock that morning. As I said, we could hear Savage through the door, shouting that the canary had disappeared, so when the door was opened, I immediately took the precaution of looking around the room. Before I'd finished, Lord Empingham had joined us, and insisted that Savage should be searched. Now, at that point, Savage had not yet left the room.

'The search proved that the golden canary was not on his person, and it was not in the Tower Room either – I can vouch for that myself. It had been there the night before, when Mr Snaresdon locked it in, but it was not there in the morning, when I searched the place. Both the keys were accounted for – Lord Empingham was adamant there were no others – and I checked the windows myself: all of them were firmly rusted shut. And so, Miss Flotsam, although I cannot explain how the bird was made to vanish, I can only state that, unless he is a magician, Savage did not remove the Empingham Canary from that room.'

I heard Miss Coburg give a low chuckle.

'Well, Miss Flotsam, that is surely a puzzle worthy of Mr Holmes! The doors and windows all locked, yet the canary gone. I cannot imagine that he will ever have come across anything quite like that before.'

'Oh, no, Miss,' I assured her, 'Mr Holmes comes across that sort of thing all the time. You'd be surprised how many mysterious things seem to occur in locked rooms. I've often heard him say that without such an improbable number of impossible crimes, he would be reduced to searching for lost dogs for a living.'

'Well, Miss Flotsam…' The artist had returned to his sketch. 'If Mr Holmes can unravel this particular mystery, I will be greatly obliged to him. Now, as for that painting, perhaps you and I could make a start in the New Year? I'm imagining a Roman bath house, and a Roman maiden lolling in the foreground near the water… No, *two* Roman maidens. Or perhaps even three…'

'Mr Alma Tadema!' Miss Coburg's voice was stern. 'You are forgetting. That is not why Miss Flotsam is here. She is not one of your models.'

The great man's apologies were profuse, but he undoubtedly looked a little crestfallen. When I said my farewells and left them to their sitting, I could still hear him muttering about clear waters in the background and the shade of blue that would best set off my complexion.

Chapter 10

Mrs Hudson had been very insistent that I should take a hansom from St John's Wood back into town, as it would be quicker than an omnibus.

'For if you are to find Mr Denham at home, the earlier you call the better, child,' she told me firmly. 'And besides, if that carpet is *ever* to be beaten, I shall need you home no later than noon.'

However, given that Mr Denham's townhouse was only a short walk from Bridle Lane, it didn't seem so very wrong to ask the driver to drop me outside Trevelyan's. It wasn't that I was desperate to see Scraggs – of course, I wasn't – nor that I was really worried for him. It would have been nice to see him, that was all. But once again, although I found his shop glowing and warm and beautiful – if a little empty of customers – I was told that Mr Scraggs was out on business. The name of Mr Trevelyan was mentioned, and I thought it was mentioned with a hint of trepidation. Perhaps the staff of Trevelyan's were not unaware of the vacillations of its principal investor.

So I made my way to Mr Denham's house in rather subdued spirits, and on being admitted by a timid house-maid, explained that I had a note to deliver in person to the master of the house from Mr Sherlock Holmes.

That name proved – as it so often did – extremely effective at opening doors, and I was shown almost

169

immediately into a smartly furnished drawing room occupied by Mr Horace Denham and by an elegant lady in her late forties with sharp features and a rather cold gaze. It soon became evident that this was none other than Miss Lavinia Burrows, the great friend of the missing violinist, and the one who had been expecting his proposal of marriage.

'And for what reason,' she asked me, fixing me with a penetrating stare, 'did Mr Holmes require this to be delivered in person?'

'Only, Miss, because he wanted me to reassure you that, as the note says, Mr Cortado is in no danger.'

'No danger? Truly?' She scoffed quite openly at the idea. 'What exactly does the note say, Horace?'

Mr Denham had been reading Mr Holmes' message with a furrowed brow.

'It is as the girl says. He tells us that Mr Cortado is alive and well, and in no danger, and that he will have more news for us shortly.' He looked perplexed. 'I fear he is greatly mistaken. I don't understand how he could possibly have arrived at such a conclusion.'

I saw my chance to put their minds at ease.

'Well, it is all to do with the boater, sir. The boater tells us that Mr Cortado quite probably did catch the train to Bognor Regis that day.'

Miss Burrows rolled her eyes at this, and she tutted loudly.

'Oh, really, Horace! Must we listen to this? We need *action*. And I simply don't believe for a moment that the man in the boater that day at Victoria Station was Maximillian.'

'Oh, no, Miss,' I told her hastily, anxious to explain. 'The man in the boater was someone else, but that man's boater went missing on the train because Mr Cortado was worried people would see the hat and think that it was *him* on the train. Which he was, of course – on the train, I mean – but he'd got rid of his own boater to make sure he wasn't recognised. So it was just terribly bad luck that Marlo the Magnificent happened to catch the same train in the same sort of hat. That's why, when he saw the chance, Mr Cortado hid Marlo's boater, so no one would see Marlo wearing the boater and think that Marlo was Mr Cortado. And that's why, when it was confirmed that Marlo's boater was only hidden, not stolen, Mr Holmes became convinced that Marlo and Mr Cortado must *both* have gone to Bognor. But, of course, now we know Mr Cortado probably wasn't heading for Bognor at all, he was heading for Amberley, which is on the same line.'

It was clear to me, even while I was talking, that I wasn't explaining myself very well, and the blank expression on Mr Denham's face when I'd finished confirmed my fears beyond any doubt.

'But why on earth would Max sneak off to Amberley?' he asked.

I took a deep breath.

'Well, you see, Lord Empingham used to have this canary…'

But I was able to go no further before a little explosion of anger from Miss Burrows interrupted me.

'Enough of this nonsense!' she declared. 'Show her the letter, Horace.'

With a very grave air, Mr Denham reached into his pocket and passed me a piece of cream writing-paper, folded neatly in half.

'Yesterday morning, as per Maximillian's instructions, I delivered the Monteverdi violin to Miss Burrows. When she opened the case to examine the instrument, she found this.'

The note was written in a childish hand, one I recognised from the envelope we'd found in Mr Cortado's practice room. And its content was such as to put all thoughts of trains and boaters completely out of my head.

> *Your last chance has gone. We gave you every warning. Now you must pay the price. Come out and face death like a man, or die like a rat in your hole.*

I hurried back to Baker Street that morning with all sorts of different thoughts and theories running through my head, the first chased out by the second, the second by the third, and so on, until the first reappeared and the circle started again. Sometimes, however, a particularly stubborn thought would refuse to be chased away and would simply collide with the one that followed it, each rendering the other hopeless and unworkable. It was a relief to get home.

But when I did, I wasn't able to unburden myself straightaway, for Mrs Hudson had a visitor – a gentleman of middle years and athletic build, and of familiar good looks.

'Mr Raffles!' I exclaimed, pleased to see him, for he was an infrequent visitor. On seeing me, he rose hastily to his feet.

'Good day to you, Flotsam. I swear you grow more lovely by the day.'

I blushed at this, but was not in any way persuaded of its truth, for I knew Mr Raffles to be free with his compliments and a dreadful flirt – also a famous amateur cricketer, a darling of polite society, and a gentleman jewel-thief. Or to be more accurate, a former jewel-thief, for Mrs Hudson assured me that his criminal days were now well behind him. Quite how he and Mrs Hudson had become acquainted was never entirely explained to me – something to do with Lady Haslemere's emeralds, I was once told – but the two clearly shared a bond of mutual respect, and perhaps a little affection too.

'Mr Raffles was good enough to call,' Mrs Hudson explained, 'to answer some questions I had about missing treasures. It struck me, you see, that if the Empingham Canary really had been stolen by the man Savage, then he would almost certainly have attempted to dispose of it.'

'But if he did,' Mr Raffles told me, 'it wasn't in this country. It all happened a long time ago, of course, back in the days when I was still practising cover drives in a sailor suit. But the many unsavoury acquaintances I've made over the years have, between them, a long collective memory, and as far as I can tell there have never been any rumours about the Empingham bird being passed around in illicit circles.'

The gentleman held my chair for me, and when I was seated comfortably next to Mrs Hudson, he returned to his own seat and carried on.

'In contrast, those other things we've been hearing so much about recently – the Buckminster Necklace and the Rutherford Tiara – which have both also been missing for years, were familiar topics of conversation in criminal circles. I'm not saying that any acquaintance of mine knew where they were, or even who the original thieves had been, but it was generally known that both were out there, somewhere, waiting to be sold on to a suitable bidder. But the Empingham Canary – nothing.'

'Which would suggest, Flotsam,' Mrs Hudson added, 'that the canary was not stolen for mere financial gain. And that, in turn, supports Mr Alma Tadema's theory that Savage was not the guilty party.'

'So, if not him, ma'am,' I added, my brow crinkled in thought, 'I suppose it really *was* one of the guests. Perhaps because they couldn't bear to see it melted down by Lord Empingham's horrible cousin.'

'A-ha!' Mr Raffles sounded pleased. 'A compassionate criminal. A benevolent burglar. I like the sound of that.'

'And if Mr Holmes is right, ma'am, and the canary really *is* about to be returned, that would all make sense, wouldn't it?'

'Go on, Flotsam.' Mrs Hudson wasn't exactly smiling but her lips were pursed in an encouraging sort of way.

'Because that would mean they weren't really *stealing* it at all, were they, ma'am? They were simply rescuing it from Mr Snaresdon. And now that Mr Snaresdon's dead, it's safe to return it to Frawling Hall. Except...' And here my face fell. 'Except that it still doesn't belong to Lord Empingham, does it? Not unless his cousin left it to him, which seems very unlikely indeed given all the animosity between them.'

Mr Raffles was also looking a little confused.

'Apologies if I'm missing something, but could one of you explain why old Sherlock is so sure that the Empingham Canary is about to be returned?'

It was a good question, and I think my confusion must have been obvious.

'It's something to do with Christmas trees,' I told him. 'Something to do with someone damaging some trees at Frawling Hall.'

I looked up at Mrs Hudson, hoping she would help me out, but it appeared that Mr Holmes' logic was not entirely clear to her either.

'It's something to do with the height of the trees,' she said. 'Two trees of similar height were damaged, but the third, which was larger, was untouched. And I seem to remember Mr Holmes said something about ladders...'

'And a gallery,' I added excitedly. 'An entrance hall with a gallery. So perhaps the smaller trees wouldn't reach the gallery, ma'am, but the larger one would? And if someone wanted to reach the top of the tree but didn't have easy access to ladders, well, they *had* to make sure the chosen tree was big enough to reach the gallery.'

Mrs Hudson was nodding, so I hurried on.

'And of course Mr Holmes saw all that, and realised that someone was plotting to be able to reach the top of the tree, but just assumed it was because they wanted to take something *from* the top, not to put something *on* to it. After all, why would someone go to all that trouble to return something? Why not just hand it over to Lord Empingham in a neat little parcel?'

'Admission of guilt, of course.' Mr Raffles spoke with a good deal of certainty. 'Giving back stolen goods is a tricky business if you don't want the world to know you've stolen them.'

I had always thought him an extremely debonair gentleman, but for once I think he looked slightly embarrassed.

'There was an occasion once, involving a certain ageing duchess's diamond ring... Well, the whole thing was a dreadful misunderstanding, and the old dear was a kind old soul who never did an unkind thing in her life, and without going into all the details, I ended up having to slip the thing back onto her finger while she was asleep.'

'Exactly!' I could feel my excitement growing. 'So perhaps the person who took the golden canary found themselves faced with just that problem! The people staying at Frawling Hall that Christmas are hugely respectable people, and if they admit to stealing something very valuable from a fellow guest while under the same roof – whatever the motive – well, it would be terribly bad for their reputations.'

'There'd be a terrible stink,' Mr Raffles agreed. 'No one knows that better than me. It is a prospect I have often had to contemplate.'

Mrs Hudson eyed him sternly.

'Of course, they could simply have returned it anonymously through the post,' she pointed out.

'Well, yes,' I conceded, a little put out. 'Although they may have been worried about postmarks and things, not to mention entrusting something so hugely precious to the mail.'

'Pah!' Mr Raffles gave a little, derisive snort. 'Anonymously through the post, Mrs H? Where's the joy in that? Where's the showmanship? Where's the *coup de théâtre*?' He waved his hand airily. 'This fellow has magicked the thing away from under the nose of its keepers, from behind a locked door, from a tower with walls three feet thick, and you expect him to return it by simply popping it in the post? Why, it would be a betrayal of his art! But to engineer things so that the Empingham Canary reappears without warning on top of the Empingham Christmas tree, as if by wizardry, after twenty-three years away... Well, I tell you, whoever the thief is, I admire his panache!'

He leaned back in his chair, evidently rather pleased by the scenario he had described.

'And now, Mrs H,' he concluded, 'if I can't help you with anything else, how about a small glass of that aged amontillado which I know you keep hidden away for special callers?'

Such a glass was provided without demure, and while Mr Raffles was still swirling it beneath his nose in anticipation, Mrs Hudson directed my attention to a cream envelope propped up on the dresser.

'It came while you were away, Flottie. From Miss Peters, I imagine, judging by the violet ink.'

It was indeed from Miss Peters, and its tone was exultant. Yet strangely it left me feeling peculiar – a little sad, and a little disappointed, and a little as though somewhere very distant – so distant that I'd hardly even noticed it – a star had been put out.

'Bad news, Flottie?' Mrs Hudson asked gently.

'No, not at all,' I replied, trying to sound as bright as I could. 'At least not really. She's only telling me that Clara Fazakerley has realised she isn't in love with Dumpty Boynton after all. Something to do with watching him play with a puppy, and not entirely liking the way he was doing it, then suddenly realising that she had never really loved him in the first place. She thought she'd fallen in love with him all at once, the first time they danced together. But now she thinks it was just the music, and too much claret cup, and him paying her so many compliments, so that she imagined the whole thing. Miss Peters is ever so pleased.'

'But you are not?'

Mrs Hudson's voice remained very gentle.

'Oh, no, ma'am. I mean, yes, ma'am. I mean, it doesn't really matter to me either way. It's just…'

And I paused, unsure how to explain myself. Unsure, even, of what I was trying to explain.

'You see, ma'am, Clara Fazakerley sounds like a terribly foolish young woman, and according to Miss Peters she was spouting all sorts of nonsense about how hugely in love she was, so I'm not really surprised she's changed her mind. It's just… It's just…Well, I suppose a part of me would like to think that perhaps sometimes it does happen in that way – that two people meet, and talk, and within a few minutes, they both feel something that never goes away. They both just *know*, and don't ever have to think about it. I know I'm just being silly, and mawkish, and terribly sentimental, but, well, it would make things so much *easier*…'

Mrs Hudson made no reply, but reached out and laid her hand over mine, while Mr Raffles drained his sherry.

'For the next three nights, I shall be dining in the Long Room at Lord's,' he remarked. 'A series of testimonial dinners. And I can tell you with absolute certainty, that there won't be a sherry served there that's half as good as this one. Now, Flotsam,' he went on, 'I don't know if it's any consolation, but assuming that this Dumpty Boynton is in fact the Humphrey Boynton who I've been introduced to on a couple of occasions, I'd say your friend is very well out of it. He's a show-off and a braggard, and a rather poor card player to boot. He mixes with some dubious characters, and I've heard that he's taken the lease of Old Mackenzie's workshop by the docks, so I wouldn't be surprised if he's up to some scheme that will get him into trouble.'

And I couldn't help but agree that Clara Fazakerley was indeed well out of it.

Dumpty Boynton didn't sound like a very nice man. It was good that she'd realised. So there was nothing to feel sad about at all.

—

That afternoon, we beat the carpet from Mr Holmes' study.

It was no minor undertaking, for a good deal of heavy furniture had to be moved, and it was a very heavy carpet. But Mrs Hudson was quite capable of hefting considerable weights even without my help, and between us we had it hanging in the area outside the kitchen before the clocks had struck two. Down there, below street level, the low winter sun couldn't reach us, but it was warm work and I felt better for it.

By three o'clock we had the carpet back upstairs, and by four o'clock, when it was dark outside, the study looked ship-shape, with the furniture back in place and a fire ablaze in the hearth.

'For it's another very cold night, Flottie,' Mrs Hudson explained, 'and it would be just like Mr Holmes to return home without any warning.'

While we worked, we talked, and I told her all about my meeting with Mr Alma Tadema, and about my rather less comfortable encounter with Mr Denham and Miss Lavinia Burrows.

'I don't think they're very happy with Mr Holmes, ma'am – and they certainly weren't happy with me. I didn't explain about the boater very well, you see. And they don't like Mr Holmes telling them that Mr Cortado is in no danger, because that note is really very sinister, and does make it seem that Mr Cortado left his house that day knowing that he was going to meet a terrible fate.'

'That is certainly what the note suggests, Flotsam,' Mrs Hudson agreed, giving the carpet another hefty whack.

'In a way, though, I think they are willing to believe that Mr Cortado really *did* catch a train that day, because after receiving such a note it would make sense for him to suddenly disappear. But they wouldn't even listen to anything about Frawling Hall, ma'am, or the Empingham Canary. They believe, if their friend is still alive, he must simply be fleeing for his life.'

'Well, Flottie, it's not impossible that they're right. Maximillian Cortado *might* have committed some terrible indiscretion, and *might* have been forced to become a fugitive from an evil and ruthless gang. That is certainly the option that his friends would prefer to believe.'

'But Mrs Hudson, ma'am, why would they prefer to believe that? It would mean Mr Cortado is in terrible danger!'

'Indeed, Flotsam. However, it would seem there are really only two alternatives. His friends must either believe that he left home that day hoping to get away from a terrible but nameless threat, or that he left home hoping to get away from them. And if you are Miss Lavinia Burrows, I imagine you would probably prefer to believe the former than the latter.'

'But the note, ma'am... The threatening note. It arrived in the post on the very day he disappeared.'

Mrs Hudson put down her carpet-beater and brushed her hands against her apron.

'Yes, that note... I rather think, Flottie, that the great violinist is guilty of an unforgivable failure of courage. You know, it seems to me that we still know very little about him. Only what you have been told by his butler.'

'By Shapps, ma'am? But surely his butler would know him as well as anyone?'

At this Mrs Hudson narrowed her eyes and looked at me with startling severity.

'If you believe that, Flotsam, then your education has been woefully lacking. His butler will know him well, yes. But I won't feel I have a full picture of the man until I have spoken to the woman whose job it is to have his rooms tidied and his shirts cleaned and his meals cooked just so. In other words, until I have talked to his housekeeper. Now, while we get this carpet back in place, I want you to tell me again everything Mr Alma Tadema told you about that night at Frawling Hall...'

And so we talked as we worked, or rather I talked and Mrs Hudson listened, for she rarely interrupted, not even to ask a question. Even when I'd finished, she continued to work in silence but I could tell by the very small furrow between her eyebrows that she was still considering the things I'd told her. It wasn't until the gentlemen's study was spick and span that she returned to the subject.

'Time for a wash, Flotsam. And then, if I put the kettle on, perhaps you could run over to Mrs Macfarlane's to see if she could spare one or two of her orange peel pies? Mrs Macfarlane is a very respectable plain baker, of course, but no one can deny that the woman is a genius when it comes to pastry. And, Flottie, as you go, have a think about Mr Alma Tadema's Harlequin suit. Because, unless I'm missing something, it seems to me a very revealing detail indeed.'

'You think it tells us something about who stole the canary, ma'am?'

'I'm no lawyer, Flotsam, and Mr Rumbelow would no doubt have an answer for us. But it rather makes me wonder whether the canary was ever actually really stolen at all.'

–

I had imagined that Mr Holmes and Dr Watson might stay down at Frawling Hall for some days, but Mrs Hudson's decision to light a fire in their study proved prescient, for the two gentlemen arrived home a little after eight o'clock that evening.

'It was only a flying visit, Flotsam,' Mr Holmes explained briskly as I took his coat, 'but we've done all that needed to be done, haven't we, Watson? And it's just as well that we returned so promptly, for as we turned into Baker Street a few moments ago, we ran into a special messenger from the Foreign Office. You remember us telling you about the German spy-ring in the Highlands, the one that is so secret even the Home Secretary has not been informed? Well, it appears the whole thing is about to kick off in earnest, and Dr Watson and I must make sure we are on tonight's Caledonian sleeper. It may prove a lengthy affair, but if all goes well, we will be back before the New Year.'

'What was that, Holmes?' Dr Watson was busy brushing grime from his bowler. 'Do you mean to say we'll miss Christmas?'

'Certainly not, my friend,' the detective told him cheerfully. 'Christmas generally proves impossible to miss. But instead of celebrating it with rather too many slices of Mrs Hudson's excellent roast goose, we shall mark the day in that remote bothy on the Knoydart peninsula, the one that overlooks Loch Nevis and smells of kippers. Assuming, of course, that my theories prove correct. If they do not, Christmas Day may find us at the bottom of the loch, instead of above it.'

'But, sir,' I replied timidly from behind the pile of overcoats that I now held in my arms, 'what about Mr Cortado? And the hens? And the Empingham Canary?'

'All sorted, Flotsam. Everything of significance, at any rate, and I don't see the need for us to take further action. We have seen Lord Empingham and have assured him that the bird is about to be returned. It was a touching scene, wasn't it, Watson?'

'It certainly was, Holmes. We were shown into his lordship's sickroom, Flotsam, and it was obvious from the first that the old fellow is in a bad way. But our good news seemed to boost his spirits considerably. I swear there was colour in his cheeks when we left that hadn't been visible on our arrival.'

Mr Holmes nodded his agreement.

'I was bold enough to predict the night of December 26th, or the morning of the 27th, as the date for his canary's reappearance, Flotsam, but of course it's impossible to be certain because we weren't able to interview the person who currently has possession of the canary. That omission, however, doesn't worry me in the slightest, as their desire to return the bird to Frawling Hall is clearly every bit as strong as his lordship's desire to have it returned. Also, Lord Empingham stated more than once that, were the bird to be restored to Frawling, he would have no desire to know the identity of the thief, so I really think nothing further needs to be done. We can simply let events take their course.'

'But what about the hens, sir? And Mr Cortado? There's been this note, you see...'

But Mr Holmes dismissed both these problems with a wave of his gloves.

'Whatever Mr Cortado's role in the disappearance of the Empingham Canary, Flotsam – if, indeed, he had any such role – he has clearly left London of his own volition. Watson and I tracked him as far as Amberley, and we know that he took a room for the night in The Black Horse Inn. He gave his name as Mr Freeman and was, by all accounts, in excellent spirits. He paid his bill and left the following morning. Where he went after that, we cannot be sure, but it wasn't to Frawling Hall, as no one there has seen any sign of him. But wherever he is, and whatever any note may say to the contrary, he is clearly in no danger and, what is more, he clearly doesn't wish to be found. As far as I'm concerned, what he does next is entirely his own business.

'As for the hens, Flotsam, I think we can all agree that those deliveries contained a message for Maximillian Cortado which was not apparent to the other recipients, and it seems obvious that the message referred in some way to that fateful Christmas gathering of Lord Empingham's. The harlequin pattern on the card would support that conclusion, as would Mr Cortado's haste to return, via Amberley station, to the environs of Frawling Hall. But the precise meaning of the message, and the motivation for Mr Cortado's strange behaviour, surely need not concern us. They are, quite probably, a private matter, and I see no reason to believe that they jeopardise the safe return of the Empingham Canary.'

'But, sir...'

My objection tailed off because, quite simply, I could find no real reason to object. Everything Mr Holmes had said was perfectly reasonable, even if it was also rather unsatisfying. It seemed that Lord Empingham was happy; that the Empingham Canary was going to be returned; and that Mr Cortado was at liberty to plough his own furrow. Even Marlo the Magnificent had got his hat back. Miss Lavinia Burrows wasn't happy, of course, but the gentle Mr Denham, who had clearly admired her for a great many years, was now free to press his suit, so perhaps both would find happiness in the end.

It was only after the two gentlemen had left for Euston Station, in great haste, with their bags rather badly packed, that I thought of Mr Alma Tadema. The outcome which seemed so satisfactory to Mr Holmes would be of no comfort at all to the artist; even the return of the canary to Lord Empingham would not prevent the shadow of suspicion hanging over him, in his own mind at least, for the rest of his days.

But only one thing could help with that – an explanation of how his lordship's canary had flown from its tower that winter's evening, through locked windows or solid walls, and had vanished into the night, never to be seen again.

And none of us seemed any closer to explaining it than those house guests had been, twenty-three years ago. Not me, not Mrs Hudson, not Sherlock Holmes.

Not even with the chickens to help us.

Chapter 11

It was not unusual for Mr Holmes and Dr Watson to be absent from Baker Street, often for some days, often at short notice. But a great many of those absences were so spontaneous and ill-defined that Mrs Hudson and I lived in constant expectation of the gentlemen's unannounced return. So to awake certain in the knowledge that the two gentlemen would be gone for a fortnight or more was unusual and perhaps even rather deflating. I couldn't help but feel that the place would be a little too quiet without them.

However, if their abrupt departure for the Highlands seemed to me to bring an end to our involvement in the Canary Affair, Mrs Hudson evidently saw things very differently. That morning, perhaps sensing that my spirits were a little low, she announced an expedition to Trevelyan's to do some additional shopping for Christmas provisions, followed by a little window-shopping in the dress-makers' establishments south of Oxford Street – something to which she knew I was very partial.

'And after that, Flottie, I thought perhaps we would wander down to Bromley Place. Mr Cortado is perfectly free to disappear if he wishes, but I gave my word to Miss Laura Epps – or rather to Mrs Lawrence Alma Tadema, as I must learn to call her – that we would explain the business of those hens to her husband's satisfaction. And since Mr Cortado and the hens would appear to be quite particularly linked, I feel it only right that we should investigate a little further.'

I had no argument at all to make with that reasoning, and had scuttled off to fetch my hat and coat almost before she'd finished talking.

It was a glorious day – clear winter skies of duck-egg blue, but a blue somehow so vast and intense it would have astounded the duck that laid it; low sunshine so bright that cabbies drove with their caps pulled down to their noses; sunlight flashing off omnibus windows and ruffling the waters of the Serpentine; so cold that even at noon you could see your breath in front of you.

At Trevelyan's, we bought marzipan fruits and plums in brandy, and a tiny box of very perfect chocolate mice that Mrs Hudson insisted was just for me. By the tea counter, we caught sight of Scraggs, talking very enthusiastically to a group of three finely dressed ladies who appeared to be hanging on his every word. I caught his eye as we passed and was rewarded with a grin and something that might even have been a very discreet wink, one that sent me on my way strangely light-footed.

Then despite the cold, we spent more than half an hour gazing at hats and dresses in shop windows, admiring the brilliant silks in shades of aquamarine and vermillion and verdigris, and chuckling together at the more absurd fashions we encountered. By the time we arrived in Bromley Place, although the sky was no longer cloudless, I felt the winter could do its worst.

This time we did not call at the front door of Mr Cortado's house. Mrs Hudson guided me firmly to the servants' door at the bottom of the area steps, a door which was opened for us, after a polite knock, by a woman of

Mrs Hudson's age and Mrs Hudson's shape, and dressed in clothes that might easily have been Mrs Hudson's, so that I was reminded of two very similar battleships meeting on manoeuvres.

This was Mrs Henderson, Mr Cortado's housekeeper, and thankfully her voice was nothing at all like Mrs Hudson's, being rather high-pitched and a bit breathless, so that as soon as she spoke the resemblance seemed to vanish away.

'Mrs Hudson? My goodness! Weren't you once at Trendlesham Manor? My sister's girl was a parlour maid there for a year or two, and she always spoke most highly of you...'

While this and other mutual compliments were being exchanged, Mrs Henderson ushered us indoors, through a kitchen that was notably darker and colder than our own, to a little sitting room that was evidently for her own exclusive use.

'Forgive the general air of desolation,' she remarked sadly, as she encouraged us to sit. 'Ours has been rather a small establishment ever since the master's wife passed away, especially as he does so little in the way of entertaining and increasingly takes meals at his club. And of course, now that he has left us...'

She broke off.

'Oh, it's a terrible thing, Mrs Hudson! He's been good enough to leave us well provided for, with wages paid and the like, even though there's precious little for us to do here now. But it feels mighty strange living in this empty house, not knowing what's become of him. The two housemaids have already given notice and gone to new positions, saying that this place had begun to give them the creeps. And I daresay I'd do likewise, if only I could be sure the master was safe and well.'

'If it's any consolation, Mrs Henderson, Mr Holmes is convinced that no harm has befallen Mr Cortado.'

'You've no idea what a relief it is to hear you say it, Mrs Hudson. Why I've been housekeeper here since he and his wife moved in, nearly fifteen years ago, and there's been plenty of times I was that close to giving my notice, but I always stayed on the master's account, him being such a kind gentleman. I suppose you might say I felt sorry for him.'

'Sorry for him, Mrs Henderson?' Mrs Hudson contrived to sound surprised without sounding over-eager to hear more. 'I would have thought him more to be envied than pitied, what with his great success as a musician, his ample means, a devoted wife...'

I watched Mrs Henderson pull a face.

'Well, you'd think so, wouldn't you, Mrs Hudson? But it was no life for him, really it wasn't. Just practice, practice, practice, and Mrs Cortado the strictest taskmaster, always keeping him up to the mark. If you ask Shapps, he'll tell you that the master was devoted to his art, but there's many a time I've wondered if that violin of his wasn't more of an enemy than a friend. And I can't count the number of times I've seen him out there in the square at night looking up at the stars. "The master's longing for what's lost," that's what I always used to say.'

'But that, presumably, was after the death of his wife, Mrs Henderson? That must surely be the loss you're referring to.'

Our hostess shifted a little uncomfortably in her seat.

'I'm afraid to say, Mrs Hudson, that I was making that particular remark long before Mrs Cortado's passing.

The master never displayed even the slightest trace of discontent, of course. Never a cross word, never a raised voice. A perfect gentleman at all times, always respectful and courteous to his wife, terribly kind to his servants. Endlessly patient. But those walks of his, especially after dark in the winter... He never went very far, only to the far side of the square, where I suppose he thought he was unobserved. And then, if it was a clear night, he would stand and look up at the sky. I've often wondered what went through his head when he was doing it. And always it seemed to me he was thinking about something he'd lost. His youth, I used to think, for there must have been a time when he did more than just play the violin.'

All three of us sat in silence for a moment, pondering those words, then Mrs Hudson spoke very softly.

'Mr Holmes thinks it very unlikely that Mr Cortado will ever come back,' she said.

Mrs Henderson nodded.

'And perhaps that's for the best. He's free of it all now. That wretched violin has gone to Miss Burrows, and he's out of reach of her scolding. If Mr Holmes is really sure he's safe...'

'The last report of Mr Cortado was that he was enjoying the hospitality of a country inn under an assumed name, and was in very good spirits.'

Mrs Henderson reached out and rested her fingers on Mrs Hudson's hand.

'It's a great weight off my mind, Mrs Hudson. It really is.' Then she cleared her throat a little awkwardly and withdrew her hand. 'My sister tells me there's a family near her in Sevenoaks looking for a housekeeper. I've been thinking of dropping them a line.'

And with that, the conversation turned to references and letters of recommendation, and Mrs Henderson's reluctance to take a position in any household which simultaneously contained cats *and* dogs *and* children.

'It would seem, Flotsam,' Mrs Hudson mused, after we had said our farewells and were crossing Bromley Place, 'that Mr Cortado might not ever really have been the person his friend Mr Denham imagined.'

'No, ma'am,' I agreed. 'Just think of it. All that time working so hard at the violin. A lifetime, really. And never really loving it. I wonder what he *was* thinking about on those winter nights, when he was looking up at the stars.'

I hadn't really meant it as a question, so I was more than a little surprised when Mrs Hudson offered me an answer.

'It is, of course, impossible to say, Flotsam. But it seems to me quite possible that he was thinking of a certain night at Frawling Hall.'

And then, infuriatingly, she refused to say another word on the subject, on the flimsy grounds that she might very well be mistaken.

Sometimes, for all her many virtues and kindnesses, she really could be quite as annoying as Sherlock Holmes.

—

When I'd woken up that morning, I'd been worried that our rooms in Baker Street might feel too quiet without the presence of Dr Watson and Mr Holmes to enliven them. By the time Mrs Hudson and I had returned home from our expedition, and had spent a quiet afternoon tidying up and dusting, the air of calm that prevailed began to seem most restful. An uneventful evening beckoned; Mrs

Hudson had letters to write, and I had a pile of books to explore. Our kitchen was well stocked with good things to eat, the coals were glowing, and it was surely far too cold outside for any idle callers to disturb us.

And so we remained undisturbed – content and at peace, all thoughts of hens and canaries far from our minds – until around ten o'clock, when an urgent telegram from Scotland, addressed to Mrs Hudson, was delivered to our door by a small, very out-of-breath young boy.

In person, Mr Holmes was often extremely succinct, much preferring action to words, but when composing telegrams he was never afraid to use as many words as were needed to convey his message clearly, regardless of the extra cost. This time, however, I was struck at once that the great detective had erred rather too far on the side of economy.

HAVE RECEIVED WORD LORD EMPINGHAM SINKING FAST STOP DOCTORS FEAR MAY NOT SURVIVE TILL CHRISTMAS STOP PLEASE TRAVEL FRAWLING AT EARLIEST OPPORTUNITY STOP URGE OWNER OF CANARY TO DELIVER TO LORDSHIP WITHOUT DELAY STOP HAVE WIRED FRAWLING TO EXPECT YOU STOP WATSON AND I UNCONTACTABLE IN WILDERNESS FROM TONIGHT STOP RELYING ON YOU STOP

HOLMES

'The owner of the canary, ma'am?' I asked, reading and re-reading the note with a sort of horrified fascination. 'The owner? But Mr Holmes doesn't tell us who the owner *is*!'

'Indeed, Flotsam,' Mrs Hudson agreed drily, 'I had noticed the omission myself. Mr Holmes clearly assumes that we have followed his lines of reasoning ourselves, and have followed them every bit as far as he has. It is a great compliment to us both, Flottie.'

But I didn't feel flattered, just appalled.

'Compliment or not, ma'am, it doesn't help us! Lord Empingham is on his death bed and we have no idea where the canary is or who has it. What can we possibly do?'

'Well, my girl, there is one very obvious thing to do, and that is to pack our bags now, ready for an early start. We can wire from Victoria to reserve rooms in Frawling, but the important thing is to make sure we're on the first train.'

'But, Mrs Hudson, ma'am, what on earth will we do when we get there?'

'Oh, that's very simple, Flotsam. I think it's time we sorted out this business of the Empingham Canary once and for all.'

–

And so, the following morning, while the countryside was still shrouded in darkness, we caught the train to Amberley. It was, of course, the Bognor train, but there was no sign of Marlo the Magnificent or anyone else in straw boaters. In fact, at that hour, there were very few passengers at all. It was bitterly cold, and a layer of thick cloud meant that, above the street lights, there was no moon and no stars.

You would think such a journey – a hasty dash to the bedside of a dying peer on the orders of the nation's greatest detective, with a mystery to solve and a treasure to find – would have filled me with uncontainable excitement. I should, by rights, have been alert to every detail of my surroundings. But it had been an early start, and with so much to occupy my thoughts I hadn't slept very well, and there was nothing to see through the carriage windows other than our own reflections in the darkness. I confess that I dozed off almost as soon as the train pulled out of Victoria.

When I awoke, my head resting comfortably on Mrs Hudson's shoulder, the darkness outside had begun to dissipate and I watched the hard-frosted fields slip past, and the smoke rising from the chimneys of unknown villages.

'Amberley next stop,' Mrs Hudson informed me, and it seemed to come all too soon, for the train was warm and comfortable, and the weather outside was neither. The cold air that rushed in to greet us as we disembarked seemed to have an extra edge to it, and for the first time that winter I could feel snow in the air. Not actually falling – only that sense, born of low light and dark cloud and low mercury, that from some distant point it was approaching.

A man with a dog-cart was found at the station to take us on to the village of Frawling, and the journey was not a very long one, but my nose was red and my fingers white inside my gloves by the time the tall chimneys of Frawling Hall were glimpsed above the trees.

There were two inns in Frawling, one at each end of the village, and Mrs Hudson had reserved rooms at The George, having ascertained from Mr Holmes' copy of the *Sussex Gazetteer* that it was the one closer to the big house. It turned out, on inspection, that despite its regal name

The George was the humbler of the two establishments, but was nevertheless the favoured retreat of villagers and farm workers in need of a pint of ale to wash away the rigours of the day. The Plough Hotel, in contrast, was a fine coaching inn of the sort frequented by local farmers on market day or by ladies down from London looking for somewhere to take tea.

'No matter, Flotsam,' Mrs Hudson reassured me. 'The George is clean and comfortable enough, and will suit us very well. And by way of reward, when the Empingham Canary is back in Lord Empingham's hands, I will treat you to tea at The Plough. Now, five minutes to unpack and then we should be setting out for the hall. If Mr Holmes' telegram is to be believed, they will be expecting us.'

They were. Our approach on foot up the short drive – the one that led from the village to the rear of the hall – was observed from the house, and by the time we had reached the edge of the gravel sweep, a very tall, thin woman was advancing to greet us. This individual, it turned out, was the housekeeper of Frawling Hall, a Mrs Dempsey by name. She seemed relieved to see us.

'You must be Mrs Hudson! I thought it as soon as we saw you on the drive! I said to Bessy, 'Bessy, there she is!' and I was right! We're so pleased to see you. And you must be Flotsam? I said to Bessy you must be. Mr Holmes' telegram mentioned you by name. We were so excited when it arrived! Hawkins – he's the butler here – took it straight up to his lordship the moment it arrived, then brought the news straight down to the rest of us. When we heard that Mr Holmes was sending someone to us who would know exactly where to find his lordship's canary – well, it seemed like a miracle!'

I cast an anxious glance at Mrs Hudson, but she seemed unperturbed by the expectations being placed upon her shoulders.

'We're pleased to be of assistance, aren't we, Flottie? Although of course Mr Holmes doesn't yet know *precisely* where the canary is. If he did, he would simply have informed his lordship of the location by telegram. But he has a shrewd idea of who we need to speak to, and if you will allow us to ask one or two questions, then we should have the whole matter cleared up in no time.'

'Of course!' Mrs Dempsey closed her eyes in something very close to bliss. 'I told Betty it would be like this. I said, "Betty, they can't know for sure or they'd have told us by now. But they'll have their ways, they will, they'll have their ways, and everything's going to be as right as rain." Because, of course, we've all read so many things about Mr Holmes! Hawkins reads *The Strand* magazine, you see, and is very good about passing it around. And we all want to know, is it true that Dr Watson doesn't actually write those accounts anymore? Adamson, our new footman, claims that some writer fellow does it for him because the doctor's too busy.'

Mrs Hudson met this enquiry with sphinx-like impenetrability.

'I couldn't possibly say. Now, it is interesting that you mention a new footman. I'd been given the impression that here at Frawling Hall there are relatively few comings and goings in the servants' hall.'

'That's right, Mrs Hudson.'

Mrs Dempsey had been leading us towards the house, and now we paused at the large back door. Above it, the old walls of Frawling Hall rose into a frenzy of turrets and battlements. I could see at once that it was not the sort of building that a purist would treasure. It seemed to me less a single house, more a gluing-together of different structures, all of them built at different times and conceived in different styles – and this was before I had even seen the old tower, the one I'd heard so much about, which stood at the front of the building and rather forward of most of it, and which didn't match in either materials or design any other, later addition. Perhaps to disguise this, more recent owners had peppered the top of the house with artificial battlements, creating the effect of an ancient and lopsided face topped by a slightly uneven crown.

While my eyes ranged over the walls above me, taking in the eccentricity of it all, Mrs Dempsey continued to answer Mrs Hudson's question about servants.

'It's very true that the staff here are loyal to his lordship. I've never known a single person leave for better work or better pay elsewhere. Born in Frawling, stay in Frawling, that's the motto here. But, of course, people *do* leave. The housemaids insist on getting married, and so sometimes do the footmen, and every fifteen years or so we need a new cook. But mostly the gaps are filled by people from the village. I said as much to Bessy just the other day. "Jobs here tend to stay in the family," I told her, "and you and me are the living proof." My aunt was housekeeper before me, you see, and her mother before her, and Bessy's mother and all three of her aunts were housemaids here at one time or another.'

'A contented servants' hall is generally the sign of a well-run establishment,' Mrs Hudson opined judiciously. 'But, as you say, it's inevitable that sometimes you must hire staff who are not known to you personally. I wonder, for instance, how many new staff of that sort you have taken on in the last year?'

'Well, let me see...'

While Mrs Dempsey considered the question, I found myself recalling Mr Holmes' words on first reading that article about damaged Christmas trees. '*I would urge him to look for a member of his own domestic staff less than three hundred and fifty-two days into their employment...*' At the time it had seemed a bizarre announcement, but now I could see that he simply meant someone who hadn't been at Frawling Hall for any previous Christmases.

'Well, there's Adamson, who I've mentioned. He's only been with us a couple of months but came highly recommended by a French count, no less! He's less experienced than Turner and Tipton, but a very quick learner. And there's Martha, the scullery maid, who came to us from Hanthrop Manor because the cook there had taken to drink. The gardeners have all been here for years, but there was a new assistant groundsman back in February, a young man called Roscoe who's an impudent fellow, and from Somerset. And then there's Goodman, who's a sort of under-butler really. The truth is that Hawkins is getting a little too old for the job but refuses to retire, so his lordship insisted that we took on someone to help with his duties.'

'So Mr Hawkins has been the butler here for some time?' Mrs Hudson asked. Once again it seemed no more than an innocent question born of a general interest in Frawling's domestic arrangements.

'For nearly fifty years! He was Lord Empingham's butler before my great aunt was housekeeper, and he's still here now. Rather frail, I'm afraid, nowadays, and not really to be trusted with a tray, but still very sharp. He's the only one of us, apart from his lordship, of course, who remembers the golden canary. He says it was ever so beautiful.'

'How fascinating!' Mrs Hudson looked at me, clearly pleased at this news. 'Flotsam and I would love to talk to him about it, wouldn't we, Flottie? And perhaps you could arrange for us to have a word with those newer members of staff, too?'

Mrs Dempsey looked a little surprised.

'Well, if you really want to, Mrs Hudson. I'd have to ask the Head Gardener about Roscoe, but Martha and Goodman are both around somewhere. You may have to wait a day or two to speak to Adamson, because he's been sent up to Glenlarrig with some family items. Glenlarrig is where his lordship's cousin, Mr Welsby, lives, some-where north of Inverness. When his lordship passes away, Frawling Hall passes to Mr Welsby, because of the entail, but none of us here like to think about it. He's a kind old gentleman apparently, but of course, as I was saying to Bessy only last week, nothing at all like his lordship.'

'A cousin, you say, Mrs Dempsey? I believe Lord Empingham had another cousin, did he not? A Mr Snaresdon?'

'That's right, Mrs Hudson. A terrible man by all accounts, although I never met him, what with him living overseas for so long. He died in the autumn, or so we're told, though the news only reached us quite recently. But, of course, he was never due to inherit Frawling because, although he was always *called* a cousin, he was... well, he was born on the wrong side of the blanket, as it were.'

Mrs Dempsey suddenly seemed to notice that we were still standing in the cold outside the servants' door.

'Goodness!' she exclaimed. 'What am I thinking? Come in! Come in! Let's get you both warm. I'll get Bessy to bring some tea at once. And Hawkins said, if anyone comes from Mr Holmes, to send them to his pantry at eleven o'clock. He's generally resting at that hour, but not today. He says there's someone he wants you to meet.'

Chapter 12

Between arriving at Frawling Hall and waiting on Mr Hawkins in his pantry, there was barely time to drink the tea that Bessy brought us and to take in our remarkable surroundings.

The kitchen at Frawling was a truly cavernous affair, with vaulted ceilings and an ancient fireplace so large that it was easy to imagine a whole deer being turned on a spit. In such a space, the more recent fittings seemed strangely out of place, and although, as Mrs Hudson pointed out, it was comfortably equipped to feed a modern dinner party of twenty or thirty guests, it was easier to imagine the preparation of some vast medieval feast, with steaming cauldrons and roasting meats and probably a swan being plucked somewhere in a corner. It was something of a relief when Mrs Dempsey led us through it, and begged us to make ourselves comfortable in her own little sitting-room.

I had expected Bessy, the young woman who made tea for us, to be of the garrulous sort, given the frequency with which Mrs Dempsey referred to their conversations. In reality, she proved to be almost completely silent. When Mrs Hudson asked her how she liked working at Frawling Hall, she mumbled something that may have been 'very much, ma'am' and quickly disappeared again.

There was no time to talk to Martha, or to any of the other recently arrived staff, before Mrs Dempsey returned and led us down a long subterranean corridor to a small, comfortably furnished room with a good fire, where Hawkins the butler awaited us with his guest.

There was no doubting which of the two was Hawkins – it was apparent from the way he rose as we entered and offered us seats next to the fire, and Madeira, and slices of almond cake, all with exemplary courtesy and a certain, stately dignity. It was hard to guess how old he was, but he did seem truly ancient – eighty, if a day, I estimated – and his joints almost seemed to creak as he moved; his eyes, however, were bright and clear. It was easy to imagine he remained every bit as sharp as Mrs Dempsey had suggested.

His companion, by contrast, was a thick-set man who I judged to be in his late sixties, with a mass of grey, curly hair, red cheeks, a neatly trimmed moustache, and no discernible neck. It came as no great surprise to me when he was introduced as Inspector Dickinson, retired, once of Scotland Yard. If there was a way retired police inspectors were supposed to look, Inspector Dickinson embodied it.

'I'm an Arundel man by birth,' he explained, 'and I happened to be down here visiting when the whole canary business blew up. That's why I was on the scene so quick. And when I was too old for police work, it was an easy enough decision to retire back here, to one of those nice little thatched houses in Amberley. When Hawkins here sent me a message saying that Mr Sherlock Holmes himself was involved, and that the bird was going to reappear, well, as you can imagine, I was over like a shot. I've had no shortage of unsolved cases in my time, but there's never been one quite like this.'

He paused, and the old butler cleared his throat politely.

'Mrs Hudson, I invited the inspector to meet you,' he explained, 'because I know that, like me, he continues to find the whole affair of his lordship's canary most unsettling, even after all these years. And while the return of the bird would be most gratifying – indeed, more than gratifying, for it would allow his lordship to die a happy man – both the inspector and I agree that the return of the bird in itself would not entirely put our minds to rest.'

'That's exactly it, Mr Hawkins,' the inspector concurred. 'You see, ma'am, I've had years to think about it, and it still unsettles me. It's like a little shadow that never quite goes away. It isn't right, you see. It just isn't right.'

'What exactly isn't right, Inspector?' Mrs Hudson asked softly.

The inspector puffed out his cheeks and shook his head, and there was something in the way he did it that gave me a sense of long- and deeply-held frustration.

'All this time I've been going over it and over it, ma'am. It nags at me every time I pass the turning to Frawling, every time I hear his lordship's name. My wife says it's spoiling my retirement, and I think, in a way, she's right. Perhaps I'll never be able to retire properly until I understand it. You see, no one *could* have stolen the bird, and yet it's gone. So that's what isn't right, ma'am. It isn't right that an object made of solid gold simply vanished into thin air.'

Between them, the two gentlemen told their story.

The butler went first, Mr Hawkins giving us his own account of that fateful Christmas – the decorating of the hall, the preparations for the ball, the arrival of the guests; the heavy snow on Boxing Day and the jarring intrusion of Lord Empingham's cousin; removing the canary from the Christmas tree and presenting it to Mr Snaresdon at dinner; having a bed made up in the Tower Room for the man referred to as Savage; serving drinks in the library until the guests retired.

It was this latter part of the evening that most interested Mrs Hudson.

'You say the guests gathered in the library for drinks, Mr Hawkins. Was that before or after Mr Savage had been locked into the Tower Room?'

'Afterwards, ma'am. I accompanied Mr Snaresdon and Lord Empingham to the Tower Room immediately after they rose from the dinner table. And the man Savage too, of course. He came with us, with the canary in its box. The bed had already been turned down by then. I had sent a maid up to prepare the room in advance, and she had lighted the oil lamp and closed the shutters. Mr Snaresdon, however, was unhappy with this arrangement and instructed me to open the shutters on the east window. This was so that observers in the main body of the house would be afforded a view into the room for as long as the lamp was burning. I believe Mr Snaresdon felt this extra measure would make it harder for any thief to operate undetected. Were anyone to enter the room while its occupant slept, he must either do so in darkness or must show a light, and Mr Snaresdon was correct that a moving lantern in the Tower Room would be very obvious to anyone looking across from the main house.'

'So I take it there was no moon that night?' Mrs Hudson asked. 'The thief would definitely have required a lantern?'

The butler took his time to answer, narrowing his eyes in his effort to recall.

'It had been snowing all day, and there was no moon when I took the gentlemen up to the Tower Room. But later... Well, I couldn't say for sure. As I recall the skies had cleared by the time I retired for the night. Yes, I'm sure they did. There was very little moon though. It was not a bright night. But there may have been enough light to move around by an open window.'

Mrs Hudson pondered this for a moment.

'You say Mr Snaresdon called for the shutters to be opened on the east window. Do I take it that there were other windows?'

'There is a west window, ma'am, but it is very high up the wall. Too high to be reached without a ladder, and for that reason the shutter on that window tends to remain closed all year round. The Tower Room is cold and barely furnished, and is rarely used. In fact, it has not been used since that day. His lordship will not allow it.'

'Excuse me, sir...' I wasn't sure it was my place to interrupt, but it seemed important. 'When I spoke to Mr Alma Tadema, one of the gentlemen who was staying here that night, he told me that he had checked all the windows in that room, and that they were all rusted up. But presumably he couldn't really have checked the west window, not if it was impossible to reach?'

'The Dutch gentleman?' It was Inspector Dickinson who replied. 'I remember him very well. Most helpful he was. When I arrived on the scene, he explained that he'd checked the east window and had found it sealed shut, but had been unable to reach the shutter to check the other window, even by climbing on the bedside chair. I therefore took the precaution of calling for a ladder and, not much liking heights myself, I held it for him while he checked the other window. And just to be on the safe side, in case you think the Dutch gentleman might have been pulling a fast one, I sent a constable up the ladder to check a second time after he'd gone. So you can rest assured, young lady, that both windows were rusted shut, and the only way the golden canary could have left that room would have been through the door.'

I think he could tell from my expression that I was about to ask another question, so he smiled and carried on.

'And if you're thinking that perhaps it didn't leave the room that night, that it could have been hidden somewhere all along, well, you can go and see for yourself. The floor is solid stone. The only furniture was the bed, a bedside chair with the oil lamp on it, and a simple washstand. It didn't take very much searching. Something could have been concealed in the window alcoves, behind the shutters when they were closed, but as we've explained, one set of shutters was open, and two different people climbed up and checked behind the other.'

Mrs Hudson listened to this patiently, then turned back to the old butler.

'So you showed the gentlemen up to the room, Mr Hawkins. What happened then?'

'Well, Mrs Hudson, Mr Snaresdon took a look around the room to satisfy himself that there was nothing untoward concealed there. "No trickery," was the phrase he used. He too noticed the closed shutters on the high window and demanded to see behind them. I offered to call for a ladder but he said it was no matter, and asked Savage to assist him with what I believe is called "a leg up". This enabled him to reach the shutter and open it, and to reassure himself that no one was concealed behind it. I should point out, Mrs Hudson, that the walls are very thick, so the window aperture behind that shutter would be deep enough to hold a man, assuming he had some means of getting up there. But the window is not a wide one. It would be a cramped space for anyone to remain in for any period of time.'

'Thank you, Mr Hawkins. And once Mr Snaresdon was satisfied, did you then leave the gentleman to it?'

'We left the room together, ma'am. First Mr Snaresdon asked Savage to show him the canary again, and when the case was opened, he made some unsavoury remark to his lordship about how, by sunset the next day, the ornament would be no more than a small bar of bullion. Then Mr Savage remained in the room with the canary, and Mr Snaresdon locked him in. The two gentlemen descended to the library, where Mr Snaresdon discovered that the door between the tower and the library had no lock of any sort. That was why he demanded that drinks should be served there, instead of in the drawing room, so that he could keep an eye on the door himself. To my surprise, his lordship agreed.'

'And did all the guests join him there, Mr Hawkins?'

'Very few of the ladies, ma'am. I think only Mrs Snaresdon, at her husband's insistence. But all the gentlemen were there, for a little while at least. By ten o'clock, the party had broken up, with Mr Snaresdon and the Earl of Brabham the last to leave. Neither seemed to find the other very good company. I was then able to extinguish the lamps and supervise the locking up of the house.'

The old man smiled a little ruefully.

'It must seem strange to you, Mrs Hudson, that I can recall the order of events so clearly, but I replayed them in my head a great many times in the days that followed, and have continued to do so, many times, since then.'

Inspector Dickinson was nodding in a way that suggested that he too had recalled the details so often over the years that they were imprinted upon his mind.

'So you see, ma'am, the canary was, without any doubt, locked in the Tower Room with the man Savage. And it was still there at around midnight, when Mr Snaresdon and Mr Alma Tadema went to the tower together to check. Mr Snaresdon had neglected to take his key, but they spoke to Savage through the door and he told them it was definitely still in its case.'

'But, Inspector,' I broke in, excited, 'Savage might not have been telling the truth. If he really did steal the canary in some unknown way, then he may very well have been lying. And since you were never able to interview him, I don't suppose we can ever be sure.'

This seemed to please the inspector considerably, because he was smiling as he held up a finger and wagged it.

'Ah, but that's where you're wrong, Miss. I *was* able to interview Savage.'

Mrs Hudson and I exchanged glances.

'Inspector,' she said, 'we were told that he'd fled from Frawling before the police arrived.'

'Very true, ma'am. It turns out that he was a wanted man. He and some of the other ruffians who used to associate with Mr Snaresdon had given a beating to someone who owed that gentleman money. Very nearly killed him, they did. His name really *was* Savage, by the way. Eustace Savage. And I heard nothing more of him from that day on, until about two months before I retired from the force, when I came upon him in Pentonville Prison. He was serving a sentence there for a different beating, and I'd been there interviewing another convict on quite another matter. It was pure chance that I recognised his name.'

Inspector Dickinson leaned forward in his armchair and gave his moustache a quick rub with his forefinger.

'He proved very willing to talk. He was a sick man by then, you see, with only months to live and still with another ten years to serve, so it was clear to both of us he was never getting out. Which is important, I think, because it meant he had no reason to hide anything. Even if he'd confessed, I don't suppose I'd have bothered charging him, not if he'd told me truthfully what had happened to the golden bird. But he didn't confess. Far from it. He told me his version of events, and it was clear from the way he told me that he was just as baffled by the whole affair as I was.'

The fire was still blazing in the grate, and I still had a little Madeira in my glass. I sipped it as I listened to the inspector tell the dead man's tale.

'According to Savage, he'd checked the room a second time after he'd been locked in. Not the high window, because he couldn't climb up that far without help, but under the bed and in all the other obvious places. He told me quite frankly that he thought his master was overly concerned about the safety of the bird – "a bit cracked about it," was the phrase he used – and so, after that final check, he lay down on the bed – under the covers and still in his clothes because it was bitterly cold up there – then blew out the lamp and went to sleep.

'He was awakened at around midnight, as Mr Alma Tadema has no doubt told you, Miss, by Mr Snaresdon thumping on his door and rattling the lock. He'd been sleeping heavily, so the banging gave him a nasty start, he said. But after a bit of fumbling, he got the lamp lit again, and the canary was still there, still in its box, right next to his bed. After that, given that Mr Snaresdon was in such a state, Savage decided he better hadn't go back to sleep, so he lay there with the light on reading a pocket edition of Keats' verse, for the next six hours.'

I must have demonstrated some surprise at this detail, because the inspector smiled at me.

'Yes, Miss. I was also surprised, both at his choice of reading matter and at how long he stuck at it. But apparently Savage was very fond of Keats. He insisted on quoting me a number of sonnets to demonstrate.'

Inspector Dickinson was not drinking Madeira. His glass contained something that looked very like whisky-and-soda-water, and he took another sip of this before continuing.

'Anyway, Savage claimed he carried on reading until he could be certain, from the lights in the East Wing, that the servants were up and about. Then, reasoning that no burglar would be operating once the house had wakened for the day, he checked on the canary again, blew out the light and fell asleep almost instantly. He remembers hearing the church clock strike six just a moment or two after he blew out the light.'

The inspector paused, and I could sense we were nearing the end of his tale.

'Savage told me that he didn't sleep for very long after that. A rather fitful sleep, I gather. He awoke properly at about ten minutes before seven o'clock, to discover the box containing the canary empty, and the bird gone. His first thought, apparently, was that Mr Snaresdon must have retrieved it himself, but when he tried the door, he found it still locked, and it was then that he attempted to raise the alarm. He had not been shouting for many minutes before Mr Snaresdon arrived with the Dutch gentleman to unlock the door. And that was that, Mrs Hudson. The canary was never seen again.'

He paused, and Mr Hawkins took up the tale.

'I can confirm one part of Savage's story, Mrs Hudson, because I know the lamp was indeed lit in the Tower Room for most of the night. I couldn't sleep, you see. I felt uneasy about having a man like Mr Snaresdon in the house, so I ended up sitting in my armchair, dozing fitfully, but often looking up at the window of the Tower Room.'

'And were you aware of anyone moving around the house during the course of your vigil?' Mrs Hudson asked quickly.

'No, ma'am. That's how I can be sure the domestic staff took no part in events that night, for to reach the tower from the servants' quarters they would have to pass my room and would surely have awoken me.'

'And you noticed no movement of any sort in the Tower Room?'

The old man shook his head.

'No, ma'am. But I did see the light extinguished there at almost exactly six o'clock in the morning. By then I was up and about my duties, and I was on my way to the library because I feared that room had been left in a less than tidy state. The corridor that leads there from the servants' hall affords a good view out across the lawn towards the tower, and given the circumstances, it was natural I should look up. It was still pitch-black outside, of course, so the lighted window was very obvious. When I saw the light suddenly go out, it did occur to me that Mr Savage must be ending his watch.'

'I see, Mr Hawkins. And did you observe anything unusual that morning? Anything that gave you cause for concern?'

'I found the library in a much worse state than I had expected, Mrs Hudson. Someone had taken one of the Queen Anne chairs and had forced it beneath the handle of the door which led to the tower, presumably in an effort to secure it. And a decanter had been smashed. I found shards of glass everywhere. There was even a shard of glass resting on the back of the chair. I later discovered, of course, that Mr Snaresdon had put it there deliberately.'

'And then, Mr Hawkins?'

'I removed the chair from behind the door, then went to find the housemaid. I helped her clear up the broken glass, then left her to the task of cleaning the rest of the room. She was still at work when a footman put his head around the door and asked her if she could hear someone shouting in the tower. She agreed she *had* heard something coming from the tower, but hadn't thought it her place to remark on it, so the footman went to raise the alarm, and it was Mr Snaresdon and Mr Alma Tadema who came to let Savage out. And that, of course, is when the bird's disappearance became known.'

'So it seems to me...' My thoughts were racing. 'Well, if the canary couldn't have been concealed *in* the room, then it must have been removed *from* the room. And if the only way it could be removed from the room was through the door...'

'Then the person who took it must have opened the door!' Inspector Dickinson finished my sentence with great enthusiasm. 'Those were my thoughts exactly, Miss.

214

And as the only way to open the door was with a key, then the thief must clearly have had a key. So, as you can imagine, I spent a lot of time asking questions about keys.'

This part of his story seemed to please him greatly, and he sat a little straighter in his chair.

'At first I thought there must have been a *third* key to the door, but Lord Empingham and Mr Hawkins here were adamant that only two existed and that it was quite impossible that any copy could have been made of either. And, although I didn't for a moment question the word of either gentleman, I did think it my duty to make sure, so I arranged for every locksmith within forty miles of here to be questioned. As you will see for yourself, Mrs Hudson, it is an ancient and unusual key, and it was the general opinion of the locksmiths that to make a working replica would be no easy task.'

The inspector looked at ease now, as though confident that he was on safe ground.

'And so, Mrs Hudson, I was left with only two possibilities. The first: that either Lord Empingham or Mr Snaresdon used their own key to enter the Tower Room that night. The second: that the thief must have obtained one of their keys without their knowledge. Now, I was duty-bound to consider the former possibility, but, try as I might, I couldn't make any sense of it. Lord Empingham's reputation was at stake – he risked disgrace if it became widely known that a guest had been robbed beneath his roof, especially if it was known that the object stolen was one for which he had a particular attachment. And, of course, he'd been adamant that no third key could exist. If he really had been the thief, it would have been in his interest to suggest the opposite.

'As for Mr Snaresdon, well, stealing his own possession made no sense at all. It wasn't insured. He had nothing to gain from its disappearance. And all those present insisted that he had been genuinely angry and embarrassed when it became clear the canary had really gone. He'd made such a song and dance about how he was going to melt it down, you see, purely to spite Lord Empingham. To have it known that the thing had been stolen from under his nose immediately afterwards made him something of a laughing stock.'

Mrs Hudson nodded thoughtfully, apparently content to accept the inspector's reasoning.

'And so, Inspector, you concluded that the person who stole the canary had obtained one of those keys by stealth?'

'Precisely, ma'am. It must be so. Unfortunately, both men had stated publicly that they intended to sleep with their keys beneath their pillows, so a thief would have known exactly where to look. To extract one of them in the night, while its keeper slept, would have been a daring and delicate task, but not impossible. But that was not the whole of it, of course, because the thief also had to return the key again when the deed had been done. Both men found their keys safely beneath their pillows the following morning.'

For a second time, the inspector raised his finger and wagged it, and I could tell that he was about to tell us something that pleased him greatly.

'It struck me, ma'am, that the whole case would become much clearer if I could work out which of the two keys had been used. The two gentlemen, you see, slept in very different parts of the house. Mr Snaresdon and his wife were in the East Wing, along with Mr and Mrs Alma Tadema, the Toukens, the Steels and Lord and Lady

Brabham. The other guests were in the West Wing, which is where Lord Empingham has his rooms. So I examined the lock and both keys with great care, hoping they might give up some secret. And do you know what I noticed, ma'am?'

Mrs Hudson did not, and even if she had, would surely not have spoiled the inspector's revelation by saying so.

'I noticed the smell!' He leaned back in his chair, savouring the moment. 'I noticed it first when I examined the lock in the door of the Tower Room – a very faint scent that I recognised as gentlemen's hair oil. And it occurred to me at once that the thief must have been responsible for it. In order to make sure that he could turn the key silently, he must have introduced – in some manner or another – the only lubricant he had to hand. That lubricant being hair oil, if you follow me, ma'am. It would explain why Savage was never wakened by the turning of the key in the lock.'

He paused, enjoying the moment.

'And when I examined the keys, ma'am... Or rather, I should say, when I *sniffed* the keys, guess which one smelled of hair oil? Of course, you cannot. It is an unfair question. So I will tell you, ma'am. *Both* keys smelled of hair oil!'

And with that, he sat back in triumph, beaming with pride at what Mr Raffles would no doubt have called his *coup de théâtre*.

Chapter 13

Tucked away in Mr Hawkins' pantry, it was easy to forget about the world outside. Along the corridor, in the kitchen, the cook and the scullery maids were no doubt busy preparing lunch, to be served to Lord Empingham in his sickroom. Outside, the raw December wind would still be blowing, perhaps even colder than before. Somewhere in London, Mr Alma Tadema would be painting, and Miss Burrows would be wondering about Mr Cortado, and the Earl of Brabham had probably forgotten all about his hen. As I sat and listened to Inspector Dickinson tell his tale, all those things seemed very far away.

'Both keys, you say?' Mrs Hudson sounded suitably surprised. 'You are suggesting, Inspector, that both keys were used in the lock that night?'

'That's right, ma'am. Now, of course, you're going to tell me that only one was used that night, while the other must have been used to open the door in the morning. And that's what I thought myself at first, ma'am, until I noticed tiny smears on the tips of both keys, as if both had been pressed into wet oil, which had subsequently dried. But when I inserted a similar key into the lock and pushed it all the way in, no smear was left on its tip. From which I inferred, ma'am, that the lubricant introduced into the lock by the thief had hardened in the course of the night, and that only keys used during the night could have become smeared in that way.'

Inspector Dickinson puffed out his chest like a robin in winter-time. He was clearly enormously proud of this minute observation, and I knew that if Mr Holmes had been present, the great detective would have been quick to congratulate him.

'Very pleased with this deduction, I was, ma'am,' the inspector continued, 'but that's where the whole thing stopped making sense. I mean, our thief would have been running a tremendous risk in attempting to take *one* key from beneath a pillow while someone was sleeping on it, so why on earth would they attempt the feat twice? And even if the thief was confident he could do it without waking either man, why would he want to? After all, one key was all he needed. Why would he steal one key, cross the house in darkness, go right past the tower he intended to rob, carry on all the way to the other wing, steal the second key, return to the tower, then use one key to open the door and the other to lock it again? And then there's the whole problem of opportunity...'

Mrs Hudson was nodding slowly.

'You are going to point out, Inspector, that between Savage going to sleep with the canary by his side at six o'clock in the morning, and awaking at ten to seven to find the canary gone, there was no opportunity for anyone to enter the tower and steal the canary?'

'Precisely, ma'am!' The inspector looked hugely relieved that my companion understood his dilemma. 'When Savage was woken at midnight, the canary was still in its box. The oil lamp illuminated the room very clearly, so he was quite certain of the fact. No one could have crept into the tower after that, because the library door was wedged closed, and Mr Snaresdon's little piece of glass proves that the chair wasn't moved all night. Besides, Savage stayed awake till six o'clock with the canary safely by his side, and only a few seconds after he turned out his light, Hawkins entered the library. The chair was still in place. Hawkins remained there for a few minutes, lighting the lamps so that he could survey all the broken crystal, then moving the chair back to its proper position. Then he went for the maid. Tell them how long you were gone, Mr Hawkins.'

'Two minutes, sir. At the very most. And very probably less.' The old butler spoke with absolute certainty. 'The housemaid was already on her way to the library, you see. We returned there together, and from that point onwards, probably till nightfall that night, the library was never left unattended.'

Inspector Dickinson looked at Mrs Hudson, then at me, then back at Mrs Hudson.

'So it doesn't really matter who had the keys, ma'am. Because to have stolen the bird, the thief must have been waiting for the very moment Mr Hawkins left the library after moving the chair. Then they needed to enter the library and cross it, run all the way up the tower using the old spiral staircase, which is tricky to negotiate at the best of times; then unlock the door very quietly; enter the room, locate the canary without waking Savage, and leave again, pausing to turn the lock behind them. Then they needed to get down the stairs again; and to have been clear of the library before Mr Hawkins returned with the maid some two minutes later.'

He shook his head.

'Well, I tried it myself, Mrs Hudson. I tried it many times, and I had every single one of my constables try it too. It simply isn't possible. It's at least forty seconds up all the steps, and fractionally longer down again. That leaves almost no time at all for unlocking the door, locating the canary and relocking the door, letting alone getting completely clear of the library too. The best time anyone managed, in broad daylight, was nearly four minutes. So I am certain of two very simple facts, Mrs Hudson. One, that the canary must have been carried off in the very short period of time between Mr Hawkins moving the chair from behind the library door and him returning to the library with the maid. And two, that in the period of time available, it was absolutely impossible for any thief to carry out the crime.'

We left the two men sitting comfortably in the butler's pantry, still discussing the impenetrability of the problem of the Empingham Canary. Inspector Dickinson had proposed to accompany us to the Tower Room, to show us the scene of the crime, but before Mrs Hudson could either accept or decline his offer, we had been interrupted by the housekeeper, Mrs Dempsey, with the news that Lord Empingham himself wished to see us.

His lordship's sickroom on the first floor of Frawling Hall had once been one of the principal entertaining rooms. It occupied a large portion of the front of the house, overlooking formal gardens and fountains, with views of the park beyond, and must once have been as bright and full of light as any room in the county. But now the windows were hung with thick drapes, and the interior was shrouded in a deep, sombre shade.

In such a vast room, Lord Empingham's four-poster bed seemed tiny and a little out of place. It had been placed as far from the windows as possible, near an enormous fireplace in which burned an enormous fire. It was the sort of blaze that should have made the room insufferably hot, but the size of the room and its many ancient windows must have made it hard to heat. Standing close to the fire, it was hard to breathe; but at the far end of the room, where we entered, the air still felt uncomfortably chilly.

It was clear at first glance that Lord Empingham was a very sick man. His skin was grey and his cheeks hollow, and the hand he extended in greeting was skeletally thin. But he managed a smile of welcome, then leaned back and closed his eyes.

'I am told you might be able to bring me my canary,' he said, in little more than a whisper. 'I was long ago resigned to its loss. To see it again… To see it once more, even if just for a moment, would mean a great deal.'

He paused to allow himself five or six heavy breaths.

'It must seem absurd, that it means so much to me. That little bird. But I loved it as a child. And as an adult too. It means the world to me. It reminds me of my grandfather, who I loved.'

And, of course, at various times it *had* struck me as rather absurd that so many people had made such a fuss about an ornament, even one made of solid gold. Somehow, though, in that dark room, looking at that gaunt face, and hearing the old man's words, I felt a lump rising in my throat, and I was grateful to Mrs Hudson for finding the right words of comfort and reassurance, promising that we would do everything in our power to reunite him with the Empingham Canary.

'As I told Mr Holmes, I do not care who took it. One of the Harlequins. I don't know which. Trying to save the bird, I think, from that dreadful man.'

'One of the Harlequins, sir?' Mrs Hudson asked, very, very gently.

'I saw him, you see. That morning. Before all the fuss. He must have been putting back the key. I stirred in my sleep. Not really awake, but saw him slipping from my room. Like a shadow, and masked. But dressed as Harlequin. Never told anyone. If he saved the bird, good luck to him. But I would so much like to see it again.'

And quite suddenly Lord Empingham was asleep, his breathing still rasping, but even. The nurse who sat beside his bed smiled at us.

'He sleeps more and more,' she told us. Then, as if as an after-thought, she added a request of her own.

'Do find his bird for him, if you possibly can.'

Mrs Dempsey was waiting for us outside his lordship's sickroom, accompanied by a young woman in the uniform of a housemaid.

'Ah, Mrs Hudson!' she called out as we emerged from the sepulchral gloom. 'I thought you couldn't be much longer. I said to Bessy, "Bessy, his lordship won't keep them long, for he simply isn't well enough," so I thought I'd come and find you. This is Martha.'

She gestured towards the maid, a quietly pretty young woman who looked rather anxious about being summoned into our presence.

'Martha has been with us for six months, Mrs Hudson, and you mentioned that you would like to talk to all the newer staff. Martha, you may show Mrs Hudson and Flotsam to my sitting room and talk to them there. And when you've finished, perhaps you would be so good as to go and find Goodman or young Roscoe the groundsman, as Mrs Hudson would like to talk to them too.'

Martha did as she was told, and as she led us to the housekeeper's room, Mrs Hudson chatted cheerfully to her about the most trivial matters. By the time the young woman was settled in one of Mrs Dempsey's comfortable chairs, she seemed a little less nervous and a little more capable of answering questions.

Which is just as well, because Mrs Hudson's first question was rather a surprising one.

'Now, tell me, Martha, where were you born?'

'Me, ma'am?' The young woman gulped. 'Near Aldershot, ma'am.'

'And your parents were from those parts?'

'Yes, ma'am. That is to say, my mum was, ma'am. My dad is from Guildford by birth.'

'Very good.' Mrs Hudson brushed her hands together briskly. 'That is all I really need to know. But perhaps you could tell me a little about some of the other staff here? Mr Goodman, for instance, the under-butler. What do you know of him?'

Martha looked a little flustered by this sudden change of direction, but rallied gamely.

'He's a ginger, ma'am. I mean, he has red hair. And he talks about roses a lot. Apparently, his father wins prizes for his tea roses at the Arundel show.'

Mrs Hudson seemed absolutely delighted to hear of this horticultural feat.

'Excellent!' she declared. 'That is just the sort of information I was hoping for. Now, what about Roscoe, the groundsman?'

Martha blushed a little.

'I really couldn't say, ma'am.'

Mrs Hudson regarded her for a moment.

'Very well. And Adamson, the new footman?'

Martha blushed rather more.

'I couldn't say, ma'am.'

'Nothing, Martha? For instance, have you ever heard either of those two young men talk about their employment before they came here? Or about their families? Or about any adventures that have befallen them?'

'No, ma'am.'

And after saying this, she closed her lips so firmly that I think both Mrs Hudson and I realised there was nothing more to be gleaned from her.

'Then perhaps, Martha, if Adamson is not yet back from his errand in Scotland, you could tell us where we could find Roscoe? Flotsam and I would very much like to speak to him.'

'He's probably... Well, ma'am, he may not be...' Martha seemed to find this request peculiarly challenging. 'That is to say, ma'am, I really don't know. You'd have to ask Mr Hanson, ma'am. He's the head gardener. He'll be in his shed, ma'am, on the edge of the woods. His shed, ma'am? Yes, I can point the way...'

'Thank you, Martha.' Mrs Hudson rose to her feet. 'But before we go and find the head gardener, perhaps you could arrange for us to visit the Tower Room? Please tell Mrs Dempsey that there's no need for her to accompany us. And then, I think, Flotsam and I will find our way down to the front entrance. We have yet to see either the Great Hall or the famous Empingham Christmas tree.'

–

I had heard so much about the library at Frawling Hall, and about the door that led from there to the tower, that it felt strange to encounter it in real life. Strange, also, that it wasn't hugely different from how I'd imagined it – a large, book-lined room, furnished with leather armchairs and ottomans, dotted with small tables and with plant-stands bearing a variety of lush and leafy greenery.

The actual door from the library to the tower was a little disappointing, however. I had imagined a tiny, arched doorway, so low that people had to stoop to use it, with a door of gnarled and knotty timbers; whereas it was, in fact, a perfectly unobtrusive modern door, resolutely rectangular and unromantic, and in keeping with the rest of the library.

Beyond it, however, my medieval flights of fancy proved remarkably accurate. The spiral steps that twisted up the tower were irregular and treacherous, the stones hollowed in the middle by five hundred years of footfall. They were steep too, with no rail and nothing to hold on to. The only light came from the arrow slits that punctured the thick stonework. It was hard not to agree with Inspector Dickinson that to ascend or descend them in a hurry, especially at night, would be a reckless undertaking.

At the top of the spiral, the door to the Tower Room also lived up to expectation, proving every bit as solid and ancient as I'd hoped, and the heavy, iron lock – turned by a key longer than my hand – was clearly one designed to withstand heavy battering.

And the Tower Room itself? Well, it was as simple as we'd been told – a plain circle with walls of unadorned stone, containing a single, iron-framed bed, a chair with a lamp on it, an unembellished washstand and absolutely nothing else. The shutters on one window were open, affording a view of the East Wing of Frawling Hall. The shutter on the other – the high window – was firmly closed. And it was very, very cold – horribly cold – much colder than it had felt outside in the open air.

Mrs Hudson and I stood in the centre of the room and looked up at the shuttered window.

'I think this is all very straightforward, is it not, Flotsam?'

I considered the question carefully before I nodded, because I wanted to be sure I was sure.

'Yes, ma'am. Those stairs are terrible. Inspector Dickinson is quite right that there wasn't time for a thief to get up here and steal away the canary that morning. So it's obvious what must have happened. I admit I got a little confused when he told us how high this window was, but when he told us *both* keys had oil on them, well, it all made sense – the hens, Mr Cortado disappearing, everything.'

My companion nodded.

'Yes. And the Harlequin mask explains why there were so many hens, doesn't it, Flottie? Then, of course, because we know Mrs Alma Tadema is happily married…'

'…Then there was only one person who could have sent them, ma'am.' It felt as though we had solved nearly all of the puzzle. 'I'd love to know where that person is now,' I added wistfully.

'Somewhere indicated by seven stars, Flotsam. No doubt we will work it out, but for now I think the seven stars are the only thing we still don't understand.'

I frowned, because for me it was not the only thing.

'Why *hens*, ma'am? Why not, say, canaries?' I paused, then answered my own question. 'Of course, I can see that canaries would have been the wrong thing. They would have been too obvious. But why hens?'

My companion smiled.

'The Empingham Canary disappeared on the 27th December, Flottie.'

I thought about it for a moment, then smiled. When stated so plainly, it seemed obvious. Then I nodded towards the closed shutter above our heads.

'Do we need a ladder, ma'am?'

'Surely not, Flotsam! It is a while since I've climbed a wall, or indeed anything else, but I remember the principles.'

She positioned herself under the high window with her back against the stone wall, and laced her fingers together to make a step.

'Up you go, my girl!'

With Mrs Hudson's strong arms launching me upwards it was surprisingly easy to open the shutter, and to scramble onto the ledge that lay behind it.

'Blimey, ma'am. It's incredibly dusty,' I told her. 'Are you going to come up?'

Bracing myself against the stonework, I leaned down and reached out my arm. Mrs Hudson took it in a firm grip just below the elbow, then placed the tip of one of her boots against the stone wall, before releasing me and stepping back.

'No, Flotsam, I shan't attempt it. My climbing days are well and truly behind me. But were I as young and supple as you are, I don't think it would be beyond me. What do you see up there?'

'It really is a very narrow space,' I told her, looking around me. 'There's not enough room to stand. If you did come up, ma'am, we'd practically have to sit on top of each other to fit in. And it's *really* cold. Even colder up here, pressed against the window, than it is down there, where you are.'

'So what do you think, Flottie?' Mrs Hudson asked, peering up at me.

I looked out at the bare hills that peeped above the tree-tops, and tried to imagine them covered in snow, the sky above them dark and full of stars. I tried to imagine time passing, the stars turning, my world reduced to nothing but sky and snow and the narrow nook where I sheltered. Then I thought of Clara Fazakerley and her silly infatuation with Dumpty Boynton, and marvelled that it had ever upset me.

'I think, ma'am,' I told her, 'that it's far and away the most romantic thing I've ever heard of.'

Chapter 14

The great entrance hall at Frawling was very grand, and it was hard for someone as dusty as I was to stand in the middle of it and not feel a little self-conscious.

Pleasingly, it was every bit as high and as cavernous as I'd imagined it, although it did not feature a grand staircase in its centre, rather two sets of stairs, one from the left of the hall, the other from the right, both leading to a great gallery-landing that ran around the whole width of the hall and joined the two staircases.

In the space between the two stairs, in the very centre of the hall, stood Lord Empingham's Christmas tree. It was enormous, at least thirty feet tall, as large as any I had ever seen, so tall that its top branches were at the same level as the gallery above us. A small army of servants were at work at its foot with ribbons and bows and step ladders, and I could understand why the decorating of the tree began so many days before Christmas. It was clearly no small task. The very top branch, where once the Empingham Canary would have perched, was still bare. It would be an easy task to decorate it from the gallery. One need only to reach out over the railing to add a bow or a star to the top of the tree.

Mrs Dempsey, who had joined us as we passed through the servants' hall, must have noticed my expression.

'Marvellous, isn't it?' she whispered, a note of admiration in her voice. 'Bigger than any we've had in all my time here. His lordship refused to allow a tree like this one after… Well, you know, after the *incident*. But this year, well, for one reason or another, there were no smaller trees to be had.'

I agreed that it was indeed a magnificent object, and Mrs Hudson nodded her agreement, and I thought we would leave the Great Hall then, to go and find the head gardener. But before we did, Mrs Hudson turned to the housekeeper.

'I wonder, Mrs Dempsey, if I may just ask you two further questions? The first relates to something his lordship said to us earlier. He mentioned seeing a masked person in a Harlequin suit in his bedroom, early in the morning, the day his golden ornament was stolen. I wonder if this is the first you've heard of any such sighting?'

'Oh, dear me, no, Mrs Hudson!' She smiled, but it was a rather sad smile. 'Although never before by his lordship. I imagine he is simply confused. You see, there have been so many rumours about that morning. I heard all about them from my great aunt, who was the housekeeper back then. You see, she claims that she saw a figure in a Harlequin suit in the East Wing sometime after six that morning, but she admits it was dark and the figure was at the far end of a corridor and deep in shadow. His lordship's room in those days was in the *West Wing*, so he couldn't possibly have seen it too. Her story has become exaggerated and amplified over the years, so that it's become a bit of a legend now. If ever anything gets mislaid here at Frawling, there's always someone below stairs who'll say that Harlequin must have taken it. I suppose his lordship must have heard those stories too.'

She paused, but Mrs Hudson seemed to be contemplating the bare branch at the top of the Christmas tree, so Mrs Dempsey went on.

'Was there something else, Mrs Hudson? You said you had a second question to ask me.'

'Oh, yes, indeed.' Mrs Hudson blinked and looked away from the tree. 'An unusual request, I'm afraid. As you know, Flotsam and I are just going to ask the head gardener one or two things about his assistant groundsman. Then, after that, depending on what answers we get, I wondered if you would mind very much if we searched the bedroom of your new footman?'

We found Mr Hanson in his shed, exactly as Martha had predicted. To reach it, we had to follow a footpath that led us around the walled garden and through a small orchard, to a building that nestled in a fold of the ground where the park met woodland. It was still only early afternoon – although it already felt like a very long day – but the clouds were so dark that the day was growing murky. I felt again the sense that snow was on its way.

The head gardener's shed was a far finer building than I'd expected. It was, in reality, a substantial stone-built barn which had been divided into two parts – the larger part held various pieces of mystifying horticultural equipment of the sort that might be pulled by horses; in the other, a spacious workshop had been created, and that was where we found Mr Hanson, seated on a stool at a work bench, peering at a large map of the estate.

I don't know if Mr Hanson was in an ill-temper before we arrived, but it was clear from the moment we mentioned the name of his assistant groundsman that we had not improved his mood.

'Roscoe?' he growled, if it is possible to growl such a word. 'I'll tell you all you need to know about John Roscoe!'

And with that he spat on the ground, clearly feeling that no further eloquence on his part was required.

Mrs Hudson, however, was hoping for rather more information on the subject. She persisted with a number of questions, from which we learned that Roscoe had come from Lord Tottenham's estate in Somerset; that he had come recommended by the gardener there, a man who Hanson now considered a knave and a liar; that Roscoe had indeed been good with trees, but that in almost every other way he had been unsuitable for the job.

'Irresponsible, lazy, always looking for a way to evade his duties. Never trusted him. We don't like that sort round here.'

Mr Hanson did concede that the young man knew one or two things about softwood husbandry, but the list of his defects went on: impertinent; over-fond of a drink; never to be found anywhere near the woods if there was an opportunity to be sniffing after the housemaids. Enjoyed low company. Frequently late for work. Suspected of selling off oak saplings on the quiet.

'Goodness, Mr Hanson!' Mrs Hudson exclaimed, when this litany of shortcomings came to an end. 'I'm surprised he remains in your employment.'

'Doesn't,' the gardener replied shortly. 'Finally gave him notice. Good riddance to him. Told him he had till the end of the week to clear out his cottage and go. Laughed in my face, he did. Called me a muck-shovelling sourpuss. Almost got him with the rake, but he was too quick for me.'

Mr Hanson paused.

'Wouldn't be at all surprised if it was him who ruined them conifers.'

'The conifers, Mr Hanson? You mean that pair of Christmas trees we read about, the ones that were deliberately damaged?'

'Don't mean those,' he replied gruffly. 'Mean the others. Come. I'll show you.'

He led us from the shed and into the woods, walking quickly and making no concessions for the rough ground or for our skirts. As he walked, he continued to deliver occasional additional comments on John Roscoe's failings.

'Didn't like his waistcoats. Too fancy. Never trusted him. Bad as they come. That girl Martha lost a ring. Gold. Mother's wedding ring. Dropped it in the woods. Canoodling, she was. With Roscoe. Had to confess. Nearly lost her place. Should have warned him off then. Scoundrel... Didn't damage them first two trees. Drinking in The George, he was. All night. Both nights. Could have done the others though. Don't know why.'

We followed him through bare, wintry woodland, then reached a little plantation of fir trees, planted neatly in short rows. Mr Hanson spat in their direction.

'Dreadful things. Worse than weeds. Only grow 'em because his lordship insists. For Christmas.' He indicated the first line. 'Them's the little ones. Next line, them's next year's. And here...'

We passed the first two lines of conifers, and the gardener gave a sweeping wave of his hand.

'Here's the ones I grew for this year. Just the size his lordship wanted. Not too big, not too small. And look at 'em. Ruined. All of 'em. The whole row. Roscoe's handiwork, I'll be bound. Just look.'

We looked.

It wasn't hard to work out what Mr Hanson wanted us to see, nor why the sight embittered him. If I had worked and planned for so long to deliver trees of the perfect height at the perfect time, I would have felt bitter too. Because every tree in the line – every tree that had been grown to the required height – had been liberally splashed with great splodges of white paint.

Beyond them, a line of really tall trees – tall enough to reach to the gallery in Frawling Hall – remained green and pristine.

Who painted all the Christmas trees?

'Please, sir,' I told the gardener meekly, 'I think I've met Mr Roscoe. He came up to London one day and was terribly drunk. But I'm absolutely certain he didn't paint these trees. In fact, I'm sure this is quite as much a mystery to him as it is to you.'

—

Later that afternoon, to Mrs Dempsey's evident horror, we ransacked the room of the junior footman.

Perhaps 'ransacked' is too strong a word, for we made every attempt to tidy things up as we went, but there was no denying the thoroughness of our search. We turned out his drawers and emptied the trunk we found beneath his bed. We ran our hands over all his clothes, even his under-garments, in case anything was concealed in them. We took his spare uniforms from his little wardrobe and checked behind them for hidden compartments. We delved into his pillows and examined his mattress. We lifted his carpet and checked beneath it for loose floorboards. We even looked behind the picture on the wall – a rather drab print of Frawling Hall with a damp stain where the front door should have been.

'Because, Flotsam,' Mrs Hudson mused as we worked, 'we can rule out Martha, and we can rule out Goodman, and I think it's obvious that John Roscoe is no angel. So, we're left with Adamson, and I think we both knew it was him from the first moment Mrs Dempsey mentioned him, because he'd made it so obvious. But it *might* have been coincidence, and we were right to check, just as we are right to take every measure necessary to recover the Empingham Canary while Lord Empingham is still well enough to receive it. I'm sure the young gentleman will forgive us. Now, if not here, where could it be? For he would surely not have taken it with him, Flotsam.'

'No, ma'am, but it could be anywhere!' The task felt hopeless. 'Anywhere in the whole of Frawling Hall. Could we not attempt to send a telegram, ma'am, to wherever he is in Scotland? Just to make sure he understands the urgency?'

Mrs Hudson nodded briskly.

'Indeed, Flotsam. We shall be at the office when it opens in the morning, and must pray that our cable reaches him before he begins his journey back to Frawling. But the truth is that his lordship may have only hours to live, so time is against us. Now, Mrs Dempsey says Adamson sometimes helps the boy clean the boots. It is a forlorn hope, but let us go and search the boot room...'

It proved a fruitless task, not helped by the presence of Mrs Dempsey, asking over and over again – and not unreasonably – why her newest footman might know the whereabouts of Lord Empingham's lost treasure.

'Turner's been with us eighteen years, Mrs Hudson, and Tipton for twelve. If it were one of those two, I could understand. But Adamson...'

Mrs Hudson, however, carried on searching, saying only that Adamson could explain it all on his return. It wasn't until four o'clock that we gave up our search, telling Mrs Dempsey that we would return the following morning. It struck me that the housekeeper was every bit as relieved to see us go as she had been to see us arrive.

And I for one was pleased to set off back to our rooms at The George. The snow I was expecting still hadn't come, and if anything, the dark clouds were beginning to fracture. In one or two places, through the gaps, we could glimpse stars.

Even so, it was a dark night, and we said very little as we walked. My head was full of all the things that had become clear to me so suddenly that day, and I imagined all over again, in vivid pictures, how the Empingham Canary had come to vanish from Frawling Hall. The more I looked for a fault in my reasoning, the less fault I could find. It all seemed utterly certain, yet highly improbable at the same time. But no more improbable, I reflected, than a great many of Mr Holmes' other cases. At least there were no snakes involved, or twins, or exotic foreign rodents.

We reached The George much more quickly than I expected, and its lights were bright and welcoming. Even at that early hour I could hear a good-natured hubbub of voices coming from the public bar, and the thought of our tidy bedroom and a blazing hearth was undoubtedly tempting. But for some reason, I was reluctant to go in, and Mrs Hudson seemed to sense as much.

'Do you need a little time alone with your thoughts, young lady? Well, that's no bad thing. I shall go in and make sure there's a fire, and check that they're getting a good dinner ready for us, for Mrs Dempsey's little sandwiches were hardly a proper lunch. But by all means take a turn around the village if you wish. It can be good to think things over while they're still fresh in your mind.'

So, with a grateful little smile, I continued with my walk. At first I headed into the village, towards The Plough Hotel, thinking there would be more to see in that direction. But I was in the mood for solitude, so after only a few yards I changed my mind and retraced my steps, back past The George, back to where the shorter of Frawling Hall's two drives branched away from the lane.

There, I paused. The iron gates that stood at the end of the short drive were still open and the gatehouse lay in darkness, apparently unoccupied. I could have continued on, in the direction of Amberley, but the road ahead was dark, and there was nothing to prevent me turning towards the Hall instead. I had it in my mind that I would like to go back and stand beneath the old tower, and look up at the west window where such an amazing discovery had been made, so long ago. Twenty-three years ago. And still not forgotten. I thought of the hens and smiled.

There were very few lights in the windows of Frawling Hall as I approached. Where once Lord Empingham's guests would have been gathering to celebrate Christmas, where once there would have been vivacity and laughter, and an army of servants run off their feet, now the hall lay almost in darkness. I thought of the old peer, lying in his sickroom, and I hoped he was sleeping. If not, perhaps he was thinking of his grandfather. Because since meeting him, it had occurred to me that his part of the story was about love too. Not love for the bird, as I'd always thought; the bird was only a thing. But it was a thing which brought him close to a lost loved one, a slim golden thread connecting him to a happy past. And the thought filled me once again with that sense of frustration. Time was so short, and the bird was surely so near.

But the sight of the tower calmed me. I suppose, over the years, something so old, and so unchanging, grows its own cloak of serenity. As I stood looking up at it, I noticed that the snow clouds were mostly gone and there were stars again, just as there had been on that other night so long ago.

Without really thinking, I looked up at them and played with the patterns they made. I knew so few of them. The North Star. Cassiopeia. Orion's Belt. The Plough.

And, of course, it came to me then with such a crushing sense of the obvious that it seemed utterly impossible I hadn't seen it before. A signature, an address and a message. The harlequin pattern for a signature; a man's name for the address; and seven stars for the message. Seven stars. The Plough.

That little scribble had been telling the recipients where to look.

And the sender was here. Right under my nose. Had been here all along, just waiting to be found.

How had I been so dull? How could I possibly not have realised?

I set off back up the drive at a run, my skirts hoisted to my knees and the gravel flying beneath my feet. Of course, I should have paced myself, for it was a long way to the village, and a long way to The Plough, and I had not gone very far before my heart was pounding and I was gasping for breath. But even then, I pushed on, as fast as I could, driven by the thought that perhaps the slightest delay might prove disastrous, that perhaps my quarry might already be on the brink of departing. I would stop at The George to alert Mrs Hudson, and then the two of us would dash to The Plough together.

Of course, we might be too late. We might already be too late. It was some days since the hens had been delivered.

But I ran anyway, tormented by the thought that there might be someone waiting at the The Plough who could tell me exactly where Lord Empingham's bird was hidden.

And it was at that very moment that I saw the two figures ahead of me in the darkness.

They were standing in the lane, in deep shadow, just beyond the gatehouse. Had I not been repeating to myself the need for vigilance, I probably wouldn't have noticed them – I would probably have crashed onwards, panting and noisy, and they might very well have withdrawn unseen into the shadow to let me pass.

But I did see them, and before they saw me.

At first, I thought they were a pair of young lovers who had wandered from the village in search of solitude. The held each other so closely that their bodies merged into one shadow. But I could make out her head, raised, and his head, lowered to hers, in a long, tender kiss, and I could see them remain that way, very still and very quiet and very tender, while I stood, desperately trying to control my breathing.

They were perhaps, twenty yards away, and I was about to cough loudly and tactfully, to alert them to my presence, when they stepped apart and I heard her speak, and something in her voice told me at once that this was no ordinary pair of village sweethearts.

'Take care.' She said it softly, so softly I could barely hear. But I knew at once she was the woman I was looking for.

I saw him nod, and he must have said something I couldn't hear, and the pair exchanged a swift and silent kiss before he swung a small bag onto his shoulder and set off up the lane, towards Amberley.

She stood and watched him go, so intently that she didn't hear me approach. When I spoke, I saw her jump visibly.

'Please, ma'am,' I said, still very breathless. 'My name is Flotsam, and I know Mr Sherlock Holmes, and, well, it's all too complicated to explain now, but you need to know, ma'am, that we know about the canary, and about your plan to put it back, and, ma'am, I can't tell you what a beautiful story it is, and how daring and brave I think you are!'

For her, it must have been the most extraordinary and unexpected encounter, and yet she made no effort to challenge me, or question me, or offer any sort of denial. I couldn't see her face very clearly in the darkness, but I think she smiled.

'Thank you,' she replied simply. 'It is a great compliment.'

Her voice was low and full of amusement, and rather lovely.

'But the thing is, ma'am, that his lordship is much sicker than people realise, and I think you planned for it to be placed on the tree on Boxing Day night, which would be perfect, of course, only Lord Empingham may not live that long. In fact, he may not last even a day or two, so we absolutely must give him the bird as soon as possible, or it will be too late, but we looked and we couldn't find it, and your son is in Scotland and doesn't know how urgent it is. So I will explain everything later on, or tomorrow, but please, ma'am, *please*, if you know where he's hidden the canary, do tell me!'

Again, I expected questions or objections or bluster, but she simply listened and replied.

'Very well, Flotsam. I'm told it's in a small wooden box beneath the bed of a very pretty housemaid called Martha. My son thought it safer than his own room.'

I nodded, my chest still heaving.

'I know Martha. If you will excuse me, ma'am, I'd better go at once...'

But as I turned to go, she called my name.

'Miss Flotsam! Please give his lordship my compliments. And please tell him we did it for him.'

'I will, ma'am,' I promised, 'I will.'

And I turned and hurried back to the Hall, leaving behind me, still in the shadows, the woman who stole the Empingham Canary.

Chapter 15

My hasty return to the servants' hall at Frawling did not create quite the stir I'd expected.

I'd imagined myself bursting in, out of the darkness, ideally accompanied by a flurry of snow, so suddenly and so dramatically that every face would be turned in my direction and the entire staff of Frawling Hall would marvel at the news I brought them.

And I did indeed burst through the door without knocking, but when I did, I discovered the big room entirely empty but for the silent Bessy, seated at the big wooden table, reading what appeared to be a penny novel. She did rise to her feet on my entrance, but made no comment at all; she simply looked quite surprised.

'Bessy!' I declared. 'I must find Martha! I know where to find Lord Empingham's canary!'

The young woman nodded politely at this, but didn't seem to think any reply was required, so I carried on.

'Where is Martha? We must find her at once!'

This direct request appeared to galvanise her, because she put down her novel rather hurriedly and nodded upwards with her head.

'In her room, Miss. I'll take you.'

She did, at least, seem to understand my desire for haste, because she led me to the top of the house at a brisk pace, up a series of back-stairs, until we reached a narrow corridor that ran beneath the eaves, with a series of small rooms opening off it. In one of them, her door open, I could see Martha laying out a clean uniform.

If my dramatic entrance had left Bessy unmoved, just the sight of me approaching her room was enough to make Martha drop the apron she held and to step back, away from the door. I think it must have been the expression on my face, or perhaps something preying on her conscience, because before I could say a word she was already stumbling through a complicated series of apologies.

'I'm so sorry, Miss, I really am. I knew it must be wrong. And I thought today I should have said something. But he told me it was private so I didn't, although I knew I should have done. And then, when I heard you were searching through his things, I felt even worse. But I promised him. And it can't be anything bad if it's him, because I know he isn't wicked, I know it, I know it!'

This declaration, coming as it did from a young lady who had reportedly been stepping out with John Roscoe only a month or two before, suggested that a striking transferal of her affections had recently taken place.

'It is nothing bad, Martha,' I assured her, 'but it is something tremendously important, and tremendously valuable too. Did Adamson tell you what it is?'

She shook her head, still looking anxious and perhaps also a little tearful.

'No, Miss. He just gave me a box and told me to put it under my bed, and to keep it safe, and not to tell anyone because it was very precious.'

'And the box, Martha!' I cried, trying my best not to sound impatient. 'Do you still have it?'

'Yes, Miss. It's right here, Miss.' And I watched as she knelt and produced from under her bed a simple wooden box, no more than twelve inches long and twelve inches wide. She placed it quietly on the bed and stood back, allowing me to approach it.

So there I stood, and suddenly all my urgency was gone. After twenty-three years of looking, the Empingham Canary had been tracked to this little box in this little attic room. And now it was up to me to open the box.

I was aware the room was very quiet. I don't know if Martha and Bessy had guessed what the box contained, but I rather think they must have done, because it seemed that all three of us were, at the very same moment, holding our breath.

And then I stepped forward and opened the lid.

Martha's scream was not a loud one – perhaps really no more than a very scared squeak – but in that silence it seemed both alarming and ear-piercing. I think even Bessy gasped. I might have done both, or either, but in fact I think I simply stood in silence and stared.

The box was empty.

The canary wasn't there.

'What's happened, Miss? What's happened?' Suddenly the words were flowing out of Martha. 'Why's it empty? What was it? Was it really his lordship's bird? How could it be? After all these years? How did Adamson come to have it? Where's it gone?'

'I rather think, Martha,' I explained, 'that someone has taken it. And I don't think it was Adamson, or he wouldn't have left the box.'

I took a deep breath and straightened and looked the young woman very firmly in the eye.

'Think very carefully, Martha. Did you ever tell anyone else about the box under the bed?'

Even before she began to answer, the truth was obvious. She began to swallow very hard.

'I'd been stepping out with someone, Miss. John Roscoe, the groundsman. Oh, Miss!' She burst into tears. 'He used to say ever such nice things to me, Miss, and he used to kiss me ever so often, out in the woods. And then last month he didn't try and kiss me anymore, he'd go off to The George instead, and I'm sure it was because of Trissy Morton who works behind the bar there. So one day, just to make him stop and talk to me, I told him that Adamson had something very valuable and it was under my bed. I don't know why I did, because Adamson is much nicer than Roscoe. Quite a gentleman, really. And Roscoe laughed and told me I should learn to keep a secret. And I never told another soul, I swear, Miss.'

'Roscoe...' Different thoughts were whirling through my brain. The young man so disliked by his employer. The drunkard I'd met in London. Martha's missing ring.

Two rings... Gave them to Humphrey. A very good egg, Humphrey...

'Oh, my word!' I declared, my mind no longer racing, but all at once very calm and very clear. 'I think I know exactly what's going to happen! Where is Roscoe now, Martha?'

But by then her tears had taken hold, and I feared I might never get an answer. Help came from a surprising direction.

'He's gone to London, Miss.' Bessy's voice, which I had barely even heard up to that point, was crisp and confident. 'On the four o'clock train from Amberley. He won't be coming back. He was given his notice, you see. Now he's packed his bags and gone. I overheard him telling Tipton he was taking something up to town for a friend, a very rich friend. Boasted that he'd be living like a gentleman from now on.'

'But did he say where? Where he was meeting his friend? It's really important!'

I must have been sounding rather shrill, but Bessy remained very calm.

'I confess I wasn't paying full attention, Miss. I remember Roscoe did say one strange thing, though, something about his friend sitting on a wall. But that's all I can remember.'

Humpty Dumpty... Surely there could be no doubt? I recalled Mr Raffles' words with perfect clarity.

Humphrey Boynton... he's taken the lease of Old Mackenzie's workshop by the docks... I wouldn't be surprised if he's up to some scheme...

I glanced anxiously at my little pocket watch. It was a little after twenty past five. If Roscoe had been on the four o'clock train... Before I'd even begun to ask my next question, Bessy had answered it.

'Next train's at five past six, Miss. And if you need to go after him, Miss, you'll have to catch that one, because after that none of the trains from the coast stop at Amberley, not until the mail train in the middle of the night.'

I looked at her, aghast.

'I do need to go after him! And straightaway! He's going to sell the Empingham Canary to someone who will melt it down! But I think tomorrow will be too late, and there's no way any of us can make it to Amberley in time to catch a five past six train!'

'Not on foot, Miss.' As I grew more and more panicky, Bessy seemed to grow ever calmer. 'And it would be no good calling for his lordship's carriage, because by the time they get it out and harness up the horses, then go round by the lanes, it will be too late. Do you ride, Miss?'

I didn't. I'd spent a good deal of my life very close to horses, mostly getting out of their way in busy London traffic, but I had never in my life attempted to sit on one. I think this shortcoming must have been clear from my expression, because Bessy continued almost without pause.

'I only ask, Miss, because my young man is an ostler here, and he's got some good horses in his care, and there's an old drover track that goes across country, much shorter than by road. And my young man's a very proper young man, Miss, and knows the track like the back of his hand, so if you didn't mind sitting in front of him, and having him hold you on board, as it were, I daresay he could get you there on time. If you leave at once.'

There are certain occasions in life when, however appalling a course of action may sound, you have no choice but to take it. This seemed to me to be one of those times. I left Martha sitting on her bed, snuffling gently next to the empty box, and followed Bessy down the stairs at an even swifter pace than we'd gone up. It seemed impossible to believe that the silent housemaid of earlier in the day and this purposeful and decisive young woman could possibly be the same person, for as we descended the stairs and set out across the yard to the stables, she continued to talk.

'I will get word to your friend at The George,' she told me, 'so that she knows what's become of you. Any special message, Miss?'

I considered this.

'Only to tell her that I'll be back tomorrow, as early as I can, because by then I'll either have good news or no news, and no news will be the worst news of all. And you'd better tell her that the lady we've been looking for is staying at The Plough. She'll know what that means.'

'Very well. Now, here we are. This is Arthur. Don't worry about making conversation, Miss, because Arthur's the silent type.'

Arthur turned out to be a rather substantial individual of perhaps thirty-five, with very ruddy cheeks, and he beamed while Bessy gave him his instructions as though taking me for a ride over rough terrain in the pitch darkness was the greatest pleasure he could possibly imagine. The only replies he muttered were a series of grunts and a slight intake of breath when told the time of the train I needed to catch.

'You *can* make it, can't you, Arf?' Bessy asked him anxiously, as he threw a saddle over an attractive bay cob.

'Arr. We can make it. Not by much though. Now then, my pretty, show us a leg.'

To my great relief, this last remark was not addressed to me, nor to Bessy, but to the bay cob, who whinnied softly in reply.

'Now, Miss,' he went on, and this time he really did mean me. 'If you don't object, perhaps you'll let me give you a lift?'

And before I could reply, strong hands had closed around my waist and I found myself raised on to the cob's back, both legs on one side, and with nothing to lean back against, so that I found myself grabbing the pony's mane in alarm. Fortunately, neither Arthur nor the cob seemed to have any objection.

'One moment, Miss.' And he heaved his great bulk up into the saddle next to me, taking the reins with one arm behind me and the other in front, so that I was enclosed between them as securely as if I were being hugged by a bear. 'Now, just you hang onto my lapels, Miss, and try to balance as we go, and I'll have you at the station in a jiffy.'

I suspect that Bessy's Arthur was a sincere and honest man, but that last remark proved very far from the truth. It was, I'm afraid, a journey I would not wish to repeat, and it seemed to last forever. When the night was at its darkest or the track at its bumpiest, Arthur would slow the cob to a walk, allowing her to pick her own way. At these times, although my position felt less precarious, I was tormented by fear of missing the train. But when the sky brightened or when the path was smooth, Arthur – perhaps aware of my anxiety – urged our mount into a trot, and that was even worse, for although the sense of speed was a comfort, I felt I was being tossed like an ungainly pancake, over and over again, and only by clutching tightly to Arthur's coat could I be sure of staying on. My cheeks spent a good deal of the journey pressed against his ample midriff, which smelled strangely of both straw and carbolic soap.

Throughout the ride, my companion barely spoke a word, and perhaps his silence made the journey seem to stretch out even longer, because when the cob's hoofs finally struck the surface of a solid road, I was convinced that, not only must our train have departed, but that it must have departed long since; and I began to wonder how long it would take me to return to Frawling on foot. I felt terribly bruised and horribly achy, but a walk of double the distance would have been greatly preferable to repeating the ordeal I'd just endured.

So it was with a great deal of surprise – and not a little disbelief – that I heard Arthur announce that it could be no more than five minutes to the hour.

'Reckon Bess got it right,' he told me. 'Of the pair of us, I know I'm the chatty one. But she talks when she has to, does Bess, and when she *does* say a thing, 'tis often right.'

'But we still have to get to the station,' I pointed out.

'Two minutes along the bridleway then across the vicar's paddock and we're there,' he told me stolidly – and he must have been just about right, because the church clock was striking six when he deposited me discreetly in a shadowy corner of the station drive.

'Safe journey, Miss,' he concluded, touching his cap, then turned the cob away and began to make little kissing noises in the darkness. As I hurried towards the entrance to the station, I could hear the cob whickering contentedly back at him.

Chapter 16

At that hour on a winter's evening, Amberley station was not crowded. In fact, there were no more than half a dozen other passengers waiting for the London train, all of them a good deal tidier and less dishevelled than myself. For, quite apart from my unorthodox method of arrival, which had left me feeling a little unsteady, and aching in places that seemed to make no sense, I was still dressed in the clothes I had pulled on in Baker Street that morning – a morning that seemed so distant that I could barely believe it belonged to the same day. To say that I felt grimy would be a terrible understatement, and, apart from the purse in my coat pocket, I had no possessions and no baggage. When the train pulled in, I was delighted to find an empty third-class carriage where nobody would peer at me strangely.

I'd expected the train to be something of a sanctuary. From the moment Arthur had lifted me onto his horse until the moment he deposited me safely back on to the ground, the prospect of a steady seat on a modern train had seemed like paradise, and I'd been praying for my ordeal-by-pony to end. But, as so often with ill-considered prayers, the thing I'd longed for didn't prove very much better than the thing I'd had before. It was true, of course, that my physical discomfort was very much less, but my anxiety – which had seemed acute enough when fretting about missing the train – was suddenly very much greater.

Because now, as I looked ahead to my arrival in London, it occurred to me that this rash journey, rushed into without any real consideration or forethought, and with no plan worth mentioning, had limited prospects of success.

The more I tried to make this thought go away, the more strongly it persisted, so for over an hour and a half I sat alone, chafing with impatience, willing the train to move forward faster, agonising at every stop along the way, yet all the time dreading my arrival and the decision I must make about what to do next.

I had no doubt that John Roscoe was a thief – if usually only a petty one – and that he took advantage of his trips to London to sell on any little valuables he'd purloined. That ring of Martha's... What had he said to me so drunkenly in Baker Street that night? I found I could remember his exact words. *Had a ring. Two rings. Not rings anymore...* And it was that last sentence which sent a stab of panic rushing through me, because it surely suggested that Roscoe's so-called friend was not only someone who bought stolen goods, but also someone in the habit of melting things down. All that discussion of the Buckminster Smelter had made me an expert in the economics of selling stolen jewels, enough to know that something as recognisable as the Empingham Canary – almost unsellable in its existing form – could very easily be destroyed forever, turned into a small and featureless lump of gold.

That was the fate Lord Empingham's horrible cousin had intended for it all those years ago. That was the fate it had been rescued from. And now, just as it was about to be returned to Frawling, just when it was about to be returned to the top of Lord Empingham's Christmas tree, that was the fate which awaited it all over again.

But there *was* still a chance, however forlorn. I remembered how Roscoe had laughed when he referred to his friend Humphrey as a good egg. Of course, I couldn't be sure that Humphrey Dumpty Boynton was the same man, but I couldn't escape the idea that he might very well be. After all, Roscoe seemed inclined to make egg jokes whenever he mentioned him; and Mr Raffles had confirmed that Mr Boynton was currently engaged in some nefarious activity down at the docks. He'd even told me where: Old Mackenzie's workshop. If I was wrong, there was nothing I could do to find Roscoe anyway. But if I was right, and if I could somehow get there, then perhaps, just perhaps…

But London's docks stretch for many miles on both sides of the river, and in that jungle of alleyways and warehouses and hidden yards, a single workshop would be impossible to find.

Mr Raffles could tell me where to look, of course, if only I could find him. It wasn't too far from Victoria Station to Albany, where Mr Raffles had his rooms, and I had thought that tracking him down would be the easy part. It was only when the train was already running through the darkened suburbs of the metropolis that I recalled something Mr Raffles had told us in the kitchen at Baker Street. Something about dining in the Long Room at Lord's. Well, I could certainly save time by going directly there. But Lord's Cricket Ground was on the edge of Regent's Park, in St John's Wood, and that meant travelling across town northwards, in exactly the wrong direction. It was a diversion that would add, well, *ages* to my journey, and Roscoe was already two hours ahead of me.

Yet, however much I fretted at the prospect, I could see no alternative, so after a hasty and undignified dash across Victoria Station towards the nearest cab rank, the address I gasped to the driver was that of the famous cricket ground.

With hindsight, I think perhaps I was lucky with the traffic. At that time on a winter's evening, so close to Christmas, I could have expected Park Lane to be almost unpassable with carriages, but we passed along the length of Hyde Park with barely a pause. Things were a little slower on the Edgware Road but even there the north-bound traffic was flowing fairly smoothly. Nevertheless, the journey seemed painfully slow, made much worse by the knowledge that with every minute I spent travelling away from the docks, John Roscoe might be getting closer to them. He might be there already. The Empingham Canary might already be no more.

I tried not to think of it, clinging instead to the arguments in my favour. Dumpty Boynton was a young man about town; he didn't spend his evenings lurking in a dingy workshop by the Thames. And he certainly didn't do his own dirty work; he may be receiving stolen goods, he may have arranged premises in which they could be broken up and melted down, but it was hardly likely that he donned a workman's smock and did the job himself. So perhaps Roscoe wouldn't be going to the docks at all. Much more likely, he would be looking for his so-called friend somewhere in town. And even if they agreed a price, and the canary changed hands, then perhaps Dumpty Boynton would be in no hurry. At the very least, he could finish his evening. Maybe he would want to keep the canary for a few days, like a hunter keeps a trophy.

In which case, dashing to St John's Wood, then back to the docks, was a silly, panicky waste of time, and for a moment I almost called up to the driver to turn the cab around. I would be better to hunt down Mr Boynton for myself. Miss Peters would know where he lived. If he was out in company, she would probably know where I could find him. Then I could confront him, demand the canary's return...

It was at that point I slipped back into my seat, realising how hopeless it was, how helpless I was. Perhaps if Mrs Hudson were with me, or Mr Holmes and Dr Watson, such a confrontation might bear fruit. But without their support, what could I do? Even if I were able to argue my way into his presence, who would listen to me? A grubby housemaid, clearly a bit overwrought, babbling about canaries and eggs, all based on something a drunkard had told her while hanging off the Baker Street railings... It wasn't hard to imagine the contemptuous ease with which a cool young gentleman could dismiss it all. Dumpty Boynton, whose brother was in the Guards, dabbling in stolen goods? Young Humphrey, who danced so well, concealing a long-lost, priceless treasure? Put like that, it sounded totally absurd, even to me.

By the time I arrived at Lord's, the thrill of the chase had drained from me completely. All the fire and urgency which had sustained me through the horrible horse-ride with Arthur, all the agitation and frustration which had plagued me on the train to Victoria — all of them were gone, leaving me feeling strangely hollow and very alone. It was all pointless. I should have gone to Mrs Hudson at The George, and had a good night's sleep, and then we could have gone to the police together. She would have found a way to make us believed. And although the wheels would have turned very slowly – probably too slowly to save Lord Empingham's bird – they would at least have turned.

Instead, I had come a long way, in a dreadful hurry, and had no real idea of anything useful I could do next. Worse than the feeling of being so alone was the feeling of being so foolish.

And if I had hoped to find an ally at Lord's I was to be disappointed. The ground itself was is darkness, of course, deep in its winter hibernation, but the cab driver dropped me near the members' entrance where there were lights showing and an old man in uniform guarding the gate. I delved deep into my purse to pay the driver, and only as I watched him drive away did it occur to me that I should have asked him to wait. The streets around Lord's were very quiet; finding a hansom to take me back into town wasn't going to be easy.

But Mr Raffles would surely help me. Cold and alone, I clung to that hope – but it was a hope that evaporated within only a few seconds, when in reply to my enquiry the doorman informed me that Mr Raffles hadn't been seen all evening.

'He's expected, Miss, I know that. But I haven't seen him yet. Could be here any minute, but you never know with Mr Raffles. Comes to these testimonials out of a sense of duty, but if he were to get into a good game of cards, for instance… Well, I wouldn't like to guess how long you'll have to wait. As I say, you never can tell with Mr Raffles.'

It was then that my luck changed because, as we were speaking, a smartly dressed young gentleman in evening dress had approached at a brisk pace from the direction of the Lord's Tavern, and now he touched his hat in my direction.

'Mr Raffles, Miss? What do you want with him?'

I explained that he was an acquaintance of mine, and that I urgently needed a piece of information from him. In reply, he held out his hand.

'My name is Manders, and Raffles is a very old friend of mine. But I'm afraid you're out of luck tonight. I've been sent with his apologies. I believe he's gone out of town. Something of a last-minute thing.'

The distress this news caused me must have been evident, because he eyed me with a great deal of sympathy.

'If I may be so bold, what exactly was it that you wanted to know?'

And so I explained I was looking for a place Mr Raffles had described as Old Mackenzie's workshop, and that it was somewhere by the docks, and that I really had to get there as urgently as possible.

'Mackenzie's?' Mr Manders looked surprised. 'Why, that's the place young Humpty Boynton's taken, isn't it? He's enjoying himself enormously, dropping hints at the club about some devilry he's up to down there. Of course, we're not supposed to know where exactly, but Raffles dug around and discovered it was Mackenzie's. It's on Mustard Street, by Shadwell Basin. Here, I'll jot down the address for you.'

He produced a tiny notebook from inside his jacket and began to scribble something with a pencil.

'Although I should say, Miss, that if it's Humpty Dumpty you're after, you won't find him down there. Not right now, at any rate. He was at the club when I left, and he was very bucked up, babbling about having had a visitor who'd brought him the most tremendous bit of good news. Most of his crowd are bound for the Pemmingtons' ball tonight, and although he told me he had something pressing to attend to and might duck out early, I imagine he'll have to give the Pemmingtons an hour or two at least.'

Two minutes earlier, I had felt in a state of utter dejection, but my brief encounter with Mr Raffles' friend changed everything. I felt the energy flooding back into me, and with it, all the urgency that had launched me upon my unlikely expedition in the first place. Mr Boynton had just had a visitor, and a tremendous piece of good news. But he wasn't doing anything about it. Not straightaway. He might still be caught.

'Please, sir,' I asked eagerly, 'do you know the address of the Pemmingtons? I think that's where I need to go.'

'Of course. They're by St James's Park.' Mr Manders had been about to pass me the page torn from his notebook, but now he paused and added a second address to it. As he did so, we heard a slightly drunken voice calling to him from the direction of the Lord's pavilion.

'Is that you, Bunny? Get yourself up here. We were just talking about your skills as a cricketer. Kortright's going to bowl oranges at you...'

Mr Manders and the doorman exchanged rather rueful smiles, then the gentleman turned to me and, touching his hat, wished me well.

I had been right about the difficulty in finding a hansom. The streets around Lord's seemed eerily still. The big houses were all set back from the road with their shutters closed, so there were only the street lamps to light the way, their yellow light picking out the sparkle of frost beneath my feet.

My first thought was to head back to the Edgware Road, where the chances of a cab would be much greater. But the sight of those big houses reminded me of another visit to St John's Wood, only a few days earlier, and I realised I was already very close to the house of Mr Alma Tadema. Without really thinking of what I would say, or of how he could help me, or of whether calling uninvited at such an hour was at all proper, I turned my footsteps in that direction. I had no idea whether or not he and his wife kept a carriage. But at the very least they might have a footman who would help me flag down a cab.

If my encounter with Mr Manders felt like a change of luck, the sight that greeted me when I turned into Grove End Road proved that Fate had, indeed, decided to smile upon me. For there, parked firmly outside the front gate of Mr Alma Tadema's residence, dark and massive in the gaslight, was a very impressive carriage; and into that carriage was being helped, by an attentive footman, a figure I recognised at once.

'Miss Coburg!' I cried, my voice shockingly loud in the quiet street, and I scampered forward, with great haste but no great dignity, into her presence.

To my relief, she recognised me. Our encounter in the artist's studio had been, for me, a memorable one, but I had no idea if it had made a similar impression on her. However, after looking up at the sound of my cry, her face broadened into a smile.

'Goodness gracious! Miss Flotsam! Whatever are you doing here, all by yourself, at this hour?'

'I've found the Empingham Canary, ma'am! I know exactly who stole it. But now I've lost it again. And I need to get to the Pemmingtons' ball, and there are no carriages, and… and…'

And I burst into tears.

Chapter 17

After that, things seemed to happen very quickly.

Miss Coburg swept me into her carriage without any hesitation at all, and before she'd even asked my reasons had instructed her coachman to drive to the Pemmingtons' house in St James's. She then positioned me beside her, facing forward, on perhaps the deepest, most comfortable carriage cushion I had ever encountered, and instructed her companion, Miss Dalrymple, to provide me with a handkerchief. This lady, who I recognised as the silent chaperone from the studio, did as exactly as she was bid, and although her silent gaze did not exactly express approval, she didn't appear hostile either. She simply regarded me with extreme surprise, as though I were some inexplicable force of nature which had blown itself in through the carriage door.

'Now, Miss Flotsam,' my rescuer began as we lurched into motion, 'if you feel a little recovered, perhaps you would like to tell me how I can help?'

My lapse into tears had been a very temporary one, brought on, I think, by finding myself at last in the company of a friend, albeit one of very short acquaintance. I was already drying my eyes and apologising, explaining that I had been up before five to catch the earliest train to Amberley with Mrs Hudson, and now I was back again, but by myself, and perhaps rather more tired than I'd thought.

'And can it really be true, Miss Flotsam, that in the course of one day at Frawling Hall, you have solved a puzzle that has remained a mystery for the last twenty-three years?'

'Oh, no, ma'am. I mean, yes, in a way, but of course we'd already found out a great deal before we even went to Frawling. That thing Mr Alma Tadema told us about his Harlequin suit, for instance. I didn't see it at first, but I think Mrs Hudson did, and of course once I thought about it, it made the identity of the thief very obvious. But nothing seemed to make sense of the hens, until we heard about the high window, and then everything fitted into place, even the keys that smelled of hair oil, and…'

'Miss Flotsam.' Miss Coburg's voice was firm but not unkind. 'I really think you had better start at the beginning.'

And she was right, of course, but in my exhausted state it was hard to work out where the beginning was.

'Well, ma'am, first there were the hens. And, of course, Mr Cortado disappearing…'

'I think it would help me greatly,' Miss Coburg replied, 'if you were to start in Frawling Hall, that Christmas, twenty-three years ago, when the Empingham Canary disappeared. It is no doubt a failing of mine, but I do like to be given things in a nice, simple order.'

Which seemed only fair. So I cast my mind back to the story Mr Alma Tadema had told us in his studio, and I began there.

'If you remember, ma'am, it all began when Lord Empingham's horrid cousin, Mr Snaresdon, insisted that the canary should be locked away for the night, with his man Savage to guard it. As Mr Alma Tadema remembers all too well, it was a terrible insult to the assembled company, and I rather wonder if it was the cause of everything that followed. If Mr Snaresdon had been content to leave the bird on the tree that night, and hadn't made any threats about melting it down, I think he would probably have been able to carry it away with him, safe and sound, the following day.

'But he did make those threats, ma'am, which was horribly cruel of him, and I suppose everyone there was repelled at the thought that something so beautiful should be destroyed out of spite. And, of course, they must have felt for their host, because the destruction of the bird would have broken his heart. So when Mr Snaresdon made that ridiculous fuss about locking Savage in the Tower Room to prevent any of the guests stealing the canary, well, ma'am, I imagine that to some of those present that night, it might have sounded rather like a challenge.'

Miss Coburg smiled.

'I imagine it would. If I were a daring young man faced with behaviour of that sort, I like to think I would have had a try for it myself.'

'Yes, ma'am. And, of course, all the gentlemen there that night *were* young men, weren't they? The Earl of Brabham was the oldest, and although nowadays it's rather hard to imagine him ever being young, back then he was still in his thirties. Their wives were all young, too, of course.'

'Their wives, Miss Flotsam? But surely you aren't suggesting...?'

A jolt of the carriage interrupted her question, so I hurried on.

'After dinner that night, ma'am, Mr Snaresdon and Lord Empingham locked Savage in the Tower Room with the canary. There were only two keys, and each of the gentlemen retained one, stating publicly that they intended to sleep with them beneath their pillows to ensure that there could be no foul play of any sort.'

'Another challenge, surely, Miss Flotsam?' Miss Coburg was smiling again. 'I find myself liking this thief more and more.'

'Yes, ma'am. So do I. Anyway, drinks were served in the library after that, but by ten o'clock the party had retired and the house was being put to bed. Now, ma'am, if you *had* been there, and if you really did want to have a go at snatching the canary from under Mr Snaresdon's nose, what would you do next?'

'That's simple, Miss Flotsam. I would wait until I was confident everyone else was asleep, then I would attempt to creep out and steal one of the keys.'

'And which key would you steal, ma'am? Bearing in mind that Lord Empingham and Mr Snaresdon were sleeping at different ends of the house.'

'Why, the nearest one, I suppose.' Miss Coburg considered the problem. 'The more creeping about you do, the greater the likelihood that someone will spot you.'

I nodded my agreement.

'And, forgiving the personal question, ma'am, what would you wear for this adventure?'

'You mean clothes?' Again Miss Coburg took her time to think. 'Well, I would slip on whatever practical clothing came to hand. For a man, that would be easy. But of course, there's a danger I might be spotted, so it would be sensible to wear something that wouldn't easily identify me. And in this case...'

I watched her face changing as realisation dawned.

'Exactly, ma'am. Every gentleman staying at Frawling Hall that night, with the exception of Mr Snaresdon and Mr Savage, had brought with him his own Harlequin suit and mask. Now, the whole point of those suits is that they all look exactly the same. The ladies, who have to dress as Columbina, are expected to appear in outfits that set them apart, but for the gentlemen it's easy – all they have to do is bring a simple suit in black and white diamonds – something that looks a bit like pyjamas – with a mask to match.'

Miss Coburg had clearly grasped the point.

'So, Miss Flotsam, if I wished to make sure that I would not be identified as I crept around the corridors of Frawling Hall, my Harlequin suit would be the obvious choice.'

'But what if you didn't have one, ma'am?'

'Every gentleman *did* have one, Miss Flotsam. Excepting Mr Snaresdon, of course, who surely didn't plan to rob himself, and Mr Savage, who was locked up in the tower.'

I nodded happily.

'Yes, ma'am. That's how we could be so absolutely sure of the thief's identity. It was someone who didn't have a Harlequin suit of their own. That's why they borrowed Mr Alma Tadema's. And as all the gentlemen had their own suits...'

Miss Coburg was a very fine lady, so it would be wrong to say that she gaped. But for a moment, at least, her jaw did drop a little.

'A woman!'

Even Miss Dalrymple appeared surprised. She was sunk so deeply in the shadow of the opposite seat that I'd almost forgotten about her, but now she muttered beneath her breath something which sounded like 'Lordy me!'

'But which one?' Miss Coburg asked, still looking a little astonished. 'No, wait! I'm not thinking straight. Whichever lady it was, she would surely have taken her own husband's suit, rather than run the risk of stealing one from a stranger. So if Mr Alma Tadema's Harlequin suit was the one used, well, it must have been *Mrs* Alma Tadema who took it!'

But there was no triumph in Miss Coburg's voice, and she was shaking her head.

'No, Miss Flotsam, that can't be right. I know Laura Alma Tadema too well, and I know how deeply puzzled and anxious she is about this whole affair. And although an admirable woman, she is surely not capable of such an impulsive and reckless undertaking.'

'I agree, ma'am. And it was Mrs Alma Tadema who first came to us in Baker Street to ask Mr Holmes to investigate. But if not her, it must have been the only lady staying in Frawling Hall that night whose husband didn't have a Harlequin suit of his own. There was only one. It must have been Mr Snaresdon's own wife.'

My companion leaned back onto the deep velvet cushions and took my hand, as if to indicate that she needed a moment or two to digest the news. I was dimly aware that the carriage was moving very slowly, and realised that we were edging our way down the Edgware Road, one small part of a long queue of carriages, all of them heading into town. Just then, however, our slow progress didn't upset me. It felt good, for a little while at least, to sit somewhere safe and comfortable, in the company of someone kind who wished to hear my tale.

'She was the young Greek lady,' my companion recalled. 'We were discussing the whole business only this afternoon, and Mrs Alma Tadema clearly took a liking to her. But can you really be so certain, Miss Flotsam?'

'Well, ma'am, according to Hawkins, the butler, Mrs Snaresdon was the only lady who joined the gentlemen in the library after dinner, so none of the others would have known that Mr Alma Tadema's Harlequin suit was going to be hanging behind his bedroom door, awaiting alterations.'

'But, Miss Flotsam, even assuming she had the courage, and the daring, and the imagination, to come up with such a plan, why on earth would she want to steal from her own husband?'

'For the same reason, I suppose, ma'am, that all the other guests wanted to. Because she knew him to be a brute who was about to destroy a very beautiful work of art. Because she wanted to spare Lord Empingham the pain of seeing his canary melted down. Because she wanted to see her husband taken down a peg or two.' I shrugged. 'Quite simply, I suppose, because she didn't like him very much, and didn't like what he intended, and loved the idea of doing something about it.'

'But to run such a risk... To dare so much...'

'Indeed, ma'am. From what I've heard of her husband, he would not have taken kindly to it.'

Miss Coburg frowned.

'All this is very well, Miss Flotsam, and I understand the significance of the missing Harlequin suit. But even if Mrs Snaresdon did indeed plan to steal her husband's ornament, how could she have done it? We both heard our painter friend explain to us why it was impossible that the canary could ever have been removed from the tower.'

'Yes, ma'am. Mr Alma Tadema thinks it was impossible because he knows Savage still had the bird at midnight. And no one could have entered the tower at all between midnight until a little after six o'clock in the morning, because Mr Snaresdon had booby-trapped the library door with a Queen Anne chair. Then, after the butler moved the chair, it was probably less than two minutes before the housemaid entered the library and started to clean it, and no one could have left the tower unobserved after that. But that little gap between the butler moving the chair and returning with the maid was far too short for someone to enter the library, climb the tower, steal the bird and get away again.'

'My point precisely, Miss Flotsam!' Miss Coburg declared triumphantly. 'So Mrs Snaresdon couldn't have done it.'

'But you see, ma'am, Mrs Snaresdon was already in the tower. She didn't have to climb the tower and steal the bird, then escape again, all in that little two-minute space of time. By the time the butler moved the chair, she was already waiting to make her escape.'

'But how *could* she have been, Miss Flotsam? As I remember it, Savage was woken up at midnight, and told his master that everything was in order. And, as you've just said, no one could possibly have entered his room after that until the butler moved the chair the following morning. So if Savage was telling the truth...'

I nodded.

'Inspector Dickinson believes he *was* telling the truth, ma'am. And I think so too. You see, Mrs Snaresdon *was* in the room when Savage woke up, he just didn't know it.'

'You mean she was hidden?'

'Yes, ma'am. But the only place she could have been hidden was behind the shutter on the west window. And today, when I saw for myself how high the west window was, that was when the hens made sense.'

'The hens, Miss Flotsam?' She said it faintly. 'Mr Alma Tadema has told me all about the unexpected deliveries of poultry. But I confess myself utterly bewildered as to their relevance.'

The more questions Miss Coburg asked, the more I warmed to her, and I reassured her that I too had found the hens the most difficult thing to explain.

'Until I heard about the height of the west window, ma'am. Too high for someone to reach unaided. Then it all became clear.'

Miss Coburg gave a despairing shrug of her shoulders, and with a little wave of her hand bade me to continue.

'Well, ma'am, it's really quite simple. Mrs Snaresdon waited until her husband was asleep and slipped the key from under his pillow. She knew Mr Alma Tadema's Harlequin suit would be hanging behind his bedroom door, and the rooms she and her husband had been given were very close to his, so she stole in and took it and put it on, along with the mask too, of course. Then she crept to the library, entered the tower and slipped into the Tower Room.

'She wouldn't have risked a lantern, because she knew Savage had been told to sleep with one set of shutters open, which meant that someone moving around with a light could be seen from other parts of the house. But the clouds had cleared, and although there was no moon, there was light reflected from the snow, so once her eyes were accustomed to it, she must have been able to see enough to make her way up the tower stairs and into the room at the top. This was all just before midnight, ma'am.'

'I see.' Miss Coburg was all attention. 'And, of course, something disturbed her husband at around that time, didn't it? I suppose he must have heard her in the corridor. So he stumbled out of bed and went to rouse Mr Alma Tadema. And if I recall correctly, they spent a minute or two searching up and down the corridors before they went to the tower.'

'Exactly, ma'am. Mr Snaresdon and his wife had been given adjoining rooms, so he didn't notice she was gone, and luckily for her, he didn't think to take his key with him. It's scary to think of it, though, isn't it? She must have been there, in the Tower Room, tiptoeing around in the shadows, when she heard him storming up the stairs, shouting for Savage, demanding to know if everything was all right. But we know Savage was sleeping heavily. It took a little while to rouse him, and longer for him to light the lamp.'

'During which time she hid.' Miss Coburg smiled sweetly, her face lit up by the fleeting glow of a street lamp. 'Except there was nowhere to hide, because you've already told me that the window with the closed shutter was too high for her to reach.'

'Too high for her to reach *unaided*,' I corrected her patiently. 'But she wasn't unaided. She had a companion.'

'An accomplice!' Miss Coburg said it with great relish, clearly delighted at the turn the story had taken.

'No, ma'am. Not an accomplice. Just someone she'd bumped into.'

My companion took a very deep breath.

'Are you trying to tell me, Miss Flotsam, that there were *two* thieves at work in the Tower Room that night?

And that neither had been aware of the intentions of the other?'

'Yes, ma'am. Of course, it did cross my mind that Mrs Snaresdon might somehow have known one of the other members of the party. But it would have been a remarkable coincidence, as she was only recently arrived from Greece, and came from very different circles. And also, of course, there was the business of the two keys.'

'Two keys?'

Miss Coburg sounded resigned, as though new and strange revelations had been coming with such frequency that they no longer surprised her.

'Yes, ma'am. It's a bit complicated, but Inspector Dickinson proved that both keys had been used that night. Now, if the two thieves were working together, why would they have needed both keys? To steal one was risky enough, but to take both – well, it's just pointless and unnecessary. And the same applies to actually stealing the canary. Why did they both need to go into the Tower Room? Much more sensible for one to keep watch in the library, to distract anyone who came along.'

'Perhaps they were afraid of that man Savage?' Miss Coburg suggested. 'They may have felt that two pairs of hands were needed, in case it came to a struggle.'

'But they weren't those sort of thieves, ma'am. They were relying on stealth. So it would have been much more sensible for one to creep in and for one to keep watch. I think that when Mrs Snaresdon arrived in the Tower Room, she either disturbed another Harlequin in the act of stealing the canary, or she was disturbed by one. It must have been an alarming moment for them both. And of course, before either of them could get away, perhaps at the very moment they encountered each other, they heard Mr Snaresdon storming up the stairs.'

I was interrupted by a little grunt, which came not from Miss Coburg but from Miss Dalrymple, and which was followed once again by a muttered, 'Lordy me!'

'They must have only had a few seconds,' I went on. 'Surely not even half a minute. But I stood in that room earlier today, ma'am, and it's very obvious that there's only one place to hide. Even in semi-darkness it would have been obvious. What's remarkable is that they must have realised it together, and worked together – two strangers, each helping the other, barely exchanging a word for fear of waking Savage. It's a high window, ma'am, and a small ledge, but they must have managed to get up there, and to pull the shutter closed behind them, before Savage was properly awake.'

'And this other thief, Miss Flotsam – if indeed such another thief really existed – have you been able to work out his identity too?'

'Oh, yes, ma'am. That's very obvious. It must have been Mr Cortado. When his friend came to see Mr Holmes in Baker Street, we were given a description of a man who had no interests in anything but the violin, and no real passion for anything but practice. That Mr Cortado seemed rather a sorry fellow, I thought. But I see now that there had once been a very different Mr Cortado, the one Mr Raffles once knew, who before his marriage had been a dashing fellow. Dashing enough to rise to the challenge presented by the horrible Mr Snaresdon. He and Mrs Snaresdon didn't compare notes, ma'am, but they both formed the same plan at the same time, and they both had the nerve to carry it out. I think they deserved their luck.'

Miss Coburg nodded.

'I said I liked this thief, and now it turns out that I like *two* thieves, not one. My grandmother would be scandalised! But it *was* luck, wasn't it, Miss Flotsam? Tremendous luck. For if either had been trapped in the Tower Room alone, they would certainly have been discovered.'

'Yes, ma'am. But they weren't so lucky after that. They must have expected Savage to fall asleep again fairly quickly, and then they'd have been able to creep down from their window ledge, and steal the canary and escape. Instead, he started reading Keats, ma'am, and he carried on doing it for *six hours*. I mean, ma'am, I don't mind a little bit of Keats myself, but six hours of it is surely more than most people would be able to bear.'

'And the two Harlequins remained trapped behind their shutter for all that time?'

'Yes, ma'am.'

When I'd first begun to piece it all together, that scene had struck me as remarkable, and when I paused to imagine it all over again, it seemed no less so. The two of them together in the darkness, time limping by, and the terrible, relentless cold. Outside, only the snow and the stars.

'It's not a very big window ledge,' I explained. 'Only really big enough for one. They must have been squeezed very close together. And it must have been freezing. Savage was sleeping under blankets, in his clothes, but those two were in thin Harlequin suits. It seems to me...'

I felt myself blushing.

'It seems to me, ma'am, that if they hadn't been pressed so closely together, they couldn't have stayed up there so long. One person alone would have frozen. But the two of them...'

I blushed again.

'I suppose, if they wrapped themselves around each other... Well, bodies are very warm, aren't they, ma'am?'

For the first time, Miss Coburg appeared a little disapproving, pursing her lips and narrowing her eyes slightly until she looked a bit like the Queen.

'Well, really, Miss Flotsam! Mrs Snaresdon was a married woman! To allow such proximity, even for a short time would be... No, I cannot approve of such conduct!'

But then she paused, and I watched her face soften, and she stopped looking like the Queen. I saw a little smile play at the corner of her lips.

'And yet...'

She hesitated.

'And yet, Miss Flotsam, the picture you paint reminds me of things I used to imagine when I was a child. My family are rather stern, you see – famously so – and propriety is valued above all things. But when I was a child of eight or nine, I would read improper novels borrowed from the servants, and I would imagine myself escaping from my world dressed as a cabin boy and setting sail for the Indies. Or stowing away with a companion, and crouching, hidden in the fo'c'sle, while a tall ship sailed into the night. Or wandering the souks of Samarkand disguised as Ali Baba, and dazzling a beautiful princess with my daring.'

She smiled and sighed and smiled again, then shook her head as if embarrassed by her own imaginings.

'More pertinently, of course, we must remember that Mrs Snaresdon was Greek, so I suppose some allowances must be made.'

It occurred to me that Mr Cortado had also been married and had also been prepared to remain hidden in very compromising circumstances, but Miss Coburg seemed more prepared to forgive him his improprieties.

'I think she was terribly unhappy, ma'am. I think they both were.' I imagined again the two of them, holding each other in silence, watching the stars. 'And I think something happened that night that neither of them ever forgot. A connection, I suppose.'

I didn't really have the words for it. But Miss Coburg did.

'A coming-home?'

'Yes, ma'am. A coming-home. That's it exactly.'

'You're a romantic, Miss Flotsam. But can you really be so sure? Theirs could simply be a tale of two irresponsible people who found themselves in a predicament of their own making, and had to wait in extreme discomfort until a very fierce man fell asleep and allowed them to escape.'

'Oh, no, ma'am! It was much more than that. We know it was, because of the hens.'

'Ah, yes. The hens.' Miss Coburg sighed. 'Tell me about the hens.'

'Well, don't you see, ma'am, the timing of the hens isn't just coincidence. After so many years, there was a reason why she sent them now.'

'She? So you believe Mrs Snaresdon sent the hens?'

'Well, of course, ma'am. After her husband died. That was a couple of months ago, you see, and for Mrs Snaresdon it must have changed everything. First of all, there was the canary. While her husband was alive, it had to be kept hidden at all costs, but with him gone it was finally safe to return it. I suppose it belongs to her now, or to her son perhaps – who seems to have inherited her sense of adventure, because he got himself a job as a footman at Frawling Hall.'

'Good lord! Why on earth would he have done that?'

'So that he could return the canary in person, of course. Because he had to do it anonymously, in a way that didn't draw attention to the fact that it was his mother who'd stolen it. And he's clearly a young man with a certain sense of style, because his plan was to return it to the top of the tree on the anniversary of its disappearance. But to make sure he could reach the top of the tree from the gallery at Frawling Hall, he had to damage two small Christmas trees and throw paint over a load of others.'

Miss Coburg eyed me sternly.

'Have you actually spoken to this man? Or is this just speculation on your part, Miss Flotsam?'

'Well, I admit I haven't spoken to him yet, ma'am, but he did call himself "Adam's son", which is a fairly big clue.'

My rescuer took a deep breath.

'Very well, Miss Flotsam. Now, get back to Mrs Snaresdon and the hens.'

'Well, ma'am, it would seem that she and her son must have begun planning the return of the canary almost as soon as her husband died. And it seems that the next thing she did was to send a message to the man in the Harlequin suit. It's as if she'd been waiting all that time for the moment when she was free. As soon as she was, she sent her message.'

'But not only to him, Miss Flotsam. She seems to have sent the same message to half the gentlemen there. If this is the love story you suppose, would she not have been a little more selective with her gifts?'

Again the image rose before me of the two figures, both dressed as Harlequin, pressed close together on their dark window ledge.

'I think, ma'am, that she didn't know for certain who he was.'

I expected this suggestion to be greeted with derision. Even as I said it, I knew it sounded a little absurd. But instead Miss Coburg stayed silent, her face full of thought.

'He was masked, wasn't he, Miss Flotsam?' she said at last. 'And it was dark. If they spoke at all, even if it was only a few words exchanged in whispers, then *he* would have known *her*. Her accent would have betrayed her. But one athletic young man in a party of athletic young men... Is it really possible that when they parted that morning, after so long in such close company, she still didn't know his name?'

'I think so, ma'am. But she did know he was married, because all the gentlemen were married except Mr Grey-Wilson, who had his arm in a sling, so she could be sure he wasn't the Harlequin. Then, if you remember, her husband took her back to Greece only a few days later, and they never returned, so she would never have encountered any of the gentlemen again. But I think she must have followed the careers of all those young men from a distance. It would have been easy to do, because all are prominent figures in their own way.'

'And finding herself a widow, Miss Flotsam, she decided upon a most bizarre way of contacting them all.'

'Not all of them, ma'am. Only the ones she knew were no longer married. All the gentlemen who received hens are widowers, except for one who is divorced. She made no effort to contact the married men, you see, only the men she knew to be free. And the messages weren't bizarre at all, ma'am. They *seem* bizarre to the rest of us, but I don't think that was the case for Mr Cortado. I think he understood her message at once. Perhaps he'd even been waiting for it.'

Miss Coburg looked puzzled.

'I understand why she sent a card with a harlequin pattern, Miss Flotsam, but what of the rest of it? What meaning could Mr Cortado see that the rest of us couldn't? And why on earth hens?'

'*French* hens, ma'am. The Empingham Canary was stolen on the third day of Christmas. But I suppose three French hens would have been too obvious, or just too hard to arrange. And then there were the little stars she drew on the cards. Seven stars. If you know your astronomy, ma'am, the Plough is made up of seven stars. I really should have seen it sooner, but I think Mr Cortado worked it out quickly enough, because two days later, having attempted to put his affairs in order, he walked away from everything and caught a train to Amberley.'

Once again I saw Miss Coburg's expression turn to one of disapproval.

'I understand Mr Cortado was about to become engaged.'

'Yes, ma'am. *Everyone* knew Mr Cortado was about to become engaged. That was his problem. Everyone was expecting it, which made it very hard for him to withdraw without humiliating the lady in question. And I think he was desperate to avoid that, which is why he decided to simply disappear. He left behind a rather silly message which was intended to suggest that some grim fate had befallen him.'

'Even so, Miss Flotsam, and leaving aside the questionable way in which he managed his disappearance, it was a very sudden change of heart.'

I thought of everything I'd been told about Miss Lavinia Burrows, and remembered my own brief encounter with her.

'I suspect his heart had never for a moment belonged to Miss Burrows, ma'am. But he had spent so many years living up to his wife's expectations, I don't think he could see any other path. Miss Burrows was clearly very dedicated to the advancement of his career. Perhaps more dedicated to his work than she was to him. And to Mr Cortado it must have felt as though his work was all he had. Until he received the hen.'

Miss Coburg nodded slowly, not really looking at me.

'We do not all get to choose our own paths, Miss Flotsam. I know a little about what it is like to steer a course charted by others.'

'But if the chance came, ma'am? If by a miracle someone you'd spent years thinking about suddenly reappeared and offered you an escape, wouldn't you take it? If you saw the opportunity to marry the person who…'

But she interrupted me.

'I shall never marry, Miss Flotsam. Circumstances will never allow. But perhaps the dreaming schoolgirl within me has not been utterly extinguished, because I am not entirely without sympathy for Mr Cortado. That dream – to slip the leash and wander the dusty roads in search of adventure – it can be very strong. So tell me, what has become of this famous violinist now?'

'I saw him this very evening, ma'am. From a distance, with Mrs Snaresdon. They looked… happy.'

I had turned away from my companion, looking out of the carriage window at the lines of shops and houses. We were making slow progress, and had still not quite reached the Marble Arch. When I turned back, I realised that Miss Coburg was looking at me strangely.

'Why does it feel, Miss Flotsam, as though the story of Mrs Snaresdon and Mr Cortado means rather more to you than just the solution of a puzzle? I said before that you were a romantic, but I sense it's something more.'

And I suppose she was right. But it was all mixed up in my head. The funny feeling I had when I thought about Scraggs' shop failing… All that silliness about Clara Fazakerley… Maximillian Cortado practising on his violin all day, every day, never complaining, but sometimes walking out to look up at the stars. The same stars. The ones he'd seen that night, from the tower of Frawling Hall.

And to my surprise, I found I was saying it all aloud. Perhaps because Miss Coburg, although friendly, was a stranger, someone I'd probably never see again; perhaps because she appeared practical and business-like, and not at all sentimental. I told her about Scraggs and his shop, and how Trevelyan's would close if people didn't start going there very soon; about how Scraggs had told Mrs Hudson that, if he lost everything, he'd have to go for a soldier. I told her about Clara Fazakerley, and her infatuation with Dumpty Boynton, and how everyone had known it was just a young woman being foolish, but how I'd found myself wanting it not to be, for reasons I couldn't really understand; and how, when it was, I felt stupidly sad.

'I suppose, ma'am, it's because Clara Fazakerley seemed to find it all so simple. I think I just liked the idea of someone *knowing*. For certain. Straightaway. Without any doubts or complications. And being so happy about it. Because I don't seem to know anything at all, or else I know too many things and they all confuse each other.

And then, when I worked out that Mrs Snaresdon and Mr Cortado had been trapped together for one night, and had never forgotten it, and how, so many years later, Mr Cortado had simply taken off his boater and caught the train to Amberley... Well, I suppose, ma'am, I wanted it to be true, and it seems it *is* true, and I'm glad it is. But perhaps I'm a little jealous too. Jealous of so much *certainty*.'

I stopped, but Miss Coburg didn't say anything. I realised she was still holding my hand, and she seemed to be looking out into the night. Miss Dalrymple, from the shadow opposite, was watching her.

'I think, Flotsam, love comes to us in many different ways. We don't choose how, or who. All we can do is welcome it when it comes, and cherish it for as long as it lasts.'

She gave my hand a little shake, and smiled.

'And as for the young gentleman friend you've mentioned, well, I'd urge you not to worry. He sounds an admirable young man. I'm quite certain his venture will prosper.'

Which was kind, I thought, but not as reassuring as she intended. Miss Coburg struck me as sensible and perhaps even rather wise, but when it came to the fate of Trevelyan's, no quantity of kind-hearted words could make a difference.

Then suddenly the carriage began to gather pace, and I saw we had reached Hyde Park. There would be time later to fret about Trevelyan's. I had a canary to save.

Chapter 18

The Pemmingtons' house in St James's was one of those very fine houses so surrounded by other fine houses that you barely noticed it. Until, of course, you passed it when a ball was in progress, when its windows blazed and its front door stood open behind a small battalion of footmen, and a little queue of carriages formed and re-formed for two dozen yards on either side.

Miss Coburg had given her coachman instructions to make haste, and I don't know what arguments he used to accomplish it, but he seemed to impress the footmen so greatly with a sense of our urgency that we were waved forward to the front of the queue with barely a moment lost.

'No, Miss Flotsam.' Miss Coburg held out a restraining finger when I made to get down from the carriage. 'Newton will go in and make enquiries. You should remain with me until we know if the man you're seeking is actually here. Mr Boynton, I think you said? No, I don't know him. I expect we move in different circles. But if he's here, I'm sure we can flush him out.'

Her footman disappeared up the front steps with some haste, and when he reappeared some short time later, he was accompanied by an elderly gentleman in very smart evening dress with a moustache that would have made a walrus proud, a gentleman who, to my great surprise, turned out to be none other than Mr Pemmington himself. I would have expected the sort of man who owned such a house and who threw such a ball to be far too grand to deal with my enquiry in person, but he proved remarkably obliging and willing to help, approaching our carriage window with an extravagantly courteous bow, and addressing himself in the most respectful manner to Miss Coburg, until that lady indicated with a nod that it was to me he needed to speak.

'I fear, madam,' he began, with another little bow, 'that Mr Humphrey Boynton has already departed. He is an acquaintance of my son's, who tells me he had urgent business to attend to. I regret, madam, he gave no indication of the nature of his business, except in the most colloquial terms.' Mr Pemmington looked a little embarrassed. 'I believe he told my boy that he had what he called a very hot potato on his hands, and he needed to take it somewhere to, in his words, er, *get it mashed.*'

I felt my heart begin to sink, but remembered that I did at least have an address for the place where this act of violence was going to take place. It seemed that, after all, I would have to follow him to his lair.

'The young man danced with several ladies, ma'am,' Mr Pemmington continued, 'and I have asked my daughter to make enquiries, in case he mentioned his next destination to any of them.'

Having made this report, he retired with another little bow, and I turned hurriedly to Miss Coburg.

'I shall have to go to Shadwell Basin, ma'am!' I told her, explaining about Mr Boynton's workshop in Mustard Street. 'I think he really does have the bird, and that he's going to do something terrible.'

'He must be stopped,' my companion agreed firmly, 'but Miss Flotsam, you cannot possibly go alone.' She glanced rapidly across at Miss Dalrymple, who was shaking her head. 'And I regret that I cannot accompany you to such a place, and on such a mission. I am a woman who enjoys many privileges, but there are certain boundaries I know not to cross. Were my family to discover that I had taken myself off to the docks, at night, with only you for company, why, there would be a terrible outcry!'

I completely understood, and it had never actually occurred to me that she might accompany me to so disreputable a location. So I explained to her that I would surely be able to find a hansom cab to take me, and that I was already more than grateful for all the help she'd given me.

'But, Miss Flotsam, I really cannot permit it. What can you do, alone, even if you were to find this gentleman? You would be placing yourself in terrible danger.'

I reached out and took hold of the carriage door handle.

'Really, ma'am, I must try. I've been to worse places than Shadwell Basin. I'm sure I'll be all right. And I haven't a moment to lose.'

Miss Coburg studied me carefully for a moment, and seemed to make a decision.

'Very well.' Her footman was still waiting respectfully on the pavement, and she signalled for him to help me down. 'Please hail a cab for Miss Flotsam, Newton. And then – I believe we are just around the corner from Carlton House Terrace? In that case, I would like to call at No 10.'

I said my farewell from the pavement, and thanked my rescuer all over again, then made haste to the place, twenty yards further along the street, where Newton was flagging down a passing hansom.

As I approached him, I heard an excited and familiar voice calling my name, and I turned to see none other than Miss Hetty Peters scurrying after me, pulling on her coat as she did so, while trying not to drop an expensive-looking fur muff which was wedged rather awkwardly under one armpit.

'Oh, Flottie! I knew it must be you! Here, will you please take this while I try to get my arm through this sleeve? That's right, the muff, not the coat... Perfect! Now, where are we going? And why are you looking for Dumpty Boynton? Because he's not at all the sort of company you ought to be keeping, Flottie. When I heard Grace Pemmington saying that her father was trying to find him because a lady was outside asking and apparently it was urgent... Well, it's a most peculiar thing for a host and his daughter to be running around asking about in the middle of their own ball, so it was obvious that something important and peculiar was up, and I did just wonder who the lady might be, so I peeped out of the window, and saw you getting down from a very grand carriage, although, of course, I couldn't be sure it was you from up there, but I thought it was, and, well, here I am! Where are we going?'

'But Hetty,' I replied, aware that Newton, the footman, was regarding her with a rather strange expression, 'shouldn't you be at the ball?'

I confess I was extraordinarily pleased to see her, but for a young lady to dash away from an engagement on a whim, unaccompanied and without explanation, was probably not the sort of conduct a respectable footman often encountered.

'No one will miss me in the slightest, Flottie! And to be honest, I'm delighted to get away. Rupert isn't here because he's at the Christmas gathering of the Entomology Society, which I think is to do with insects, although it might be snakes or, knowing Rupert, quite possibly slugs, but my uncle *is* here because he and Mr Pemmington once stalked tigers together, or maybe deer or otters, I can never remember. And of course I can never really enjoy myself at a gathering when Uncle's present because I'm always slightly afraid that someone will mention Tariff Reform and that he'll explode by the rum punch.'

She aimed a dazzling smile at Newton, and allowed him to hand her into the hansom, without once pausing for breath.

'Thank you so much! Of course, Flottie, if I had stayed, I might have danced with the Billington boys, which is always quite fun, but they're still moping around after the Portman girl, whose eyes really *are* rather like forest pools, and, to make matters worse, I'm afraid Potty Peasmarsh has developed something of a soft spot for me, because he's been following me around all evening trying to show me his magic tricks again, even though he only really knows two, and I worked out ages ago how they were both done. I think he does it because he really doesn't have any conversation at all, poor lamb, and so I told him it was time for *me* to vanish, and please would he tell my uncle that I'd gone home with a headache. Now, back to Dumpty Boynton. He *is* a cad, isn't he? And you're about to prove it!'

So, as Newton nodded to the cab driver and our hansom pulled away, I started to explain to her about the Empingham Canary, and the strange coincidence of Roscoe, the Frawling groundsman, being drunk in Baker Street, and asked her if she thought it was possible that Dumpty Boynton might really be dabbling in stolen goods.

'Goodness me, yes,' she replied without hesitation. 'That's exactly the sort of thing he'd do. He likes to think of himself as the bad boy, you see, who can look down on everyone else because he's just so clever and naughty. I blame Eton. No, really, I do. His cousin is an Etonian too, and makes up his own dance steps, because doing the same dance steps as everyone else is beneath him, and if he treads on your toes while he's doing them, he just smirks, as if to say that you're lucky to have your toes trodden on by someone so brilliant. And don't even start me on that dreadful Boating Song...'

It was strangely calming to have Miss Peters beside me, prattling away, as the cab picked up speed along the Embankment. Gradually, as we continued eastwards past Blackfriars, the streets grew quieter. It began to feel colder too, and as we left the festive, brightly adorned streets of Westminster behind us, Hetty and I huddled a little closer together for warmth. All along Queen Victoria Street, heading towards the City, then along Cannon Street, Miss Peters kept up a happy stream of chatter, asking questions about Frawling Hall, marvelling at Dumpty Boynton's depravity, and eager to know more about my rescuer.

'Miss Coburg, you say, Flottie? I'm not sure I know any Coburgs. And you're sure she was not going to the Pemmingtons' ball?'

'Very sure, Hetty. When I left her she was about to pay a visit to a friend in Carlton House Terrace.'

This seemed to puzzle Miss Peters greatly.

'Carlton House Terrace? What sort of person lives there? Perhaps, Flottie, she is a *courtesan*?'

The idea seemed to please her greatly.

After Eastcheap, as we neared Tower Hill, we both grew quieter. Here we could smell the river, and as we entered East Smithfield, we could glimpse St Katharine's Dock through the gaps between warehouses – tall masts and rigging, and even at that time of night, the scraping of winches and the calls of dockers unloading cargo. Somewhere overhead a gull cried in the darkness, and I shivered. This was a strange place to be seeking someone who'd just left the Pemmingtons' ball.

Shadwell Basin lay in darkness, and the streets around it were much quieter than around St Katherine's. To reach it we had to leave St George Street, then turn right, into the heart of the docklands, where the narrow lanes were flanked by dark warehouses, so high they blocked out the stars. Our driver was getting a little restive now, keen to be dropping us so he could return to more salubrious spots.

'Nearly there,' he told us curtly as we rattled over a bridge that connected two wharfs. The water beneath us was still, and black as mud. We passed a street called Milk Yard and a minute or so later the cab drew to a halt.

'Mustard Street,' the driver announced. 'You sure this is the place, Miss?'

I looked around. Mustard Street was another narrow lane, as dark as the others, lined with towering warehouses and workshops. About halfway along it, a brazier was burning, and gathered around the glowing coals were half a dozen muffled figures, their heads turned towards us, watching.

'Yes, I think this is the place,' I told him.

'You sure, Miss? There's a public house in Shadwell that's respectable enough. Sure you don't want me to drop you there?'

I glanced across at Miss Peters, who was looking at me hopefully. I looked down Mustard Street again, at the group of men watching us. And, just for a moment, nothing sounded nicer than a respectable public house. But I'd been to worse places than Mustard Street, and somewhere in its darkness the Empingham Canary lay waiting.

'We're quite sure,' I told the driver.

I watched him drive away, hoping that I hadn't made a terrible mistake.

'I have to say, Flottie,' Miss Peters told me, in a much smaller voice than usual, 'that all of a sudden the Pemmingtons' ball doesn't seem quite so unattractive. Looking at those gentlemen over there by that big fire thing, I really think I might prefer an evening with Potty Peasmarsh.'

She said it lightly, but neither of us were unaware of the danger we were in. I think I was on the brink of suggesting that we should simply turn away after all, and follow the cab towards busier, brighter streets. We could repair to the brightness of Shadwell High Street, perhaps, and look for a policeman to help us. But just as my resolution was wavering, a small, dark-skinned woman, very shabbily dressed, emerged from beneath an archway only a few yards ahead of us, carrying what appeared to be a basket of fish.

'Excuse me,' I called to her. 'Do you know where we can find Old Mackenzie's workshop?'

She turned in surprise at the sound of my voice, then looked even more surprised when she saw the two of us standing there.

'Mackenzie's? Yes, dearie. It's just up there. Them fellas will show you.'

She took another look at us.

'But what business could you two young ladies have in a place like that?' she asked.

'We're looking for someone,' I told her firmly. 'It's really important.'

She hesitated, then nodded towards the men at the brazier.

'Go and ask Big John. He'll show you.'

Big John proved to be neither very big nor particularly small, but he did have an impressive series of scars all across one side of his face. He wasn't the sort of person I would normally have approached for directions. He watched us with a blank stare as we approached, and when I asked him for Old Mackenzie's workshop, he looked at me just as blankly.

'I'm looking for Mr Boynton,' I added. 'Humphrey. Humpty Dumpty. The Egg,' I added, guessing desperately.

'Ah! The Egg.' He looked relieved. 'Should have said that straightaway. But how can I be sure you're not police?'

This was evidently a ridiculous question, and it struck me that Big John's was not the most powerful of intellects.

'Do we look like the police?' I sighed.

I heard his companions chuckle.

'Can't be too careful, John,' one of them sniggered. 'That one looks just like a Scotland Yard inspector to me.'

'Itching to get the cuffs on you, she is,' suggested another with a laugh.

'She might be hiding a truncheon in that muff,' added a third.

This remark, which could perhaps be understood in more ways than one, was met with general hilarity by everyone except Big John.

'Second arch on the right,' he muttered gruffly. 'He's just arrived. He's got Big Alf firing up the furnace for him.'

The inhabitants of Mustard Street were clearly not the most original thinkers when it came to nicknames, but I wasn't going to be the one to point it out. Instead, I simply smiled politely and drew Miss Peters with me in the direction he'd indicated. We were, it seemed, safe — for a little while, at least.

When I look back on that evening, I realise how important it was that we had surprise on our side. Had Humphrey Boynton entertained even the smallest fear of being followed, he could simply have slid the bolt in the heavy door that guarded Old Mackenzie's workshop, and that one act would surely have thwarted us. We would have been left helpless in the mud and muck of that alley for the whole of the freezing night.

But the door was not bolted, and we didn't bother to knock. I turned the handle and shoved it open with my shoulder, all in one movement, with the result that I rather stumbled inside, and down a couple of steps, while Miss Peters stepped in after me, unruffled and with great dignity.

It was a striking scene: a low room, slightly below street level, its narrow windows blackened by soot, lit in one corner by an oil lamp, but mostly illuminated by the high flames of a fierce fire, burning in what looked like an enormous iron cauldron. The flames were being fed by a man in a leather apron and leather gloves, a man with fewer scars than Big John, and not a great deal taller, but with an infinitely more forbidding expression. His face and apron were touched with the orange glow of the flames, and all around him, littering a work bench and hanging from hooks on the walls, were bulky iron rods and metal crucibles of different sizes, and hefty moulds laid out ready to receive delivery of molten metal. At first glance, Big Alf might have been a god of the underworld at work on some infernal construction had it not been for his almost bald pate, which, with a touch of the ridiculous, caught the glow of the fire and looked like a large and strangely shiny orange.

A few feet away from him, in the corner by the oil lamp, a young gentleman in evening dress stood examining the contents of a small wooden box.

At different times I'd imagined Humphrey Boynton in different ways – either as the handsome charmer who had dallied with Miss Fazakerley, or as a scheming villain whose evil heart would clearly be reflected in his face.

Now I saw that he was neither. He was just a presentable young man with a face that was neither handsome nor hideous, the sort of face you wouldn't really notice on a crowded omnibus. Had it not been for the impeccable cut of his clothes, he would simply have been very ordinary. But careful grooming and a well-paid tailor can work their magic on even the most ordinary material, and it was not hard to see how such a man, armed with the self-confidence of wealth and an overbearing sense of entitlement, might cut a swathe through certain circles of society.

As soon as we entered the room, and before we could make out its contents, he had slammed the box shut, looking up in alarm at our unexpected intrusion.

However, his alarm turned to amusement when he realised that Miss Peters and I constituted the entire invading party, and placing the wooden box beside the lamp, he stepped forward to meet us.

'Why, Miss Peters, I believe? Miss Fazakerley's friend. You appear to have followed me from the Pemmingtons', although I cannot imagine why. A secret passion, I hope, rather than a desire to lecture me about my moral failings in trifling with your friend's affections. And this young lady is…?'

He fixed me with an arch and artificially quizzical look, one eyebrow raised, and I realised he only appeared ordinary when his face was at rest. At other times, his expression was marred by a slightly sneering smile and a look of condescension which made me itch to kick him in the shins. No amount of kicking, however, was going to win back Lord Empingham's precious bird. If it came to a struggle, it was very clear that Mr Boynton and his accomplice had a decided advantage in terms of brawn.

'My name is Flotsam,' I told him, 'and I believe you have something that isn't yours. We've come for the Empingham Canary.'

He laughed out loud at that.

'Well, really, Miss Flotsam, I have never heard anything more ridiculous in my life. I shan't even bother with the usual protestations of innocence, because I *do* have it, right here. But why on earth would I hand it over to you? Perhaps you hope to win me over with some girlish pleading? In which case, please proceed! Tell me how beautiful it is, and what a barbarian I must be to destroy it, and how old Lord Empingham will go to his grave a broken man. I shall enjoy hearing your arguments while Alfred here gets the furnace up to temperature.'

I was aware of Miss Peters looking at me expectantly, waiting for a reply that would bring the man to his knees. But, of course, I had no reply, and no plan. I had simply blundered in without any sensible forethought whatsoever.

'There's no point in melting it down,' I told him, with as much confidence as I could muster. 'The game is up. Mr Sherlock Holmes and his associates know who stole the golden canary, and they know he brought it to you.'

He moved over to the door which was still hanging open behind us, took a deliberately theatrical look up and down the street outside, and closed it firmly.

'How careless of Mr Holmes and his associates not to come in person! Had they arrived with twenty policemen to back them up, I would have had no choice but to surrender. As it is, ladies...'

He returned to the wooden box and picked it up.

'As it is, the canary remains with me. In a moment, Alfred here will set to work with his pliers and whatnot to tear the gemstones from it, and what is left will be reduced in minutes to a puddle of hot bullion. You are welcome to watch. Afterwards I will deny it all, of course, and you will have no proof. Alfred and his friends outside are surprisingly loyal – it is amazing what degree of loyalty can be purchased for a relatively small sum in this part of London. And why would anyone choose to believe a pair of silly young women when two dozen of my old school chums will be ready to testify that dear old Dumpty is a bit of a joker, but a gentleman at all times, begad! As for the fellow who sold me this...'

He stroked the box rather lovingly.

'Well, he's a nobody, but he's rich enough now to disappear completely. I can't see anyone ever getting him into a witness box.'

'But *why*?' I asked him. I suppose it was the question that most plagued me. 'Why are you doing this? You can't need the money. So what's it all *for*?'

He looked at me with utter disdain.

'Of course I don't need the money. Are we ready yet, Alfred?'

His accomplice grunted and shook his head, and Dumpty Boynton turned back to me with a shrug.

'One evening, Miss Flotsam, a couple of years back, a friend took me to watch a rather bloody heavyweight bout in Bethnal Green. Afterwards, when the crowds were milling around, some shady old man drew me to one side and asked me if I'd like to buy his ring for a guinea. Well, it was obvious from the first that it wasn't his ring, and that it was worth a lot more than a guinea, and when I asked to examine it, I realised it was a ring which belonged to old Lord Collumpton. There'd been a bit of an outcry about it being stolen by one of his servants.'

He smiled at the recollection.

'Well, it just so happened that Lord Collumpton was not my favourite person at the time. There'd been a bit of unpleasantness between me and his son over a dog, and old Collumpton, who is a supercilious stuffed shirt at the best of times, had cut me rather pointedly at the Markham Club. So instead of apprehending the man who'd accosted me, I slipped him a guinea and took the ring. I think my first idea was to return it to Collumpton and make him feel like a fool for cutting me. But before I could do that, I heard he'd been bad-mouthing me at the Army & Navy, and it struck me that a better revenge would be to take his precious heirloom and make damned certain that he would never see it again.'

He gave a little, artificial yawn, as if to suggest that the descent into criminality was a mere nothing to someone as clever and quick-witted as himself.

'I won't bore you ladies with how I went about finding someone who would do my dirty work for me, but it was surprisingly easy. I had the old devil's ring melted down and recast into a pair of gold cufflinks, which I made a point of wearing to the Markham Club whenever I knew Collumpton would be present. Made damned sure he saw them, and I can't tell you how much pleasure it gave me to flaunt his family heirloom in his face without him knowing.'

He was still holding the wooden box, and now he eyed it with a strange, twisted smile. He looked almost gleeful.

'The thing is, when I next went back to the boxing, the same fellow recognised me and tried to sell me a diamond bracelet. I bought it, no questions asked, and told him to put the word around that I'd be interested in any items pilfered from the aristocracy, and that I'd pay good prices.'

'And then you just carried on?'

The longer he talked, the more time I had to come up with some sort of plan.

In reply, he raised one fist to the level of his face, revealing a little gold stud-link on his cuff.

'Behold, the Rutherford Tiara! Or what's left of it, at least. I wore these links when I went to see Henry Rutherford, just after the news had broken that his family's famous heirloom had been melted down. Henry Rutherford once gave me a thrashing at school, but I assured him there were no hard feelings. When we shook hands, I made sure my cuffs were fully in view!'

I should have been outraged. I should have been appalled. And perhaps I was a little of both those things. But strangely, as he talked, instead of feeling angry, I began to feel oddly sorry for the man in front of me. For all his fine clothes and Society connections, Humphrey Boynton was a rather pitiful figure, so taken up with proving how superior he was to others, that he seemed to have become all hollowed out inside.

'And now, ladies,' he concluded, lowering his fist and taking the box firmly in both hands, 'if you wish to stay, you may witness the last moments of another treasure. The gemstones will be sold, of course, but the gold? Well, I thought that some of it could be fashioned into a little bauble that I would send to Lord Empingham along with a note sympathising for his loss. It would amuse me to think that part of the Empingham Canary remained on the Christmas tree at Frawling Hall, unbeknown to everyone but me.'

I began to reply to this horrible and petty little bit of cruelty, but Mr Boynton carried on.

'No, Miss Flotsam, let me stop you before you begin to protest. There's nothing you can do. I learned at school that people like me can always get away with things. We simply deny them, and the school tie does the rest. And as you two are clearly in no position to stop me, I intend to proceed as planned.'

'Come, Flottie. We should go.'

To my surprise, Miss Peters chose this moment to speak for the first time, and her tone, although resigned, was surprisingly firm.

'He's right, you see. There's nothing we can do here, and those men outside are friends of his. Let's just promise to keep quiet, and go.'

I heard Dumpty Boynton chuckle. It was a dry, ugly sound.

'Very sensible. Unpleasant things can happen to young women in places like this, can't they, Alf? Very unpleasant things. But if you two run away like good little girls, and promise to keep your mouths shut, I'll make sure my friends don't bother you as you go. So, go on. Scram!'

Miss Peters was nodding very earnestly, but to my surprise made no real movement to the door.

'We will. We *do* promise. We do. It was ever so foolish of us to come.' She paused. 'But, please, Mr Boynton, before we go, might we be allowed just a little look at Lord Empingham's canary? I've heard so much about it. Is it indeed as beautiful as they say?'

Mr Boynton smiled, clearly enjoying this little victory.

'It's not a bad piece of work, Miss Peters. See for yourself.'

And with that, he opened the lid of the wooden box and held it out to show us.

There are some moments in life you never forget, and I shall never forget my first sight of the Empingham Canary. Even in that low, dingy workshop, in that strange orange light, I understood at once why it meant so much to Lord Empingham. I had imagined it as rather gaudy – too much gold and too many jewels, a display of wealth rather than a piece of craftsmanship.

But I saw in that moment that I was entirely wrong. It was quite simply exquisite. Perhaps the best way to convey its magic is to say that when you looked at it, you didn't even notice the gold or the gems. What you saw was a bird, so perfect, so real, it might have been alive, its head slightly cocked, its wings unfurled as if poised to take flight. In that flickering light, it seemed, for a moment, to be watching me.

By my side, I heard Miss Peters gasp, and she reached out, entranced, taking the box from Mr Boynton and raising it close to her face. Mr Boynton allowed her to take it, the smile of triumph still on his lips, and I realised that the more ravished we were by the canary's beauty, the more he would enjoy the act of desecration.

'Oh, Flottie,' Miss Peters whispered, 'have you ever seen anything so lovely?'

I felt a lump forming in my throat, so I didn't reply, just shook my head.

Very quietly, and very sadly, Miss Peters closed the box.

'And truly, Mr Boynton, is there nothing we can say to stop your friend over there going about his business?'

We all looked across at Big Alf for a moment. He was standing watching us, waiting to begin. In that moment, he looked every bit as fierce and unrelenting as some brawny figure from the Underworld.

'No,' Miss Peters sighed. 'I know there is not. Come, Flottie, I really *can't* watch. I just can't.'

She thrust the box back into Mr Boynton's hands and turned to go, but I held her back.

'No, Hetty, we mustn't... I won't...'

'Flottie! There's nothing we can do. This was all a mistake. Please, let's just go. Right now. *Please!*'

I heard Mr Boynton give another low, unpleasant laugh.

'Your friend is very sensible, Miss Flotsam. But you're very welcome to stay and keep me and my associates company if you wish.'

And he tossed the heavy wooden box over to his accomplice, who caught it easily and set it down on his work bench before selecting a pair of iron rods from those hanging on the wall.

I think I must have made a move forward to stop him, because Mr Boynton moved across to block my path and simultaneously Miss Peters seized my arm.

'Please, Flottie! Let's just go.'

And dropping my arm she moved over to the door and raised her hand to the latch.

'Hetty...!' I began, pleading, but also a little outraged at the ease of her surrender. Before I could say anything else, however, three things happened at once.

Mr Boynton laughed, and gave me a little shove towards the door, as if to dismiss me.

Miss Peters succeeded in lifting the latch.

And Big Alf, by the furnace, opened the wooden box.

'Eh!' he cried out, bewildered. 'Where's it gone?'

Mr Boynton and I turned as one, and stared in his direction. He was holding the empty box in both hands, looking at us in confusion.

'*Now*, please, Flottie!' Miss Peters cried, pulling the door open with one hand and beckoning me frantically with the other, which was still hidden in her fur muff.

I think I must have been very slow to react. I remember feeling a rush of cold air as the door opened, and then almost immediately felt Mr Boynton's fingers closing around my arm. Perhaps it was his touch that roused me into action, because now it was my turn to shove *him*, and as I shook my arm free from his grasp, I pushed him away so violently that he stumbled into the oil lamp.

'*Now!*' Miss Peters called again, and this time she practically screamed it. But I needed no further urging, and as Mr Boynton struggled, cursing, to regain his balance, I was up the two steps and almost through the doorway, only to stumble and fall as I felt my ankle enclosed by a strong male hand.

'No, you don't!' a voice muttered, and I turned to see Big Alf behind me, his fist gripping me incredibly tightly.

He must have moved with surprising speed to have reached the door so quickly, and he'd had to dive to grab me, but there could be no doubting the strength of his fingers. Even though I kicked out at him as hard as I could, his hold didn't loosen, and as I squirmed on my back on the top step, still kicking desperately, he reached down to where my petticoat had ridden up, and seized my other ankle with the same steely grip.

But just as he was beginning to draw me back into the workshop, I heard Miss Peters' voice from just above my head.

'Let her go!' she cried, and I saw her step forward, above me, and aim a slap at my assailant's face.

It seemed a brave but useless piece of resistance, for Big Alf had broad shoulders and no neck, and looked like the sort of man who could take a punch, while Miss Peters' hand was not only small and rather delicate, but was still wrapped in her very soft fur muff. But to my utter astonishment, when the slap landed, I saw my captor's eyes open very wide, then turn glassy, and he crumpled to the ground as if pole-axed.

'Now!' Miss Peters cried again, as I scrambled to my feet and followed her through the door, into the darkness of the alley.

'This way!' she ordered, and was about to break into a run when I saw her stop abruptly.

After the bright glow of the furnace, Mustard Street seemed almost pitch black, and for a moment I couldn't see anything at all. Then, as I blinked, I made out a large covered wagon parked by the now-abandoned brazier, and what seemed like an endless stream of uniformed police officers emerging from it. A moustached sergeant was already approaching Miss Peters.

'Mackenzie's workshop? Thank you, Miss. Special raid. Home Secretary's orders.'

And with that he plunged inside.

Chapter 19

It felt like the middle of the night by the time Miss Peters and I found ourselves in a slow and heavy Victoria, bound for Bloomsbury Square. In fact, it probably was the middle of the night.

The confusion in Mustard Street had been considerable, with a large number of policemen running around in a great many directions. We were asked lots of questions by officers who barely had time to listen to our answers, but had very little opportunity to ask any questions ourselves. We did at least get to see Mr Boynton being led away into custody, and Big Alf too, the latter looking a little the worse for wear, as though he had chosen to put up a struggle.

In the end we were taken in hand by a very kindly sergeant whose job seemed to be to have us removed from Mustard Street as swiftly and gently as possible.

'A very pretty haul,' he informed us happily. 'As well as that bird of yours, Miss, there were five or six items of jewellery under one of the work benches which the inspector says will be easy to trace back to their owners. And the man seems to have kept a cash book of sorts, a record of his various transactions, which will probably be enough to convict him all on its own.' He shook his head. 'You'd think he'd be too clever for that, wouldn't you? But it's often the clever ones that are the most foolish. Never dream that we'll catch them, you see.'

The same sergeant led us over to a carriage, one of many now lined up in Mustard Street and the adjoining lanes, and nodded at the driver.

'Johnson here will take you home, ladies. I imagine that the inspector will want to have a word with you in the next day or two, but you should have a good rest first.'

I think it was then that Miss Peters produced the Empingham Canary from her muff, but he refused to take it.

'No, Miss. I'm told that you two ladies are best placed to restore it to its owner.'

He nodded as Miss Peters hid it again.

'That's right, Miss. You'll be safe enough in the carriage, but probably best to keep it out of sight in any case.'

He saluted as we pulled away.

'So Hetty,' I asked as we turned out of Mustard Street. 'I still don't really know how you did it.'

I said it in quite a small voice, because now I was safely in the carriage, I was suddenly aware of just how tired I was, and it felt blissfully comfortable to be sitting down, my feet stretched out in front of me, my head back, enjoying the gentle rhythm of the wheels over cobbles.

'Oh, it was very easy, Flottie.' She shuffled across, a little closer to me, so that we were sitting elbow to elbow. 'I've seen Potty Peasmarsh do it so many times. It isn't magic at all, you know. You just open the box and take the thing out and hide it. Of course, you have to do it all very quickly and quietly, but so long as the box is closed when the audience looks away and closed when it turns back, the trick works. And to be fair to Mr Boynton, it wasn't

310

very difficult to get you both to turn away while that funny man in the blacksmith's aprons was standing there looking like a very bald troll. Potty Peasmarsh doesn't have a troll, of course, but he does have a funny nervous tick which makes his face twitch, and when the twitching starts, people always look at the floor, or out of the window or somewhere, because it seems polite, so all he has to do is pretend to twitch just before he makes the thing disappear.'

She took out the canary again, and studied it. Even by the low light of the passing street lamps, it seemed to glow.

'I don't think it's damaged, Flottie,' she concluded, 'because I think I must have hit Big Alf in that soft place above his ear. And it's ever so heavy, you know. I wasn't at all surprised to see him collapse like that.'

'We were very lucky, though, weren't we, Hetty?' I could feel my eyes growing heavy, as I let myself lean against her shoulder. 'I mean, with the police arriving like that, just at the right time, on the very night we happened to be there. I mean, what were the chances of that?'

'Well, that's just what I thought, Flottie,' I heard her reply, as I allowed my eyes to close for a moment. It really had been a very, very long day. 'I mean, when I saw all those officers, Flottie dear, it just seemed to be too good to be true. And then it came to me! I remembered what sort of person lives in Carlton House Terrace.'

I think I heard the words, but I was already beyond making sense of them. Before we had even left the docks, I was dozing, slumped rather heavily on Hetty Peters' arm.

I didn't go back to Baker Street that night. I was awoken by Carrington, the Earl of Brabham's butler, who helped me from the carriage and explained that a room was being prepared for me there, in Bloomsbury Square. I remember Rupert Spencer welcoming us into the library where there was brandy and hot tea already laid out, but I was far too tired for either. Too tired, even, to be particularly alarmed when the Earl of Brabham himself, clad in a vivid tartan dressing gown, put his head around the library door and demanded to know what was going on. When Mr Spencer explained very calmly that the Empingham Canary had finally been recovered after twenty-three years missing, he simply puffed into his moustache.

'It has, has it? About time. It was that Greek woman, I suppose? Always suspected her. Striking young thing. Had a glint in her eye. Surprised it's taken so long to work it out.'

And when I ventured to point out that the same lady had sent him his chicken, he looked rather pleased.

'Ha! You see! Told you all along it was a prank, not an error! Funny sense of humour, these foreigners. Don't understand Rugby football. Think posting hens is funny. Don't drink enough whisky.'

And that was almost the last thing I remember, although I do recall telling Miss Peters, as she helped me into bed, that I needed to be woken very early so that I could catch the first train back to Amberley, because Mrs Hudson would be worrying. It was, however, an instruction that she blatantly ignored, for when I woke the next morning, startled for a moment to find myself in a strange bedroom, it was already light.

In fact, it was a peculiar light that found its way through the gaps between the shutters that day – soft and oddly bright after so many dark days – and I realised, as my thoughts reordered themselves, that it had finally started to snow. Not much. Not fairy-tale snow, the sort that falls in penny novels when the author wants a cosy ending, not the extravagant snow tipped from buckets at the end of pantomimes. Just a thin, slightly lumpy covering on the grass in the centre of the square, so thin that it had already been swished from the street by the wheels of carriages, and trampled into mush on the pavements. As I peeped out through a discreet gap in the shutters, I was horrified to realise that the church clocks were striking twelve.

I would have pulled on my clothes at once and set off for Frawling Hall without delay, but for the fact that my clothes were nowhere to be found; and the night-dress I was wearing, although soft as snowflakes, was not the sort that allowed me to roam the corridors of Lord Brabham's townhouse with any sort of decorum.

So I pulled the bell, something I had never done in earnest in my life before, and waited, and after a minute or two Miss Peters arrived followed by a maid with a break-fast tray and another carrying an assortment of garments I didn't recognise.

'Your clothes are being washed,' Miss Peters told me, in a voice which suggested regret that they weren't being burned. 'Really, Flottie, they were in a terrible state, and frankly most of them smelled of horse. So I've brought some of my things for you to choose from. Nothing fancy, because I know you're funny that way. Just a few very plain and ordinary oddments.'

Miss Peters' ordinary oddments proved to be very sumptuous indeed, but they were, by her standards, relat-ively plain. In them, I looked like a very well-dressed young lady, but not the sort who would excite excessive attention on an omnibus.

'And you have no need to rush off to Bognor or wherever, Flottie, dear,' Miss Peters assured me. 'Tele-grams have been exchanged. Flocks of them. In all sorts of directions, from all sorts of people. I'm surprised they didn't wake you. I'm sure at one point the delivery boys must have been queueing round the square. You and I are quite famous. Or we would be, except Uncle says that a lady's name should never appear in any part of a newspaper except the engagement columns, so ours don't, which is most unfair, because I should like to be remembered as the Lady Who Snared Lord Empingham's Canary, even though Uncle says that sounds too filthy for any decent newspaper. Anyway, the most important upshot of all those telegrams is that Mrs Hudson is on her way back to London. In fact, she may already be here. She says to meet her in Baker Street. And I'm to show you this.'

It was a copy of the late edition of the morning newspaper, and I saw in the Stop Press section on the front page a single narrow line of print: *Scotland Yard report lost treasure recovered in Docklands raid.*

'Not that one,' Miss Peters told me impatiently. 'You already know that. This one.'

The item she pointed to was also a small one, at the foot of the first column.

STRANGE EVENT IN HIGHLANDS

Reports reach our Edinburgh office of a large explosion in the waters of Loch Nevis. No casualties have been reported, but a great number of fish are reported destroyed. Police state that several individuals have been arrested but will be offering no further comment.

'Apparently, Flottie,' Miss Peters informed me, slightly sceptically, 'you will know what it means.'

I did, a bit, although I wasn't really supposed to.

'I think what it really means,' I explained, 'is that Mr Holmes and Dr Watson will be on their way home.'

—

I knew at once that I was not the first to arrive back in Baker Street. The shutters were open and the chimney was smoking, and although the thin powdering of snow on the roof hardly transformed our dwelling into the magical cottage of winters' tales, my heart nevertheless gave a little joyful leap as I approached. I'd only been away one night, but it felt much, much longer. It was good to be home.

Miss Peters had declined to accompany me, explaining that she had a busy day ahead of her.

'For I have a fitting at two, Flottie, dear, with the French lady who created the Portman Dress, as everyone's calling it, and if I'm not there on the dot, Lady Stanswick's daughter will take my place, because she's told everyone that she plans to wait outside in her carriage between now and Christmas, if that's what it takes to get a fitting. And before that, I have to see Clara Fazakerley and explain to her that the man she thought felt like sunlight on a tiny frozen hand is really an odious little schemer with horrid taste in cufflinks. I suspect the news will rather buck her up.'

I'd expected to find Mrs Hudson alone, but as I made my way down the area steps, I was aware of voices in the kitchen, and when I opened the door, I found the fire burning brightly and Mrs Hudson seated at the big table pouring tea for a lady I realised, with something of a shock, was none other than Theodora Snaresdon, the original purloiner, and also the saviour, of the Empingham Canary.

315

She recognised me at once, and rose to greet me with a winning smile.

'So you are Flotsam!' she declared. 'We meet again, but this time in the daylight. I had no idea before how pretty you are!'

I blushed a little at that, but I might have said the same, for I had barely been able to see her face in the darkness, and now that I could see her properly, I realised that the attractive young wife remembered by Mrs Alma Tadema had grown over time into a striking, indeed rather beautiful, woman. Her dark hair, tinged with grey, framed a face of timeless distinction, but it was her eyes that stood out. They had a brightness to them, a sparkle and a vivacity that seemed to draw you in. The Earl of Brabham had obviously seen it too. A glint, he had called it. Whatever it was, when she met your eyes with hers, you felt compelled to smile.

'Mrs Snaresdon and I became acquainted yesterday evening,' Mrs Hudson explained, rising to fetch an extra cup and saucer. 'Shortly after I received your message. We had a good long chat in a private room at The Plough, which serves a very fair veal pie and a quite passable claret. Then, this morning, when I told her about your exploits last night – as described in Mr Spencer's telegrams – she insisted on accompanying me back to town.'

Mrs Snaresdon turned to me with more of that smile.

'It is true, Flotsam, because it seems to me that I owe you an explanation in person. And so, perhaps, does Maximillian – Mr Cortado. But first, is it really true that you rescued the bird?'

In reply, I reached into the very plain carpet bag that I had carried with me from Bloomsbury Square. It is probable that no carpet bag in history has ever been gripped as tightly as I had gripped that one, all the way across town, until the kitchen door was closed safely behind me. Now I produced from it a small parcel wrapped in old newspapers, and from the old newspapers I produced Lord Empingham's little bird. Very gently, I placed it in the centre of the table, next to the tea tray.

'Ah, it is beautiful, is it not?' Our guest turned her smile towards the ornament. 'Sometimes, when my husband was away from home, I would creep up to the attic of our villa, to the place where it was hidden, and would allow myself a minute – never more – just to look at it.'

Mrs Hudson put down the teapot and pulled her chair a little closer to the table, as if to examine it more closely.

'It is indeed a very fine piece of work,' she agreed, then reached out and touched our guest's hand in a peculiarly moving and heartfelt gesture. 'It is not just Lord Empingham who owes you his thanks,' she added. 'We all do.'

Mrs Snaresdon nodded to herself for a moment, her eyes still on the bird.

'When something so beautiful is destroyed, the whole world is diminished, is it not?'

Then she looked up and smiled at us both.

'But it is not just me to thank. Maximillian too. Without him, there would be no little golden bird to delight us.'

'Please, ma'am,' I asked, a little anxious that it might be an indelicate question, 'where is Mr Cortado now?'

'He also is in London, Flotsam. He returned with us. He has gone to explain himself to Miss Burrows and to his friend, Mr Denham. I told him that he must, that he could not simply disappear. I told him that he does not have to explain himself to the world, but he should explain to those who are closest to him. He is, I think, a little ashamed, but of course, it is really me who is to blame. The arrival of my hen, out of the blue sky as it were, caused him great agonies of conscience.'

She pushed her tea cup to one side and reached out to touch the wing of the little bird, almost as if to reassure herself that it was not about to take flight. Then she leaned back in her chair and addressed me again.

'But, please, Flotsam, before I speak of Maximillian, let me explain to you, as I have explained to Mrs Hudson, how all this has come about.'

And so I pulled my chair closer to the table, and felt the warmth of the fire on my face as I heard the story of the Empingham Canary told by Theodora Snaresdon herself. Outside, snow had begun to fall on the area steps but I barely noticed it. Mrs Snaresdon spoke softly, but rarely hesitated, as though the events she described were as fresh in her mind as on the day they'd taken place.

'I never loved my husband, of course,' she began. 'You must think me dreadful to state it so plainly, but our marriage was never more than a transaction, an agreement reached between Adam Snaresdon and my father, who was, if possible, a man even less lovable. But do not think I complained, Flotsam. I welcomed the marriage. To escape what I had known before, at any price, seemed like a blessing. And my husband, of course, never expected or required my love. I was a purchased chattel, nothing more. And so I came with him to England, and in time, after not very many months, to Frawling Hall...'

I shivered slightly as she described her journey to Frawling, through ever increasing amounts of snow, with only Mr Snaresdon and Mr Savage for company. Her husband, she explained, seemed that night like a man demented, so great was his haste to reach Frawling Hall. The pleasure he had shown on hearing of his substantial inheritance from the sixth Lord Empingham had been nothing to his glee on learning that with it came the golden canary, the most prized possession of his cousin. And nothing, he declared, was going to stand in the way of him claiming what was rightfully his.

'I do not know why he hated his cousin so,' Mrs Snaresdon told us sadly. 'I think perhaps because Hugo was a lord, and legitimate, and content, while my husband was none of those things. Also, perhaps simply because my husband liked to hate. It gave him great energy. He took a pleasure in it.'

I heard again the description of that evening at Frawling Hall, Adam Snaresdon's cruel demands, his relish in offending his host, in challenging everyone, in rubbing his triumph in their faces.

'It was at dinner that night that I knew I must stop him,' she told us calmly. 'His anger was so ugly, so pointless. I looked around the table and realised that no one would blame me. They would all be pleased the bird was saved. So that night I would slip out of bed and go to the tower and steal it away while my husband's big brute slept. It would be easy. Then I would hide the bird in Frawling Hall, and when my husband was safely in Greece I would write to Lord Empingham, telling him where to find it, and no harm would be done.'

She pulled a little face, part rueful smile, part mock horror at her own naivety.

'So that is what I did, Flotsam. First, I went to the room next door, where the Dutch painter slept. I knew his costume for the ball was hanging behind his bedroom door and it was very easy to reach in and remove it. These suits were all the same, all black and white diamonds, and I knew if anyone saw me in such a costume, they would think I must be a man, but they would not know which one.

'It was easy, also, to remove the key from beneath my husband's pillow. My husband slept like a pig, all heavy and grunting. I think this made me a little careless, because on leaving I let the door bang a little, and later I realised my husband must have woken. I took with me, in the pocket of my suit, a bottle of my husband's hair oil. I did this because the key looked very old and rusty, and I thought it would not turn quietly. But the oil worked well, because the key made no sound. In only a very few minutes, I found myself standing over the sleeping Savage.'

As Mrs Snaresdon talked, I pictured the scene. That bare stone room, very dark and freezing cold; Savage asleep in his bed; and the wraith-like figure of Theodora Snaresdon stepping quietly around him, searching for the bird.

'I had no lamp, of course,' she went on. 'I felt safer in the shadows, and I knew that to show a light in the room where Savage slept was impossible because it would be seen through the open shutters. But I was not worried. There was a little light from outside, from the stars and the snow, and I knew the canary could not be very hidden because there was nowhere to hide it. So I waited for a moment while my eyes grew accustomed to the room, and very quickly I could make out the box, on the floor, just beside the bed. The box was open, and I almost had the canary in my hands when I heard a sound that sent a thousand tremors through my body. I heard the sound of the door opening.'

I already knew what happened, and why and how, but I still found myself holding my breath.

'I had not thought to lock the door behind me, or even to fully close it, but I had removed the key from the lock and put it in my pocket. So whoever came behind me found the door not locked but ajar, and I knew it was not my husband, for he would have been shouting and stamping and cursing, not creeping so silently that there was not a sound as he entered. And even in the darkness I could see that I was face to face with another masked Harlequin, exactly like myself.'

It must have been the most heart-stopping of moments, but Mrs Snaresdon smiled to herself as she recalled it.

'I think for a few seconds he was too surprised to speak, but then I heard him say to himself the words, "*Good God!*", and to me, in a whisper, "*We've both had the same idea.*" But there was no time for reply, for at that exact instant we heard the door at the foot of the tower banging open, and we heard my husband's voice roaring at Savage to wake up.'

'You must have been so frightened, ma'am,' I told her, but Mrs Snaresdon shook her head.

'There was no time. No time to speak, no time to feel fear. We looked at each other, me and my Harlequin, and I could tell he thought as quickly as I did, because, without a moment's hesitation, he took his key and locked the door behind us, then we both looked up at the high window at exactly the same time, and I heard him whisper, "*Leg up!*"

'So I placed myself beneath the window and cupped my hands as I had seen the small boys do in Athens when stealing apples, and I managed to lift him as he reached upwards for the latch on the shutter. It was a struggle for me, with my strength, for although he was not a big man, he was still heavy. But he was very quick, and almost before I could wobble, his weight was gone, and he was up on the window ledge, reaching down for me. Thankfully, he was strong, for he pulled me up very easily. But to get me onto the ledge, which was so small, he had to reach around me, with his hands in places where a gentleman would not usually touch a lady without invitation, and as I landed on top of him in the window and pulled the shutter closed behind us, I heard him whisper, "*Good God! You're a woman!*"'

Mrs Snaresdon paused and smiled at me.

'I fear, perhaps, Flotsam, this will shock you very much. But I must in honesty tell you that I did not mind at all where his hands were. Nor did I mind my body on his, all tangled up with him. I'm afraid to say I liked it very much. And not just in *that* way, the way a man can sometimes make a woman feel with his touch. It was much more.'

She was looking away now, looking out of the little window, at the snow falling. She seemed to be searching for the words she needed.

'You see, there was an instant – I remember it to this very day – an instant as I was reaching for the ledge, and his hands closed around me to lift me, when I felt *safe*, Flotsam. It sounds a little thing, to feel safe. But for me it was strange and shocking, like a shiver through my whole body. Because I think in my whole life, as a child, as a wife, I had never before felt this feeling.'

She gave a little shrug, and nodded to herself.

'And still I felt it, pressed against him there, as we heard the banging on the door and Savage stirring. I should have been terrified. To be caught in such a place in such a way... My husband was not a gentle man, Flotsam.

Anyone who knew him knew also to fear his anger. But I was not frightened, up there on my ledge. We could see a line of light below the shutter, so we knew Savage had lit his lamp, and we could hear my husband's roars. But I felt that nothing bad could happen to me, up there, with him, this stranger in a mask.

'So we stayed totally still, Flotsam, even though we were most improperly entwined. And we listened. We heard Savage tell my husband the bird was safe, and we heard my husband go away. And we waited, still not moving, for Savage to put out the light and go to sleep. But Savage would not sleep. The light remained burning. We heard him turn the pages of a book, and still we waited.'

She sighed and said nothing for a moment, remembering. Then she smiled again.

'In the end, we had to move, to rearrange ourselves into positions where the cramp would not get us. We did it so slowly, so quietly, inch by inch, until we were resting against each other, my back against his chest and our faces very close. It was very dark, too, remember. He was no more than an outline against the window. And still we did not dare to speak.

'The following day Savage told the household that he had remained awake for all those long hours, but thank the Lord, it wasn't true. I know, because after a long time we heard his breath grow loud, and we could tell he was dozing. But even then we did not move at first. In the end I signalled towards the shutter, suggesting we might try to escape, but my Harlequin shook his head.

'"Not while the lamp is on," he whispered. "The butler is awake in the West Wing. He can see into the room. We should wait." And so we waited longer. Outside, we could make out trees and snow and stars. We watched them together. A voice in my brain told me that we should take our chance between Savage's snores. But at the same time, I confess that I was happy to stay. My Harlequin had thought to throw on a cloak before he ventured out, and as the cold grew worse, he wrapped it around us both. Without it, I don't know how we would have survived. We had to hold each other very close for warmth. Our breath was freezing on the glass. And yet I was strangely content.

'Soon we heard Savage snuffle himself awake, and once again we heard the pages of a book turning, then gradually he fell asleep again.

'"He may never turn down the lamp," I whispered. Those were the first words I had spoken to my fellow thief, and I felt him turn his head towards me.

'"Why, you're Snaresdon's wife!" he whispered, because my accent betrayed me. And I knew he was about to tell me who he was. He even reached up to take off his mask, but I stopped him.

'"No!" I told him. "I must not know. If they ever catch me, if they ever question me, even if my husband uses his belt, I cannot tell them, because I do not know. It is better."

'"The brute!" he replied, and I felt his arm tighten around me.'

Mrs Snaresdon's eyes had drifted back to the window, but now she gave herself a little shake and turned to me.

'After that, Flotsam, while the Savage snored, we talked. Only in whispers, in little, broken sentences, but we spoke of things, we confessed things… We spoke in a way that perhaps only strangers can. From time to time,

Savage would wake again, and we would wait, and when the heavy breathing began again, we would continue.

'I told him everything about my life, about why I had married such a man and why I must stay married to him, and about all my fears and hopes. And he talked too. Not about the details of his own world, for I wouldn't let him. But he spoke of his dreams, his longing to wander the world, to see all seven seas, perhaps in the end to settle where the waters are warm and to grow the most beautiful and exotic flowers in a little garden of his own. And he spoke too of his regrets. A marriage entered into because he hadn't known how to say no. A path laid out for him, expectations, a grey road ahead. I knew, of course, just as he knew, that he must walk that road. He was too honourable not to. He had a wife. He had made vows.'

'And you, ma'am? Was it the same for you? Was that why you stayed, even though Mr Snaresdon was so horrible?'

She smiled a little sadly.

'For me, Flotsam, it was something more. I had discovered only a few days earlier that I was expecting a child. And legally that child too would be my husband's. So I had to stay, for my son's sake. And I have never regretted it.'

'But surely, ma'am, in all those hours, even in the dark, you must have learned something that told you who your stranger was?'

'Perhaps I didn't want to, Flotsam. I knew even then that if we were somehow to escape from our impossible position, he and I would part with the dawn; I knew I would spend the rest of my life far from these shores. But also, I knew that I would always remember those hours, and I would always wonder how my life might have been different had I spent it with such a one as my Harlequin. No, not such a one. That very one. No other. But if I were to know his name, Flotsam, if I were to have a real person to fix my dreams upon, the pain might be too great to bear. Much better for me if he remained a shadow, a mystery. The dream of a winter night.'

Mrs Hudson cleared her throat.

'But you knew, of course, that the gentleman was not Mr Alma Tadema.'

'Of course, Mrs Hudson. I knew from his voice that he was not the Dutch painter. Nor was he Mr Grey-Wilson, whose arm was in a sling. But I had not even spoken to any of the other young men. I knew only their names.'

'And how was it, ma'am,' I asked, 'that you were the one who ended up in possession of the bird?'

'It was something we spoke of, Flotsam, that night, in our whispered conference. Oh, we spoke of so much! We watched the stars appear, and I told him the names of the constellations we could see. And some of the things we spoke were foolish things, nonsense. But he made me laugh. Yes, cramped in the freezing cold, trapped like rats, he made me laugh! Even though I had to laugh in silence. And the longer we were there, the more I could feel the warmth coming from him. Such warmth. Not the warmth of his body, although I could feel that too. No, it was a different sort of warmth – a warmth of understanding and tenderness and kindness, like a soft heat radiating out from him. It felt...'

Here she broke off, and I saw her eyes were glistening.

'You will think me foolish, Flotsam.' She paused. 'But it felt like I'd always thought love would feel.'

We were all silent for a moment then, until Mrs Snaresdon gave a little toss of her head.

'But I haven't answered your question, Flotsam. We also talked about practicalities. About what time the servants would wake. About how long it would take to return the keys and reach our rooms. About when it would grow light. He made me understand what I had not bothered to think about, that making the canary disappear was no small thing. There would be police and questions. We risked a very great scandal. And the little bird could not simply be returned to Lord Empingham, as I had carelessly imagined. Not while it remained, in law, my husband's. His lordship would simply feel obliged to give it back.

'So I made my stranger promise that the theft would be mine, and mine alone. I wasn't even sure it *was* a theft, because I was my husband's possession, and legally all my belongings belonged to him. How could I steal from him what could never be said to be mine, only his? And how could my husband be stolen from, if the missing object remained beneath his roof, in the custody of a wife who belonged to him?'

She laughed at the thought.

'I don't think my Harlequin agreed with my legal arguments, but he agreed to abide by my decision. Then, as the night began to draw to an end, we knew that we must take our chance, light or no light. Only then did we speak of the future.

'"If I am ever free," he said. "If *you* are ever free…"

'"If I am ever free," I told him, "and if I know you to be free also, then I will come for you dressed as Harlequin, with a canary on my finger, and will make you return here with me and stand beneath this tower."

"'Not a canary!" he said. "Scotland Yard will be waiting and you will betray us both," and we laughed silently together.

"'Then another bird," I told him. "Some bird nothing like a canary, so you will know it's me."

"'But how will you know it's *me*," he asked, "if I cannot even tell you my name?"

'So I promised him, Flotsam, that I would find a way. That if both our worlds changed, I would seek him out. And I did.'

I considered this for a moment, and my heart felt very full.

'And then, ma'am, at six o'clock, Savage turned out the lamp, and you were able to escape?'

'Yes, Flotsam. It was as if the gods finally smiled upon us. Getting down was not easy though, especially in silence. I remember that my legs were so cramped they would barely support me. But it seemed lighter in the room than in our little window prison, so to unlock the door and take the bird took us only a few seconds. Then we crept down the tower steps, being careful to make no noise, because we were afraid the servants would already be awake, and just as we reached the door into the library, we heard someone on the other side of the door, moving something. So we waited again, until we heard the person leave the library, and we seized our moment.

'And then, Flotsam, we came to that point, by the Christmas tree in the Great Hall, where our paths separated. There was no time for a goodbye, but as I moved away, he reached out and caught my hand. He was still little more than a masked shadow. "*Find me*," I heard him say. "*If the time is ever right for us, find me. Or send for me and I will come.*" And then we parted.'

She looked down at her fingertips.

'And twenty-three years later, I waited at The Plough, not knowing if he *would* come, after so many years. Not knowing if he had understood my message, not even knowing if he had received it, for I sent messages only to the gentlemen who were no longer married, and I could not be sure my Harlequin was one of them. He might have been preparing for Christmas with his wife, unaware of the birds I was sending across London.

'But then I received a message at The Plough that a gentleman was asking for me. And although I had never seen his face before, I knew at once it was him. He was unshaven, and had only the clothes he stood up in, but what did I care? We walked in the lanes, and his voice was exactly as I remembered it, and I felt it again – that warmth, that sense that he had found in me someone who was special to him. In the evening he returned to Amberley, but he came back the next day, and we talked all day – about the past, yes, but about the future too, and about all the dreams we had shared back then which were still only dreams to us now.'

She looked up at Mrs Hudson for a moment, almost as if for reassurance.

'And now it is agreed. We are to stay in London for a few more days while Maximillian puts his affairs properly in order. And then we shall return to Greece, to a little village I've always loved, where my husband rarely let us go, and Maximillian will plant his garden, and perhaps, while it grows, we will travel. To Egypt, to the Holy Land, to the Istrian coast.'

'And your son?' I asked. 'You haven't even mentioned him. Is he still in Scotland on business for Lord Empingham?'

'Ah! My Theo!' Her expression changed to a different sort of joy. 'We are very close, he and I. We have always been close. And nothing I have done, with the hens and the canary, has been done without the two of us planning it together. In Athens he is considered a very promising student of medicine, but here, it seems, he has become an excellent footman! And that, of course, was his idea. He speaks English like an Englishman, and he loved the idea of returning Lord Empingham's bird to the top of its tree on the third day of Christmas, the day it disappeared. Of course, we had no idea that Lord Empingham was so ill. In Frawling this morning, I heard them say that he may not last till Christmas Day.'

'Which is a timely reminder, Flottie,' Mrs Hudson said, beginning to move the tea things back to the tray, 'that you and I have one last task to complete before we can relax and enjoy the festive season. I have taken rooms at The Plough. If we catch the ten to five train, we can be in Frawling in time to return this object to Lord Empingham before bedtime.'

And so once again we travelled to Amberley. It was only one day since I had left it, rattled and a little bruised from my night-time horse ride, but I returned in very different spirits, carrying with me a long-lost object of unimaginable value in an old carpet bag. I felt rather proud of myself.

It would be wrong of me to dwell too long on our interview with Lord Empingham. He was a very old man entering the last weeks of his life, and what was said – the questions and answers that passed between us – the tears that were shed – are all things that should properly remain within the walls of Frawling Hall. Needless to say, his joy on seeing the little bird once again was very great, but I can't really describe the moment he finally took it in his hand because I was, to use a phrase beloved of Scraggs, weeping buckets. Even Mrs Hudson's jaw appeared to tremble a little, and Lord Empingham allowed the tears to roll down his cheeks without shame.

Cradling the Empingham Canary in his palm seemed to change him. His gaunt, clenched face seemed to soften. His features relaxed. I had wondered beforehand if seeing his lost treasure might give his lordship a new lease of life, but now I realised that the opposite was true. We had given him peace. He could begin to let go.

He gave orders for the bird to be taken from him and placed without delay on top of the Christmas tree in the Great Hall. And then, he told his attendant, he wished to follow it, wished to be carried down to the Great Hall for one last time.

'Only one wish remains to me now,' he explained, 'and that is to behold it once more in the place I best remember it. I think I can die content, knowing it is there, at the very heart of Frawling Hall, watching over me. Yes, indeed. I can go to my grave in peace if my little bird is safely upon its perch.'

We didn't stay with him for very long, because we could see that he was tiring, and that he longed to be carried down to the Great Hall. I had wondered if we might accompany him, but Mrs Hudson steered me away.

'It is a private moment, Flottie. Let his lordship enjoy it alone.'

Just as we were leaving his sickroom, however, Lord Empingham called me back.

'I forgot to ask you, child, if there is any way in which I can repay you for everything you've done for me. Anything at all. If there is, you have only to ask, for without you, there would be no bird to comfort me in my last hours.'

Even before he'd finished speaking, I knew, with a horrible, stabbing certainty, what I most wanted to say.

You have only to ask…

Sick as he was, infirm as he was, I knew he meant it. He had given me his word, and even in those last days, his word was still his bond.

I could even imagine the scene. I could hear the news-boys' cries and see their papers waved aloft: *Lost treasure to go on show in London store! Empingham Canary to decorate tree at Trevelyan's!* I could see the crowds thronging the shop and filling the street outside, the carriages jostling to drop their passengers; and the little golden bird looking down on it all. I could see Scraggs, no longer frowning, his venture saved. And it needn't be for long. It need only be for a day or two. Two days away from Frawling Hall would be enough.

And then I looked at the old man's face as he lay there, still gaunt and shrunken, but tranquil and at ease now in a way he hadn't been before.

I can die in peace, knowing it is there…

But he would let me take it if I asked.

Whatever it cost him, he would keep his word.

I had only to ask.

I thought of Scraggs.

I had only to ask.

I took a very deep breath, then touched the old man's hand with my fingertips.

'No, sir,' I replied. 'There's nothing.'

There remains very little more to tell about the Empingham Canary. Mrs Hudson and I returned to London the following day on the ten o'clock train. We didn't return to Frawling Hall before we left, because there was nothing else for us to do there, and nothing else to say. I didn't tell Mrs Hudson of the choice I'd made. I was never again to cradle the little golden bird in my hands.

Even so, despite the regrets that clawed away at me whenever I stopped to think about them, the return journey was a happy one. It would have been difficult, after witnessing at close quarters Lord Empingham's simple joy, not to feel uplifted, and with only five days left before Christmas Day itself, the train was full of passengers travelling in festive mood – two ladies from Arundel with presents for their cousins; a mother with three small children spending Christmas with an aunt; an old man delivering freshly cut mistletoe to his daughter's house in Clapham; even a vicar bound for St Martin's, fretting over his Yuletide sermon.

And within very few minutes of arriving in Baker Street, we felt properly at home again. Mrs Hudson set to work with the energy of a Fury, airing rooms, opening and closing windows and shutters, lighting fires, and setting upon the stove a large pan of mulled cider to warm us after our journey. Since that first snowfall, the skies had remained clear, but with the clear skies had come a plunge in temperatures. I hadn't felt properly warm since Clapham Junction.

Various communications awaited us on the doormat, perhaps the most pressing being a telegram from Mr Holmes confirming that he and Dr Watson had concluded their business in the Highlands and would be returning to London before nightfall. This information, of course, called for additional preparations. Shopping lists needed to be prepared, menus considered and food bought in; fires needed to be lit in both their bedrooms, which had a tendency to grow musty in winter; the study needed dusting, the smears on its mirror polished away, and its armchairs checked for old snuff and nail clippings. Fresh antimacassars had to be located in the airing-cupboard, and dirty ones dispatched to the laundry. In summary, much hard work, and a great deal of running around, was required. It was not till late afternoon that Mrs Hudson and I sat down properly to draw our breath.

I confess I had hoped to see Mrs Snaresdon again on our return to London, because I can't deny her story had touched me strangely. But instead of that lady in person, we found a note from her, thanking me again for my assistance in recovering the bird, and telling us the outcome of Mr Cortado's visit to Miss Burrows.

It had clearly been a frosty encounter. The great violinist had written in advance to both Mr Denham and Miss Burrows, explaining his position in full and apologising to them both for his lack of frankness. As a result, when he called upon Miss Burrows at her home, he found Mr Denham already in attendance.

'It would seem,' Mrs Snaresdon wrote, 'that Maximillian's letters had brought the two old friends together in a way he had not expected, for he discovered the pair holding hands in the drawing room. Miss Burrows told my Harlequin she had been woefully deceived in him, that she had thought him a fellow worshipper at the altar of great music, that no true musician could ever walk away from his craft, and that she never wished to see or hear of him again. Mr Denham said almost nothing, mumbled a few words about his great disappointment, and never let go of Miss Burrows' hand. Miss Burrows insisted on Maximillian taking away the Monteverdi violin, an object he'd hoped never again to lay a finger on. Walking away from Kensington he saw a ragged urchin playing the fiddle for pennies on the street corner, who was apparently delighted to agree an exchange...'

'A happy ending for one small boy, and perhaps for Mr Denham too,' Mrs Hudson observed, perhaps somewhat doubtfully, as she folded the letter away.

'I hope so, ma'am. I really do think he has admired Miss Burrows for a very long time. So he must know what she's like.'

We toasted their future happiness in Dundee cake.

The other note awaiting us was for me, from Scraggs, a hurried missive in his scrawly handwriting. Rather stupidly, I found myself flushing as I read it.

'It's a very nice note,' I told Mrs Hudson, as I stowed it in my apron pocket. 'He says the Round Pond has frozen, and asks if I'd like to go skating tomorrow. We do it every year, if you remember. There's always music and hot chestnuts, and it's lovely just before Christmas. I thought he'd be too busy this year.'

Or too worried, perhaps, but I didn't say that bit aloud.

'You must certainly go,' Mrs Hudson told me sternly. 'A bit of time on the ice will do you both good. Did he mention a time?'

'He suggests I find him at Trevelyan's after lunch. I did wonder, ma'am,' I went on, changing the subject, 'if Mr Cortado might be persuaded to play one last concert before his retirement. Perhaps for the customers at Trevelyan's. But I suppose, if he really has given up his violin...'

Mrs Hudson nodded.

'I fear, Flotsam, that those days are already behind him, even if he had the time for such a performance before he sails. Once you have shrugged off an old skin, it can be hard to put it on again. And remember, by slipping quietly into retirement without attracting any notice, he can spare Miss Burrows many awkward questions about their expected engagement, questions which would certainly be asked of her if he were to make a much-publicised swansong from a London shop.'

And I had to agree. The violinist was honour-bound to disappear from London society as quietly and as unobtrusively as possible.

'Do you think he and Mrs Snaresdon can be happy together, ma'am?' I wondered. 'I mean, I know how romantic it all is, but they don't really know each other at all.'

To my surprise, Mrs Hudson didn't answer my question at first. She rose from the table and reached down a pair of sherry glasses, then poured us each a very small drop of something rich and dark, which smelled of raisins and vanilla. Without a word, she raised hers towards mine and we clinked our glasses together.

'Here's to you, child,' she said, before taking her first sip. 'And as for our Harlequins, well, always remember, Flottie, love arrives in people's lives at unexpected times and in all sorts of unexpected ways.' She smiled at me. 'Let us wish them well.'

So we did.

<hr>

The return of Mr Holmes and Dr Watson that evening also added to the growing sense of festivity. They arrived tired, and rather dirty, but Dr Watson was bearing a large haggis he had purchased in Crianlarich and Mr Holmes had a new and rather fine blackthorn stick.

'We have been an awfully long way,' he observed, pulling off his gloves, 'for a very short stay. And to be perfectly frank, our time could have been better spent.'

'Don't know what you mean, Holmes,' Dr Watson grunted. 'Got your man, didn't you? Got your men, I should say. General Windermere was delighted.'

'Very true, Watson. But if the general had been a little bit more forthcoming with the facts, we should never have needed to travel north in the first place. As soon as he mentioned the cormorants on Loch Nevis, the significance of the Macedonian boatman in Mallaig became obvious. If he had only thought to mention them in his letter, we could have remained comfortably by our own fireside.'

Dr Watson shrugged and handed me his deerstalker.

'Still, Holmes, the ringleader's stick makes a damned fine souvenir, and we did get to witness the big bang. I'd have been sorry to miss that.'

'That is true, my friend.' Mr Holmes looked pleased at the recollection. 'As the general says, it was a blast that will have echoed in Berlin. Now, lead the way upstairs, Watson, while Flotsam tell us how the Empingham Canary, which should have been safely under guard at Frawling Hall, came to be recovered from the depths of London's docklands. It was, I assume, the footman who had it in his possession, Flotsam? The other three servants seemed unlikely candidates…'

And so I told them everything, and my explanation must have been quite lengthy, because by the time I'd finished, and supper had been brought up to them, then cleared away again, it was already bedtime.

Given the general air of goodwill and high spirits that prevailed, I should have gone to my bed in a buoyant mood. But when I lay down to sleep, I remembered that next day I was to go skating with Scraggs, and began to feel a little rush of joy at the prospect; but before the joy could rush very far, I recalled all Scraggs' difficulties, and the possible collapse of Trevelyan's, and those thoughts hit me with the sort of sickening, achy feeling you get from a punch in the stomach. And then, to make it worse, I thought of Lord Empingham's offer; and I had to scrunch up my eyes to stop myself imagining his golden canary on top of Trevelyan's Christmas tree.

When I did finally sleep, my dreams were muddled and at one point I was standing in front of Trevelyan's, watching the shutters being put up, while a shop-girl explained to me that they'd been forced to close because they had sold out of hens.

It was not a good night.

The next day, the twentieth of December, found me in a restless and unsettled mood. The two gentlemen slept late, then set out in a hurry to breakfast with Lord Caithness at the Clamberers' Club. At Mrs Hudson's suggestion, Dr Watson's haggis was taken with them as a gift for their host; she waved off all three with a contented smile.

The hours that followed hung heavily on me. More than once Mrs Hudson urged me to take a break from housework, and she tried to suggest various unnecessary errands that would have taken me out of the house. But I wasn't in the mood for the bustle of the city, or the festive window displays, or all the talk of Christmas. Instead, with grim determination, I scrubbed at the grout of the bathroom floor and tried not to think of my rendezvous with Scraggs.

Then, to make matters worse, just when I was preparing to leave for Trevelyan's, the Earl of Brabham's carriage pulled up outside, and Miss Peters emerged in her usual high spirits, carrying a neatly ribboned parcel containing my clean clothes. When she heard where I was heading, she insisted on taking me there in the carriage.

'For it's freezing cold outside, Flottie, and ever so busy, and if you walk, you're bound to get splashed by a hansom just as you arrive, so that you'll end up muddy and wet, as well as cold, and probably quite smelly too, and generally no good to anyone. Whereas the carriage is really quite cosy, and Carrington won't mind at all because he enjoys the traffic. He treats it a bit like jousting...'

It was easier to say 'yes' than to say 'no', and if I wasn't in the mood for conversation, Miss Peters didn't seem to notice, for she chattered incessantly about the dress that was going to be even more beautiful than the Portman Dress, and about what to buy as a gift for a man who preferred caterpillars to cravats.

Or perhaps she did notice my mood but chattered anyway. With Miss Peters, you could never really be sure.

The first indication I had that anything unusual was taking place was when our carriage drew to a halt as we tried to turn into Beak Street.

'Seems like a proper jam ahead, Miss,' Carrington called down. 'I'll try to go round.'

But halfway along Brewer Street, we stopped again, and I could see from peering out of the window that a long line of carriages stretched ahead of us, all of them stationary.

'Might be an accident, Miss,' Carrington informed me, and I heard him whistle to a young match-seller. 'Some sort of big event, apparently, Miss,' he told us after a muttered conference. 'The boy isn't sure what. Here, lad,' he added, 'hold the horses for a minute while I go and find out.'

Carrington was away for a surprisingly long time, during which the carriages ahead of us stayed exactly where they were. 'Like cows waiting for milking,' the match-boy told us. But had we been a herd of cows, those of us at the rear would, by then, have been mooing our frustration at those in front, instead of stewing in well-mannered, silent impatience. When Carrington returned, he still looked a little perplexed.

'They're stuck like this all the way up to Bridle Lane. That's where you're heading, isn't it, Miss? I didn't want to leave the horses any longer, but it seems there's some sort of event taking place at the new shop there, and the crowds are queuing in the street. I passed any number of fancy carriages, Miss, all determined to get there, however long they have to wait. You'd be better off walking.'

So we walked, and found that Carrington's observations about the fanciness of the carriages had been correct. As we passed the stationary vehicles, Miss Peters might have been ticking names off the guest list at a Society event.

'The McDougalls... The Pomfrets... The De Courcy-Trouvilles... Lady Greasby... Lady Montmorency... That funny Italian contessa who once danced with Garibaldi... Really, Flottie, I have a funny feeling about this...'

But what the funny feeling was I couldn't say, because at that point we turned the corner into Bridle Lane and were greeted by the sight of an enormous crowd gathered around the front doors of Trevelyan's, its members desperately pressing to get in while a dogged cordon of policemen just about succeeded in keeping them out.

'Store's full!' we heard one of those officers shout. 'It's one out, one in. Nice orderly queue, please! Careful with that umbrella, thank you, madam.'

All along the narrow street, stationary carriages waited, and at the front of the line, separated from the crowd by a second blue line of constabulary, was an enormous and oddly familiar black carriage.

'Why, Flottie!' Miss Peters declared. 'Isn't that…?'

But she didn't need to finish the question, for she could already see that I was nodding. Marked in bright colours on the carriage door was an impressive and instantly familiar crest, and that afternoon, in bright winter sunlight, it seemed impossible to believe that I hadn't noticed it before, when it had been parked beneath a gas-lamp in St John's Wood.

'So that explains all those policemen!' Miss Peters exclaimed. 'No, Flottie, not these policemen here. I mean the ones the other night, in Mustard Street. Of course, I worked out how they came to be there, obviously, but I couldn't really work out how your friend had managed it.'

We were being jostled now, as pedestrians of all kinds pushed past us towards Trevelyan's. Perhaps it was the crowds confusing me, but I could only look back at Miss Peters in bewilderment.

'Carlton House Terrace, Flottie!'

She said it with such emphasis that I felt sure it should mean something to me.

'You told me your friend was going there, remember, instead of going to the Pemmingtons' ball, and I wondered who she might be visiting at that sort of address, and then, of course, when all those policemen arrived in Mustard Street, I remembered that Rupert has a friend who collects moths, and possibly beetles too, who lives in Carlton House Terrace. He's a pale, ordinary-looking sort of fellow with whiskers, and Rupert once told me that, when he isn't bothering beetles, he's also the Home Secretary.'

She paused to allow a lady in a very large hat to sway past us.

'So I could see how the policemen came to be there. But the thing was, Flottie, I couldn't see how your friend Miss Coburg could persuade someone like the Home Secretary to send so many officers to such a grubby little place so quickly, because he must be quite a busy man, what with all his moths and things, and it isn't as though just anyone can knock on his door and ask him to send round an army of constables. And I'd never even heard of anyone called Coburg, which was even more puzzling, because I do know an awful lot of people, you know. But when you stop thinking of *Coburg* and start thinking of *Saxe-Coburg and Gotha*, well, it all makes sense, doesn't it, Flottie?'

Ahead of us, I was aware of growing excitement near the doors of Trevelyan's, as the people in the crowd began to cheer and wave their hats in the air. Someone was clearly leaving, and I could feel my jaw dropping in a most unseemly way.

'Princess Victoria!' I whispered.

Miss Peters beamed.

'Well, I rather think it must have been, Flottie. She does match your description, doesn't she? And that *is* her carriage. And the royal family are very keen on that Dutch painter of yours, which is odd really, isn't it, because some of his paintings are really rather rude. And you definitely told me that her grandmother was rather strict, and wouldn't approve of her heading off to the docks with you at night, which does make sense, of course, because if your father is the Prince of Wales and your grandmother is, well, the Queen, then being allowed to pay visits in St John's Wood with only a chaperone for company must be considered terribly, terribly *modern*, but going off to meet Big John and Big Alf in Mustard Street would probably be enough to have you thrown into the Tower.'

'Princess Victoria!' I said again stupidly, and a man in a flat cap who was passing at that moment winked and nodded to me.

'That's right, love,' he confirmed. 'Arrived late morning, she did, all unannounced like, but word had already got around. Must like the place, 'cos she's been in there near on two hours. I've just come along to give her a good cheer, like.'

He tipped his cap at me, and pressed forward into the crowd, and as I watched him go, I could feel my face flushing the deepest, darkest red.

'But Hetty, all those things I told her…' I think I might have shut my eyes as I recalled all the confidences that had spilled out of me. 'I just prattled away. I told her all about Frawling Hall and all about being a housemaid, and – oh, Hetty! – I think I must have gone on and on and on about Scraggs.'

'Yes, Flottie…' Miss Peters was standing on her tiptoes and attempting to peer over the crowd. 'I rather think you must have done.'

And then, of course, I recalled how certain Miss Coburg had been that Trevelyan's would prosper, and how readily I had dismissed her comment as a trivial but well-meaning commonplace, and how I probably hadn't disguised that very well, or perhaps hadn't actually disguised it at all. And then I think I flushed even more deeply than before.

Ahead of us, the royal carriage had begun to pull away from the kerb, and the crowds were parting to let it pass. Even so, its progress was slow, and as it approached us, I was able to see that the footman in attendance was none other than Newton, who had been on the box when Miss Coburg rescued me in St John's Wood. As the people around us on the pavement pulled off their hats in respect, it seemed to me that his eye met mine for a moment before he looked down, perhaps to make some communication to his passenger. Maybe I imagined it, though; I'll never know for sure. But as the big carriage rumbled past, it seemed to me that I glimpsed a face inside, leaning forward, turned to the window, and a white-gloved hand raised slightly as if in greeting.

I'm still not sure how I found my way into Trevelyan's that day. Miss Peters didn't even attempt it, declaring that the cost of entry would almost certainly be a good dress ruined, but that she would most definitely return the next day to see what all the fuss was about. I didn't attempt to dissuade her, but battled on alone until I found myself part of a little group that might have been a queue and which was suddenly and surprisingly called forward by one of the constables.

The crush inside the shop was less great than outside, but it was still quite hard for me to recognise the elegant, empty rooms with which I'd become so familiar. Shoppers thronged every aisle and every corner, and had even filled the gallery, where a string quartet was battling to assert itself over the chorus of excited voices. The shiny shop-counters which I so admired were almost completely obscured by the smart ladies and gentlemen who pressed around them, and it was very difficult to stand still and take proper stock of my surroundings because of the great many elegantly wrapped parcels that were being manoeuvred towards the doors by helpful shop-boys or over-burdened footmen.

Above everything rose an elegant and rather beautiful fir tree, ribboned and adorned with red baubles of blown glass. The top of the tree was tied with a simple bow of red velvet, and the sight of it made me giggle with joy. No golden bird, no Empingham Canary. But no such bird was necessary, after all, to draw the crowds to Trevelyan's. I found myself thinking of Lord Empingham, and let out a deep, deep breath – you might almost have thought I'd been holding it in ever since I left Frawling. But now I could breathe. In fact, I could do better than that – I could laugh, and I did, all by myself in the middle of the crowd, so that anyone who noticed me must have thought me drunk, or light-headed, or both.

It must have been only a very short time after I stopped laughing – while I was still smiling up at the Christmas tree – that I felt someone in the crowd take my hand, and I turned around in surprise, and there was Scraggs. And I didn't say anything to him at first, just smiled and laughed again, and reached up and placed my palm on his cheek, and left it there. And I didn't feel any sudden jolt of the sort Mrs Snaresdon had described, nor did I feel as though I was stroking moonbeams with my fingertips, like Miss

Fazakerley. But it didn't matter, not one little bit. It didn't matter what I knew, or didn't know. I liked the way it felt.

'Come on, Flot,' he said, grinning at me. 'They don't need me here today. Let's go skating.'

And I think I might have shut my eyes for an instant, because I thought I was going to laugh *and* cry, both at once. But I didn't. I just nodded.

'Yes,' I said. 'Let's.'

Author's Note

Readers may be interested to know that Sir Lawrence Alma Tadema's completed pencil drawing of the Princess Victoria is now held in the Royal Collection.

It was presented to her by the artist some twenty-three years after his first London home was partially destroyed by an explosion on the Regent's Canal.

The works of both Lawrence and Laura Alma Tadema fell dramatically from fashion in the twentieth century. Their second London home, the lavish and remarkable residence (and studio) in St John's Wood, was later turned into flats.

Cricket, however, is still played at Lord's.